Entre Nous: The Goosefoot Chronicles

a fictionalized memoir

by

Lydia Riantee Rand

Wild Ocean Press
San Francisco

Book graphics by James Maxwell

*

Rand, Lydia Riantee,
Entre Nous: The Goosefoot Chronicles

Published by Wild Ocean Press, San Francisco, California
www.wildoceanpress.com

Printed in the United States of America
First Printing

ISBN: 978-0-9841304-7-4

Distributed by Small Press Distribution, Inc., Berkeley, California
http://www.spdbooks.org

To my parents and my brother who offered me the gift of their stories;

To my friend and first editor Neva Beach, for her literary wisdom and encouragement to put these stories down in English when I was switching from French;

To my husband Charles and my children Tatyana, Arianne and Kyle, who supported me and persuaded me to go on when I was ready to give up;

To my writer's group for their patience and perceptive critique;

To my friend and final editor, Christy Wagner, for her invaluable time and support, and for the stupendous job she did of weeding and clearing the path to a more complete understanding of the story's deep meaning.

From the Tao ~

The secret waits for the insight
of eyes unclouded by longing.

Those who are bound by desire
see only the outward container.

These two come paired
but distinct by their names.
Of all things profound
say their pairing is deepest.

The gate to the root of the world.

INTRODUCTION

I have described this memoir as fictionalized because although the personal memories retold in it are true to what I recall and to the stories my parents told me of their background, there is always a large margin of error as studies about memory have shown. It is fiction inasmuch as I made up some of the events I suspected but was never sure happened. This book has been a long time in the making and in the process I came to realize that some of the occurrences I didn't know about but fabricated turned out to be true. There is no ultimate truth, only points of view. I believe it is time to give up distinctions between memoir, fiction and essay, time to move on to a genre that includes them all.

I changed the names of people involved for privacy and took the liberty of introducing a character, an obscure saint whose original story is known by the locals in the village of Lerné in the Loire Valley, as a confidante to the main character. I have also given a voice to characters that are dead in order to tell the stories they communicated to me while alive and to imagine their take on things from their new point of view.

To indigenous people, as with my family in the Italian Dolomites, the myths of their tradition are not just tales or metaphors but true events that happened in a distant past and serve as a roadmap to guide them throughout their lives. In Western society where our indigenous myths are lost or disregarded except as objects of curiosity and study, we have to re-dream or generate our own myths so that our lives can make sense. That is my goal and I hope my readers are willing to take the leap and be guided through the labyrinthine minds of a not-so-simple family of immigrants.

Orsolina

We all come from a village; we are a village.   —Sainte Némoise

1

VILLAGE LIFE

In which Orsolina tells how she came to Lerné after her brother's death, how she tries to connect with Némoise, the saint in the Lerné church; where Némoise asks questions about Orsolina's mother Angela, her brother Pietro and where Orsolina recalls scenes of their early history, in which she muses about loyalty and tells stories about Lerné and the villagers, the local drinking place, Fricaut the baker, the hunchback nurse; where she describes Angela's love of bed and fluff, how Angela sits in her house at the center of everything, how she, Orsolina, put an ocean between herself and her mother because of too much invasive love; where we understand that Némoise loves enigmas and rhymes, often answering a question with a question.

About three days ago, my brother Pietro passed away. I was with him all the way until the end. I witnessed the shriveling of his ashen body, his fragile bones, like those of birds, protruding. I saw the dark blossom of his sex. I recognized the fear in his eyes, the timidity of his soul. It numbed me.

At dawn I went to the church across from my mother's house. "When do we really die?" I asked Sainte Némoise. "Before or after what we identify as the moment of death? Does our body only exist because we believe in death? Are the body and death part of the same illusion?" But Némoise today remains silent. I insist: "When do the dead really die?" She still does not show any sign of hearing me.

Is it three or four days ago that Pietro left his body behind? It might even be five. He was in his early fifties, too young to die. Even though I witnessed his rapid decline and held him as he took his last breath, I don't perceive him as dead even now. I am not sure. It's like a mistake that will be corrected at any moment. The phone will ring, and I will hear his voice.

I have left two daughters and a son with their father at the place that has become my home on the other side of the ocean, to attend my brother's last days. California, my new world! But all that seems so far away it is like another lifetime. I know my children are in good hands. I cannot let myself feel the pain of their absence.

After Pietro's death I entered a different reality. I could no longer count in terms of days. Since the funeral couldn't take place without my mother and me, it must be less than three days. I know for sure that Pietro died a year to the day after our father Giovanni. The family made a big deal of that fact, but I don't remember the exact date of my father's death either.

We are a family of Italian immigrants to France, the Spiazzis. We call ourselves a tribe. Pietro is actually my half-brother on my father's side, but I always considered him a full brother. He was born in Italy, but when he was nine our father kidnapped him from his mother to bring him to Paris. I was born four years after that.

The way I remember it, Pietro opened the door for me when I first came to this earth. There were people in white, I felt the sting of a slap on my back, the intense light burned my eyes, but my brother laughed with rapture because he recognized me as the one he had been waiting for. His bliss took the burning pain away, and I could breathe.

"How funny you looked," he told me later, "with your lopsided red face and a full head of jet black hair sticking up like a crown."

I am convinced that I saw him first when I opened my eyes, but attending a birth was not an accepted practice for family at the time. I always meant to ask him if he actually was present at my birth. I never inquired and he is dead now.

Once, I was fooling around, "what if, in some other lifetime you had been my father, what if, in some other place, you really were my husband?" I asked.

"I waited a long time for you to appear in my life," he said in a whisper. "I was a little angry at you because you didn't respond to my call as fast as we had agreed upon," he went on, raising his voice. "How patient I have been with you. I gave you the time you needed to be a baby, sucking and howling and filling your diapers with regularity. I let you pretend that you hadn't instantly recognized me."

He clowned and made a show of being angry because he was embarrassed about mentioning a past-life connection. I remember, but was it remembrance, dream, or pure imagination, that during the first months of my life he quietly watched me concentrate on things, clutching the objects I eventually succeeded in bringing into focus, trying to reach, hold and grab them even though I was only interested in him.

"I knew you were only pretending to be a baby," he teased, "because the minute I opened the door for you to come into being, you made the sign we had agreed upon before coming here."

"Yes" I answered. "I heard that I raised my right hand and touched my forehead right in the middle. But are you sure it was not just serendipity?"

Now I am not sure of anything. I might have constructed this conversation later and it became a memory. We all have a tendency to do that.

Pietro's pancreatic cancer was already well advanced by the time it was discovered. It went fast. When Pietro's wife, Simone, called me to tell me it might be the end I left my children in the care of their father, caught a plane from San Francisco to Paris. There I saw Pietro in the hospital, barely recognizable. His doctor told the family that an operation might be possible but not right away, that Pietro should go home and rest first. The whole family was in turmoil. Pietro wanted to go to Lerné, the village in the Loire Valley where my parents moved after they retired, to regain some strength before the operation. His whole family and I went with him, but after four days he was in such pain and discomfort we took him back to Paris.

Two days later Pietro died in our arms. The next day Simone put me back on the train to Lerné. I am to bring my mother, Angela, to Paris for the funeral.

The church in Lerné is dark and damp. A musty smell pervades. In the corner where the worm-eaten polychrome statue of Némoise stands in a niche, the tuffa walls are green with algae.

I consider Némoise my patron saint. I never miss a visit to the church when I come to the village of Lerné, although in general, I don't have much use for anything having to do with the Catholic religion. Némoise has a goosefoot however, and the story of how she got it intrigues me. Even though sanctified, she is an eccentric saint—aren't they all in one way or another? And I suspect that there is much more to her story than is told.

I wish I had someone like her in Northern California where I have made my home, someone who would answer me when I ask questions.

Actually Némoise mostly answers my questions with her own. She does this to get me to give myself the answers I seek. She speaks in a high-pitched, supersonic voice, somewhat like the buzzing of a mosquito. "You can't have a question to which you don't already have the answer," she once told me.

I don't hear Némoise loud and clear like *Jeanne d'Arc* heard Saint Michael, Saint Catherine or Saint Margaret. It's often just that tiny voice in my head. I can't ignore Joan of Arc standing across the nave from where I am, in full armor, brandishing her sword, but she never speaks to me.

In California I have many friends I can confide in, spirits that guide me, but with Némoise, I use a different language, my tongue goes places that were once familiar. Némoise is my mother tongue, she is France.

Even in Paris the connection with her is never as strong as it is here, in the church of Lerné. When I leave the gentle land of France I seem to lose touch with Némoise altogether. She vanishes. So my tongue finds the more precise places, the more direct constructions, the active verbs, and I speak the language of adventure and ambition, a masculine tongue that creates new words, new worlds, my English tongue.

This morning just before waking up in my mother's house in Lerné, I had a dream about Pietro. I tell Némoise about it. In the dream he walked through the village enveloped in a green fog. He traveled the morning sky in slow motion, searching into every farm, disfigured with rage. He looked for our father, or maybe somebody else. He yelled that someone had robbed him of twenty years. He was in pain.

I woke up with a start, but couldn't move. A blue light flickered all over my room. I remained paralyzed and panic seized me. I could not shift any parts of my body. After a while I was able to wiggle my right toe. Then I rolled over and surrendered to the somnolence that spread through my being. Stories gathered inside my body like flesh around bones. Then clouds burst and a storm broke out. A welcomed rain. I woke up a second time, cried and cried. Until that moment, I hadn't found my tears.

When things are too hard in my life, I go to Némoise. She feeds me villagers' stories as pacifiers or maybe as parables. My mother also takes refuge in stories. It's easier to deal with other people's drama than one's own, easier to understand and accept.

"Are you using tales as a way to show me something about myself?" I ask Némoise. "Is there any difference between waking and dreaming? Are we supposed to look at the material reality as a metaphor for the spiritual one and vice versa?" Usually Némoise likes to engage in those kinds of discussions, but this time she doesn't answer.

In the past, she helped me put all the pieces of me together. My Italian country relatives think of me as a complicated city girl; to my sophisticated French city friends I am a naïve country girl. My family mostly thinks that I am a foolish risk taker. In North America, my new country, I am thought of as a wild, daring, strong woman. Némoise knows who I really am.

Finally, I feel Némoise coming to life. It starts as an undulation around her statue as I sit contemplating her from one of the pews, then turns into a vibration within my body. After that, thoughts flood me.

Lerné is only a village of adoption for our family. We came from Italy, kept immigrating to France, to America. I have cousins in Australia, Switzerland, Argentina. Ever since my parents moved to Lerné I have tried to understand this village and its inhabitants, their connection to the land, what is left of nature in this farming country. I do that whenever I move to a new place.

People from Lerné feel secure in a life regulated by unchanging chores—feed the animals, milk the cows, turn over the compost, go to the fields. Measured by the rhythm of church bells and barking dogs, the days feel safe. Villagers deviate little from a habitual course, they endure without complaints the feudal system that still rules them. Their personalities form around constantly irritated ancestral wounds, just like pearls inside oysters: only death will reveal their hidden treasure.

So you know there is a treasure here. Tu te souviens de la fable, de La Fontaine, Le Laboureur et ses Enfants?

Yes, I do remember the fable about the poor cultivator on his deathbed telling his heirs to keep plowing the soil because a treasure was hidden under; but it's not easy to find the hidden treasure since it's a metaphorical one. I watch farmers moving slowly throughout their days, never straying too far from their land or looking too deep. They easily submit to suffering and misfortune, that's just life. Their hard work seems meant to rub off the smell of poverty that clings to them in spite of the prosperity that tentatively came into the country since the war.

A barely perceptible scent of barnyard, pig stall, sperm and sweat lingers. Not so long ago families crowded ten to a room. Blackened walls, no running water, outdoor toilet, cows in the basement as the only source of heat, and no medical coverage—when you get very sick, you die.

"Isn't that what they try to forget," I ask Némoise, "when they buy the newest farm machinery and work long hours in the fields, often way into the night? Isn't it release from serfdom they seek when they borrow from the bank to remodel their houses to look like those of the rich?"

Qu'est-ce-que tu en penses? And how do you see your mother fitting into village life? She is not a farmer, not a villager, not a gardener. Do you really even know your mother?

MY MOTHER

Of course I know my mother. Well, sort of. Angela comes from a village herself, but hers was set on a castle-crowned hill in Emilia Romagna where people are much more open and friendly. She spent most of her adult life in Paris, an immigrant in an Italian neighborhood, where she became more of a city person. Later in life her husband, my father, bought this house in Lerné to spend his weekends hunting—in more ways than one since he was an incorrigible womanizer. As a family we spent our vacations here, and when my parents retired they moved to their Lerné house.

My mother hated it at first, the closed and suspicious villagers, the lack of any entertainment. Now she never wants to leave it. She'll let me take her to Paris for Pietro's funeral, but she would rather stay here. I sense that there is something she is afraid of in Paris, something she is not telling, or that she would rather not know.

In any case, she likes to feel village life around her, sluggish and subdued; that is safe. She wraps it around her body like she does with those endless lengths of soft winter shawls she knits for herself during lonely evenings. She loves to witness the daily drama from the gentleness of her bed, sinking into her own imprint in the wool mattress and comforted by the weight of the eiderdown on her legs.

She never forgets to fluff up the pillows before surrendering her head to their downiness. "I love you, bed," she murmurs each time she slips in between the ironed sheets. Then she draws the village in, using it like an extra blanket—not that my mother is a pleasure seeker or anything like that, quite the contrary.

In anything but bedding she is rather frugal and stark, frigid even. I often suspect the fluff and feather to be more of a way to protect herself and keep life's overwhelming sensuality at bay, also to be repaid for all the deprivation of her childhood. She was raised among the poorest of the poor, lived with her family in a rundown house people named *sin pan,* breadless. "We didn't have a pot to piss in nor a window to throw it out of," is the way she describes it.

The rough wood of the pew is hard and I have to shift my weight to find a more comfortable position. I get a side view of Némoise. She breaks my heart, this little peasant girl in country attire, one worm-eaten arm reaching to the heavens, her goosefoot barely recognizable—carpenter ants having munched on it to their heart's content. Meanwhile, *Jeanne d'Arc* is freshly restored, repainted and she retains all her initial spunk.

My mother's house in Lerné sits at the center of everything. The church bell right across the street rings one stroke for each hour right on the hour, then again one minute later for good measure. It practically deafens those who sleep in the room next to it, but Angela uses the other bedroom, on the garden side, and the sound comes to her pleasantly muffled, just loud enough to hold her dreams afloat while keeping her in a semi-consciousness that allows her to feel how delicious sleep is.

There are other sounds that succeed in fishing her mind out of the collective sea, the butcher's loud honk, the baker's morning call, the grocer's ancient klaxon. They feed her lonely soul better than a companion would. Her life passion has always been me, her one and only child, but the burden of her love drove me away.

I put an ocean between her and myself, became American. She had to find her inspiration elsewhere. After the stroke that left my father stranded on a chair, she became a martyr, rushing to his side every time he banged on his table demanding immediate service, never showing her exhaustion or protesting when he became unreasonable and refused what she offered, complained that it was not what he had asked for. This martyrdom lasted until he died; she had a talent for it.

MY BROTHER PIETRO

Et Pietro alors! What about Pietro? Is he a martyr also? What is his place in all this?

Pietro seldom came to Lerné. He already had his own family by the time our parents moved to the village. I can picture the wedding photo of him and his wife Simone sitting on the mantle in our dining room. I don't know why Angela keeps it there. For me it brings back the memory of that dreadful evening.

After the newlyweds had left for their one-day honeymoon and the guests scattered, my parents and I went back home. In the car, my father Giovanni, who was a little drunk, kept insisting that my mother had arranged a secret meeting with a handsome uncle of the bride. When we arrived home he had worked himself into a fit.

"I've watched the two of you all day, dancing and laughing and making fun of me. Don't think I am such a fool. I could see how attracted you were to him. Tell the truth, you fell in love with him. What did he promise you, that asshole? He's married, you know. I'll kill him." My mother refused to deal with his drunken craziness and was leaving the room when he grabbed his hunting gun out of a nearby cabinet.

I hollered in terror, "Please, Daddy, don't kill her." My mother turned around and saw the gun. She started to scream. My father was so agitated that we couldn't make sense of his shouting. It took us a few minutes to realize that he was not pointing the gun at my mother but attempting to put the barrel into his own mouth.

Everything became frozen in that moment, a black and white snapshot of Angela who had rushed over to Giovanni and was pulling on the gun with all her might while yelling for help. I pulling on my mother's dress, shrieking.

Angela succeeded in taking the gun away from Giovanni and he collapsed on the couch, sobbing like a baby. That night I switched allegiance from my brother Pietro to my father. I would make him happy. He needed me, whereas Pietro had betrayed me, leaving me much too soon in the hands of ignorant parents to go and get married.

After that everything quieted down. My mother went to her room and offered to take me into her bed, a favor I would have been glad for at any other time, but I refused. My father's sobbing slowly resumed. I sat by him on the couch when he passed out, rubbing his head until the first light of morning.

Pietro became the betrayer in my mind, and my resentment of him for abandoning me remained stuck like a chicken bone in a dog's throat, turning a strong bark into a cowardly yelp. But somewhere I knew that Pietro was the one being betrayed; he had always been.

Tell me Némoise, why do I have to go over the most painful scenes time and time again? Why don't I have control over my own memories?

Is it a form of exorcism, the healing that seals a schism? You go all the way into the pain, each time with less charge, less strain.

You are a poet Némoise.

LOYALTY
A wind coming through the open door makes the candles on the main altar flicker. Shadows move.

Let's get back to the subject of switching loyalties, I tell Némoise so as to be the one directing the course of our interaction for a change. On that fateful night after the wedding my loyalty went from Pietro to Giovanni, but it was not the first time it happened.

In my earliest memories, I find myself enraptured with my young mother, the silk of her hair, the sweetness of her scent, a gentle taste of peaches in my mouth. A picture of her standing under a blossoming tree, wearing a flowered chiffon dress and enfolding me, a baby, in the world of her arms stands out. Maybe it's a photo in my mother's old album.

In the picture the sun breaks into golden fishes bouncing off leaves, spots of light fall on my mother's face, on her clothes. Everything is purring. I drift into the flowers on the dress, they expand and become the blossoms on the tree. Diffused feelings come into awareness for the first time.

Out there the world is familiar and friendly. My bliss creates it. The shifting light picks up elements of the surroundings and sends them off like fireworks of goodwill. It's the voice of the tree that makes me conscious of my mother's love, of my love for her. My head on her chest, I follow with a finger the soft skin in her cleavage. From the faint sound of her heart beating against my cheek I derive the courage to see the world outside myself, a world bright with colors dancing around the glistening tree. I love my mother so much and I have so much time to discover the world out there, a world so separate and yet so close.

Tu vois, there are also blissful memories.

Yes, I am thankful for that.

In those early days, I could only concentrate on one person at a time. As I started to walk and talk, my attention shifted from my mother to Pietro, my half-brother, whenever he came around. Angela shrank away into the background but didn't resent him for that. She only had good things to say about her stepson, he was a good boy who never gave her any trouble. She took good care of him, was always fair and respectful of his young manhood. They had a good relationship. But she never felt she had the right to intervene when Giovanni punished his son unfairly. I wonder if there was something she knew and never told, but because of that a distance always remained between them. And on that fateful night after the wedding, Giovanni became my only focus.

In the back of the church the wind moves in through a side door that remains open in the summer, pushing some dead leaves that roll across the center aisle. As it squeezes through a narrow opening on a side chapel, it finds its plaintive voice. Autumn already? I shiver and tighten my jersey around my shoulders.

Now Angela looms big again. Despite her frail appearance she is the survivor, the keeper of the family's memories and secrets. She holds all the keys; my childhood hope chest would be closed forever if it weren't for her.

Tu parles surtout de toi! Everything you tell is mostly about you. Tell us more about your mother, would you?

MY MOTHER LOOMS BIG

Yes, of course. Angela was always worried. I remember her many warnings as I entered the different stages of life, but also how she passed along her own kind of wisdom.

"When a woman is young," she cautioned in my early twenties, "men try to take advantage of her. They get their pleasure and discard her when they are tired of it." When I entered mid-life she predicted, "You'll see as you get older. You become invisible as a woman. Younger generations have no respect for the wisdom of age these days. After fifty, you've lost all your appeal and are of no value. There is no compassion for your frailty after sixty, you are just an elderly lady incapable of clear thinking. Past seventy you might as well be dead and if you aren't, you should be. Unless, of course, you are famous, then you remain young forever."

So my mother, who used to be beautiful, learned to nourish herself, in her older years, with the village bustle, the gossip on the square in front of her house, the sound of bells. She doesn't have much else since I live so far away.

I pause but there is only silence. I was probably too judgmental again!

I walk out of the church and into the heat. The wind that made me shiver inside is actually a hot wind from the south. I cross the road and enter the common courtyard through the large portal between two stone buildings.

Houses in Lerné are built that way, four or five to a communal courtyard and garden. My mother shares her courtyard with a cheerful hunchback nurse, a somber carpenter who makes his musical saw whine every evening, a jolly baker and his wife, and finally the *Société,* a gathering place for village men.

In the summer everyone eats late and my mother tries to adjust to that custom, but her tendency is to have her dinner very early. It's the crunching of the gravel when the nurse comes home at six o'clock that tells Angela it's time to have her last meal of the day, but on holidays when the family gets together around the long table she does not care how late we eat. On one of those days we usually make gnocchi.

Making gnocchi under my mother's directions is an event the whole family is eager to be part of. It is the glue that binds us together as a tribe, and if a member cannot participate for one reason or another he feels as dejected as if he had been cast off for good. If it's not the day the butcher-on-wheels comes through Lerné, someone has to drive my mother to her favorite butcher in Thizay in the early morning to get a big chunk of brisket and a few *os à moelle*, those large leg bones full of marrow. She knows just how to handle the simple, powerful piece of meat.

She comes home and pulls out her big *cocotte* to brown the meat on all sides. She then fries bacon in butter and *fait sauter* just the right amount of onions in it. They have to be translucent but not brown, that is an absolute rule; a few cloves of garlic follow. Later she dices fresh toma- toes and adds a profusion of them along with spices, a *bouquet garni* from her garden and a cup of her best *Chinon* wine. This is to simmer all day and as the *fumet* rises, the aroma drives us mad with desire but we are for- bidden to pick up the lid and dip a chunk of bread in the sauce for it would spoil the magic.

When her back is turned, however, we never miss the opportunity, for the simmering dish is infused with the knowing tenderness of the generations. And then comes the sacred moment, the ritual we would remind each other of all through the year, the communion. We all stand around the long table, which is well scrubbed, powdered with flour and at the center of which my mother has piled a mountain of mashed potatoes. She makes a hole in the center of the mound and breaks two eggs into it. Then she adds some flour a little at a time and kneads the whole thing vigorously. Only she knows the amount of flour that makes the dough just right, for to follow a recipe with proportions is unknown to her, but she has the utmost respect for the firmness of the long tubes of dough we must roll on the table. Firm but not too hard; the gnocchi once cooked are to be sublime little sponges drinking up the sauce and returning its full flavor to our salivating mouths.

Some of us roll the tubes of dough and cut them into small chunks, others more expert gently push the chunks onto a floured fork and curl them around—they look somewhat like ridged wood shavings. The gnocchi then are deposited like delicate shells onto large platters and soon the whole table is covered with those full platters. Finally comes the tricky part: the gnocchi are to be very gently dropped into a humongous *marmite* of boiling water without touching each other. They drop to the bottom but as soon as they rise to the surface a large *écumoire* seizes them and deposits them into the sublime sauce whose meat had been removed and cut into chunks to be served on top of the dish.

Finally we sit together at the table and pass the freshly grated parmesan around. As we partake of the food our eating has a religious significance and no one says a word as we slowly savor every nuance and inhale the bouquet.

The rest of the time Angela eats her dinner early and alone. Inviting neighbors and friends to her table is not a concept she can understand. Only the rich do that, it's a privilege not available to everyone. In turn she is never invited anywhere except for a cup of coffee or a glass of wine. Villagers' food is reserved for their family.

Her courtyard is never entirely quiet. The baker works till the wee hours of morning with his radio turned on all night long. It keeps her insomnia company. She likes that. The *Société*, on the other hand, is a bother to her. A poor excuse for a local bar, it was created decades ago as a hunting club but does not have much atmosphere. Most village men go for a drink there three times a day. They talk animatedly about politics, taxes, the corrupt government, the poor crops, the price of wheat. They play cards, *Pétanque* or *Boule de Fort*. Bottles are uncorked in mid-morning, at lunchtime, at five o'clock, sometimes after dinner.

For the longest time women were not allowed to set foot in the *Société*. A sign on the door read, *Interdit aux femmes et aux chiens,* forbidden to women and dogs. When the right of women to frequent the place was finally voted in, they refused to honor it.

There are no cash transactions at the *Société,* only tabs. People write down with chalk on a blackboard how many beers they had, how many bottles of wine they opened. Each member has his own way of handling the chalk, with confidence and authority, or as an afterthought, hesitantly. Some make it screech annoyingly. My mother recognizes each man by the rhythm of his writing. She can also tell who is opening a bottle from the way the cork pops, she sniffs out whether it's wine, cider or beer that has been uncorked and identifies the forgetful or dishonest man who hasn't written his name down after opening a bottle.

My mother goes to bed earlier than most but hardly sleeps. Propped up with pillows she makes out from the sound of steps on the gravel who crosses the courtyard to enter the *Société* after dinner. She knows the ones to watch out for, never fails to catch the drinker—too lazy to climb to the toilet on the first floor—stepping out and pissing from behind the hedge into her garden.

Her outrage springs her into action and she rises from her fluffy bed to catch the man in the act, bombarding him from her window with a steady barrage of insults until his penis arrested in midair shuts down and dribbles pitifully. The sheepish man reduced to eternal shame puts away his half-relieved instrument with a hangdog look, for he knows he will have to endure the sarcasm of his drinking companions watching from behind the *Société*'s glass door.

There is no end to what Angela assures me she can hear when all windows and doors are opened in the summer; she can hear the clinking of silverware against plates in the carpenter's house, she can hear sobs from the cemetery nearly a block away and assures me it's her friend Blanche crying; she can hear the love chats of Fricaut the baker next door; she can gather every word of the juicy gossip from the butcher-on-wheels delivery van on the village square; she can hear the envy simmering behind the flattery at the greengrocer's across from it. But she never hears what she doesn't want to hear.

During the good season she keeps her windows open so as to listen to the village from the comfort of her overstuffed armchair. She uses her sense of smell like a thread she spins out toward the center of action, connecting it back to her web and wrapping the juicy morsels for later. She knows more about most people than they would ever wish anyone to know, but the ones who particularly tickle her fancy are those who don't care what she knows, the *bon-vivants* and wild ones who are not bothered by the venom of forked tongues, the impetuous ones who can't help but take risks.

"Just like you," she accuses whenever we are on the subject. And, according to her, they live too loudly, laugh too much. Just like me.

One man in particular draws my mother out of the habit-struck dullness she has chosen in order to avoid the blows life deals to those who stand out in any way, it's Fricaut the baker.

ngela

Live each day as if it were the last, leave no room for regrets.
—*Sainte Némoise*

2

MY VILLAGERS: FRICAUT, the best of bread, the best in bed, BLANCHE & her homonym, JOJO the gravedigger

In which Angela instead of getting ready for the train muses about Fricaut the baker, her neighbor, his affairs, his sexual prowess, his pranks, his offerings to Némoise, also about other villagers, her friend Blanche dealing with her son's suicide in her own way, her daily visits to the cemetery, the book of her namesake opened on the grave, and finally about Jojo the gravedigger and his obsession with death and burial; where Angela spies on Orsolina's diary and expresses her distrust of too much analysis with not enough real information; in which she may allude to the family secret she has kept from her daughter.

From my window I see Fricaut busying himself. In a little while he will come to pick up my daughter and me to drive us to the train station.

He is the village baker, my neighbor, a half-breed Gypsy with deep dark eyes and a jet-black pompadour. Men in Lerné distrust him, as they distrusted my husband and me when we first came to settle in this village. Villagers didn't like our foreign accent, in their minds Italians were over-sexed thieves. It took them ten years to let me pass the threshold of their houses. Another ten to invite me in for a drink. I don't like them much.

I met Fricaut's mother, a beautiful Gypsy woman, *une Manouche*. I liked her immediately, but nobody else did in the village. The people of her tribe disowned her, for she has committed the unforgivable sin of falling in love and settling into a stagnant life with a *sédentaire*, as the traveling people contemptuously call those who never move away from the place where they were born. She can never go back to her tribe. She is an outcast.

Women in the village may not approve of his mother, but they just love Fricaut and he is crazy about them all, whether young or old, fat or skinny, tall or petite. Sometimes he comes and talks to me. I encourage him to seduce wives while their husbands are out drinking. Being cuckolded is what those selfish drunkards deserve.

He flirts shamelessly with his lady customers while selling them the best bread in the region. He offers pastries so divine, women who taste them melt into a puddle of pure delight, and they long to surrender, like bread dough, to his expert hands. He knows when they are baked just right, when they are ready to offer him their hearts . . . and the secret in-between their legs.

I heard a little singsong a youngster was broadcasting through the village:

> *His cock rises in the morning,*
> *and bread is not the only thing*
> *that is baked in the evening. . .*

If I were younger, I might go for him, even though there is something that disturbs me about his looks. From the waist up he is a perfect dark Adonis, strong handsome features, broad shoulders, the athletic build of a tall man, but from the waist down he is very short, with small legs that don't belong to his upper body. However I hear from certain ladies that the important part of him matches the upper.

If he were my lover, I would keep him in bed to avoid looking at his legs. But he is in his mid-forties and I am in my early seventies, even if I look younger than my age as I am told. My hair is white, I keep it very short, my sharp face and thin lips give me an air of sternness and frigidity according to Orsolina.

Although he told me much in the past about his most passionate affairs, he is bashful when it comes to details nowadays. I don't know why. He hardly ever lets me in on his illicit liaisons anymore, but I know much more than he thinks.

Fricaut hardly ever sleeps. I hear him whistling along with his radio till two or three in the morning while preparing his dough and dividing it into loaves. As the bread rises, he catches a few hours of sleep right at the foot of his kneading trough where he has dragged a folding bed. He wakes up to light the fire under his brick oven and lets it heat up. He might catch a little more sleep as the bread bakes, but at six o'clock on the dot he is up to start his deliveries.

He brings bread to isolated farms. Even at that early hour, most of the men are already working in the fields. Along with warm bread, he offers the ladies the deep well of his languorous eyes, the dark velvet of his melodious voice and the hot fire of his wondrous cock.

I don't know what kind of arrangements he has with the farmers' wives he enflames, what secret code they use so as not to be surprised in their lovemaking, but he never gets caught. To absolve him, I must add that he never makes love without passion.

I often point out Fricaut's mistresses and his illegitimate children to my daughter Orsolina when we take walks together, something we both love to do. I can tell that she does not really believe me. I am not sure how many women Fricaut services on his morning runs, but many of the youngsters around the village look an awful lot like him.

When I tell her that Fricaut is always fervent about love, that he never has an affair without passion, Orsolina answers that passion has nothing to do with love. "It tries to disguise the fear of death as desire. It's a means of self-deification, and no one can sustain a steady diet of it without eventually experiencing a fall." She always has complicated theories about everything, most of which I hardly understand.

Once a month Fricaut takes me along with him to the big market in Chinon. First we have to make his deliveries, fresh bread is sacred and must get to the people daily no matter what. He never takes a day off. Triumphant, he drives his bread van into farm courtyards, honking savagely like a drummer leading the troops to battle. He immediately notices whether the tractor is still sitting there, in which case the husband is home— whether the milk vats are lined up against the barn wall ready for the pick-up, which means that the driver from the dairy will appear.

If the men are home they invite him to drink with them—straight shots of *goutte,* a seventy-degree proof alcohol distilled from fruit. They chase it down with coffee. It's their opinion that this gets rid of the night's cobwebs and cuts through the morning chill.

Farmers like Fricaut because he makes them laugh; he is not afraid of seeming a fool. When men are not around, however, he loves to laugh with women.

He was not always shy about the juicy details. He showed me old love letters from the time when he was apprenticing to become a baker, declarations from his bosses' wives, overflowing with passionate revelations and luscious descriptions.

"Straight out of *Nous Deux*," he said proudly as he handed me an enflamed letter a baker's wife had slipped into his pocket during one of his apprenticeships—he and I share a love of romance novels. It was not his first conquest. He had already acquired some skills during a previous apprenticeship when he was sixteen.

As his story went, the fiery woman's husband was out making deliveries, but the shop was already opened. Customers filed in steadily and soon she was out of hot morning bread. She went to the bakery kitchen in the back to get the bread that Fricaut had just taken out of the oven. She was standing next to the big kneading machine when he sneaked behind her and whispered, "The letter you put in my pocket set my body on fire."

Meanwhile his fingers gently climbed up her leg, pulling her skirt up inch by inch, crawling to the inside of the thigh, gently pushing her panties aside and moving into the crotch, ever so slowly. The woman was trembling so hard her legs were giving way. In a weak voice she kept murmuring an unconvincing, "No, no, please, not here," while shaking her head. But as he gently parted the lips and introduced a probing finger inside her folds, her *non* became weaker and weaker and her legs opened wider as if they had a will of their own.

In the throes of passion they made love right there on the floor of the bakery, the excitement mounting with the urgency of the danger, her *non, non* rising in intensity until it ascended to a glorious, *"oui, oui, give it, give it to me, oh, you are so big, give it, I am all yours."* Anyone could have walked in on them at any moment, husband or customers, but they no longer cared.

He was nineteen or twenty by the time he had his last affair as an apprentice. My understanding is that the baker's wife was about twenty years older than he. "Quite a live wire," Fricaut commented. "She wanted hot sex all the time, kept asking for more any chance we got. I could barely keep up."

Come to think of it, I got plenty of details about that story also. "When she first made advances I couldn't believe my luck for she was quite a catch, very shapely and just ripe enough, soft like a plum," he told me. But he couldn't reconcile himself with the betrayal involved because he liked the baker, and he didn't go along with it right away.

She pursued him on any occasion, came through the kitchen bakery many times a day to bring her husband something to eat or drink, squeezing herself between the apprentice and the kneading trough as she went, rubbing her generous breasts against him. He'd get aroused but remained stoic and didn't respond until she handed him such a graphic note he could no longer control himself.

Always these notes! I guess it's the written word that makes him fall. Fricaut rationalized, as he often did to assuage his guilt, that his boss was really a bastard, that he mistreated his wife and exploited him.

Whenever the husband went away on deliveries, the bakery kitchen was on fire. The passionate couple did it above, below, on top of or under tables, even in the brick oven when it was still warm, sperm and juices flying around. They did it with dough and pastry dildoes, using Chantilly cream, smearing it on bodies and into orifices to be licked clean by eager tongues.

Eventually Fricaut fell in love with the woman who is now his wife. The Black-Panther-of-the-Green-Eyes he calls her. To hear her talking you would think she had explored every aspect of gallantry, that she had *le feu au cul,* her pussy was on fire, that she was a hot number, a *baiseuse.* But in fact she is totally frigid and does not give a hoot about her husband's escapades as long as he leaves her alone, sexually speaking.

From the very beginning of their relationship she'd read magazines over his shoulder or yawn widely when he made love to her. That seriously dampened his flame. He can't even get it up for her anymore.

Fricaut's passionate mistress tried to kill him when he told her he was getting married. He had to run away like a thief in the night, leaving a month's salary behind.

My daughter would be shocked by these graphic descriptions, especially coming from me. There is hardly anybody, no matter how old, who can handle an association of their parents with sex. Orsolina would be angry with Fricaut for telling me all this. He must sense that and that's probably why he doesn't give me any details anymore. I know he is secretly in love with my Orsolina.

She thinks I am a prude, a frigid woman who despises men and hates sex. I suppose it's my fault if she thinks of me that way. I worked hard at making her believe that sex was no fun. I had good reasons for that. I could tell the minute she was born that she was wild and greedy for sensations. She couldn't stay away from the teat. I was afraid that if I didn't reduce her fire early she would get into all kinds of trouble later and I wouldn't be able to control her.

But here I am, thinking about Fricaut and his affairs when I should be getting ready to go to Paris with Orsolina. If she catches me sitting here looking out the window instead of packing she'll be annoyed. The truth is I don't really want to go to Paris or even think about Pietro's funeral. I have attended enough funerals in my life. Pietro himself didn't like funerals, so I'd rather remember Fricaut and his fornications.

After his first taste of sex Fricaut could never get enough. What followed was a long chain of love affairs, one link hooking the next. Women would hear about his prowess and become anxious to be one of those he had his way with, or who had their way with him. "Women taught me everything I know," he boasts. And he took his apprenticeship of love as seriously as his bread and pastry making, an absolutely necessary ingredient in the art of living.

What remains a mystery to me is what brings such a pagan and sworn anti-clerical to the church before anyone is up in the wee hours of morning. He started a few years ago. I spied on him once. He went in with a baguette in his hand. Got out without it. I was very curious. I entered the church soon after, looking for the baguette. I found it in front of Sainte Némoise's altar. Then I understood.

He must put the first baguette to come out of his oven as an offering to Némoise. What is his special connection with that saint? Does he consider her a pagan deity who will help him with his trade? Does he want to lure her and make love to her in dreams? What is it with that saint anyway? I know that my daughter also has some special relationship with Némoise.

At first it enraged the priest to find that baguette when it was no longer fresh. I heard him ranting about it to Madame Manceau across the road, "It's a scandal to offer food to saints as though they were pagan deities. And such an obvious sinful symbol at that!" But now that he found out that the baguette appears every morning, he picks it up for his breakfast.

On his way back from the church, if Fricaut finds laundry left on the line in villagers' courtyards, and if perchance there happens to be women's underwear drying there, the baker never misses the opportunity to put a carrot in the crotches of those underpants large enough to receive it—most farmwomen don't bother with cute panties.

The outraged complaints from the women whose underpants have been chosen is all pretense, they actually are flattered by such a choice, but the exasperation from the women who never get Fricaut's attention is even louder. It feeds the town gossip.

I really have no business thinking about Fricaut now. I had better get ready for the trip to Paris or Orsolina will chastise me; I hope she does not ask too many questions while on the train, especially about Pietro. I can pack my suitcase, but can't stop my mind from wandering.

BLANCHE
There is a woman in the village Fricaut never touched although she

is dying of love for him. Her name is Blanche. She likes me and wants to be my friend, maybe because in our different ways we both are strangers in Lerné. She is no spring chicken, but the age difference wouldn't be of concern to him. He is used to mature women who need the vigor of youth to resurrect their ardor dulled by a stuffy husband.

It's not her seniority that keeps him away from Blanche, but rather a certain air about her that distinguishes her from other villagers. She is not from around here and since most country folks never move away from the place where they were born, they distrust those who come from afar. Blanche came to the village about ten years ago. Because she is more re-fined than the crude farmwomen with their rough hands and inclination for graphic jokes she is thought of as standoffish. What no one knows is that she is rather shy and that those solid women frighten her. She certainly is not distant with me. She comes to my house often to have coffee and she invites me to hers.

Her husband has more means than most people around here and that disturbs the villagers, especially since they don't know exactly what he does. He is away from home a lot and she is lonely. He is her second husband, and that's to be distrusted here where you are supposed to be married once and for all. Her only son who died very tragically a year back was from her first marriage. I hear that the stepfather was hard on the boy, strict, abusive even, and that he made his wife's life miserable because of it. He was probably jealous of this son she adored.

The circumstances of the teen's death started a frenzy of specu-lation. Some maintained that his suicide was drug related, others said that it was to escape his stepfather's punishment for wrecking the car he had borrowed without permission. Others yet suggested that his stepfather had forced on him a fiancée the young man didn't like. Whatever the reason, on his eighteenth birthday, he took his life with his stepfather's hunting gun.

It was Sunday morning in early November a year ago. I remember because the last leaves were falling and the smell of decay and smoke hung in the air. His parents never missed the Sunday Mass, and he usually went with them, but on that day he complained that he didn't feel well and wanted to stay home.

As soon as they left he made his bed, covered his velvet bedspread with layers of white sheets and tablecloths, wrapped his head in thick white towels and shot himself through the mouth. By the time his parents came back, he was getting stiff.

I was impressed by the meticulous way in which the young man had prepared himself and the bed so as not to ruin his mother's decor. She is a fine housekeeper. Everything in her home matches and is impeccably clean. Her son obviously wanted to make sure that the blood wouldn't permanently soil any of the rugs, cushions or tapestries. I am sure he chose white so everything could be bleached.

What a considerate young man he was, not unlike Pietro had been with me. How could Pietro leave now, only a year after his father? That is not so thoughtful. And why, if he had to die, didn't he do it in Lerné so I could have him next to me and visit him in the cemetery? He wanted to be here for the last weeks of his life, but the family had to transport him in urgency when he started to get worse so that he ended up dying in Paris instead of in my house.

I might be better off not having seen Pietro's dead body. My friend Blanche went mad when she found her son. Forgetting her overwhelming distaste for anything that leaked, her irrational fear of blood, she threw herself on his body. It took four men to get her off, covered with her son's blood. When they relaxed their hold she escaped again, throwing herself against the wall and banging her head with great force until she lost consciousness.

When she came to, the body of her son had been taken to the morgue, the bloody sheets and towels removed. Blanche never talked to her husband again. She forbade the cleaning lady to scrub off the over-looked spot of blood that had splattered the wall in spite of her son's precautions. She actually framed that spot. Rumor has it that she found a letter from him in a purse she seldom used, but she never showed it to anyone or talked about it.

Now she visits his grave daily in any weather, arms loaded with red roses and white lilies. She had a greenhouse built around the tomb-stone so that exotic plants and tropical flowers could thrive. Every now and then she adds a new memorial plaque engraved with his picture, a sculpture or bas-relief depicting ascending angels, cupids, doves with lily of the valley sprigs in their beaks. She writes short poems to him and has them carved in white marble.

She also took to putting one red rose in front of Némoise's statue in the church. What is all this going on about *Sainte* Némoise lately? In the past it was only the old crones in the village who seemed to have an attachment to the saint, but now. . .

Anyway, a few weeks after the burial, a leather bound book appeared among the flowers. It was opened to the first page. I was visiting my husband's grave fairly regularly at the time and the two tombstones were next to each other so I noticed the book immediately. Beautifully illustrated, a tale was written in large characters on parchment. It told the story of a countess of Chavigny named Blanche who lived in the Lerné castle a long time ago and fell in love with a knight called Tristan. At one time that tale about a jealous husband who tricked his unfaithful wife into eating her lover's heart had been known to everyone, but forgotten.

Every day the book was open to a new page so whoever was interested could read the tale. Women told each other and those who had nothing better to do while their husbands drank at the *societé,* gathered in the cemetery during late afternoons.

After the last page was turned, the book was removed and a ceramic bleeding heart was put in its place. Those who had come to the cemetery day after day to follow the story wondered what was meant by all that. The grieved mother was seen kissing the heart while pounding hard on her own. Had she gone insane? Did she believe that her son's heart and the knight's heart were one and the same? Did she mistake herself for her namesake?

Oh, I wish Pietro were buried here so I could visit him and remind him of the village's stories and tales just like Blanche is doing with her son. He must be so lonely in an anonymous cemetery in Paris.

I had lots of time to think about villagers during the lonely years I spent caring for my husband Giovanni. I came to believe that Blanche tormented her heart with her unreturned passion for the baker as an act of contrition. Meanwhile, Fricaut is molesting his own heart with a secret love for my daughter Orsolina.

I am good at reading hearts. I know that he will never tell her about his love. He thinks her too good for him, sophisticated, well read and well traveled, when he barely finished middle school and has never gone anywhere out of the region. Besides, she has her own family and would never give Fricaut the time of day. He is sorely aware of all that but is obviously attracted to what he thinks he can't get. Romantic and tragic, Fricaut the womanizer thrives in this role as the victim of love. I am good at reading hearts.

JOJO THE GRAVEDIGGER

I have a few other friends in the village besides Blanche and Fricaut. One of them is a man called Jojo. I met him through Marcel, a neighbor of mine about Pietro's age whom I became very fond of over the years. When Marcel introduced me to his uncle Jojo he proudly added,

"You know, everyone says that my uncle is quite an artist."

Jojo is in his late forties, one of Fricaut's buddies. He is as tall as Fricaut is short, dark skinned, lanky and always a little disheveled. He often comes to visit the bakery's kitchen. Since I live next door, he stops by and brings me vegetables from his garden. People say that he is no more than a pathetic drunk, a blabbermouth and a lecher, but whenever I watch him tend his garden in the early morning hours before the wine has replaced the blood in his veins, I can't help but notice the way he talks to each new blossom, the marvel in his eyes as he caresses each little start. It makes me forgive his drunkenness and irritating behavior.

Jojo used to carve on tombstones. He was good at it. He had the right touch, but there is not much need for this kind of carving any longer. Except for Blanche, most people nowadays order cheap gravestones of particle granite with smooth tops and square edges. "Death is not what it used to be," says Jojo. "People won't pay for bas-reliefs, for fancy crosses with angels flying around. They don't want any engraved words of regret, no doves holding lilies, no white marble book or frame carved around a suitable photograph. They don't even buy a Virgin Mary or a baby Jesus to adorn their tombstones. All they want is a name, and maybe, if the deceased is lucky, they'll stick an occasional bunch of glass flowers in a container of sand placed right in the middle as if to mark the bellybutton of the defunct."

Jojo doesn't find much in this line of work any longer, so he resorts to digging graves, repairing roofs, putting up fences, building sheds, painting walls for anybody who wishes to hire him. When the day begins to bear heavily on him, he goes over to the *Societé* where corks joyously pop. He vowed not to touch the stuff until the bell rang twelve, but then he allows himself all he needs to lighten his grief for his lost art.

One morning while digging a grave, he reflected that since he was such an exceptionally tall man there wouldn't be a coffin to fit him when he died. He decided to go over to his friend Coco, the coffin and cabinet-maker to talk it over. He ended up ordering one the very next day out of mahogany. When Coco delivered the coffin, Jojo stored it under his kitchen table where he could admire it daily. "I love the discreet shine on the exotic wood. It's all hand rubbed and French-varnished you know, none of that plasticky acrylic stuff."

Jojo never married and, as far as I know, never had a girlfriend. He makes such a fuss over Joan of Arc I suspect that he is in love with *La Pucelle* and that he keeps himself for her. When I tell him about Némoise's recent popularity he points out the neglect in which that saint is kept compared to the statue of Joan as portrayed in the church, the thrust of her big sword so realistic. With contempt he remarks, "As far as virgins' fame goes, Joan definitely wins the race." When I tease him about Saint Michael being Joan's only true love he gets all upset.

Jojo takes his three meals a day sitting alone at the kitchen table, feet resting on the coffin. As he thoroughly masticates his food in the slow way of folks around here, you never know what he'll come up with! One year he had a bright idea but kept it to himself until his birthday.

On that day, he put on his best clothes and asked four of his drinking buddies over to help him do a prank. The open coffin was on the table. Jojo climbed on a chair and lay down in it. He told his amazed friends about his plan and gave precise directions.

They would have to take some of the heavy-scented flowers he had picked for the occasion and display them all around him in the coffin before sliding the lid back on. They would carry the coffin on their shoulders to a partly dug grave in the cemetery. Jojo was ready for the next death at all times, always a hole ahead of himself. They solemnly would lower the box into the hole, trying to shed a tear or two as they threw a few handfuls of dirt down on the lid.

The first year the show was staged, Jojo waited for his friends to bring him back up. He had rigged up a system of ropes for that purpose. He waited and waited but his friends, no longer spring chickens, were having a hell of a time figuring out how to raise the heavy coffin with the ropes. Jojo finally burst out of it, scolding them and ordering them to give him a hand. When he was out of the hole he declared, "I can't compliment you, my dear friends, for the quality of your performance. I hope you do better next year." And they fortified themselves with a few liters of wine.

The next year, when they had ironed out the wrinkles, Jojo praised his friends declaring, "This calls for a celebration, let's go on a round of the missions," and he took his buddies from bar to bar in Chinon, treating them to all they could drink.

This has become a yearly tradition. Jojo tells the story of how it all began to whomever wants to hear it. "I won't be a witness to my own burial once I am already dead," he concludes. "I might as well have that pleasure now, when my eyes and ears and nostrils are still wide open." Lauding the virtue of making friends with one's own death, he goes on and on, enrolling quite a following for the next year's burial.

I keep having these recollections about my friends and neighbors in the village. Maybe it's to avoid thinking about Pietro. My daughter believes that I never think for myself, that I never have an original thought. I heard her say to a friend, "My mother uses a stick language, the language of conventional clichés." More of her theories!

A few days ago I picked up Orsolina's journal she had left on the dining room table after she went out. I opened it to this:

Uneducated people live in survival mode and never develop enough language to express what they feel because they don't fully grasp the symbols representing feelings or ideas. People who can't read probably don't think much, their imagination is a desert. They live in inner silence, don't develop concepts, have no understanding of their motives and never question who they are.

What cannot be expressed is not felt. Like children, they only understand pictures and simplistic stories. They live in the moment, follow their instinct, make decisions from their guts, hardly ever using their minds. As I write this trying to understand un primaire, a one-dimensional, uneducated person, I see that I might just as well be describing an actualized being, someone totally living in the present—and that is what many sophisticates are striving for.

I didn't want to go any further. Didn't need to. I had an idea who my daughter was talking about. Orsolina too often forgets that although my brothers and sisters were illiterate, nuns took me in and taught me well. She forgets that although my French might be rudimentary, I can speak, read and write Italian fluently. There is no end to what my daughter doesn't know. She doesn't know that I won't talk about Pietro's death because I cannot tell anyone what I know.

ietro

This life is like a dream of a dream; real life is elsewhere.
—Sainte Némoise

3

ORSOLINA AND THE GYPSIES

In which Pietro, Orsolina's beloved brother, speaks from the other side one day after he died, situating himself and Némoise in the spirit world, describing how he entered the tunnel, the gentle place where he rests now, the spirit guide who is with him, appearing and disappearing, and who reminds him of Fricaut the Gypsy; also where he reminisces about his sister Orsolina, her fascination with hoodlums and Gypsies, her boldness, and why he would never deal with the whole truth in his lifetime, how he died of invasive cancer.

It's my turn. I have things to say but haven't been allowed to have a voice yet. It was often like that in my lifetime. I've learned to watch out or someone would take over, speak for me.

Without a body to hold me down I can be in more than one place at once. I just found that out. I can be discovering the spirit world while still trying to figure out things on earth. My body just died yesterday in the morning, but from where I stand it could be years.

Némoise, the saint from Lerné Orsolina is so fond of, likes to be the director of the play and inform the public supposedly as a fair witness, but she has her own take on things. In the world where I am now she is no more a saint than anyone else. Even Catholics could never pin her down as to whose side she was really on, God or the Devil. Evanescent as mist, capricious as a river over rocks, she slips in and out of one reality after another, moves from one spiritual heaven to the next. Right now she seems to spend most of her time on earth, she may be stuck, not in one of her incarnations but in an interpretation of incarnation.

So from an earthly point of view it is the first day after I passed away. There is someone here with me; someone very patient who seems intent on guiding me, for things can get confusing. I feel him as masculine but I am not sure. He is mostly eyes, deep orbs of kindness in an egg shape made of light filaments. Nobody has told me but I know his name is Yamill. Something about his energy reminds me of Gypsies, of Fricaut the baker in particular, even though Yamill feels more like a giant than a semi-dwarf.

He informs me that after death people mostly go where they believed they would go while they were alive. There are many paradises and purgatories on all different reality levels. Every religion has its own heaven and hell, but there are others, non-religious ones. Yamill says it will take me a while to figure things out, but that here time doesn't count, doesn't even exist. He tells me that for now I still have to finish things with some people on earth, so I will remain on the planet until the day of my funeral and even come back at different times after that.

My sister Orsolina is one of the people I still have to resolve things with, I know that. She is on my mind a lot in a different sort of way. Like Némoise, Orsolina is continually on the move and refuses to be accounted for; she won't be pinned down, always gallops ahead of herself, does not like the sedentary life. So Gypsy-like the both of them!

I have often wondered why Orsolina had to emigrate like our parents and move to America, so far away from us all? Our parents did it out of necessity, but she was educated and provided for, had no good reason to follow in their steps. Was immigration a fate she couldn't escape? I will have to ask Yamill when he reappears. He tends to vanish for long periods of time, and then shows up when least expected, hardly ever when I call him though, and he doesn't always answer my questions.

Right now, having gone through the difficult passage, I am in what seems like a pleasant waiting place, lingering here until the next step is shown to me.

Soon after I died, things were strange and very frightening. Such blackness and total immobility to start with, no sense of self or direction, a void. I think that on my last day, when I mentioned the black hole in front of me to Orsolina, I really scared her. She told me to look for a light, even just a glimmer, but I didn't see anything like that for a long time. When I did, I could no longer communicate with her.

After a while a gentle but irresistible current pushed me towards a gleam of light directing me into a tunnel made of dark gray clouds. On each side of it there were openings like doorways, with scripts I didn't recognize suspended above each one. At that point I had a little more control over my navigation and I could have gone through any of those entrances, but I chose not to. At the end of the tunnel I met what I believed was my guardian angel because he was a form surrounded by a white halo. I trusted him immediately.

It was Yamill. I was awed by the totality of his presence. The association I made with Gypsies came later when I was in the waiting place reviewing parts of my life, and I remembered how fond Orsolina and I were of Gypsies, daunted by their mystery, wishing to learn their strange ways.

I recall one day when in spite of Angela's advice my sister and I visited the Gypsy camp. Our father Giovanni had flat out forbidden us and I was too scared of him to disobey like she did, even though I was thirteen years older than she was. She talked me into it though.

Outside the village of Lerné Gypsies camped all summer, along rivers, on the edge of forests or at the *friche,* a big meadow on the outskirts of the village where an ancient custom granted them the right to park their caravans for weeks at a time.

That spring, Orsolina and I watched as the first caravans drove through Lerné. Within a day or two, slower wagons pulled by horses followed. Mangy dogs tied to the rear licked the feet of dirty, half-naked children riding in the back, legs hanging down.

In the past, the tradition was for some of the Gypsy men to walk down the streets to announce the caravans' arrival and the various wonders Gypsies would offer, how they could foretell health, happiness and love, divine secrets. People were glad to see them arrive, for they provided entertainment, could repair their pots and pans and cane their broken wicker chairs. Since the advent of TV however, and private transportation made accessible to all, people ceased to be interested and became suspicious of what Gypsies had to propose.

No sooner was the camp set up than hip-swinging young women in gaudy clothes and cheaply bleached hair flocked into the villages and towns of the area selling baskets made from rushes and reeds. They stood on street corners, hands on hips, self-assured, their stance scorning the disapproving passersby. "Here I am and I have no problem with that, so why should you?" they seemed to say.

Pubescent girls with bundles swung over their shoulders wove their way towards the nearby farms demanding petty cash to feed their starving grandmothers or their ailing brothers, and trying to introduce themselves inside of houses under one pretense or another in order to pinch what they could.

In Lerné, the word preceded the Gypsies and went around in a hurry: the *Manouches* are coming. Beware! Don't let them into your house, not even in the courtyard if they ask for a pail of water. Only a fool would let the wolf into the poultry. Gypsies will steal your chicken, your cattle, your kettles, and your children. If you meet them at the market, hang on to your billfold. If they offer to cane your chairs watch out. If they want to read your fortune, don't allow them in your house or storage shed. Tools will disappear under their skirts or in their pockets in a split second. Always be on the lookout.

"They are quick. They know lots of magic tricks. Count your chicks. Grab a stick. Hold your dick," children sang.

And just to make sure no Gypsy got a free ride, farmer's wives would tear their discarded clothes to pieces before taking them to the dump where Gypsies would have a chance to retrieve them.

All this fuss didn't ruffle the ill-mannered *Manouches* though. They were never short of *amour-propre*. Their self-esteem was very good thank you, they acted cocky around villagers and town dwellers, showed no respect for those *sédentaires* who never moved away from one place. Only around their campfire did they let go of their arrogance.

It was there that Orsolina and I longed to join them, at a time when they took it easy, ate and talked, made music and sang, gambled, joked or fell silent. We'd observed them from afar, unnoticed, saw the huge bonfires they lit and how the wind curled the flames in twisted tongues. At times fist fighting and wrestling occurred, someone would throw out a remark that drew laughter, another would play guitar and sing. Smoke traveling sideways enshrouded them all in a strange phantasmagoria as we watched, wishing to be part of the festivities.

In the old days the more daring villagers went to the camp for a game of dice, but nowadays no one would ever visit a Gypsy camp at night and *Manouches* only went to villages under the cover of darkness to snatch poultry or pilfer vegetables in gardens. Very aware of how the sedentary people locked safely inside their houses feared them because they were dark and different, they roamed without restraint then.

"They are free and have nothing to lose, so they are capable of anything," Angela would comment. Indeed Gypsies considered freedom their most precious possession, and that it should represent such a threat tickled them no end. I learned all that when I got to know them better.

If Gypsies were seen in the village at night, any felony that occurred in the last few months would be added to the long list of their ill doings and they might be denied the right to camp. So they snuck around in their most invisible skin.

To villagers, the *Manouches* were a necessary evil like inclement weather, something they had to live with for the months of summer because they could be hired for harvesting. After the harvest season was over, the nomads would disappear for another year and it was good riddance.

Orsolina had theories about everything, and Gypsies didn't escape her scrutiny. She wrote me a letter, years after all this had happened.

I think that it's the Gypsies' capacity for prolonged silence, even more than their freedom that makes sedentary people uneasy. To me they exist in a time of their own where life is simple, responsibilities nonexistent, possessions scarce. Nothing weighs them down, they don't presume to carry any personal weight and have no need for recognition. They come and go where the wind blows, happy just being, not having to be saved or justified. They get their guidance by reading omens hidden behind minor incidents. When I got to know some of them better I realized that they carry no guilt.

They come upon the things they need here and there as they gather rushes for their baskets or visit dumps. What they don't find they steal. They use things, then discard them. It's the same with stories; they tell them and then forget. There cannot be any accumulation when you are always moving.

Obviously Orsolina romanticized Gypsies. She often threatened to run away with them when things were not right at home because she believed the Gypsy realm was one where children were free.

She had often begged me to go with her to the *Manouche* camp when she was a kid, but it was only years later, on a short visit from Paris to my parents in Lerné that I had the guts to grant Orsolina her wish. I was married by then and had my own children. She had just turned fourteen. After dinner she announced, "We are going for a walk." Fortunately our parents didn't ask to come along.

We took the direction of the Thizay forest where we knew the Gypsies had made their camp at the *friche* a few days earlier. As we came closer to the camp, Orsolina's hand gripped mine tightly. I asked her if she were scared and wanted to go back. She didn't bother to answer.

We came to the crossroads marked by the gigantic rusty cross that was like an accusing finger pointed towards the heavens. Jesus was much bigger than life, horribly realistic, haggard and caved in, rags hanging down from his hips.

"I know that there is power in martyrdom, but it's time to get off it, time to take the old boy down from his cross and look at redemption,"

Orsolina joked. Leaning against the huge slab that cemented the cross, a young Gypsy was smoking a cigarette. He must have been in his early twenties, darkly handsome, acting cool. He whistled his admiration when Orsolina walked by him and I noticed for the first time that she was becoming a woman.

We veered left and came in full sight of the camp. There it was: trailers, horses, dogs, adults and naked children, wailing babies, all in a big circle around a bonfire. Colorful clothes were drying on lines; the wind and the fire's reflections on this laundry gave it an uncanny life. An animated group sat around the fire gambling for money, one man was throwing dice on the ground. Another man played a lonesome tune on the harmonica. There was swearing and cheering. A woman sang in a raw voice. An acrid smell of smoked meat and cedar incense rose from the camp, mixed with the strong odors of horses and unwashed bodies.

Our unexpected appearance brought everything to a stop. The silence shimmered between them and us like a wave of heat rising from hot pavement. I noticed glimpses of irony in the eyes lit by the flame. In the smoke and wavering of the heat, faces were distorted and I thought I saw demons. Everything, everyone was in suspension, waiting for our next move. Protective, I stepped in front of Orsolina. Then we stood there, frozen.

A Gypsy began tinkering, as if to break the spell. I felt the earth under me jump forward like an enormous animal. A wave of sickness came upon me. I closed my eyes. When I looked again Orsolina was in their circle and I was left out, cold and drained. To reach Orsolina's side I would have to make my way through the hanging laundry that had become alive, through those rows of sarcastic eyes. I didn't have enough strength to try. I looked gloomily at my extremities. They seemed so far away.

The Gypsies were welcoming Orsolina and gesturing for me to join in. The sight of pale-skinned outsiders daring to break the fearsome taboo and meet them on their own turf amused them immensely. Their curiosity was not held in check by the usual standards of civility and good manners. They had to know the how and why of everything and asked Orsolina very personal questions in their coarse and vulgar way, staring her right in the face. They giggled and nudged each other with each answer.

They spoke a special slang, a piecemeal language collected from many tongues, similar to the one used by hoodlums and carnies in Paris, barely comprehensible to outsiders. It dawned on me, when I saw how fluent Orsolina was in this jargon, that during her school year in Paris she must have been running around with the youngsters from a nearby *bidonville,* a ghetto where kids had adopted the Gypsy slang.

Her admiration for hooligans' provocative and gutsy ways had been obvious to me, but I had no idea how far her familiarity with them extended. Obviously she had not let me in on all of her escapades. The only reason she had apprised me of her secret life at all was because I followed her once, when she had told Angela she was going to study with a friend.

She ran the few blocks east to the tough district on the edge of Montreuil and Bagnolet. There, past the blocks of low-cost housing, an area of vacant greenery belted Paris and separated it from the suburbs of small houses with gardens. Before she reached Bagnolet she stopped in *la zone,* an empty lot where wild weeds grew freely.

I heard that in the past monarchs had purposefully left this area vacant so the cavalry could encircle Paris with ease and suppress the rebellion of a perpetually dissatisfied Parisian population. Nowadays it was used by vagabonds who made shelters of tin and cardboard, by bums and winos who drank around big bonfires, and by vagrants of all kind who cooked food and played cards. A few low-class prostitutes offered their services, dealers their drugs. Gypsies could camp there and no one bothered them. Children ran free. Teenagers hung out and necked. Junk accumulated.

And there Orsolina met her friends, some gang kids from the neighborhood who knew her by name. I figured that she had gone there often and the image of my sister, the good little Catholic girl from a re-spectable family of artisans, was shattered. Something had happened to her to which I had been blind.

The same thing was happening right there at the Gypsy camp under my very eyes. The delighted and amazed Gypsies cheered when they realized she spoke their slang. They forgot all about me.

The young man we had met at the cross came back. He was watch-ing Orsolina closely and she was aware of it. She was also conscious of my discomfort, but she'd been holding a grudge and I believe this was a challenge on her part. Ever since my marriage she had kept a certain distance between us. I knew she resented Simone for taking me away from her but the birth of my second child, Amélie, a baby daughter, ticked her off even more. She could accept a boy in my life, but not a girl. Now I watched her getting bolder, more outrageous, outspoken and vulgar—like a Gypsy. Once in a while she glanced in my direction to see what I would do.

It was as though I were seeing her for the first time. To break the spell I forced myself to step into the circle and tell Orsolina, "Time to go home. Our parents are waiting for us." I took her hand, but the handsome Gypsy interfered,

"Mommy and Daddy are waiting for us, they forbid us. . ." he mimicked in a baby voice looking at Orsolina.

Then directly to me, "Don't you see she doesn't want to go," he said obviously challenging me to a fight.

If I didn't want to pass for a coward I had no choice. I got ready to punch him but Orsolina, knowing he was much fiercer than I was, intervened. She put herself between us.

"He is my big brother, but don't mind him," she joked, "I raised him wrong." And everyone laughed.

Then she turned around and challenged my adversary, coming on to him and daring him, cajoling and insulting him in the same breath,

"Look at you, man. You think you are such a stud. But when it comes down to it, I bet you don't dare to take a real chick on. You are so cool, but I'd like to see you put your money where your mouth is."

She seemed surprised at herself, only discovering as she went along what she would say or do next. The Gypsy loved it. He was challenged all right, irritated and aroused at the same time, laughing and teasing. "Come on chickee. You're not ripe yet, still wet behind the ears. I bet you don't even know how to really kiss, *rouler un patin* that is, tongue and all."

She picked up the provocation. "Try me," she answered taking a few steps towards him. She stood there for a moment, very close, looking up into his eyes, then in front of the whole Gypsy camp and under my disbelieving eyes she encircled his waist and brought her lips to his, kissing him so fully and passionately he could barely catch his breath. After a while she pushed him away, took my hand and announced, "We are going home now." No one stopped us or said another word.

I never mentioned this episode again, just as I never mentioned many other things that took place during my life, things I would have liked to clarify. I was ashamed and it was my way when I was alive to push aside the things that bothered me, hoping they would disappear. The habit of burying things, silently enduring and giving in, makes for a weak personality.

I believed I was a coward and cowards were supposed to avoid confrontations. So I did. At all cost. Toward the end of my life, I couldn't even handle the way people looked at me. When I appeared so dreadfully malnourished and sunken, when death was written all over me, I asked my family not to push me around the village in my wheelchair anymore. They pleaded with me, but I wouldn't give in.

"It's good for you to see people, talk to them, have a little distraction, forget your illness for a while," my wife Simone would advise. But in spite of them all I stayed inside or in the enclosed part of the garden. I couldn't stand the sick fascination in villagers' eyes. Not that they were pleased to see the disease progress, no, their pleasure was in being able to glimpse the alien entity that was eating me up, this from within the security of their own healthy bodies. They were like children going to a freak show, like a crowd gathering for a public execution. If Gypsies came by however, I welcomed them. There was no shame in being seen through their eyes.

Fricaut the baker returned from a vacation at one point. He didn't know I was in Lerné and when he came upon me in the garden he thought he was seeing the ghost of my father. That greatly disturbed me. I didn't want to know I was dying and wouldn't give my family a chance to tell me it was the big C choking me to death. Even now I remain confused about what was going on at the time of my death. I sensed that there was a door that was not to be opened because no one could deal with what was behind it.

When I was healthy I thought that after death, all secrets would be revealed and everything about life would become clear. I believed that I suddenly would acquire some new knowledge about others and myself, that people on this side would not lie. It's not so. It has only been one day since I died though—at least I imagine that it has only been a day because it's difficult to count in terms of days here—and even though the secret of life hasn't been revealed, I have already understood something I hadn't in my lifetime about people projecting their own darkness onto others, veiling them in their own shadow.

All the family secrets have not been disclosed to me, but I am glad for it because the idea of a total unveiling makes me edgy and confused. I did believe I was a coward and maybe I still have that in me. Maybe I want to continue lying about something.

I have come to other understandings though; one day can be an eternity over here. When the horror of life becomes too intolerable, burying things is the only way to survive. In my own life the wounds had not been as horrible as some, and I had the capacity to heal them. Instead I chose to hide them in order not to make any waves. I never asked in life the questions that obsessed me. I died of invasive cancer.

 **émoise**

4

THE CHURCH IN LERNÉ
In which Némoise introduces herself, tells the story of Némoise the shepherdess and how she got her goosefoot, talks about her canonization; where she describes her place in the Lerné church and the limited faith of the priest.

Je me présente. Let me introduce myself. I was canonized three centuries ago. It took the church more than three hundred years to debate whether I deserved to be a saint. Evidently, to acquire a goosefoot as an answer to prayer—which saved me from ignominy—was not enough of a miracle for the Catholic Church. It needed two more.

Je n'ai oublié aucune de mes incarnations. I remember all my incarnations. When the three miracles were accepted as such, the clergy gave me a place in the village church, in a little niche in the darkest corner of the dampest wing while all the other saints, like Martin, Francis and Joan were enthroned in the lighter, more traveled center aisle. Here they are now, polished and shiny while I am termite-eaten and colorless because the paint on my polychrome wood is scaling off. However, my story, more original and powerful than theirs, is written in beautiful gothic letters on parchment, framed in silver and hung on the church wall right under the carving that represents my incarnation as Némoise. No such information can be found about those others anywhere in the church.

The educated travelers who come this far walk right by the other saints without paying them much attention. Even the big Christ figure and the Mater Dolorosa do not distract them from their purpose. Holding the guidebook that directs them to me, they go straight to the dark corner where my likeness stands. My presence here is the only thing that makes this 12th century church remarkable, for they are as common as *centimes* in this area. Under my statue, at the end of the written story, following the explanations about how and where I was found, one can read these mysterious words:

Tu es Némoise, ni noble ni bourgeoise,
au pouvoir décrété par l'honheur
tu opposes celui du coeur.
Quel sera mon sort, O Némoise
pour la vie et pour la mort.

You are Némoise, neither noble nor bourgeoise,
To the righteous decrees of honor
You oppose the power of candor.
What will be my fate, O Némoise,
In life and in death.

The old women of the village still mouth this chant when they come to me asking to be healed, or to protect their daughters against the soiling by males. As long as I keep my power, virgins may not know the shackling heat of passion:

Némoise n'est ni grivoise ni courtoise.
Sur le pouvoir du Seigneur
Sa pureté triomphe sur l'heure.
Némoise, Némoise, à la vie, à la mort

Némoise, neither courtesan nor saucy courtier,
Doesn't pay court to noblemen's power
Over which her purity triumphs instantly.
Némoise, Némoise, to the life and to the death.

They repeat these rhymes endlessly while rolling the beads of the rosary between their fingers. They believe it protects them from demons. If the new priest knew about this surviving custom from pagan times he would be horrified. I notice how uneasy he is when someone more curious or inventive than the rest of his flock asks him questions about God, especially if that person seems to have developed a personal relationship with the Creator. They might understand something he doesn't!

On the other hand our clergyman has no problem dealing with Christ. Everything that has to do with the Son of God, with His life and message is in the scriptures, easy to follow and repeat daily. Our Lord lived in the flesh, and that is something one can trust, something real. God on the other hand is too vast and too vague a concept to be reduced to priest's size. It remains inaccessible to him.

Every Sunday the priest leads the congregation in glorious hymns. He has a beautiful deep baritone and loves to show it off. Those hymns, so familiar and unthreatening, have become his only rendition of the divine. As the chanting rises toward the stained glass windows and reaches the place where colors lighten and heaven opens, the old women in the front row mutter incantations under their breath or gnaw the inside of their cheeks.

NÉMOISE THE SHEPHERDESS

Il était une bergère, et ran et ran petit patapan, says the song. Here is my story as told in the village. I was, at the beginning of the 14th century, the raven-haired daughter of a small landowner from the illustrious family of de Baussay. My father oversaw the farming on the estate he had inherited. I was dismayed that even though he was oppressed by the demands of the overbearing lord to whom he was vassal, he had little compassion and exploited the serfs who worked for him. I didn't wish to be part of this injustice and very early on showed disdain for the things of this world, an affinity for frugality and contemplation.

When I came of age I showed no disposition for marriage or family life, no interest in house or possessions. All I wanted to do was to run barefoot and free with humble shepherds and shepherdesses through hills and forests, sleep under the purring of the stars. All I wanted to do was to accompany our flock of sheep and goats wherever it went. Animals obey the will of God in all simplicity and innocence and I wanted to follow their example. Renouncing my rank in the provincial nobility, I embraced the humble condition of shepherdess so as to allow the Spirit of God to guide me. Fortunately my father was not unsympathetic to my calling and he allowed me to leave home.

Je gardais les moutons. I took shepherding into my heart as I would have embraced Jesus, had I taken the religious vows, but more joyously, without the sense of doom young women getting locked forever behind heavy doors can't help but feel as they enter the convent. The companions I spent my days with were the young and the very old, the maimed and the handicapped, for shepherding, in our county of rolling hills, was reserved for those with too little strength or vigor to work in the fields, those without land or fortune. My shepherd friends were among the lowest of the low.

I became skilled at recognizing Spirit wherever it moved, feeling it when it touched people, animals or plants. I could even detect it in rocks, following its dance within the dense matter. When night fell I studied the sky to read the messages contained in the special positioning of the stars. I learned all there was to know about this art from an old shepherd—we simply called him the Old Man. Later, I could divine on my own.

I loved roaming the countryside, answering to no master, having no servants to impede, with their demanding subservience, the flow of the life force pouring through me. I received signals from the things I looked at or touched. At first the Old Man also shared his knowledge about what healing plants to gather in forests or meadows, at what season, what time of week, hour of day. He showed me where and how to dry them so they might retain all their potency. After a while I found my own way into the vegetal kingdom.

Standing quietly next to a living plant I would become as vast as the earth and was given knowledge about what ailment that plant could heal. They called me the *guérisseuse* the one who knows the secrets of healing.

At night my companions and I sat around a campfire roasting the small animals the young ones had caught in their snares, letting the songs taught by a woman we titled the Ancient One because she was even older than the Old Man rise from deep within our throats, catching many spirit voices as they went up with the smoke. Because she was very, very old, the Ancient One had become the song, and her singing had many more voices than ours. When she made us the gift of the Sacred Song she also passed on its power. We sang it first forward, and then backward to know the truth.

J'étais une conteuse. I knew many stories of fairies, elves and gnomes, but I also made up new ones, because the children were always hungry for more. I loved their luminous eyes growing bigger and bigger in the light from the fire. Later I would pass on the storytelling to them and form what we called the sacred hoop. We sat in a circle around the fire holding hands, allowing Spirit to flow through us. Then, the Ancient One would start telling a story. At one point, she would stop and pass on the telling to the person on her left with a little squeeze of her hand, and that person would continue the tale. It went on in that way all around the circle until the yarn was finished.

Un jour d'infamie. One day, I had ventured far from the others and climbed over a ridge to get my flock to better pastures when suddenly I heard a horse galloping behind me. The Lord to whom my father was vassal rode at full speed towards me. Only just before hitting me did he make his horse veer away. The animal's sweaty and strong-smelling flank actually brushed against me and I lost my balance. I had been crossing paths with this rider daily for weeks and was perplexed by the intensity with which he looked at me each time.

I stood up, I was not hurt. He had not gone a hundred yards before he made an abrupt turn and galloped back towards me. Slowing his horse down at the last moment, he bent over and grabbed me by the waist as he went by. I screamed and tried to loosen his grip, but he threw me across his saddle and held me, galloping farther and farther away from my flock.

My screams were in vain, no one could hear me. He continued galloping through the forest and only dismounted when we came to an isolated clearing. I pretended to be docile, but as soon as he relaxed his grip I escaped, running as fast as I could towards some thickets. He was on my heels, cursing, catching up rapidly. Terrified, I appealed to the Highest Power, I prayed to be saved from the tragic fate of the raped girl who, soiled and banned for the rest of her life, carried this incurable wound at the very center of her. I wanted to be untarnished and whole in front of God, without a hole in my inner body through which my power would leak out.

Qui m'a répondu? I don't know if it was God or the fairies I prayed to, if it was Jesus I begged to come to my rescue, or a lesser deity, a saint, my guardian angel or my guiding spirit, for I was in such a panic I would have prayed to whomever had the power to save me now and forever from man's desire.

Whoever it was found nothing better to do than to turn my lovely foot into the enormous webbed one of a goose. I felt the change as a tingling at first, followed by an eruption that caused me great pain, a stretching and rearranging of bones, ligaments and flesh. I let out a cry.

When he caught up with me and saw my new foot the horrified lord became so repulsed that he quit the chase, turned around and ran the other way as fast as he could, stumbling and, thinking he was dealing with the Devil, muttering prayers for mercy.

J'avais le pouvoir de changer de forme. When, later, the Ancient One taught me how to change shape at night and roam the fields and forests in animal skin I was able to learn easily. I became owl in order to peer into the villagers' windows, partake in their joys and travails. I became fox to outsmart the arrogant ones, she-wolf to nurse the abandoned babies, and badger to punish the rapists by biting off their balls at the moment of rape. I turned into rabbit at night to sneak into children's rooms and snuggle with them, whispering into their dreams.

J'étais une araignée. Before long I learned to spin threads that bound villagers to me and I made a web. As spider, I sat at the center of my web and each time I felt a little tug, I rushed my attention to the spot. I am a devourer of stories, always on the lookout for a new one. In this way I was apprised of every villager's movements, every one of their feelings. Forever alert, I became aware of the goings on in the humblest huts and the mightiest castles. My goosefoot gave me a mission. While still alive as Némoise I vowed to come back from the other side and help humans free themselves.

Over the centuries I heard every story in the county and became a collector of them. *Ma patte d'oie m'a donnée la connaissance.* The knowledge of my many incarnations seems to have come with the goosefoot. Was it the gift that came along with the infirmity, or was the goosefoot a tool of prophecy?

Némoise

5

THE TWO OTHER MIRACLES

In which Némoise tells of the two other miracles needed by the church to canonize her and how her champion, father Fracout makes it possible; where the story of father Fracout (who has similarities with Fricaut) reveals that his free spirit and belief that carnal love is a gift from God makes l'Abbé come to a bad end.

Cependant, c'était seulement un premier miracle! Besides the Goosefoot miracle the Church needed two more in order to canonize me. When the question of my sanctity came up two centuries after my death, I had a champion, a short and dark *Abbé* of uncertain origins who shepherded the Catholic flocks of five communes. A free spirit and, according to gossip, quite a favorite of the ladies, Father Fracout believed that carnal love was a gift from God and should be performed as an act of worship. This eventually caused his demise but not before he made my canonization possible.

Le deuxième miracle fut accompli grâce à lui! Because he was aware that many folks had been cured of minor ailments and that occasionally one major healing happened, he staged a big event in order to have witnesses of authority validate a miracle. He invited the Archbishop who had come to inaugurate the placement of Joan of Arc's statue in the Lerné church to lead Mass after a most elaborate Easter procession.

And sure enough, a mother who had heard of those healings came from a nearby village with her paralyzed son, knelt in front of my likeness and was granted her prayer. The boy stood up from his chair and walked shakily toward his mother with extended arms crying, "I can walk, I can walk." The mother fell on her knees and sobbed, "Thank you, Némoise, thank you for this miracle."

Le troisième miracle. The third miracle needed for my canonization was accomplished when the Cardinal of the province became very ill with some mysterious ailment and slowly declined until he became "just a shadow of himself," people said. Doctors gave him up for lost, but *l'Abbé Fracout* begged him to try the succor of Némoise.

"Please take me there on a stretcher," he asked his attendants.

When he and his retinue had prayed for a while in front of my statue, the Cardinal suddenly started trembling all over. When the shaking receded he got up from his stretcher and walked like a man in good health. "I feel so strong," he said in amazement, and he continued to feel better and better during the following weeks. Eventually he was completely cured.

So it was that *l'Abbé Fracout* made my miracles public, but he couldn't save himself.

It was after he had engineered the miracles that Father Fracout ran into trouble. He was appointed confessor of the nuns in a nearby convent and became the object of the Mother Superior's sexual fantasies. A hunch-back with a beautiful face but a twisted mind, she ran the place with an iron hand and the penances she gave the nuns she supervised were more like tortures. He knew of her as a frustrated woman, vicious and unreliable, so when she chose him as her personal confessor he declined.

"I am afraid of the temptation in which such a position would put me," he lied.

But she fixated on him, and when he continued to refuse her obvious advances she felt utterly humiliated because she knew he preached the benefits of carnal love. She swore to take revenge.

"The devil torments me every night and he performs all kinds of perversions on my body," she told the confessor who took the position *l'Abbé Fracout* would have held.

"Have you seen his face?" he asked.

"Yes," she screamed feverishly, "the face was of. . ." she hesitated, "Father Fracout." Then she threw herself on the ground, squirming and screaming and tearing her clothes with such hysteria that some of the nuns caught the frenzy and started yelling that they were possessed also. After much ado and trials with false witnesses, and because his liberal ideas won him many enemies, Fracout was put to the question and burned at the stake.

Giovanni

Death defies dishonesty for dishonesty cannot live in the light of its presence.
                                                          —Sainte Némoise

6

MEN ARE TOUGH WOOD, WOMEN FLOWERS

In which Giovanni, Orsolina's father, speaks of his death a year earlier, of his paralysis, of his son Pietro and first mentions the family secret, reminisces about his life in his native village, his first wife Malva, Pietro's mother, and their passion, his affair with Madeleine with whom he had a child he dismissed; where he compares the women he seduced to his second wife Angela, the good woman with whom he bloomed late in life after his stroke; in which he describes his beloved daughter Orsolina who gave him his cherished grandchild, the golden boy, Jean-Luc.

None of those still alive asked me to, but I must speak. My guide Senja is urging me to tell my story, my helpers insist that I learn to express my feelings in a better way than I did on earth.

It has only been a year since I passed away and the family already has forgotten about me—all this fuss about Pietro's sickness, Pietro's death. They didn't care that much about my demise. True, I had been dying for nine years. The sickness that killed me lasted that long, taking hold of me a little at a time, making me fall apart piece by piece. My family scolded me; "With a little will power you could shake off your lethargy and do most things for yourself instead of becoming so dependant." Damn them, I didn't want to do things for myself; I was miserable and confined. Someone owed me for that.

When I died, my family believed they got rid of the sickness and me all at once. In their mind I had become the sickness. I was like a fallen tree, a piece of furniture, already in my coffin when still alive, but now I am dead and have the power of telepathy. I have to smile when they say, "I wonder what made me think of that?" because I know it's something I communicated to them.

I know perfectly well what my son Pietro's cancer was all about. During my life, I tried many times to speak the truth about what was happening, but no one wanted to hear it. Until the end they pretended that Pietro's business partner was a good friend and not a betrayer. I must admit something I would not even allow myself to think about when I was alive. It was I who brought the snake into our lives. Still, my folks will have to face the truth someday, just like I had to.

Only a few members of the family know the story—and still, not the whole truth—but those who do keep their secret well guarded. What a fool is Pietro's wife, Simone. Doesn't she know that everyone in the family holds a piece of that truth? And when all the pieces come together her secret will be out. Even the relatives who still have no clue have this uneasy feeling—a damn nuisance, like a fish bone stuck in their throat. Eventually they'll have to cough it up in order to breathe freely again.

My poor son. I look at him lying in his coffin all white and wasted. I can see him because I am able to be in more than one place at once. Even though I have mostly remained in the spirit world, I have come down to earth to revisit my family five times: three days after my death, then seven days after, again thirty days and one hundred after, and now three hundred and sixty seven days after I died. This had been a tradition among the living and it is still kept in many parts of the world. At those times the dead are celebrated. I am not, however, because what should be the celebration for my visit from the spirit world is the burial of my son. My unfortunate Pietro, he aged twenty years in two months.

Fricaut the baker, our neighbor, was out of town when Pietro came to Lerné with his family, supposedly to convalesce, but as it turned out to spend the last week of his life. The baker came back home before he had a chance to talk to any of us, and he ran into Pietro dozing in his wheelchair in the garden—actually my wheelchair my son had taken over for himself. Fricaut thought he was seeing my ghost and let out a scream that woke up Pietro.

What I could never accept when I was alive is that my son does look like me in many ways, low forehead, hooked nose, high cheekbones, and strong jaw line. If I ever had any doubts about his paternity that resemblance should put them to rest, but I never could get used to his gentle eyes—for Christ sake, too soft for a man. I couldn't stand the curve of his mouth that betrayed so much kindness. I believed it was weakness. "Get off it," I'd yell to him every time he'd run to rescue people at the drop of a hat.

During my life, the earth and everything about it made total sense to me. In the last years of my sickness, however, I was no longer so sure about the most obvious things. My landscape was shifting. While still alive I never was able to understand what that shift was about.

God didn't do things right. We should keep on living as long as we are still learning something about ourselves. We should be able to go through the cycles of the seasons and turn new leaves like trees do in the spring, with a renewal after our winter. Instead, we humans have only one spring.

I was born from the rock into a hard life and damn it, I sure am not sorry about that. Our family didn't have much to eat but the mountains gave me everything I needed. From the beginning I rejected any sort of guidance and managed to raise myself, mostly in reaction to my father. I didn't like the man much. Even though I was very strong, a real man, he preferred my brother who was willing to obey, to stay home and do things the old way. Shit, I needed more adventure. Was that a sin?

Mine was a family of furniture makers and I believed that a real man was like wood, best when hard and strong. Blooming was the job of women. Never would I have believed that a man could bloom and still be a man. To me his best flowering came when he was with a woman. Women are really like men's springtime, but I never understood that until the end. Even with Angela, my deepest love, I didn't understand soon enough. I lived by her side most of my life taking her for granted.

MALVA

Angela was so different from Pietro's mother, my first wife Malva—that bitch who took men and left them when she was tired of them. There was something about the way Malva moved. Even the priest fell in love with her, and the richest man of the village, *Nodale*, of small nobility, wanted to put her up in one of his houses. No shit, she wasn't having any of that. She didn't want to be owned. She didn't need anybody; she had the strength of the mountain.

After her father's death she inherited the mill. She was queen there and certainly wouldn't lower herself to become someone's marquesa. She was like hardwood, she took what she wanted like a man and it was me she sought for a while. Fuck. I should never have married her but I was bewitched.

She was hard and soft all at once. Hard on the inside but soft to the touch. How I loved to encircle her waist when I helped her throw the grain into the hopper. How I loved to touch her silky skin, feel her smooth queenly wood against my own rough bark. What afternoons I spent there in the mill, deafened by the beating of the sifters and the scraping of the gigantic millstone that made the floor tremble. We could not hear each other over the noise. We communicated by signs and touches. We laughed a lot. Such fun we had.

And what silence when she shut off the water in the evening. All things back in order, to their rightful place, recovering their voice. Covered with flour dust we giggled, and drank wine, and fucked. We bit into whatever food she had around, and then we took little bites of each other. Later we screwed again, right there on the bags of flour.

I never gave much thought to whom she really was. I only thought about screwing, that's all. Shit, she was a woman who devoured men to the bone and I was hoping to eat her up. In the village they said she was a witch, probably because of her deep green eyes that looked at you and guessed all your desires. Those eyes took away your thoughts and your ailments and she stole your soul like a farm hand sneaks eggs away from a hen's nest to gobble them down in secret.

Malva was like a bad dream one can't awaken from, just as when I had my stroke nine years ago. All I remembered afterward was a lightning bolt striking me down. Such a bright light bursting in my head . . . then the blindness, the terror like in a childhood nightmare when you cannot move and you cannot scream, and the witch keeps gaining on you to pull out your eyes and cut off your balls.

Before my stroke, doctors kept telling me all along that I had the heart of a teenager, that my arteries were in great shape. Damn them. I knew something was wrong but believed they knew more about me than I did myself. Don't ever trust the fucking doctors!

When my marriage with Malva started to go sour, my mother kept telling me that things would settle down and work out, but they didn't. I ended up hating the damn bitch because she had used me. Twenty-five years later, I was vacationing with my new family in the village one summer. We met Malva in the street by chance and I couldn't help myself, I spat in her face. I never heard the end of it from my daughter Orsolina.

I hated Malva till the end, not quite to the end, but close. I called her *La Strega*, the witch, like my father did. He used that word to describe all the women he didn't know how to deal with, women who stepped out of line, dared to be independent and do their own thinking. The rascal passed that on to me. Not much else really.

ORSOLINA

When I was a kid, my real fathers were the old shepherds of my village. They didn't help me much as far as understanding women but they gave me so much life. I used to tell my daughter Orsolina about them when she was little. She listened to me with round eyes, like a squirrel on a branch.

She was born in Paris, but I wanted her to have the mountains in her blood, I wanted her to know my fathers. I never got tired of describing the high pastures where I spent part of the summer with the old shepherds, how they taught me not to be scared when I was alone, how to build a shelter, how to make a fire with no paper and no matches, how to read the stars. The best present they gave me was a pocketknife—what strength one feels holding a knife.

When I spoke in this way to my little daughter, my words burrowed into her small chest, and even if she didn't understand them I knew that they would be stored there for later. Even if she didn't remember where they came from, the stories would remain.

My little Orsolina, born thirteen years after her brother Pietro, was the first to help me understand that even a real man could bloom. I wouldn't have put it that way at the time, but later, during my years of immobility, I sat there mulling over my life like a cow in the stable, chewing cud at night. I understood how her birth had stirred up my heart and started to loosen the ties that held it so tightly bound. My years of sickness and the birth of her child Jean-Luc finished the job.

Orsolina came back from California—where she still lives—to bring my recently born grandson to us in Paris. Such a gift that child.

By the time many years of immobility had gone by, I began to make sense of things. So maybe the stroke was necessary. I was like the straw bale that had to be untied, winnowed to get the grains out, and crushed in a press to give flour for bread. Only then would I be good to eat. My daughter was the first to harvest me. I wanted to put that across to my little Jean-Luc, the only grandson I took time to know. I never gave Pietro's children the time of day, paid little attention to Orsolina's two daughters.

So among other things Orsolina gave me that treasured grandson, that angel who heard everything I said even when I didn't say it aloud, even though he couldn't talk yet—not just my stories but also the secrets of my soul.

After Jean-Luc was born Orsolina brought him to stay with Angela and me every summer, sometimes twice a year. The little angel understood that I was crippled and he sat at my feet for days on end. We played games. He never got tired of it. I handed him a small pastille at the end of each game and he applauded with his plump little hands. Then he wanted to ride on my wheelchair with me. He'd just as soon do nothing else but stay by me all day. I knew that he understood me.

In old age, we carry our story with us everywhere. We are never alone. My little grandson could feel that story keeping us company. He heard it even during his sleep when I watched over him. That angel of light didn't want to sleep alone and he didn't want me to be alone either. I told him that when I was a child I'd sneak into my parents' bed, on Mamma's side, this until I was ten, and he had that right also. It's inhuman to let a young child sleep alone in a room with all the witches and dark spirits roaming around.

Things were different in my day. I was lucky in that way. I hardly ever slept alone. My mother took me in her bed and breast-fed me till I was four. I always shared a room with my brother and sisters. I spent the summer months in the mountains with shepherds. I never went to bed by myself. I slept with young calves and with the other kids that tended the cows. Later I had my dorm buddies in the army, and even as bad as the prison camp during the war had been, I was not by myself.

And then there were women of course. Women! They were so delicious when ripe, just like figs. I could smell pussy from miles away and knew how to make it ripe. Women are so soft. Even in your sleep you feel their warmth, their skin, their hair . . . and how you snuggle beneath the covers with them, bury your head between their breasts. You feel like a newborn child who, immediately after birth already knows how to turn its head and nuzzle the tit, catching it in its small round mouth, sticking out the little pink tongue to suck on it.

When my little grandson wouldn't go to sleep I offered the nook of my arms as the best of cradles. There he could snuggle. His big eyes would look at me with such seriousness, as though he wanted to tell me something I didn't know. I melted under his stare. The twilight in the room would light up from that look.

I had spent my life fighting, defending my territory, dominating women, believing it was a man's way in the world. Men were tough wood and women flowers, but with this little one in my arms, it didn't seem so clear. Even the oldest, toughest of fruit trees blossoms in the spring, and the most fragile flowering bushes turn into trees if you let them grow long enough. Doesn't the tree come from the seed contained in the fruit that the flower produces? So many things I hadn't understood.

I could have bloomed better I suppose, but each time I started to soften so the flowers could open on my rough branches, my grudges and resentments would be like a late frost that killed the blossoms.

ANGELA

With my second wife Angela I bloomed very late. It took me so long to realize that guessing the desires of women, understanding them and giving them what they wanted didn't make me less of a man. More of a man in fact, more complete, a man who isn't afraid to have tits. And eventually I did grow tits from too much sitting in that chair.

What Angela and I had at the end didn't seem like much, but very few people get it in their lifetime—one for the other, always on each other's side. Total trust. A man shouldn't walk ahead and only stop to face the woman he desires in order to possess her, as I always had. Instead, he should place himself next to her so they could be side by side looking in the same direction.

When I met Angela she was a widow who hadn't lived yet. Because she had had the perfect husband, a sweetheart of a man who did everything for her, I was jealous. This man kept her from growing into womanhood. She didn't know how much men deceived women, robbed them of themselves, especially at that time. When her husband died she was still a young girl who read romantic novels and fell in love with movie stars. A tough rascal like me could easily win her over.

I was a lover. I was a dancer. I was the king of the tango. Women lined up to dance with me. I twirled them around, and then with a sudden twist of my powerful wrist I bent their waist and lowered them to the ground. How they surrendered to my touch, followed each of my moves. I was a scoundrel, yes. Bed was the best place for a man and woman to be together in my mind, and I took them there whenever I could.

I had a serious crush on Angela, this ingénue, and it was not hard to turn her head. I was still in the process of trying to get my French nationality in order to divorce Malva, a satisfaction I could never get in Italy where the church had made divorce illegal. I had a hard time convincing Angela to live with me in sin, but she finally did when I promised to give her a child, a girl preferably. She had remained childless with her first husband and was very unhappy about it.

At the beginning it was like heaven for us, cooking and singing and eating on the small balcony, taking the train to the countryside on Sunday to gather bouquets of wild jonquils, daffodils and lilies of the valley in the spring, pick wild strawberries in the summer and steal fruit from orchards.

When Angela got pregnant, I knew I had her. My old ways got the best of me. I couldn't stay home. I spent my money with other women. I even got back together with my old mistress Madeleine. Because I didn't want to lose Angela I kept her penniless so she wouldn't run away. I told her that my business was not doing well, that I was broke. I gave myself many other excuses. Having learned about life from animals, I often forgot how to be human.

Women. I marked my prey like a wild animal its territory and left my scent on each one of them. Usually when I was finished with them, I broke their hearts and didn't care. I was a beast always needing fresh blood.

MADELEINE

I found my match with Madeleine. I met her after I left Malva, before I met Angela, at a union meeting. The very first night we met I became the lover of this sophisticated woman. How she fell for me I don't know. She was an artist, but I didn't really get her kind of art.

"What's the use of all this?" I'd ask pointing to her paintings, "Who buys that shit?"

I'd get her so angry at times, "How could I fall in love with such a savage, such a gross uncultured man who doesn't even wash every day," she'd yell. It was a mania with her, all those baths she took all the time.

"Savage like our love. You can't control that. In spite of yourself you are mine," I'd answer grabbing her tits, and she'd laugh. When she laughed it was like fire moving through my body and catching my loins.

We both were fighting against fascism. She convinced me to enroll in *le Parti Communiste*. She said the two of us were locked in the same ideology, but I never understood half of what she said. During my sickness her ideas kept crossing my mind as though they had become mine, and it all started to make sense.

Our wild affair finished abruptly when she announced that she was pregnant and thinking of keeping the baby. I told her I didn't believe it was mine. She refused to see me again after that, but I heard years later that she had a daughter.

During my sickness I took a good look at those kinds of things and lost all my illusions about myself, but in the place I went to after death there is no judgment. I don't condemn myself. I just didn't know any better and was working things out from a previous lifetime. And this constant stream of memories rushing by is a habit from so many years of sitting in a wheelchair.

When my grandchild was born it was like a final grace. Those deep blue eyes, that blue light around him! I had the ability to make the stream of my memories move through his little being. Sometimes it stopped flowing. It was as though it came against an accumulation of rocks and branches that created a dam—something wanted to come through but was stuck, something I didn't want to remember.

So I had to stay there and clean up the mess of brambles before I could go on. It took some time, but I was willing to do this for my grandson. I wanted to clear everything for him. One time, in order to unblock the dam, I had to tell him about that other child I never talked about to anyone, a daughter that probably was mine and whom I never met in my lifetime.

I told it all to my little Jean-Luc, even the worst, but I let him know that by the time my hated ex-wife, Malva, died a couple of years before I did, I had changed a lot and felt something resembling compassion. I told that little grandchild of mine that the stroke allowed my most rangy growth to bear fruit.

Madeleine, my artist lover, used to say, "You have to forgive others in order to forgive yourself." At the time I thought it was all a bunch of shit. She wanted me to become aware of the pain she believed I had buried. It was hard for me to recognize pain. I called it anger, rage, hatred, especially when it came to Malva, that unfaithful bitch who, when I confronted her, cursed me in front of everyone present, calling me a bastard. That was an insult to my mother whom I loved more than anyone in the world. I knew it wasn't true, Mamma was a pure and good woman and I couldn't be a bastard. Unforgivable.

So I'd tell Madeleine, "Yes, yes, I feel the damn pain," so she'd leave me alone. I just wanted to be done with all her crap as quickly as possible so I could go back to being the animal I had always been and fuck her.

In the animal world it's the stronger that wins. There is no room for weaklings. That's why I had to be tough with my son Pietro. I believed he was too soft, too kind; he would have given his shirt away. I wanted him to toughen up, to show him that if you don't bite, you get bitten. So many times I reminded him that on the farm, the tough bull is the one we keep to the end to make strong calves. The others are killed for meat, but he couldn't or wouldn't hear. It was his nature to be kind and gentle.

To the rest of my family, except for my little daughter, I became a dragon everyone was scared of. And even Orsolina, the first time her mother took her to the top of Notre-Dame and she saw the gargoyles from close up said to Angela, "They look like *Papa* when he is angry." I never forgot a grudge, never wanted to resolve anything. I was the hardest on those close to me. I never gave up being tough, never wanted to stop fighting, but sickness and immobility got the best of me.

When I capitulated, Pietro started fighting me, and even Orsolina became impatient with me. She couldn't understand why I let myself sink so low into dependency. She wanted me to fight the indolence invading me, regain my power. But I was finished fighting. She never grasped that this apathy might have been the best thing that happened to me, the blooming of my rough wood.

After my stroke, when I realized that I would be paralyzed I wanted to die before getting subdued. In the convalescent home I tried to hang myself with my sheets, but I didn't have enough strength. Instead, something else happened. I surrendered to my condition. When I came back home I was ashamed of sharing my bed with a woman I was unable to satisfy, but even that went away.

In my younger days I possessed women and never thought that there could be something else going on between us. They would tell me I was a magnificent animal and it was true. I gave them everything I was at the time, and no more. Just a magnificent, unthinking animal that wanted to be on top. But while I sat in my chair, year after year, Angela was in charge, her standing, and me sitting. She dominated me, but I stopped caring about that also.

When I needed tending at night, she'd lean and her breasts were over me, spilling out of her nightgown, still round and white like the moon that makes the ocean rise. One night I asked if she didn't regret having my dead flesh in her bed. She answered that I was more alive every day, because my heart was coming to life.

I was really struck by this and felt so full I had to wheel myself to my sleepy little Jean-Luc in the morning and tell him all about, "My heart is coming to life. Look, I am more alive than ever."

What power he had, that tiny creature, to tie us all together. No one could resist that angel of light, that cherub with blue eyes who could hardly walk yet. What a golden child when he put his plump little arms around our necks. An immaculate angel, who raised his hand up to the sky and, babbling a few syllables in his mysterious language, gave us absolution.

Orsolina

All living things rely on the deaths of other living things.

—*Sainte Némoise*

7

COLLECTING GOSSIP AND PERFECT MOMENTS: First Stop, Azay-le-Rideau

In which Fricaut drives Orsolina and Angela to the train, how they find an empty compartment and select seats in a telling way; where the first communication with Némoise out of church happens, and where Orsolina accuses Némoise of being a shrink; in which Orsolina reminisces about being a collector of perfect moments, and reflects on how Angela loves stories also but does not approve of the way her daughter analyses everything; in which the origin of gossip is mentioned, where a disruptive woman in black with two boys gets on the train and Orsolina has a little psychic episode, inadvertently telling the future of a stranger; in which Orsolina remembers her brother's wedding and her father's attempted suicide.

My mother and I got up early this morning. A gray, foggy morning. She tells me she is ready to go to Paris now, but is she really? There is no train station in Lerné, so Fricaut the baker has offered to take us to Port-Boulet in his car. He drives much too fast, probably just to show off since we are not running late. He is always on the move, always two steps ahead of himself. I don't feel concerned about his imprudent driving though. It's easy for me to ignore recklessness on the road and lock myself into my own thoughts. Accidents will occur if they must.

I have given up trying to prevent bad things from happening, or protecting those I love with the power of my thoughts. I am tired of trying to put significance in everything I do, of attempting to find meaning to life. I am just so tired!

Fatiguée hein? What is that tiredness? Lack of purpose? Re-

member, in order not to lose meaning you have to hold life as sacred, give it significance every day.

It sounds like Némoise's voice. Would she have followed me? It's very rare when there is communication out of the church corner where her likeness is kept. I like to sit in front of her statue and talk to her when things are difficult, but seldom have done it elsewhere.

I do give life significance, but does it give it to me? I ask.

Does it?

You always answer my questions with your own. It's annoying, like a shrink can be.

For years, when I woke up in the morning and everything was so quiet, I would go deep within myself to honor the world I lived in. I gave thanks to life. It didn't really work for me though. Behind everything I did there was something that choked me and muddled all sacredness. It was a secret so secret I didn't want to know it—even if somewhere I did know it.

Némoise, Why can't I just feel God's presence instead of having to invent it?

Didn't you when you were a child?

When I was a child, I believed I was the only being on earth and that made me so lonely I had to invent animals, people, and gods. Am I really the only one here Némoise, the one making it all up, the one fulfilling my own prophecies about myself, or are those prophecies indelibly inscribed in my genes, only slightly modified through the course of ancestry? Must I erase everything that is written on my blackboard in order to have a chance at a clean slate and finally be myself, be free?

Être libre! Does freedom mean that you must do away with everything, that you must no longer identify with your past experiences? To be free do you have to stop defining or identifying and only be in the moment?

No, of course, if I stopped describing I couldn't have conversations, I couldn't write, I would starve my psyche. All my life, I have been a collector of experiences, and I had to describe those experiences to others.

I collected moments of plenitude that gave me the certainty of timeless existence. Certain artists have that ability to penetrate the mystery and let me forget the futility of daily pursuits.

Ah oui, intéressant! You say that you have been a collector, speaking in the past tense. Have things changed? Is the collection of perfect moments not helping now?

That's right. I used to be a gourmet. I became a gourmand, and even a glutton for life, for people, for nature, for food, for art, for books. No longer so. I ran out of curiosity for the things of the world.

Refléchis! It may be a temporary protection? If you no longer care about life, grief and fear cannot be set in motion.

Fricaut bringing the car to an abrupt stop interrupts my thoughts. He gets out, helps us carry our luggage into the station. After brief good-byes he leaves us there. He always seems awkward around me.

After he goes, we find that there was a change of schedule and we have missed the direct train to Paris. We have to wait a couple of hours to board a slow one or else take a taxi back home and come back in mid-afternoon.

We decide to wait. Two hours in the vacuum of the waiting room. I write in my journal, my mother dozes, a stray dog sits by our feet, I feed him part of the sandwiches I brought.

When the train arrives we choose an empty compartment. There is hardly anyone on this train. I take the seat next to the window facing forward. I can't stand to ride backwards. My mother settles across from me, she will be looking at what we are leaving behind.

The train starts to roll and I watch the countryside unfold. Fields, meadows and villages rush by as the train catches speed. I make up stories about what's going on out there. Storytelling and inventing stories is an aptitude I have inherited from my ancestors. Even in childhood I capti-vated family and friends with my tales.

My mother has retreated into her fluffy cocoon. I know she can find her bed whenever she closes her eyes, and she settles into it. I don't have to look at her directly. I can see her reflection in the glass, super-imposed on the moving landscape. She is not asleep. Probably rehashing some of the latest village drama so she doesn't have to think about what's really bothering her. Like many of us in the family, she likes stories, loves to hear them and tell them. Most men, who would rather stick to the use-fulness and function of things, call that gossiping, but it's a way to make sense of one's life from the stories of others. The way my mother tells her stories, however, often feels like a judgment on me. Consciously or not, she chooses characters that are bound to trigger me. Aah, the minefields of mother/daughter communication!

Her eyes are closed now. I absorb the countryside until I fall into a doze, but the train slowing down startles me awake. A timid sun peers from under the layer of fog, battling to push through and clear the sky. At the edge of a village two men are repairing a very steep roof; one hands the slate shingles to the other. The train tracks run so close to the house I can clearly see the men's features.

The train slows even more and I realize we are close to Azay-le-Rideau, our first stop. A woman comes out of the house carrying a basket, probably *baguette et saucisson* for the ten o'clock *casse-croûte* she brings to the workers. She looks a lot like the man working on top of the roof who must be her brother. Something tells me that the other man is her husband and that the couple is not happily married. She calls out to the men.

The train rolls into the station leaving the scene behind, but a scenario unfolds in my mind. There will be an accident. The husband will roll off the roof and impale himself on the pitchfork I saw lying on top of a manure stack. I wonder what's all that about.

Tu as raison, you have seen what's about to happen. Aren't you interested to find out how you know that? Do you believe that everyone has those premonitions? Does your mother?

Is it Némoise, is it the voice-in-the-ear flooding me with questions? I just know because I know, that's all, I answer. Those kinds of things wouldn't interest my mother—just fibs, she'd say, and who cares to try and find out later if it really happened. If it did, that would be scary to her. She is only curious about the characters she knows personally. Not having much imagination, she does not fantasize or philosophize. She believes I do too much of both. She's probably right.

I am convinced that all the questions inundating me are baits from Némoise. She once told me that I have the answers to all my questions.

Oui et mieux que ça, if you care to look inside, the answer to all questions.

The train only stops for a few minutes in Azay-le-Rideau, and Angela does not bother to open her eyes. I surmise that behind her closed lids she is gathering pieces of our family history. She collects those pieces randomly from past, present and future like wildflowers strewn over fields. She loves to make bouquets from the fields and to hand them out to her friends and family along with a story.

Ever since I was born I have always been her number one concern. Giovanni and Pietro came second. The rest of the family third. Her friends came last, of hardly more importance than the people in the romance novels she read or the soaps she saw on TV.

As for the rest of the world, even now it's peopled with strangers she doesn't care about. Her frail body gives a sudden start. She has probably come against a painful thought. I empathize. Pietro was taken away out of sequence, the order of things has been disturbed. She always trusted that she would die before her children and now she fears I could be next. Without opening her eyes, she chases away the painful vision with a small wave of her hand and switches her attention to some other plot, but I know that all her thoughts end up mirroring the kingdom of death.

Némoise seems to be back. This time I don't just hear her in my head. In a flash her image superimposes itself on my mother's reflection in the glass, reaching out to me. I must be going nuts.

Tu ne veux pas croire ma voix, pourtant c'est la tienne, Why don't you believe my voice, it is your voice, why only trust reason? But let's get back to your vision. How do you think you know things that have not yet happened in your reality?

I don't really know. Something tells me. But really, those incessant questions are becoming very tiresome.

Excuse-moi, but one more question. Haven't you guessed yet?

I have now. You suggest images to me, right? You are my inner knowledge.

The train picks up speed, I am ready to stop conversing with Némoise. I ask Angela if she wants something to drink. She shakes her head, so I reach for my water bottle and take a big gulp. I am so dry.

Bien, bien! Good, I am glad you figured it out. Mais, autre chose. I am also your dreaming. Dreams dissolve quickly as you know, and are forgotten, but they will leave a trace that help shape your destiny and even change it. Another way to channel information and activate prophecy.

My attention wanders. It's hard to believe it, but I see Némoise's reflection in the window impatiently drumming her goosefoot on the floor. Too much imagination!

Prophecy is possible because thinking is not something that takes place inside the head of a person in isolation from the rest of the cosmos. Human thinking and actions develop through resonance with an evolving cosmic consciousness activated by the various energy shifts of the earth. All humans are channellers but their ability to think in that way is very limited. To be the master of your own destiny you have to step back, and from a distant point of view notice the details.

Némoise's voice trails off. Stepping back would mean getting away from my grief and looking at Pietro's death from a cosmic perspective? I am not sure I can do that. I look at my mother. In her own way she is more in touch with the cosmic plan than I am. She does not judge, accepts things as they are and goes on with life. Why do I dismiss her so much of the time? She is so touching in her innocent knowledge and I need her wise innocence. But how long will she be with me? She is the last one to remember my childhood, the last one who cares? My irritation and rejection of her overbearing concern is probably my way to prepare myself for the ultimate separation? It gives her the power of a mastodon.

She has always held me captive with guilt, so I put an ocean between us because the weight of her immense love smothered me. I expatriated myself to escape, but I carried her with me.

I remember how she used to be plump. Every year she is a little smaller, thinner, her high cheekbones more prominent, her lips, which never were full, now thinning away into non-existence. It's as though by the time death comes she wants to give it as little of herself as possible.

My eyes fall on my journal on the seat next to me. Time to write I guess.

JOURNAL

For a long time I tried to put together the puzzle that is life and the only way I could do it was to become a collector of experiences, of beautiful objects, of adventures, of knowledge, and of stories—all pieces of that puzzle—and to write about it. Even after I lost some of my interest in collecting I kept looking for perfect moments, just as I still search for flawless pebbles on the beach, small round rocks that stand out like tiny planets or are shaped like innocent hearts. I believe that any moment fully experienced takes on a life of its own.

When I am absorbed in sensory details my feelings and emotions lose their definition, my short-term memory is suspended, which allows me to experience the present directly with no interference from associations. The moment, liberated from words, detaches itself from place and time, it is perfect.

A sudden *whoosh* as the train rushes along the wall of a warehouse snatches me out of my writing. My pen falls. I see my reflection against the darkened window, Némoise is not there, probably never was. Then the light comes back in and I am gone. That woman I saw for a second, could that be me? She seemed old, tired, confused. There is a secret so secret she does not want to know what she knows.

Do you want to excavate that secret?

No. I'd rather not. I want to pick up my pen and write about those moments when a taste, a familiar melody, a slanted light, the susurrus of silk on skin, a scent—more persuasive than any of the others—brings back earlier feelings and sensations; those times when Pietro came back from his outings with friends smelling of the forest and when he picked me up to twirl me around.

Suddenly, a woman in black wearing a silly little hat slides the door of the compartment open, sticks her head in and asks, "Those seats are not taken, are they?" My mother opens one eye and responds with an unconvincing, "No." I remain silent. The woman eyes us suspiciously and retreats. Good riddance. I pick up my pen and continue writing.

When I relive moments I have the opportunity to change whatever I didn't like about the past to mend the future. In dreams I can live out tragic moments so they don't have to happen in my waking life. How do I decide what moments to re-enact?

I don't always have a choice. Some moments from my own life insist on coming back whether I like it or not. It's as though something needs to be taken away or added to make them perfect. There is a particularly insistent one nagging at me right now.

I was twelve years old then. My brother Pietro was getting married. The night before the wedding I went to bed crying. I didn't want to let him go to another woman. He was not yet gone and I already missed him.

I had been crying off and on for three days. I cried until my pillow was soaked. My wet nightclothes clung to my body. I had refused to bathe for days and smelled sour, as when sickness is about to set in. During the night my bed swam away on the ocean of all the tears in the whole world, bobbing up and down like an abandoned cork. I was lost at sea in a huge storm, but hung on fiercely. The bed eventually reached a shore and I woke up with the first light of morning.

I snapped out of the crying trance and carefully prepared to be the flower girl. I washed and dressed, combed and cologned my hair, but some tears remained permanently trapped behind my left eye, blurring my vision. As the bridal procession slowly entered the church, my heart was heavy. I held the bride's train with dignity, conscious of the impression my poise made on the guests.

As we passed the holy water font I saw the neighborhood's bad boys, my friends, who had pissed into the font earlier, hiding behind a column to watch church mice devotedly dipping their hands and crossing themselves upon entering the church.

I started giggling. To hide that giggle I lowered my head and put it in my hands as though in prayer. When the giggling stopped I raised my eyes and noticed a large painting hanging above the cross holding a tortured Jesus. It was a painting of the Annunciation; I had never really looked at it before. Small cupid-like angels were flying all around the Madonna. In the semi-darkness I couldn't be sure, but it seemed to me that one of them was blissfully pissing on the head of Jesus below.

I giggled again and something devilish made its way into my heart. "Wouldn't it be fun to step on the bride's train, trip her, make her fall and upset the wedding," I thought to myself. As soon as I got the chance I followed the suggestion. Simone, the bride, only missed a few steps, but the train got dirty.

Once again I giggled. I felt much better. It was as though that dirty train would curse the marriage. I was sure that it would not last long. I would get Pietro back. I felt sorry for the bride, but she was not pretty, she was too fat and she would lose Pietro.

After that I had fun at the reception, played with the other children. We pilfered champagne from partly empty glasses. I felt so light.

Now when I remember my lack of concern for others' feelings, I feel guilty. Guilt has always been a way for people to hook me. I know guilt to be the glue that makes sins stick to me. So I had to pay that very night for that sin when my father attempted to shoot himself. And I often ask myself: would the marriage have been perfect if it hadn't been for my curse?

Bad moments like that one I'd just as soon forget. I'd like to travel from one happy moment to the next, everything painful permanently erased from my memory, but unasked, wounding memories show up.

To make things worse the woman in the hat comes back with two obnoxious looking boys in short pants carrying large duffel bags. She gives us a dirty look and settles herself with determination on the seat next to me. She orders the boys to put their bags in the overhead rack, and then signals for them to sit across from her next to my mother. They immediately start swinging their legs and hitting the seats across from them just to make noise. I could scream.

I was not always so touchy, not always so distraught around death. Whenever I spent time with friends on the verge of death I felt like I was in a bubble. There no longer was any possibility of mistakes, no bad timing or waste of time. I was at the right place, doing the right thing, and everything was just as it ought to be. For that time I was absolved of guilt. When the usual filters are gone, one experiences uncensored reality and enters sacred time.

It has been called a state of grace.

I look out the window, make a mental collage over my reflection and the racing countryside. I superimpose icons of the past, memory bubbles, balloons full of perfect moments; I play with multiple layers of reality and meaning. I am my own master of illusions.

Angela– Trois-Volets

*Your life is changing from day to day. The water of life flows
everywhere and for each of you; be a worthy vessel. —Sainte Némoise*

8

FARMERS

*In which Angela on the train keeps pretending she is asleep while reflecting on
Orsolina, talks about farmers, describes the region, the crops, the troglodytes that captivated
her daughter and stepson, so as to remain with familiar and comfortable things; where she
reminisces about Malva, her husband's first wife, recalls a letter from her father-in-law to
Giovanni, her stepson Pietro's kidnapping and speculated retardation; in which she tells how
much she wanted a child and the selfishness of Giovanni the womanizer; where she advises her
daughter that marriage only works if a man loves a woman more than she loves him, and as
they enter the station Trois-Volets goes back for security into memories of a young neighbor
who reminds her of Pietro, tells his story at the hands of his shrew of a mother, then shows her
deep love for her daughter.*

Orsolina thinks I am asleep. I prefer it that way. I open my eyelids
a crack to watch her as she looks out the train window. I have chosen the
seat facing backward, the one she didn't want. I like to see the landscape
as it disappears. As she sits across from me looking at the oncoming
countryside I hope she won't get a notion to take my hand and talk about
Pietro. I know that she feels it is her duty to get me to grieve.

But no, she stares at a group of farmers gathered in a field. Not one
of them bothers looking at the train; they don't see the passengers, they
don't wave. One man bends down as though to check the soil. She notices
my eyes opening and points to him, "Doesn't he look just like Jojo?" I nod
a weak yes and close my eyes again.

I know my daughter well. She probably imagines that he is
listening to ancient tales rising from the earth. When he stands up he scans

the countryside questioningly. "The earth's stories don't interest him," I tell Orsolina sleepily. "He only surveys the landscape to appraise the land in terms of crops and profit, just as he acknowledges the sky only to see if it will bring the desired weather conditions. When they are in need of help for their crops, farmers may even start praying, even though they think that God does not exist. They are ready to try anything, even the things they don't believe in." Orsolina grumbles a protest:

"Why don't those farmers, if they are as greedy as you make them to be, set up watering systems in a region of streams and rivers? Why do they rely on the weather as unpredictable as it is?"

"That's the way it has always been and that's the way they are," is all I can answer. "They submit to how it is, never want to change any of the old ways." Orsolina probably believes that's how I am also. I close my eyes to indicate I don't want to engage anymore.

From the back of my house in Lerné I overlook fields. Farmers drop their activities a few times a day for a quick one at the *Societé*. I hear them curse the sun when, month after month, it hides behind low drizzling clouds and the crops are molding instead of ripening. Then I hear them curse it for shining too brightly. They curse the rain that doesn't fall to save the crops, and when the rain falls for too long, they curse it for rotting the grapes. They might have forgotten how to pray, but they sure know how to curse.

The train slows down and I instinctively open my eyes again. Orsolina notices, and leans over to be closer to me. I stiffen. I don't want her to touch me and start talking, I don't want to soften and get mushy. "You are afraid that the shards of pain will dissolve into tears and flow like rivers of grief out of some deep abyss inside of you," she once told me when I admitted that I could never cry. It's always poetic images with her, but it's true, I am afraid that if I started to cry, the tears would never stop.

When she gives up trying to communicate I breathe a sigh of relief and pretend to settle back into a doze, but I keep an eye open.

We are going through a village where a few women in purple printed pinafores are plastering the side of a house. One of them fills in a wide crack in the wall. A tall stonemason wearing the blue overalls of his *métier* taps on the rock wall of an outbuilding and listens as if expecting to hear a voice. Orsolina observes them closely and begins writing in her journal; she always keeps it close to her. I can guess that she is making up stories about those people.

I want to tell my daughter that it's not an ancient tale the man tries to release when he strikes the rock. He just sounds the solidity of those old walls half eaten by ivy, trying to locate the flaw needing repair. She has such romantic notions about peasants and their lives, but I know them differently. I am one of them.

TROGLODYTES

In our region we all live in houses made of *tuffeau,* a blond rock extracted from the cliffs by forefathers and shaped into stones. The caves made by the extraction are used even now as outbuildings for storing tools and sheltering animals. Before any dwelling was erected, local people lived in those caves made comfortable by straightening walls, carving niches for utensils and shaping chimneys going all the way up to the fields above ground. When they were finished, they furnished them with their heirlooms. Whole troglodyte villages were set up that way, hidden away from the eyes of potential invaders who could see nothing from the plains above ground because the chimneys and shafts were well disguised and concealed in the midst of bushes. The land above the dwellings was used for planting crops—no wasted space. When the troglodyte dwellers needed an area for a new child they just dug farther back into the rock and made a small room or even just an alcove big enough for a bed.

Orsolina recently took me to one of those villages kept intact by a few eccentrics who lived there—she always seems to find those kinds of places and people. They showed us how the wheat grown on the top fields was thrown down shafts directly into grinding mills, the grapes into presses to be crushed, walnuts into big vats to be compressed for oil.

The peculiar couple told us that troglodyte dwellers considered that they had no nationality, just like Gypsies. They were people of the earth who could hear and be guided by the earth; they felt related to troglodyte occupants in other parts of the world much more than to their compatriots.

In Lerné, the elders often lament the loss of this way of life, a communal life. Tools were shared, harvest done by the whole village, evenings spent in the large underground room shelling beans and peas, crushing walnuts, carding wool or spinning while a small group played music or told stories. After work was finished there even was enough time for square dancing in the gathering room, which also served as a chapel, before going to bed.

I came too late and didn't witness any of that, but I wonder if it really was such a rosy picture. I was born in Italy and the struggle for daily survival was so demanding that it consumed every minute. How destitute we were! Not even time for feeling. On the outskirts of a beautiful hillside market-town we lived as in feudal days with no facilities or hope, stuck in the belief that we would always be backward, dispossessed peasants. There was not a great variety of first names in our circles, we were given the names of dead relatives, as though we were graves for them. Ours was a life without words because we were too tired to speak, too numb to express. Reduced to living like animals in cramped quarters, tragedy for us was just in the order of things. For poor wretches like us there was always a disaster ready to happen, losing a child brought hardly more grief than losing an animal. We could not even imagine the comforts and pleasures the rich enjoyed, we just knew that the strong lived and the weak died. Pleasure and suffering were dealt in proportion to your place in the hierarchy.

What I'd like to do right now is to get into bed. I do miss my big bed. I never wanted to take this trip, be on this train. I didn't really want to go to Pietro's funeral and see his dead body. I could keep him alive in my mind if I didn't have to do that! But I can always drift back to Lerné, to the villagers, their lives. Most people have moved out of the damp troglodyte dwellings into stone houses now. Orsolina dates the beginning of what she calls forgetfulness to that time. She says that house dwellers don't hear the earth, don't understand the rock. They forgot that a chant rises from every stone that was used for their house. It must be those eccentrics she has become friendly with that put those ideas into her head. They even write for magazines about all that.

Even though I think all this is a product of overactive imaginations, the eccentric friends of Orsolina might have a point. Because they lived within the earth, troglodyte dwellers could probably hear the song of the rock. Nowadays, most people in their sterile houses no longer have time to listen to anything from the old days, but even new generations have a longing for those evenings when villagers used to exchange tales. Instead of doing something about it they let the picture on the screen capture all their imagination. It steals their eyes and silences their voices.

Pietro also was fascinated with troglodytes. I can still hear his voice talking to little Orsolina and me, "Caves remember. The rock taken out of those caves remembers the story of the giants who have left their footprints when the earth was a cooling speck of matter devoid of color and order." He recounted how the Big Water retreated, leaving its snail-shaped signature in the rock as a proof of its passage, fossilizing mushrooms, vegetables and sponges we still find in vineyards after the plow has turned the ground between the rows. We go gather them like wild flowers for a bouquet.

Pietro would go on describing the migrations of those giants that followed ruts in the landmass, while Orsolina kept round adoring eyes on him, "They drifted, unseeing, eating anything to survive, hardly ever originating acts of creativity, never dreaming." His little sister didn't tire of listening to Pietro's tales, even if she didn't understand everything—one of a kind those two—and he loved to recount them for her. Meanwhile, there are parts of the family history Pietro never talked to Orsolina about. He never told her that he found letters their grandfather Ferdinando had written his son Giovanni, defaming Pietro's mother.

PIETRO'S KIDNAPING AND FIRST YEARS IN PARIS

Malva has been acting up during your absence, the old man Ferdinando wrote Giovanni in one of the letters. *I tried to restrain her, watched her like a hawk during the day, locked her up in her bedroom at night and took the keys with me, but she climbed out of the window when everyone was asleep to meet her lover. Not even a beating could stop her. She is bringing such shame on the family's name that I must advise you to kill her.*

Your son shouldn't be raised by a whore, he should live with us, his grandparents, until you can take him with you to Paris. Don't worry about the consequences, there are plenty of folks ready to stand as witnesses to her shameful behavior. It will be considered a crime of passion here, and you'll get away with it.

I didn't know any of this until Orsolina was in my stomach. Giovanni had hidden his son from me because he was afraid that I would leave him if I knew he had a child. When he confessed, he told me everything and showed me the letters from his father. He explained why he hadn't committed the crime his father Ferdinando demanded of him, "I wouldn't risk a long jail sentence because of a bitch I despised."

At that time in Italy divorce was not allowed, so Giovanni asked for a legal separation and left Trieste to go to Paris where he had relatives. The big wave of immigration to Paris had started to empty the villages of his region, he told me. It was only much later that I met Giovanni's huge family; everybody seemed to be related in his village! In Paris he took a job with a cousin who was doing well in the furniture business and was willing to take the risk of employing an illegal alien. The big Italian family was taking over some sections of Paris. When a *paisan* had his foot in, he dragged behind him a long trail of brothers and cousins and in-laws. Anyway, Giovanni rented a room from distant relatives and there he was. He had his plan. He was determined to get a divorce from Malva. He would become French, but for now it was better for his son to stay in the village in Italy.

Ferdinando didn't give up though. He kept harassing his son. Malva had been at it again, she was having a scandalous affair with the priest of the village and had given birth to a bastard. Giovanni had to do something fast.

To pacify his father, Giovanni contacted an Italian family who boarded children for a small sum. He wrote his father that everything was set up and that he was ready to steal his son from *la putana,* but he kept procrastinating. I know him well, I am sure he was having a grand time running around, chasing women. His father would not let him forget, he kept writing.

All of a sudden one summer, (nine years had passed since the birth of his son) Giovanni went back to his village to visit his family. He told Malva he was taking his son on a day outing and would be taking the bus to Udine to show him the city the boy had never seen. From there they went on another bus to the French border, got out and crossed on foot from Claviere to Montgenèvre—local people were allowed to go back and forth between the two countries without having to show any papers. On the French side they boarded a train that took them all the way to Paris. By then Giovanni had rented the one-bedroom apartment I came to know, but I was not part of the picture yet.

Pietro had never been away from his mother, family and village; he hardly remembered this father of his and didn't speak one word of French. For weeks and months he remained confused, unsettled, often acting as if he were retarded. Giovanni rationalized his son's behavior. *The boy has been abused by his mother. He is disturbed but will slowly recover.* In order to ease the pain of the separation and help his son forget his wicked mother, he told Pietro, "Your mother is a whore, a liar and a cheat, she doesn't care about anyone but herself."

Night after night Pietro begged his father to let him sleep with him in his big bed. He was so scared and miserable Giovanni would often allow him, but Pietro snuggled up and clung to his father with a desperation that embarrassed and irritated the man. He'd push him away and turn the other way, but the boy would clutch his back, stiff and shivering. Giovanni described all this to me much later, he also said that the boy reminded him of a scared monkey and that he repulsed him. Each time it would take much patience to convince his son to let go of him and the boy eventually would fall into a deep slumber, but even in his sleep he was drawn to his father's body and held it tight.

The Italian family that agreed to take Pietro had to wait a few months for another young border to leave. During that time Giovanni had to remind himself to be patient, that it wouldn't be long now before his son took up his lodging with the family and he would no longer have to deal with this peculiar child. Everything would go back to normal then.

In the meantime he was courting me and pulling out all the stops. How charming he was. Such a gentleman, wining and dining me, taking me to ballrooms—and such a great dancer—but he never took me to his apartment until Pietro, who was sleeping on the couch in the living room at that time, moved in with the Italian family.

After Pietro left, Giovanni tried to persuade me to live with him until he got his divorce and could marry me. In order to do that, he had to become a French citizen, and this would take some time. It took a lot of talking to convince me. I was in my early thirties, widowed. My first husband's long sickness and suffering had exhausted me. I was not ready to consider another relationship, but it saddened me to remain childless. I felt the clock ticking and Giovanni knew just how to make use of that. He still didn't let on that he had a son and persuaded me that he also was ready for a child. So I did move in with him and I got pregnant right away. I was in seventh heaven and he was so attentive.

It was only when he was sure he had me that Giovanni sprang the news about his son. I was incensed. How could he lie to me about some-thing so important? How could he lead me on? Did he just want a nanny for his boy and a servant for himself? Eventually though, I got used to the idea. Or did I? I stayed because I was pregnant and the war was imminent. I was scared to be a single mother in time of war.

We moved to a bigger apartment and Pietro came to live with us. He had just turned eleven by then and I was not sure how to handle this addition to our family. I tried to do my best. Was I a good mother? There was always some distance between the boy and me and I couldn't fill that gap. Or did I? I don't know how it was for Pietro, but my heart eventually opened wide to him. When did it happen? Was it too late to heal the wounding that that occurred when he was torn away from his real mother?

It took a little more than a year for Pietro to get used to the new country and his new family. He went to school and began to learn French. Except for a few slips here and there he acted normal, and Giovanni stopped worrying about retardation.

A lock of my hair has fallen down on my face and tickles my nose. I can feel Orsolina looking at me and I still don't want to move. I am afraid that if I look into her eyes I will start to cry and if I start. . . Orsolina has those poetic ideas about why I am afraid to cry, but there is something else.

I chose the seat facing backwards because I couldn't stand to face the landscape bringing me closer to Paris and the grieving family, even though Orsolina can see every move I make that way.

I wonder sometimes about how my daughter deals with her own husband and children. Is she happy? I once told her, "A marriage works better if the man loves the woman much more that she loves him, because men have a tendency to be selfish, and they have such a sense of entitlement. It's only if they are kept on their toes and afraid to lose you that they learn to behave." I doubt if Orsolina thought much of my advice. She dismissed most of what I tried to teach her about life. In her mind I was too subdued, a good woman, and she, on the other hand, was too wild for me. We clashed.

My own mother advised me to be subservient to men and put myself in God's hands, enlist the help of miracle-working images, saints that could intercede in my favor. I did have a chance to buy my way into God's good graces through them. Candles lit on the saints' altar would help, as well as gifts of money dropped in the small slots designed for that purpose, and of course the priest would be glad to say Mass for those who had the means to make generous gifts to the church. When there was no money, our suffering might do, but our martyrdom had to be known to everyone so God could hear of it and help us escape a terrible fate.

But my mother died too young and I never had anything to do with the church after a priest tried to forcefully seduce me. So it is that I didn't escape my fate! Giovanni on the other hand said that he acted on behalf of fate when he relieved "that whore" of her firstborn; he believed that she didn't deserve his child. For people in our villages fate was accepted as blind and inescapable, there was never a possibility of changing it. I wonder what's the difference between fate and destiny. Fate seems to always be burdensome, whereas people are said to soar with their destiny. Is destiny only a privilege reserved for rich people?

The train comes to an abrupt stop and I open my eyes again. I hadn't noticed that we were entering the station *Les Trois Volets.* I wonder how it came to be named The Three Shutters. Why three when so many pale blue shutters liven up the faces of nearly every house in the county?

Outside our window a vendor is calling attention to his sandwiches and drinks. Orsolina asks me if I want something. I decline. She opens the window, leans out and buys a bottle of Perrier water. By the time she sits down I have closed my eyes again. I still don't wish to engage.

I want to keep thinking about the things I am leaving behind. I don't like to go away from the village any longer, especially in the summer, and when I do, I can't help but take some parts of it along with me. Until now it had been a good summer, dry, but not too much. Just enough to keep farmers from moaning about their crops.

It's not the first time I leave Lerné on a train, in fact I have done it so many times I can no longer count them. This time it feels different though. I had to scrub my whole house, a real spring-cleaning, then put my papers in order. I know it's ridiculous, but it felt like I wouldn't come back. Even though Orsolina was impatient, I insisted on saying goodbye to my neighbor, Marcel Miollet. I wonder what Marcel would be doing right now; probably working in his vegetable garden. I've known Marcel since he was a kid and he treats me like the mother he never really had. He is the kindest man, so generous with the food he grows. Many times a week he brings me a huge basket full of fruits and vegetables from his orchard and garden, a few pigeons or guinea hens from his fowl house.

What a sweet heart.

MARCEL MIOLLET

When I first met Marcel, his kindness reminded me of Pietro's. It was also the way he threw his head back to get his hair out of the way, the timid smile often brightening his face, his soft whistling of popular songs all throughout the day. I might have been a better mother to him than to Pietro. It's easier to know just the thing to do when the child is not your stepson.

Marcel's father had already had a stroke when Giovanni and I moved to Lerné. The man sat in a chair all day long, absent and melancholy, much like Giovanni did years later. He was not very talkative even before his sickness, letting his wife Maude make decisions so he wouldn't have to confront her in any way. She was fierce and he was a peaceful man. When he became incapacitated Marcel's mother ran the farm with an iron hand. It was not very big and she could only afford a few farm hands to help her with the work. She was never satisfied with their performance.

"Lazy bones, can't you use your head for once? What makes you so stupid?" You could hear her yell all over the village. She would insult them day in and day out. She underfed them and abused them in a hundred different ways. They hated her but deferred to her for she terrified them and they needed the work. Meanwhile her husband pined away and finally died.

Suspicious of nature, Maude trusted no one but herself, not even her only son. She did all of the transactions that involved an exchange of money. Thus, it was she who did the milk run every day, summers and winters alike, harnessing the horses at five in the morning and lifting the fifty pound milk containers into the cart to be driven on uneven icy dirt roads twenty miles from the village to the milk cooperative. She had devised a way to add to her meager income by picking up the milk vats of the villagers who didn't want to do the run themselves for a percentage of their profit.

Marcel could never forget his mother's hands in the winter, purple from the cold and raw with chilblains. When she came back in the early afternoon he had to warm up a pan of water for her to thaw her hands and feet. Then he had to rub those extremities with the paste used to massage cows' udders in order to avoid sores. His mother's feet were so cracked and callused, so deformed by the constant wear of wooden clogs that they no longer looked human. To him they were something horrible, something alien, he told me when we became better acquainted.

When Maude had recovered and eaten a bite she would go back to work on what was most pressing at the farm, roughing up everybody who stood in her way. No one could do anything right, even if they tried. If they did do good work, she suspected them of stealing from her. She held a tight purse, locked all the food in cupboards and linen in closets and kept an array of heavy keys on her belt. She even slept with them. Whenever food was needed to be prepared or beds made with new sheets, she had to be found so she could unlock the cupboards or armoires. Marcel was ashamed of her behavior toward those people he considered as possessing the qualities he himself lacked.

He tried to make up for it by being extremely polite and considerate, a thing she saw as unduly apologetic and idiotic. She accused him of meekness and he became more shy and retiring as the years went by. She constantly nagged him and complained bitterly. "How did I deserve such a son! He has no interest in the farm, no filial love."

He was the last of her children that survived, born to her late in life. He never married and stayed home with her. She had no one else to complain to and complaining was like a daily prayer she used to fend off misfortune. The fact that Marcel had learned to absent himself and not listen was a source of further irritation to her.

In the summer Marcel could retreat into his room after his work was done, but in the winter only the big room was heated in order to economize on wood, and she forbade any candles to be lit in any other room. The bedrooms were freezing cold and if she caught him trying to sneak a candle to his room she'd snarl, "I hope you are not taking this candle to your room to waste it on reading. We are not rich enough to afford this luxury."

If he read by the fireplace she'd snap, "Can't you make yourself useful? Don't you have anything better to do but sit there, gawk or read? There is wood to be brought in and you could help with the dishes, but of course you are too good for this kind of work, too smart. Always with your nose in those stupid books. What can you possibly get from all that reading?"

Maude was illiterate and had a profound distrust of books. They put lofty ideas into her son's head and didn't prepare him for the kind of work he would have to do at the farm. Since he had inherited from his father's side an excessive desire for peace at any cost and a tendency to never confront anyone, he retreated into silence. His father and grandfather had been refined gentlemen from a well-off family fallen into ill fortune. They both had married authoritarian wives. Marcel, like his father, never talked back and would immediately drop his book to do his mother's bidding.

Had Marcel rebelled just once, yelled and thrown something to show his anger it might have broken the ancestral spell and she would have backed off, I am sure of that. Encountering a worthy adversary she would have regarded him as a man to contend with and would have heard his voice. Instead she never noticed that he had one, so she pursued him with her disapproval. "Look at you," she'd say. "You are just such a weakling. How can you expect to win the respect of the hired help? They laugh at you behind your back for being so kind to them."

I saw Marcel growing up to be physically as strong as a horse and doing all the hard work that was required of him, but emotionally he had not grown up at all. So huge was his mother's presence that it occupied him entirely, leaving only very little territory where he could secretly develop his own identity, and this was only because she didn't suspect that this territory existed.

At first I just came to the farm to buy chickens, rabbits, pigeons or guinea fowls. I watched Marcel during the long winter nights, trying to read by candlelight or by the flame of the big fireplace before his mother would rouse him up with an order. "Go warm up some water so I can soak my tired feet, and while you are at it, make me an infusion." She would disturb him a dozen times, always needing something for her knitting, her sewing, her shawl against the cold, a tablet for her indigestion. My heart would fill with compassion for the young boy.

The first time I visited Marcel in his room he was sick in bed with the flu and his mother, sick also, had asked me to bring him some hot drink. The room had one small bed with a straw mattress, a shelf to store the extra set of clothes he owned for Sundays and holidays. Nothing else. He didn't have enough blankets and complained of being cold at night. He said that he could only sleep when he buried his head under the covers and let his breath warm up his body.

I brought him some blankets and took to sneaking in small presents for his comfort and pleasure: candles, books, candies, and warm slippers. I would tell his mother that I needed him to do errands for me so he could come to our house and be treated. She let him go since she knew I would give him a little money for his help, which she pocketed as soon as he returned home.

In their house the walls of the big room with the fireplace were black with age and soot. Nothing was ever done to refresh them, not even the quick white washing other peasants did every two or three years. Once Marcel suggested that he'd do the work if she bought the paint, but she exploded. "That stuff costs way too much. I refuse to spend a penny on frivolities."

The purse strings were so tight nothing could loosen them. As Marcel grew older he never had his own money because Maude never paid him for his work at the farm. Whenever he attempted to court a woman she ridiculed him in front of the help. And how could he impress a woman when he didn't even have a cent to buy the smallest of gifts?

So he resigned himself to not marrying. As years went by he became less and less able to have a thought of his own so dizzy was he with his mother's voice; his obsessive fear of her took up all his thinking. He'd rehash her rebuffs, trying to avoid being in the same room so as not to get scorned, eluding her, never talking at the table, finding excuses to be out of her sight. He wanted to be forgotten, so he became invisible to everyone except to her who would root him out wherever he went.

His head dropped down, his shoulders slumped, he never took his eyes off the ground. He lived in her shadow, as her shadow, for fifty years until she died. Then he raised his eyes, his shoulders straightened, he looked around and developed a perpetual smile on his face.

He embraced Marxist ideas and let the hired help share in the farm's profits. His mother never had any use for church or priests. "They turned your head around with their nonsense to better screw you from behind," she used to say. He didn't start going to Mass but became the priest's best friend, for he had a great curiosity for finer points of theology.

He would often invite Father Maindreville to dine with him. They endlessly discussed the state of the world, the need for humans to believe in a higher force to avoid the fear of death, but they bitterly argued about what this higher force might be, material or spiritual, and when the conversation turned to politics you could hear them slamming hard on the table.

Even in the absence of his mother Marcel could never totally break the spell of frugality. He never repainted the big room and lit only one fire, but he used many candles—until he brought in electricity—and even kept some of them burning on the altar dedicated to his mother. On a doily she had made he displayed the only photo of her he had, her locket and wedding ring, her thimble and her knitting needles. On this altar he put fresh flowers in the summer months, autumn leaves in the fall, fruit blossoms in the spring and potted plants in winter. He told everyone who would hear it that she was a saint and a martyr, that she had devoted her life to him and the people who worked for her. "She always helped the poor and comforted the needy," he'd add. After a few decades, everyone believed him, but I knew better.

"*Maman, Maman.*" Orsolina believes I am asleep and she shakes me to wake me up. I wonder why. The train is still moving, we have a ways to go. I slowly open my eyes and look around. Everything is as it should be, there is no urgency.

I look at my daughter questioningly. How I love her in spite of the annoyance she often seems to feel towards me. She is a strong, intelligent, outspoken woman, not at all like I was. I am lucky to have two great children, one from my womb, the other not. . . I forgot, that second one is gone. . .

"What is it *chérie?*"

"I am going to the *wagon-restaurant* to get some tea and pastry. Do you want to come with me or shall I bring you a treat?"

"I'll stay here and keep our seats. Please surprise me with something delicious."

I watch her open the door of the compartment and close it behind her. She is so graceful, so beautiful. Was I a good mother to her? Was I able to let her find herself as a woman, find that power I had abdicated for myself?

Orsolina

Nothing is what it seems to be; the world you perceive is a symbol,
an image in a dream.

—Sainte Némoise

9

THE BAD WOMAN – Savonnières

In which Orsolina names her early fears, mostly those inherited from Giovanni about the witch and the bad woman, Malva, who fascinates her, especially after she finds a letter from her grandfather; where Orsolina tries to figure out what is expected of a woman; where Némoise fades in and out and Orsolina recalls the most painful moments of Pietro's death; in which Némoise explains grief as a healing practice and fear as illusion; in which Orsolina describes herself as collector of dreams, and as the train leaves the Savonnières station Orsolina has a dream.

I can't keep my eyes open and fall into a slumber. A horrendous noise jerks me awake. There is pressure on my eardrums and we are in total darkness. I try to relax, tell myself it's just a tunnel. But it takes a minute for the train lights to come back on, during which panic closes in on me.

Fear was the companion of my early childhood. From the minute I was born an array of demons, monsters and witches attached themselves to me, ready to manifest at any moment. As I grew older I often dreamt of being cast upon a tormented sea, bobbing like a cork. Once, a shape emerged from the foam of that black ocean. It began to take a form quite different from the mass of monsters that were always hanging around my bed ready to pull me out and devour me if any parts of my body stuck out of the covers.

The form became a woman, maybe one of the sorceresses from my father's tales of *La Strega,* the witch from his village that haunted my early years. *La Strega* was mixed up in my mind with Giovanni's first wife, *la putana,* a woman who embodied everything that was most undesirable to adults. As I got used to her though, she was no longer so frightening to me. She was the bad woman I had been taught to hate but couldn't.

When I reached my teens it became a comfort to know there was a woman who hadn't toed the line like all the others I knew. Something perverse in me wasn't at all convinced of her evilness. I secretly wished to meet her. What did she look like? As far back as I could remember she had been in my life. Even though she had no name I recognized her whenever she was mentioned. She was the bad woman, shameless, perfidious. She had disgraced herself. She had been the shame of my father's family. She fascinated me.

I didn't doubt that what was said about her was true. She might have been a slut, a whore, a degraded bitch, and a rotten soul, but I couldn't help being curious about her. I first learned about her along with the names of things, animals and plants, the description of her irrefutable as hot or cold, sweet or sour. I didn't remember being told of her existence. She existed, that's all. In the same way as I knew about the good woman, my mother, I knew about the bad one, Pietro's mother, a diabolical woman who obviously couldn't be forgotten and remained unforgiven.

From her I learned what was acceptable for a woman and what was not. Too much freedom of choice, too much decisive power was unacceptable. A woman was meant to stay in her place and not make any waves. She was to be nice and nurturing, serve men and always smile.

At thirteen, I found an old wrinkled letter in a drawer inside my father's expired passport. The letter was from Giovanni's own father. The ink was so faded I had a hard time reading it, but from what I could understand the patriarch revealed to his son that Malva—that was the first time I learned the name of the bad woman—had slept with her own father from a very early age. My grandfather explained that this was why *la putana* had inherited the mill from her father, while her older brothers only got worthless hillside land. He was urging my father to do something about her shaming the family.

In this way the first family secret was revealed to me. I was appalled, distressed. I didn't know that a father could sleep with his own daughter. It was revolting! I had heard of such things happening among low-life people, among the down-and-out family of alcoholics that lived across from our apartment on *rue des Maraichers,* but how could it happen among our own people, in my father's village? From that time on, when my father or brother came too close to me and put their arms around my shoulders, I shuddered. Were they trying something?

Whether it was true or not I don't know, but according to those who had known her, Malva was a hysterical woman in a state of constant rut, falling for every good looking man in sight whether young or old. She drew them all into lust, even the priest, but her sexual appetites were never satisfied. It was as if she wanted to devour all those men she made love to. She couldn't get enough, couldn't be stopped by shame or law. She couldn't give it up. That was totally unacceptable.

The train slows to a stop. We enter the station of Les Savonnières. I know it is a short stop so I choose not to move.

MY BROTHER RISES OUT OF THE PAIN

The train pulls out of the Savonnnières station and is beginning to gain speed. The telephone poles along the line look as though they are falling down as we race by, a movement that becomes hypnotic. Things in the compartment have quieted down. The woman in black barks to the boys to stop kicking and after much squirming they fall asleep.

I let images drift, ideas come and go, thoughts fly by like a gaggle of geese on their way south; I watch them until they disappear. I don't make a choice of which is the most beautiful, flattering, funny or interesting but follow each one to see which direction it'll take. Sometimes I get the strange feeling that Némoise is directing that show.

I have always done that though. Riding the great current of images, not holding on to any in particular is how I work things out in times of stress. My brother's death took me unaware. I want to avoid the waves of grief that take over, each time more painful as I brace myself against them. I'd do anything to try to prevent that pain or at least dull it.

However, the images that keep coming, unasked, assault me with the most painful details of Pietro's bout with cancer. I get stuck in feelings of abandonment, of the slow untying of our connecting threads. I become stranded in remembrances: the horror of his agony, those times when forgetting all dignity he whined and demanded constant attention from his wife, begged for sympathy from his children and me. Earlier, Némoise suggested that rehearsing painful memories is my way of healing, that I should surrender to the waves of grief, "Embrace it instead of resisting it and you will find it more of a friend than a monster," she advised. It is not easy though. Where is she now when I need her? "Life is a preparation for death," she added at the time. "In what way?" I ask her now. But she doesn't answer.

Pietro didn't die the way I expected, courageously aware and powerful in that awareness. I was there at the moment of death. Two of his three children, young adults, were also present. His wife Simone was sleeping. Pietro asked to be taken to the bathroom, insisting that he didn't want the bedpan. He still was denying the fact that he was dying, still talked about healing.

His daughter Amélie and his younger son Lucien supported him on one side; I was holding him on the other. We left him on the toilet for a while until he signaled that he was finished. We resumed our positions, but half way back to the bedroom Pietro suddenly slumped over. His whole being collapsed, he became so heavy. We held him in our arms, carried him to the bedroom. He was dead.

He didn't have as Giovanni did, a peaceful mask, the glowing features of one reconciled to one's death. Instead, his face grimaced with all the pain, all the mutilations he had undergone. Torture and fear were chiseled into it as if he hadn't yet accepted his death.

I get stuck with those images even though I saw him, the day before he died, rising out of the pain. As he reached the ceiling, he hung there for a few moments. He swayed, softly humming, moved by a power he had never acknowledged before, out of the comatose confusion the morphine created, far from the big dark hole of which he was so afraid. He had been mentioning that hole for a few days, over and over, describing it with a wide movement of his hand, complaining about being pulled into it.

At that moment though, the hole no longer beckoned and Pietro had no need of wings to fly. Out of his restless sleep he rose, out of his anguish, into the original state of being.

How can you forget that?

Is it fair that just a year after my father withdrew the shield his presence on earth represented for me, my brother should do the same, leaving me so exposed?

What makes you so special? Do you think that fair is fair? Isn't it time for the child inside you to give up being eternal?

It's my passage into adulthood, I surmise.

So my mind rehearses the most painful aspects of my brother's death, a dozen times a day, in inappropriate places at inopportune moments, until it becomes a hellish vision of my own death. I go to a place so dark as to not let me even suspect the possibility of light. I am left, like Pietro, in the hands of doctors, in the prison of hospitals, alone to wither in denial. Doctors' hands are not hands I can trust, their word is skewed. Restful healing is impossible in hospitals. The medical profession doesn't know how to make whole, only to take apart; that's the way I see it.

As expectant mothers prepare themselves to successfully cope with childbirth with dreams of delivery, I could be learning to master the fear of death by going through the most frightening scenarios; all fears are contained within that one. I might be immunizing myself with repeated doses of the fear serum, making it stronger and stronger each time, until I let go of it.

I am beginning to sound like Némoise.

Yes, you are finally getting it, I think I hear her say.

Maybe I got that part of it, but now I fear the funeral. I won't know how to act and it is an act, isn't it? I could take refuge in the conventional role of the afflicted sister silently bearing her grief. Many members of the family, fearing their own vulnerability, have opted for conformity and rigidity, "Chin up." They might never be able to step out of the concrete strongbox they chose for security, and they can't allow themselves any motion that might create a fissure. Through that fissure, the light might shine on a family secret we all sense but have chosen not to investigate.

The train unexpectedly slows down, jostling my mother's head. She opens her eyes and I see terror in them, the same terror that might be in mine. Life cannot be trusted anymore. Will we die in a train accident before we even get to the funeral?

I try to chase away all fearful images.

Don't you know that they are illusions, thought forms issued from your own mind, tests of your credulity?

But they come full force and if I resist, they submerge me.

Don't resist. Do you remember when as a child you turned around and faced the beast that had been chasing you in nightmares? You asked what it wanted, and it answered that it wanted to be loved. Can't you do it now?

Right now I can't face the beast because there is something I can't bear to remember and I might be forced to. I'd rather close my eyes again and sleep.

When I wake up I write down in my journal the dream I had, something about a wind-up little toy goose that keeps going back and forth in the room where I am sitting with my boyfriend.

"Cancer is a double-reflected condition and can only be healed by a reflection on a reflection." I hear this like a sing-song coming from the toy. *"You will have to jump through the mirror and look at the reflection on the lake."* One whole wall of the room is a huge mirror. My boyfriend

is unwilling to make the jump. "We will get badly cut," he protests. I take his hand and tell him I will jump with him, but as I leap he lets go of my hand. The lake is a mirror where I can see into the past and future, but when I look back I see that my boyfriend is still on the other side. I can no longer reach him.

Dreams are part of my collections, beside perfect moments and stories. I try to hear what they tell me; this one is not easy. In the waking reality it is Pietro who made the jump to the other side while I stayed behind. Is Pietro my animus, a masculine part of me much less courageous than my feminine?

I make a small sound of discouragement. Angela is looking at me with concern, "Are you OK?" she asks. Her voice is so loving!

émoise

10

SISTERS

In which Némoise speaks of her relationship with Orsolina over lifetimes

Elle a toujours voulu une soeur. Ever since she was born Orsolina longed for a sister. *Je suis cette voix.* I am the voice of that sister, an inner voice. When technology allowed humans to spy into the womb during the fetus' development, it became known that it was fairly common for a pregnant woman to carry twins or even triplets at the beginning of her pregnancy. One or two of the fetuses would either be reabsorbed by the dominant one, dissolved into the mother's body, or become mummified in the wall of the placenta. This usually happened very early on. The sense of guilt, abandonment and incompleteness the remaining twins experienced subconsciously—often throughout their lives—became a subject of study. Orsolina read about that. *Elle s'est interessée à ces études.* Her body holds the memory of a ghost twin she shared the womb with for a while. Maybe she crushed it by taking too much space, or starved it by ingesting too much food, maybe even absorbed it.

So she created me, her sister, a childhood companion, a confidante throughout many lives—lives that run parallel and happen simultaneously with this one. As sisters we have met again and again, continuing our dance over incarnations.

# iovanni

It is through surrender that spiritual energy comes to this world.
—*Sainte Némoise.*

11

HOW I TRAVELED TO THE OTHER SIDE
In which Giovanni tells about what happened when Orsolina stayed with him night and day at the hospital, his experiences from the third day to the seventh day after he died, the speed of out of body projection, the horrible creatures he encountered, how he passed right through them, entered the tunnel, witnessed the nightmarish rooms, his terror; where he meets with a tall white-haired woman, his guide who encourages him along and points to the other helpers; in which he visits the beautiful place with crystal palaces and bejeweled pathways where he wants to stay, but his guide advises him to go on and tell his story to invisible listeners.

I was not devastated by my own death. When I witnessed my funeral I knew I would see my loved ones again. For three days—in earth time—my spirit had hovered, floating through my home, sitting with my family, not totally realizing that my body was dead. On the third day I attended the funeral Mass, followed the coffin, heard the funny stories people shared at the reception after the burial. I could tell they regretted losing me; I had been quite entertaining and even charming at one time and they happily forgot the grump I became later. Nobody mentioned my womanizing.

Between the third and seventh day I had a chance to come to Orsolina in a dream to lighten her sorrow by making a joke. I asked her what the fuss was all about since all I had done was to change address. Then my soul wandered further away from my corpse in order to visit other relatives and friends who had not been present at the funeral. On the seventh day, my perplexity lifted and I became totally aware that I was in the spirit world.

In the hospital just before my passing, Orsolina was by my side day and night. I was very confused and entered a place of total darkness, felt myself sucked into a huge black hole. I was afraid. The hole turned into a tunnel, I asked Orsolina where it led to, but she couldn't see it.

Some people I didn't know showed up. She couldn't see them either. She kept telling me to look for my mother, my sisters, any of the people I loved who had died. She said they would be able to help me, but I didn't see anyone I knew, only strangers. All of a sudden I was taken on a wild ride, everything shaking and vibrating. I could barely hold on, and I lost track of Orsolina.

The speed at which I was projected out increased until I screamed in terror. I entered a passageway. Total darkness again. I heard Orsolina's voice from far away, telling me to look for a light at the end of the tunnel, but I could see no light. I was out of control, lost, directionless.

Suddenly I came face to face with the most horrible, terrifying creatures one could imagine. I wanted to change course and turn away before I hit them, but I was pulled by a magnetic force and my rushing towards them couldn't be stopped. There was nothing to do but surrender to being torn apart by those horrifying monsters. As I submitted to my fate they burst into horrific laughter, then turned into balls of fire. When I hit the first one I passed right through it and went on towards the next, each time shrinking more and more into a sharp point of pain, this until I was only a little tip of blue light, a star traveling in a gray fog.

In that shape I progressed through the passageway. There were entrances on each side, small black doorways, and each entrance was marked by some kind of hieroglyph. I couldn't decipher any of it. Some of the openings were blocked off. Each time I passed one that wasn't closed off, I was drawn to the entry. I could look in, but once I had done that it took a great effort to resist the pull if I wanted to move on.

In the first room I looked in I witnessed a horrendous nightmare. When I was a kid, one of my teachers in Italy described Dante's inferno to us. That's what it looked like to me: in a fairly large area like a swampy cavern, decrepit, diseased and deformed people looking like corpses were packed together or piled up on each other. Entirely naked, they squirmed in this filthy mire from which deadly fumes rose. Everyone moaned and pleaded, apparently in great agony, but totally unaware of each other's pain except for the harassment of the crowding.

When I felt pulled further than I had wished into that immense cavern I was terrified. I resisted with all my might but to no avail; before I knew it I was inside, hovering over the scene. Fortunately I wasn't pulled down into it. I remained there for a long time, floating about until I stopped resisting and dared taking a closer look. I knew then I didn't belong there and felt sorry for those souls, but there was nothing I could do for them, so I went on. I simply rode the current, which got me out. All it took was to have compassion for myself and for those others, and again, to stop resisting. As I exited I realized that any of the people in there could easily get out just as I was doing. The cavern was wide open, but none of them knew that, and I couldn't tell them.

Once back in the passage I felt somewhat disoriented, a little reluctant and apprehensive to go on. I drifted, enjoying feeling free without the impairment of my maimed body, without the pain that had been with me for so long. Then I moved on and entered a kind of diffused brightness. There I floated around, weightless, suspended in air that was not really air, in a space without limits. All fears disappeared, there were no obstacles to run into.

I glided, gently pulled by the magnetic force into what I realized was The Tunnel. It was made of foamy material, different than clouds appear when seen from the earth. I kept ignoring the cavernous entrances on each side until I was tugged through a dim vent toward a small circle of brightness at the other end. That's what Orsolina was talking about, I thought, the light on the other side.

There, a tall thin woman dressed in a blue robe, her white hair long and loose, met me. Her face looked young. She reminded me of the Madonna on the altar of my mother's bedroom. I recognized her as my guide, Senja, an entity that had been with me since the beginning of my lifetimes as a human. From her presence I derived a sense of trust, a faith that I would meet allies to help me look at my last life until time came to reincarnate. Then I could choose a life in which to work off my past mistakes.

Next I entered a much lighter fog. It was as though I filtered through it, totally at ease, feeling love and empathy coming from allies I couldn't see but sensed all around. I felt secure, grateful for their attendance.

"Finally I came back home to this beautiful place again," I said to Senja. I no longer saw her but felt her presence as the moisture in the fog. I was so full of love and gratitude I lost myself in it.

I went on and came across a majestic ice palace; enormous, bright, sparkling crystals and colored jewel-like stones formed magnificent mosaics. Everything glittered. I believed I had entered into one of those tales in which castles were cut in diamonds and furniture made of emeralds. I felt at peace. I heard sounds, musical tingling, wind chimes vibrating as I moved. Angelic forms floated about in total freedom. I thought it was the paradise priests talked about and I wanted to stay, but Senja would not allow me. This is just where they made you believe you would go, but there is more you need to experience, she conveyed.

Memories of scents and tastes came to me, and unexpectedly I relived scenes that took place at the time of my stroke. It looked as though everything was projected on a screen, but I could experience all the feelings that went with it. Senja encouraged me to tell what I saw. I didn't have to keep a linear storyline like Orsolina as a writer would, but follow any picture, anything that came to me, act as if I had an audience of interested listeners.

Maybe I have.

Orsolina

*The water of life flows everywhere and for each of you. Let's stay in
the current.*
　　　　　　　　　　　　　　　　　　　　　　　　—Sainte Némoise

12

CAT AND MOUSE – Langeais
*Where in Langeais more people board the train, the subject of the war comes up and
Orsolina remembers the time of war in Paris, nursery school, the cellar where the class hides,
the rats, the scared teachers, the Gypsies in the subway, the German soldiers, the long lines
waiting for meager rations, the bombing, the fear of being orphaned, the scary encounter with
the German officer; in which she recalls how grown-ups ran like rats and she gets the inner
command to keep running.*

The train has been slowly filling up. In Langeais, a crowd boarded.
I see people circulating in the corridor looking for available seats, kids
sliding the windows down to stick their heads out and fool around. An
older man looks in, points to the empty seat questioningly, and the woman
in black nods her agreement. He comes in, says *bonjour* and sits down.
Soon the two are in conversation, and before long the subject of the war
comes up, a favorite subject for people of that generation. They are not
over it yet and maybe never will be. Am I?

*For those who went through it, the scars of war are not so easily
healed.*

I always believed that I was so young it didn't really mark me, but
someone told me recently that when you have been in a war you are never
over it, and you never stop grieving the lives lost in vain.

Most of the time days went on like they used to. My best friend
and neighbor Françoise and I went to preschool hand in hand, as usual.
The school courtyard displayed six well-aligned plane trees in two rows.

Their roots were prisoners of the asphalt, their trunks enclosed in cages like the pacing animals that broke my heart at the zoo, but their leaves were glorious. You could easily wrap your whole hand up to the wrist, make parasols or even string them as skirts. Fortunately for the trees, but not for us, the tall smooth trunks couldn't be easily climbed and anyway, we were absolutely forbidden to do so. We only had access to the foliage in autumn, when the leaves fell in soft abandon.

At recess we were led down the wide staircase from the class-rooms in rows of two, in very orderly formations. In rows of two we went to lunch, sat at two long tables on each side of the long, narrow room. We ate our meals and after lunch went to bed. Two lines of beds faced each other on each wall.

We pretended to sleep during the enforced nap because if we made too much noise recess was canceled. When we had been good however, we were led to the courtyard to play, then back up the staircase to class, always in rows of two. We were ordered to keep absolutely quiet in the classroom, but often disregarded the order, whispering and chuckling behind our hands. When caught at it we were sent to a corner of the room, facing the class. On the culprit's head the teacher planted a makeshift don-key hat kept for that purpose in her drawer. The whole class pointed and giggled.

It happened to me just once. When the teacher tried to put the donkey hat on me I kicked her. She commanded me to follow her to the principal's office. I lay down and refused to go. She dragged me by the hair, kicking and screaming all the way there. After that, I kept absolutely still to avoid such humiliation.

Then suddenly . . . a welcomed disruption! Sirens howling. Order broken. Whether it's a drill, a warning that enemy planes are flying to-wards Paris, or a real bomb alert doesn't matter. The war we have seen on newsreels has moved into the school. The war is all grownups talk about. To us it means enemy soldiers taking over our homes, sirens threatening, airplanes flying low, panic, probably bombing. . . and we are taught to run to save our lives.

So you run.

Yes, run to the cellar. Don't bother making two straight lines, don't bother walking in orderly rows, don't bother keeping quiet. Just run to the cellar any way you can, the bombs might be already falling.

The cellar, a long tunnel lit by two bare bulbs hanging down, with high narrow cement benches along the walls. We sit on the benches, our short legs dangling. Suddenly, a blackout. The bulbs die. We let out a long excited scream. It's fun to be scared, to huddle together and screech. Our short legs beat the war dance. Wooden soles of steel-shod shoes kick the benches. "Silence," yells the teacher. Our short, invisible legs will not be silenced. "Stop it. Girls, listen to me. I know it's always the boys who start this. Don't be as dumb as they are, and get the ones next to you to stop."

But neither the boys nor the girls will stop. They are no longer afraid of the teachers; in the dark, they are no bigger than us, their shaky voices lose their authority. Their threats drown in a panic we cultivate. The uproar is now formidable.

Under our breath we chant the song of liberation,
Teacher, teacher, you so mean, so bossy,
are you scared suddenly?

And our most welcome song of freedom, the song the big kids sing on the last day of school before summer vacation, comes to everyone's lips,
Vive les Vacances, plus de pénitence,
les cahiers au feu, la maîtresse au milieu!
Hooray for holidays. No more punishments.
We'll set our copybooks on fire
put teacher in the center!

Caves, cellars, tunnels and passages. By now we know these underworlds by heart. The moist darkness under the earth, comforting like a womb we are glad to return to in time of stress.
You knew them like rats know them, by smell and touch.
My friend Françoise told me that after all the neighborhood cats had met their ends in the *concierges'* frying pan, people started to eat city rodents.

Everyone I knew cheered after finishing the most frugal of meals, *"Encore un autre que les boches n'auront pas."* One more the Krauts won't get. I knew that Krauts were the bad Germans; on newsreels I had seen troops marching on the Champs Elysées as though they owned Paris. I wondered if it meant that there were no more cats or rats for all those bad German soldiers to eat.

I would not touch the meat Françoise's father, our friend and butcher, brought to us all bloody. I only wanted eggs and milk. Oats with milk, mush with milk, cereals with milk, mashed potatoes with eggs and milk and milk to drink, all that milk my mother would provide against all odds, like an excuse for her breast too soon empty. Our milk tie was still so close I remembered.

Long milk lines in the small hours of morning. Dreams of milk trains rushing through the night, sucked empty by Krauts before reaching our house. I was told that night trains also carried deportees, children who would never get any more milk.

To save me from malnutrition my mother procured a one-egg-a-day hen we named *Poulette*. Who knows how my mother got it, but *Poulette* came to live with us in our apartment in Paris. I loved the eyelets on her rusty feathers and she let me pat her. Extremely well mannered, she perched on the back of a chair most of the day, at mealtime picked crumbs at the table where she had her own plate. She used my mother's shoulder for a roost; often fell asleep against her cheek. Once she pecked one of my loose teeth, swallowed it before I could cry out.

Wasn't the war a time of fear and tragedy?

To us kids the war was a long game of hide and seek, cat and mouse. The Krauts had black, shiny boots that clacked. Grownups said that the foreign rhythm of those boots molested our pavement, that it was like a slap in our face. I imagined the Krauts to be like the cat with the black boots and long overcoat, who cracked its whip and smacked the mouse in my picture book. I knew that mice could be trapped to serve as food. They could also be taken away in trains, never to be seen again.

I watched those boots beating the cement floor of the subway, ready to trample what was in their way. The Kraut-cat had a long black raincoat, even on sunny days. The mice were always running underground. Mice believed that the biggest threat always came from the sky; they blackened all windows so as not be seen. Poor mice, so scared when they had to go out in the light of day to find food. When mice were caught by the cat, they were always surprised. Why me?

You didn't run fast enough, that's why.

An older friend who liked to scare me said that a bomb had dropped a few blocks away and dead bodies had to be dug out, others were buried in their cellars for days. I wondered how it felt to be trapped like mice or rats under your own house.

I heard someone say that *la faim* had driven orphaned children to make kindling out of the frames of torn down buildings and sell bundles in the streets to survive. Hunger was this terrible being, worse than the cats. So many of the tales and stories read to us in class or at home were about mean stepmothers, beggar children dying of cold in the street, mistreated orphans.

I wondered how it felt to be alone in the world. I questioned the dark shadow in my dreams:

What if my parents died and I survived? What would become of me?

You'd be in the streets, like those other kids, making kindling. A mistreated orphan, miserable, cold and lonely. Hunger by your side. Nothing for you to eat, no love, nothing.

Someone might adopt me.

A stepmother would only take you in to beat you. She'd make you work from morning till night, bare feet in heavy galoshes until those fell apart, then no shoes at all even in winter. You'd be blistered and chilblained, mangy, itching with scabies. Your frozen fingers would crack and turn blue. Scabs would cover your body.

No one at school would treat my diseases?

No school for the orphan, no sulfur bath for the poor. You'd be like one of the Jewish children hiding in attics, dirty and hungry. Fleas and lice would crawl all over you. You'd be wandering alone all over the country, hiding your mangy body. Bedbugs would devour you at night. No. You are no one special without your mother, you would be treated like all others!

No one would care for me?

No one! Who would take the time to fine-tooth comb your hair many times a day to get rid of lice like your mother does, peel your scabs and disinfect the oozing to treat the impetigo? Who would have the patience to tuck you in bed and keep you warm, stand in line for the foods you like? You are spoiled, difficult. No, really, you could die, no one would care!

So . . . run girl, run for your life, run like a rat, don't lose sight of your parents, don't get left behind.

My *Maman* and *Papa* forbade me to talk to anyone. Not about anything that went on in our house, not about the Jewish couple hidden in our attic, not about my brother Pietro delivering messages on his bicycle, nor about the butcher smuggling meat across Paris in the dead of night to bring it to our neighborhood people.

The butcher only delivered to the ones who could pay the price, but because we were like family and helped him in many ways, he always had something for us. He carried sacks of bloody meat on his back. Blood in the night.

People said that Germans were unnecessarily spilling our young men's blood, that the Nazis were bloodthirsty. There were many bloody battles. Blood soaked the land. I dreamt I was drowning in a river of blood.

My parents warned me never to say a word to German soldiers.

Et le boche alors? What about that German officer?

Yes, that was scary. One day in the subway a German officer sat across from my mother and me. He bent over, gently patted my cheek and, smiling to my mother, said in French with an accent very different from the one my parents had, "What a cute little girl." I shoved his hand away and snarled, "Don't touch me, dirty Kraut."

My mother squeezed my hand, turning pale like the day when darkness settled on the land in mid-afternoon. On that day a cold wind started to blow from the open window and suddenly it was dusk, then nighttime. I knew that night couldn't come in the middle of the day and my chest tightened. Could this be the end of the world? My mother put the back of her hand to her forehead and with a small cry collapsed on the couch. She fainted and I thought the ghostly night had killed her. Petrified I screamed, but she came to almost immediately and comforted me. I was told later that it had been an eclipse. I would never trust eclipses after that.

Now I was afraid she was going to faint again on the subway. She held her heart. She had heard that you ended up in concentration camps for much less. She had heard that Germans took away your children and let them die alone, prey to horrible sicknesses. She had heard that torture made you confess to anything. She had heard about killing fields, gas chambers, ditches filled with corpses and her terror could summon up even more horrifying images, but the officer turned to her and said in a soft voice, "Don't worry! It's all right. I understand."

He seemed kind suddenly. I liked him in a way. My mother nodded weakly. How beautiful she was in those days.

Later I was admonished, "Never do that again. Don't say anything to anyone, ever, especially German officers, or you'll be deported. When they talk to you just answer yes or no, and be polite."

Ne dis rien à personne. Don't ever talk, little girl. Just keep running.

At night, dark shadows walked over me and threatened to crush me. During the day I saw them on the subway. I understood well that we had deadly enemies: I'd seen our neighbors following the path of spilled blood on huge maps they unrolled at night. They pinned little red flags on them to mark the enemy's advance and French flags for our victories.

Tu comprenais tout ça? Did you understand all that?

Non. Grownups said that the war was senseless, chaotic, but on newsreels the tanks paraded around in orderly formations; the war seemed so organized, unthreatening. Wise men with white hair and stern faces discussed and planned, made speeches and signed treaties. They seemed very responsible, not senseless at all. They were ready for anything in order to save France, to save us, they said.

Those men must have known of an order of things most people did not understand, just like I didn't always understand grownup talk. Some people said that our government was right to collaborate, that the Germans ran the war with discipline, method and reason. Others said that the conqueror was an assassin, extremely fastidious when planning death. I heard about dispassionate and indifferent bureaucrats.

Bon ou mauvais, bien ou mal. Good or bad? You didn't know exactly what it all meant and it was very confusing, right?

Yes. But Pietro and his friends were not confused when they talked about what Germans were doing, "They are determined to eradicate a race and conquer the world. They don't care how much blood is spilled." I thought race meant people of different colors, but the race the Germans were after was really made of people like us, even people from our neighborhood.

Sometimes I stopped trying to understand and forgot about the war. It seemed to me that for the first time adults had learned to play. I had never seen them run so much before. Running at night when they should be asleep. Running often during the day. On newsreels people ran when planes were flying low. Running to catch trains, running away from soldiers on a raid. Running like rats chased by cats. Whistle of sirens. Our allies bombing us by mistake. Airplanes coming again.

All a game.

What about the night of the bombing? Ton souvenir le plus effrayant. . .

I am awakened out of a deep sleep, my father shaking me, yelling, "Come on. Hurry up." I don't want to wake up. I want to sink deeper into the secure hollow. I refuse to break the crust, to crack the nurturing shell and emerge into the madness because I'll have to deal with the noise and terror. The urgency of the distorted voice finally gets my full attention. "Come on! Come on damn it! Wake up! Hurry! Put a coat over your jammy. Hurry! Hurry! We've got to make it to the subway. Got to make it before a bomb drops." I am dragged out of bed, half asleep, wrapped up in a blanket, pulled down the stairs.

In the subway, real rats are there already, as always. Rats obviously run faster than people. They scamper through tunnels along the deadly electric rail I have been warned never to touch. "If you ever fall down there by accident, stay away from it." I have repeated dreams about it. In the dreams I have to cross to the other side because a German is after me with his rifle, but when I want to step over the electric rail I am paralyzed. I am so afraid of it I do not even dare look at it because my eyes might burn up when in contact with the deadly current. I cannot move. Then the rats come to get me.

The subway is the rats' kingdom. They share it with brightly scarved and skirted Gypsies, magicians of this underworld, obviously immune to the deadly embrace of electricity. They walk right along it and journey through the dark tunnels under the city, bravely diving into the black passages and disappearing. I follow them in my mind as they travel with death amongst bats, spiders and rats, disregarding the traps where trains could crush them, having mastered the entanglements of rails.

You seem to know all those dangers well. Tu les connais bien!

I spell them out to myself when I travel by *métro* with my mother. Looking out the window of moving trains I take stock of all the predictable deaths that would befall me if, by accident, I fell out of the protective shell.

Gypsies, wizards, fortunetellers, animal tamers are not afraid. I know that. They are so bright they seem to glow in the dark. I watch them, barely touching the ground as they walk, swinging hips, following a music I can't hear. Sometimes they even dance and sing. Sometimes they have a monkey. I wish they would take me along with them, teach me how to have special powers like them. I want to travel their fate, read the future and the past.

Don't they scare you?

Yes, they do. I was cautioned more than once about them. They are thieves without morality. They steal children, take them away from their families and no one ever sees those kids again. "After they commit their crimes, they take the road and disappear. Never settling anywhere, always on the move, they get away with everything," says my mother to a neighbor. "Outlaws. They have no roof, no shoes and are going nowhere," the neighbor answers.

Are you not strictly forbidden to talk to the Gypsies or to answer any of their questions if they talk to you?

I do it in the secret of my heart. I often smile at them when they go by. I almost hope that they would take me away. I imagine they do.

Danger can come from talking, but not from imagining.

"Hurry! Hurry!" This time, the sirens have already finished urging.

My brother is still sleeping or pretending. He always refuses to go down with us. He says they are not real bombing, just drills. At one time a bomb must have been dropped though, because there are destroyed buildings right in our neighborhood.

    Papa shakes him. A sleepy voice answers from under the blankets, "Go by yourselves! I have already told you. I won't follow you down there even if it's for real this time. I refuse to die in the dark, like a rat, buried alive. If a bomb falls on us I want to be in my own bed, die like a human being if I am meant to die."

    Papa yells louder. His son's fatalism drives him crazy. "What do you mean, 'meant to die?' Tonight because of you delaying us we won't have time to make it to the subway. So let's go down to our own cellar and seek safety there. I tell you, you are killing your whole family."

    So run girl, keep running, and never talk to anyone about anything.

Angela

Something within remains unaffected by the transient circumstances
that make up your life and through surrender you have access to it.
—*Sainte Némoise*

13

JOURNAL READING ON TRAIN
In which Angela on finding Orsolina absent from the compartment reads her open
journal and finds out that her daughter holds her responsible for giving up on her talent as a
painter, a talent Angela admired; also where she comments on her daughter's neglect and
dismissal of her.

I open my eyes. Orsolina is still not back. She is taking her time having that tea and pastry, probably wants to be alone. She has left her journal open on her seat. I can't help but peek even though I have gotten in great trouble with her in the past about that, she actually accused me of being abusive. I keep thinking that if she leaves it open and obvious, she wants me to read it. I just take a look at what I can see without turning the pages for I don't dare touch the diary:

Not long after La Roche the countryside has begun to flatten, by now it is a plain taken over by bright red poppies stretching all the way to the horizon. I would like to paint children the color of wheat, put them in those fields, have them run wild. . . maybe a woman in a light blue dress would walk behind them carrying a basket full of fruit. Far away on the horizon storm clouds would be gathering and the slanted rays of the sun would pierce through to have fun with the foliage of trees. My brush, in adherence with the light, could search for textures, light and colors, meet them and play. No interference. I would put in there the part of me that knows love well.

I recall that parents and teachers discouraged me from being an artist, "No way to make a decent living." I am still sad about that. I was cut off early from my truest mode of expression and I dropped it right then and there, just like I did with music.

Small islands of trees emerge from the sea of wheat and poppies. A cemetery appears. As far as I can see, no agglomeration justifies this large graveyard, only cows in pastures peaceably eating the grass. I could paint that also, add a ghost town and a tombstone called 'Regret' in the cemetery.

Suddenly, the train pulls out of a narrow valley and I catch a glimpse of a magnificent castle on the other side of the river. Below the castle, a stately church with slate roof seems hard at work fending off evil spirits.

We are now entering the station of Cinq Mars la Pile. We will have a ten minute stop. I think my mother is asleep . . .

I find hardly anything about me, except maybe for that reproach. I don't exist in my daughter's eyes and I fooled myself when I thought there would be a message for me to read. But I never wanted to stop her creativity, I wish I could tell her that. I admire my daughter's visual descriptions, her poetic way of saying things, of expressing her regrets. She paints pictures with her words, such a talent! She was a very good artist when she was young and I always wondered—if she were discouraged from making a living with her art—why she gave up painting as a hobby. Now I see that she holds her father and me responsible for abandoning what she loved to do most. There are no half ways with her.

What about her violin, about music? What made her give that up, I wonder.

iovanni

It is through the devil's doing that death came to this earth; it was his first gift, limiting the realm of God's kingdom. —Sainte Némoise

14

THE WITCH

In which Giovanni, after recalling the years that followed his stroke, met his mother Orsola in the tranquil, foggy place where he seems to be suspended; where she manifests memories that she wants him to retell to his grandson, but Giovanni is careful not to scare the boy as he had his daughter Orsolina earlier; where he recalled episodes with the bad witches, the division between good and bad, Orsola's bout with witchcraft, the sleeping sickness, the village priest, the school six miles away through the snow, the curse from the evil witch, the bewitching black cat, the ghost of Nodale.

When the memories of the years that followed my stroke faded away, I stopped my unreliable telling to the invisible listeners, which my guide Senja had encouraged me to do. If they were really there, did they even care? I asked to return to the tranquil foggy place, which was becoming a familiar and comfortable home. I rested there for a while waiting for the helpers that had assisted me all along in visible or invisible form. The foggy place was like a small schoolhouse where I was the only pupil with lots of teachers. With their help I reviewed my life to determine in what ways I had succeeded or failed; where I could have made better choices; what conditions I might choose to help me work out some of my fate and progress in my next life towards embracing my true destiny. I learned that there were no wrong turns, only turning points.

I stayed in infinite time, thoughtless, weightless, holding no image, no thoughts or recollections, just suspended emptiness. Then the helpers came. Their teaching was wordless, quick images and symbols followed by sudden bursts of understanding that dissipated immediately. This went on until one of them pointed behind me.

I turned around and recognized Orsola, my mother—my daughter Orsolina was named after her—coming towards me. I was so excited I wanted to rush and embrace her, tell her how much I had missed her, but she put one finger on her mouth as she used to when I was a child and she wanted me to be quiet. She showed me a valley that lay beneath us. I looked and saw our little village of Noiaris nestled against its church.

Mamma, finger pointing like a wand, was manifesting memories of my childhood: my sleeping sickness, my meeting with the black spirit cat, my encounter with the ghost of *Nodale*. Through it all I felt such deep love for her who always saved me when I was on the brink of death.

"Forget the invisible audience," she conveyed. "I'd like you to tell those stories to the grandson you love so much—this as long as you don't forget that you also have other grandchildren."

"How will I do that?" I asked.

"Just envision him and you'll be by his side."

The image of him projected me to his bedside in the blinking of an eye. That's when I learned that I could be in two places at once.

So it's to you my grandson, my golden child that I will tell those stories, the same ones I told Orsolina when she was little; those my mother, her mother, passed on to me.

When I was a child, tales surged like genies from out of the jars the women came to fill at the village fountain. I went there to listen to gossip, to ghost stories and to tales of village drama.

Does your mother Orsolina ever tell the old stories to you my golden child? When I was still alive she tried to prevent me from staying in your room at bedtime. That mother of yours—daughter of mine—said that I was too intense and disturbed your sleep. She said I had scared the hell out of her when she was little with those tales, and she didn't want me to do the same to you. So I'd have to sneak into your room after you were already asleep.

Now I am free to come and go as I wish. I know very well that you can hear my stories without being afraid. I need to tell them to you so our myths won't be lost.

Listen to me, young fellow. The way your great-grandmother—my mother Orsola—saw it, our village of Noiaris was divided into two factions, the good one, and the bad one, the ones who worked for God, and the ones who had a pact with the Devil; our Family and the Enemy. Even after I moved to Paris *Mamma* kept me informed of the continuing battles.

There was no doctor in our village and the nearest hospital was thirty miles away. We had good witches who healed with roots and plants; in return we gave them food, wool, furniture and clothing. Bad witches like *La Strega* had a different purpose. They could force reluctant lovers to fall in love, bring on abortions, make people sick, or put them to death.

Let me talk to you like a man, my little angel, although you are only four. *La Strega* was a real knockout as well as a powerful sorceress. What a vixen! Tall and thin with big tits and a full ass, always wearing a black dress with a low cut that dipped down into her cleavage molded by her bust. I don't think your mother would approve of me telling you all this. I don't believe you can really understand it now anyway, but later you will appreciate this.

Nobody knew how old *La Strega*, my first wife's cousin, might be, but she certainly was not as young as she appeared. My mother hissed whenever she talked about her for she was a Chiapolino, the clan of our family's archenemy. Her enchantments made the balance of power tip to that clan's advantage. In the age-long battle, the Chiapolinos were often winning because of that witch's ability to make us sick and confused. *Mamma*, forever devising ways to undermine our opponent's network, burned candles to obscure saints like Niocetta, Valeria, Ilda so as to weave a web of secret alliances.

Once, when she was very young, your great-grandmother Orsola tried her hand at magic. She'd heard from a friend that it was possible to go into a daze by looking intently into a mirror, and that in that state, the incantations one voiced would have full power. With a specific invocation one could imprison a chosen victim in a bag of bran prepared for that purpose. Orsola memorized the words of the invocation.

That morning her family had ordered some wheat to be ground and the miller had returned the flour and bran side by side. When everyone was asleep she tried her magic on *La Strega*. She dragged the bag of bran to the middle of her room, locked the door tight, then she stared into the mirror and began reciting the words of the spell. When she finished she saw movement in the bag and began hitting it with a stick as if the devil was in there. Suddenly, someone tried to kick the door open. She recognized the voice of the witch on the other side, cursing her, then begging her to stop. She kept on beating the bag as hard as she could. The voice screamed in pain, moaned and groaned and only stopped when my mother's arm became too tired to go on. None of the family members heard the racket. The next day, a relative of ours who had married into the enemy clan but was still loyal to us, reported that the shrew could not get up so sore was she.

Shaken by her daring and afraid to have fallen into deadly sin, my mother promised the Virgin Mary she would never do that again. She preferred to weaken *La Strega's* power by loudly stating her crimes, believing that to name evil and reveal its true color would rob it of potency. I'm sure she confessed to the priest, and he probably absolutely forbade her to fool around with spells.

Now young one, I will tell you something that happened when I was twelve and I fell prey to a strange sickness, which made me fall asleep in the oddest places. This often put me in dangerous situations. I'd suddenly turn pale and lose all my strength. Lulled by a sound of murmuring water I slept for hours at a time. No cock ever crowed, no watchdog broke the silence, no branch rustled in the breeze and no bird song disturbed the peace. Just this rushing sound.

The slumber claimed me mostly when the low angle of the sun stretched shadows, turning small boys into giants. It's often when I wandered alone in narrow valleys or canyons, at the foot of steep mountains that this tiredness overcame me and I had to lie down. No sooner was I down than I'd enter the dusky twilight that swaddled everything in shadow. In my village, they called my sickness the Deep Sleep or the Little Death. I went to a place like that after I died, but there will be a better time to tell you about that.

How about coming along with me to see what happened the first time I entered the Deep Sleep my little one?

Look, we are coming to a huge house. Look, all around red poppies are in full bloom. The scent of herbs makes us drowsy. Watch over there that ghostly man lying on a downy couch. He gets up, takes you and me into his arms and puts us down by his side on a daybed. He pulls down our eyelids with his thumbs. His son appears on noiseless wings. He can do whatever he wants, become a boy, a toy, a monk or an acrobat, climb walls or walk through them. Let's enjoy the show he puts on for us.

"Damn *Strega*!" The sound of your great-grandmother's voice wakes us up. It is often her voice that would jerk me out of my sleep. Sometimes I came around by myself and I tell you my boy, I was always stunned to be in darkness, far away from my house. So scared I'd run back home as fast as I could to tell *Mamma*.

"Damn *Strega*." She'd always introduce whatever she had to say with that curse. "I bet it's the work of that cursed witch again!"

Yes! That witch fascinated me, but even though I was an unruly scoundrel who wanted to fear nothing, no one, her doings scared me to death.

Let me tell you more about your great-grandma, a fantastic woman. Villagers gossiped about her. They whispered that she had strange powers, that she was unreasonably attached to me, her youngest. Whenever she was confronted about some of my mischief she defended me to anyone's face. She had a sharp tongue and often got carried away.

The village priest—what a bastard he was—taught classes in our one-room schoolhouse. He hit our fingers with his ruler for any small disobedience; for bigger defiance he beat us with a stick or the leaden whip. More than once I came back home black and blue from school.

It happened one too many times and my mother, enraged, stomped to the priest's house, which was right across from ours and, brandishing her broom, she threatened to break it on his head. He believed she had gone mad and ran away from her into the street. She chased after him with her broom through the village, yelling, "If I catch you, you'll get the beating you have given my son." Later however, ashamed and repentant, she went and confessed to him since he was the only priest in the village. She gladly did the excessive penance the bastard ordered, but that didn't stop her from fighting him the next time he got out of line.

She had in common with *La Strega* her contempt for that priest. However, the witch handled it quite differently—she tried to seduce him. She flattered him, made big donations to the church, so much so that they became allies—and probably lovers—for a while and he even sent her customers for her love potions. This until something went wrong, no one ever knew what, and they became enemies again. Even so, both the priest and *La Strega* made a great show of ridiculing the attachment between *Mamma* and me, an attachment that proved very useful.

Orsola could feel danger creeping in even when I was out of her sight. A constriction in her chest, a rushing in her blood and heaviness in her bones would let her know that I was in danger. Many people felt that she had the Gift and could be a soothsayer, but ever since the time when she beat on the witch trapped in the sack, she refused to play around with spells. She used her natural instinct for identifying sicknesses as well as her knowledge of medicinal plants for her family only.

Now do you want to hear how her gift saved my life? One day I did not come back from school at the usual time. A small building behind the church served as our elementary school, but when children started middle school they had to walk the five miles to Sutrio, a town of about 2,000. Our house stood at the edge of the village of Noiaris, on the road to

Sutrio. When my mother saw all the other kids going by her window on their way home one late afternoon and I was not among them, she began to worry, but figured I had been detained.

If the priest didn't keep him after school to do some lines, he probably is catching snakes, or setting up traps, she reasoned. But her heart was squeezed; she found it difficult to breathe. The wine in the carafe left on the kitchen table started to boil, a sure sign. She set off, guided by a quivering in her heart that moved her forward and led her straight to a ditch where I was deep in sleep. A red asp had curled up on my warm skin at the opening of my shirt. The slightest movement from me could cause it to strike. She knew it would be deadly. She hissed to get the snake's attention and then clapped to scare it away. When the snake was gone she slapped my face to bring the blood back, then tweaked my ear so my spirit would return. She couldn't totally wake me up so she carried me home on her shoulders. What a tough woman she was that wiry little thing.

The witch struck again and again. Believe me, my angel, I have countless stories about that bewitching woman and her tricks. You are so quiet tonight, my golden child. You don't even whimper in your sleep, but I know you hear every one of my words. I told your mother all those stories and more, and when I came to the end of my telling, I'd often become a witch, a monster, a troll or a ghost depending on the story. I made my voice wheeze like the wind, then lowered it into a rumble. My hands turned into claws. When I pretended to eat her up, Orsolina loved it at first, but later, as I rolled my terrifying eyes, and gnashed my horrifying teeth, and made ghastly screechy sounds, she became frightened. But I couldn't stop. I roared in our dialect the words my mother scared me with, those words that frightened generation after generation of children, *Bay guay, Bay guay, Bay guay, por con'l diavol te amarei, volerei, mangerei,* something about a boogey man that loved and stole and ate children in the same breath.

At the time I believed that this made Orsolina courageous and I wouldn't stop even when she panicked. I didn't know that I had become the monster and that her terror was real. Frantic, she tried to get out of my clutches, begging me to stop, but I enjoyed her fear. To entice me, her father, out of the monster's skin, she had to quiet herself down, then ask calmly "Is that you, *Papa*?" Only then did I remember I was her father.

I believed she was fearless because of how she got over a terrifying nightmare she had about a lion wanting to eat her. It went on for months. One morning, all excited, she shouted, "*Papa*, I faced the lion and asked him what he wanted." The feline didn't answer, but as he was about to close his jaws on her throat she slowly and firmly put one hand on the lower jaw, one on the upper, and her strength prevented the lion from closing his mouth and devouring her. She had won.

Even when I still was in your world, my child, I knew better than to scare you that way. By the time you were born, things in me had softened; my tongue had taken a different turn, I didn't swear anywhere near as much. Anyway, I know you want stories more than those endless considerations I am prone to these days.

So let me tell you a few more. One took place at the end of summer, when the late season brings on crisp mornings and evenings. In a week or two at the most, the cows would be brought down from the high pastures. A stillness in the air predicted early snow; the whole world seemed suspended.

Old Renzo was the high pastures cowherd for the village. Each of the children took a turn bringing supplies to him. When my turn came I left home right after daybreak in order to reach the summit before noon. It was late afternoon when I started back. Leaves were starting to fall and I crushed them as I ran, drunk on the pungent smell. I had fun until a heavy fog caught up with me; the cold was snapping at my heels. I ran faster. I got tired and out of breath. I sat down for a minute or two to regain my strength. Overcome with sleep, I didn't get up again. I had fallen into the Little Death.

Towards dusk *Mamma* began to feel restless. Soon, the anguish crouched in her chest invaded her bones. Her blood was rushing. She started up the mountain. It was nearly dark when she got to me. The fog was too dense to see two feet ahead on the trail, but her instinct told her where I was. She slapped me back to life, then held my hand because we had to carefully pick our steps in order not to fall off a cliff. That night it froze hard, and the wolves were heard at dawn.

Again my mother cursed the witch. Imagine the vixen casting spells on me one after another. But my *Mamma* refused to go to a rival witch to return the curse as the family advised. She kept her promise never to fool around with black magic because Jesus didn't like it and Mary was protection enough. She prayed to the picture of Mary with child on her bedroom altar many times a day.

We young ones welcomed the opportunities the road to school offered. We checked our traps, collected reptiles, pollywogs, picked up wounded birds, robbed eggs from their nests and gobbled them down. I myself kept and tamed birds—an owl I named Beco that perched on my shoulder and always came back to me although I gave it total freedom, a magpie to whom I taught a few swear words, and a blackbird that could imitate any song I whistled.

I often talked my friends into *fare la scuola del bosco,* the school of the bushes, as we called it. It meant cutting classes and fooling around all day in the fields and woods. Whenever I could, I brought the tobacco I had stolen from my father's pouch to smoke with friends. Inspired by the smoke we set up a game. One of us would call out the names of all the pretty girls he could think of. He went on to pick one of the favorites and started to describe how he took off her clothes, one piece after another, while the rest of us, eyes closed to be better led on this suggestive exploration, jerked off vigorously. Then another boy would take up the lead and go on to the next girl.

Say, young fellow, you rolled over. I believe I heard you giggling in your sleep, or was it just a tiny snore? Do you think it's funny? I would love to make you laugh.

To continue with my story: every time I talked my friends into skipping school I knew I'd be accused of being a bad influence on the other children and kept after school, but I didn't care. I'd still have fun coming back home by myself an hour or two later than the others. I didn't like much filling pages after pages of repentant lines disowning my evil ways and vowing that I would not repeat the experience later, but I got used to it.

I will not call the teacher a bastard, (I had been caught a few times doing just that.)
I will not talk my schoolmates into skipping school.
I will not kick the principal.
I will not draw naked women during math.
I will not fart in class.
I will not make fun of the teacher during or after class.
And others. . .

Here is another story you will enjoy. On a cold winter day, I had been kept at school even later than usual. The snow had been falling for hours. When I started for home I could barely distinguish the road from the fields. All footprints had been erased. A heavy frost from the night before had hardened the old snow enough so I could walk on it without sinking.

I ran through fields, kicking the five or six inches of new powder or dragging my feet to make the snow unfurl like a cape behind me. Sparkling, feather-light particles expanded my outlines. I made believe I was flying. I built huge mounds and turned them into strange creatures. I made mysterious signs in the virgin snow to be read by sky creatures. I created snow angels: taking a great big breath I shoved my face in the powder, surrendering to the bite for as long as it took for the imprint of my face to hold. I flapped my arms on each side of me. When I raised my face out of the snow, the mold was left intact, and the fluttering of my arms gave an impression of vibrating wings. But that day it bothered me when I noticed how much like a death mask the imprint was.

Before I knew it the snow was turning gray. I had only walked halfway to my village and the light was getting so low I was afraid I would not make it home before dark. The trees were motionless.

A large black cat came up behind me and began rubbing against my legs. I stopped for a minute, bent down to pet it, then went on. The cat continued to rub and slide against me, wrapping my legs in a voluptuous figure eight without hindering my walk. It managed to always be out of the way of my leg as I stepped forward. I watched his maneuver closely. To begin with, I had questioned the presence of this cat so far away from any house walking in the fresh powder—cats hate snow, they have a horror of getting wet, they usually distrust strangers—but I enjoyed that presence. The animal seemed to grow larger by the minute.

The wind had come up. It carried a call from very far. Someone was yelling my name. I turned around and made out my mother's figure in the far distance gesturing for me to come to her; her silhouette was elf-like on the horizon and barely distinguishable. Only then did I realize that I had strayed from the road and was going the wrong way, deeper towards the forest. I felt as if I'd suddenly woken up from a dream. I started to run towards my *Mamma*, then remembered the cat and looked back. Nothing. I looked in the four directions, pondering how something so black could disappear on a white background. There were not even any tracks.

When I got to my mother, she hugged me as though I had come back from a long journey.

"Did you see the black cat?" I asked her.

"What cat?" She was amazed for a moment then recovered and carried on. "That damn shrew! She wants you dead, but I'll wring her neck before she succeeds."

I tell you, that slut really had it in for me. You sigh, my little angel. Are you tired of all this? No, I see the beginning of a smile on your soft little mouth. Do you want just a last story before I retire? I see that you do. I'll finish off with a ghost story. I don't think this one had anything to do with *La Strega*.

In our Dolomite mountains, the custom was for younger brothers to leave home and seek their fortune elsewhere so they could send money back to the family. The eldest stayed to help tend the farm he would inherit later. It was a way of putting a stop to the parceling that had made some of the land practically unusable; sometimes our hay fields were divided into long strips only a scythe's swing wide.

The younger brothers resented this custom, they were jealous of their eldest brothers. You know my dear one, had I stayed, you would still be breaking your back doing farm work on infertile ground like your cousins do.

I left home at sixteen, headed for Trieste to find work and only visited my family once a year. I was nineteen when I had the following adventure during one visit that I meant as a surprise for my mother's birthday. Because of this I didn't write her that I was coming. The closest bus stop was in Sutrio so I was walking home on the very same road I took to go to school, the road where the black cat had appeared.

It was high noon in the heat of summer. The sun beat on my head and dwarfed my shadow. I had forgotten my cap and I smiled at the thought that *Mamma* would reprimand me. The grass was parched, the wild flowers languished, and the intense heat rose in wavelets above the road, jumbling outlines. The landscape seemed undecided as to what form to take. The chirping of the cicadas was intense. As a child I had learned to tell the temperature by the rate of their trill within the span of one minute.

Halfway home I saw a peasant coming towards me carrying a scythe. I should have known anyone using that road at that hour, but I couldn't figure out who it was. No one—except for the young men forced to seek work elsewhere—ever left our villages, and no one ever visited them either. Besides, this man, obviously on his way to get some hay, had to be a villager.

As the figure came closer I recognized his walk but I still couldn't place him. Very disturbing. Only when he was about to pass me did I get it. In front of me stood *il Signor Nodale*, the richest man in our village, the land owner whose sharecroppers worked his fields while he sat in his big, cool house with soft hands, clean nails and fancy clothes, served by wife, daughter and maids. Never in his life had he worked the land.

He ignored me. As he passed me I called, "Good day, *Signor Nodale*. Don't you recognize me? What brings you here in the heat of day when every man alive is taking a nap? You are not really going to work the fields, are you? Is there something wrong?"

He continued on without a word, his face blank, his eyes absent.

He never glanced at me or slowed down. The man must've been very preoccupied, or for some reason, angry with me. He was known for his good manners though—very strange.

Imagining the surprise of the family I would soon embrace I forgot about *Nodale*. Just before I reached the last curve leading to the village I heard the death knell toll. Who had died? I prayed it was not Mother or a member of my family or a close friend.

The mourners were gathered on the square to follow the coffin into the church. I spotted my mother in the crowd and ran to her, hugged her tight and asked, "Who died?"

"You must have left before my letter telling you about this arrived. Don't worry. It's just *il Signor Nodale*." I gasped.

No one in the village had much love for that exploiter of others, abusive to his relatives, but it was traditional for everyone to attend all funerals. *Mamma* whispered, "His heart stopped while he was taking a crap. Imagine that! Never did a day's work in his life. How could his heart be so tired?"

"Maybe tired of being so fucking hard," I answered.

rsolina

When human beings function without the frequency of love, they annihilate the energy that inhabits them. If for millions of years powers occupied the earth and existed without love they would kill the earth.   —*Sainte Némoise*

15

MAMAN MATHILDE – Les Fondettes
In which Orsolina recalls the air raids in Paris and being sent to Maman Mathilde, the abusive woman at the foster farm, the cruelty of the children to each other and to animals, the kindness of her little friend the martyred child, the punishments, the walks in the forest she is banned from, the visit from Pietro and his stories of the exodus in front of the German troops, later a visit from Giovanni on leave from the army, his bout with the Resistance; where Orsolina wakes up in a hospital on the day of the liberation of Paris and we are introduced to the Jewish doctor who saved her; in which she tells of her out-of-body experience when going under ether and the ecstasy of her awakening as her brother Pietro points to Allies flying in formation..

Just before we get to Les Fondettes the train tracks run parallel to the road. A troop of soldiers led by a nervous sergeant marches in the middle of the street. I turn around and follow them for as long as I can. Whenever I see soldiers, I go back to being a child in the war again.

Isn't the war forever inscribed in your psyche in spite of your denial of it?

Yes it is. When too many air drills shortened our nights, when the rumor of our city being razed by bombers seemed serious, when the booted cats had multiplied and insulted our pavement too openly, when the food was so bad and scarce it was hard to stay healthy, for some even hard to stay alive, when the chances of survival in the capital became too slim, when women were needed to do the work of the absent men in factories, I was sent to the country like many other children.

Foster farms were made available. "Farmers never suffer from the war. They always have plenty to eat and are not quick to share what they have," sneered envious city dwellers. "On top of it they pick up some extra money from the worried families of city kids." In spite of their misgivings though, *citadins* did entrust their kids to the selfish farmers.

Raconte! Tell about the farm.

The farm ideally, was away from main highways, from railroads, from large towns and even important villages, away from the risk of being strategic. All I knew was that it was away from my parents, away from love. That, I was told, was safety.

I had never left my mother before. When she tried to prepare me for the fact that I was going away, we were in the subway. I listened to her, following with one finger the Celtic border on the white enamel panels by my seat, hoping to work up some magic. "And you will be coming also, right?" I asked her.

She did come with me to the train station where many other mothers had brought their children. On the quay we were taken over by women in uniform who led us to the train. Some kids were screaming, hanging on to their mothers and refusing to let go. The mothers had tears rolling down their cheeks as the social workers forcibly separated them from their desperate children. I remained silent. My mother cried.

We all went by train to Sées, a town in Normandy. From there I was put in a bus in the care of the driver. I was the only passenger. He helped me out next to an isolated farm outside a hamlet called Cerisier. By the gate of the farm a man in a cap was waiting for me. He said to call him *Papa Henri* and asked for my name. He took me by the hand.

Four other children from different cities were already there in the farmers' charge. We were all told to call the farmers *Maman Mathilde* and *Papa Henri* as he had already informed me.

What was your first impression of Mathilde?

Always dressed in black, compact, robust and sharp *Maman Mathilde* was a tough peasant whose womb had never spoken. A long, thin, silent man with a thick mustache, *Papa Henri* wore his cap even inside the house. All the animals were kept in the barn, including cats that took care of the mouse and rat population. Dogs were always chained at the entrance gate to deal with possible thieves. We were not to play with them.

We soon became acquainted with Mathilde's whip. Its leather strap on our bare butts fell hard, but it did not seem so bad compared with the utter desolation of her disapproval when she had decided on a subtler course of action. Were we paying for the child she never could have, for the child she never had been? Somehow I knew we were paying.

My dues were larger than those of the others.

Why was that?

Because my Italian family was related to the traitors, the enemies. "When we trusted them they stuck a knife into our back," I heard *Maman Mathilde* say to a neighbor while pointing to me. And she kept her most subtle punishments just for me.

Too young to understand the making and unmaking of alliances, the politics of war, I was not aware that we had more than one enemy. I had never met my family in Italy and never suspected that I could be anything but French like all my friends—even though my parents often slipped into a foreign tongue so familiar I barely noticed the difference.

Mathilde believed that my people and I were at fault, just like the Jews—that accursed race—who were totally responsible for the war according to her. I encountered hatred for the first time; it became a supportive friend who kept me going in a time of loneliness and despair.

Did you have another kind of friend?

In the group of children, Pierre, a red-haired boy soft, gentle and submissive, Mathilde's favorite child, also her favorite victim for the physical beatings, became my best friend. He was an orphan and she knew she had no parents to answer to. We learned later that she adopted him when the war was over.

Pierre loved me without condition; when allowed, he'd always choose to sit next to me. He took my side against any of the other children if a dispute arose. Of the six other children under Mathilde's care, he was the only one who gave a hoot about me. He'd even share the small chocolate squares or candies he would seldom get—those treats were more precious than life to us—because I got them even less often than he did.

Maman Mathilde, stick in hand, her black apron with a print of barely perceptible dark gray flowers tightly wrapped around her, defined our territory. Smoothing the ground with her worn-out clog she drew on it with her stick.

We were absolutely forbidden to venture any farther than the farmhouse's courtyard, enclosed like a fortress between thick, high walls, barns and outbuildings. To the north, a gate guarded the only opening onto a small country road—the place I had come through when I first arrived. We were not to ever pass that gate. On the other side of the farmhouse an arched passage closed by a heavy, studded door led to a south orchard and meadow. The meadow marked the absolute outer limit of our domain. We spent most of our free time there, leaning against the door, because it was the only place where Mathilde's eye could not follow us.

Flocks of crows often landed to raid the fields that had just been tilled on the other side of the fence. When they flew low over us, Pierre would become agitated. "Quick, quick, please hurry up and cover my red hair," he would urge.

"What with?" I would ask.

"Anything, your skirt, your hanky, I don't care, hurry up so the crows don't get me!"

Someone had told him that crows hated red hair and would attack anyone afflicted with that condition. I'd comply to calm him down, unconvinced of the danger.

Not having one single toy between all of us, we'd invent various games around the gifts presented to us by the meadow: rocks, bones, sticks, branches from the thick bushes skirting its edges, flowers, dead insects from the tall grasses. We had a very orderly, fully organized insect cemetery with rows and rows of graves along broad alleys.

That's when your cruel games began.

We plucked the wings from the flies we caught so as to have soldiers and armies, and having grounded forever those winged creatures, we obtained control over their awkward, mutilated bodies. Many died at the front and were buried, others scattered in panic during battles. To the heroes left we gave freedom in the evening.

One of the boys started to steal mice from the cats and finished them off so we could have larger corpses in our cemetery, then he caught small chicks and wrung their necks so they kept the mice company. Often, a few chickens disappeared anyway, caught by a hawk or eaten by a snake, so Mathilde never thought anything of it.

One day, the devious girl no one liked was accused of tattling and brought to court by the children, then judged rather expediently. The judgment was solemnly read from a scrap of blank paper. She was guilty. The sentence was immediately executed. The two strong boys forcibly sat her down on a red ant's hill and kept her there until she screamed and begged for mercy. Her legs were swollen for days, but Mathilde never noticed.

Maman Mathilde was a witch. I was sure that she had put a spell on me. She often guessed my thoughts, especially when I had done something wrong. Every morning, in spite of my efforts and prayers, I would wake up urgently to the feel of pee in my bed and spend the next hour in agony. How to dry the sheets, conceal the urine-soaked mattress? I would try to rinse the sheets in the porcelain washbasin with a little water I poured from the ewer. But what about the mattress? How to correct that awful accident? Could I dry the sheet and cover the mattress before she came in and found out?

Had you been a bed wetter before that?

I had been clean long before I came to the farm. My mother, having applied herself to my education with extreme patience and stubbornness, proudly boasted that I had been toilet trained before I was eight months old. It was her big accomplishment; few babies were successfully taught so young, but now her training failed me.

Through the open doorway, Mathilde's shadow spilled into the room every morning. She knew I had done it without ever looking. I pleaded guilty and begged to be forgiven. "I won't do it again, I promise." But we both knew I couldn't help it. She would remain silent for a while and my heart sank as I waited for her sentence.

"You need a punishment!" meant physical beating.

"You need a correction," meant the other kind of punishment, deprivation of everything I loved.

She terrified me. I hated her with all my heart and it was hatred that gave my heart a boost, shoved it back to a strong place in my chest. From there I felt it going up to my throat, ready to pounce, come out, scream, kick and bite like the devil himself, but terror subdued the frightful urge to strike, promising this heart of mine a future revenge. I tirelessly fondled that prospect and although it remained vague, it was a fire I could warm myself by.

You had been banished from your loving home and now you were deprived and beaten?

Yes, it was no longer a game. I hated the war as much as I hated Mathilde. Not much was offered for reward and enjoyment. There were walks in the forest, sometimes a Mother Goose story read by *Papa Henri*, and mostly the chocolate my mother sent in small packages at great cost and sacrifice. I hardly ever got any of it because I was 'corrected.'

Half of it was distributed fairly among the other children, half locked in the huge cupboard for later, but we never saw it again. Chocolate was my favorite thing in the world, but as the other children ate theirs in front of me, I knew I couldn't beg them directly for a little piece. I tried to trick them, pretended to play *Maman et bébé*. I'd stumble and fall, then whined in a little baby's voice, "Mommy, Mommy me hurt myself. Me want chocolate," hoping they'd share. But without fail, they handed me a leaf from a tree. *"Tiens bébé!* Here is some chocolate. Poor baby! Show me your owie." And they'd blow on the make-believe hurt. If he was not in the barn doing chores though, Pierre would often share his chocolate with me.

When it was time for the weekly forest walk, I'd be punished again and wouldn't be allowed to come along. I stayed home with *Papa Henri*. I went on a walk a few times only, probably so I would know what I was missing. As Mathilde and the children disappeared into the forest, I followed them step-by-step in my mind's eye.

Across the road from the courtyard, surrounded on three sides by the forest, lay an immense meadow in the center of which stood an ancient oak tree. This giant sheltered, in its hollow heart, a swarm of the biggest black hornets we had ever seen. Awed by the size of both tree and *frelons,* the children kept a respectful distance. Mathilde had warned that if by accident we aroused the insects' anger, their army would attack and pierce us with poisonous darts. More than five stings would kill us.

In spite of the danger, the oak tree, so powerful and securely root-ed, fascinated us. There it stood, serene amidst a rustling of leaves and the buzzing of hornets, worshipful like an old woman in church, surrounded with a pale light that seemed to have its source at the heart of the tree. I'd go to the gate from where I could stare at the oak and stay there the whole time *les promeneurs* were gone. Sometimes *Papa Henri* called me away from that spot.

The forest stretched past the meadow and a determined little trail led straight through, lined with huge bracken ferns, heather and scotch broom. Something mysterious lurked there, something exciting. The worst danger was the vipers. They hid in the grass. My mother had a deadly fear of them that she passed on to me. *"Les vipères sont dans les fougères"* she'd tell me. Yes, in the ferns, but also behind the fringe of heather, pro-tected from sight by polished holly bushes, I was sure that the vipers lay in wait for the leg that would venture close enough.

As a rule, Mathilde would never let us run, convinced that it would get us too excited, wild and unruly, that freedom of movement was bad for us and could easily turn us into out-of-control imps. But at a certain place in the forest she would let go of control and allow us to run, not too fast, not too far, but we could make-believe we were knights galloping on horses and fighting the enemy.

We had to remember though, these woods were the home of the Resistance; there were courageous men hiding in the *maquis*. If we wanted to sing without disrupting them it would have to be patriotic songs. Mathilde told us the *boches* would have us arrested if they heard those songs, but she wanted us to be brave. The Krauts would have a hard time finding us in such a thick forest anyway, and the partisans would get them first. So we sang,

"Ce sont ceux du maquis, ceux de la résistance,
ce sont ceux du maquis, combattent pour le pays..."

And we picked ferns that towered over our heads to be our scepters, our parasols, our fancy umbrellas. We sliced the ferns to uncover the message hidden in the milk inside their stems. I loved the smell sticking to my fingers; the forest's sweet and pungent juices. Beetles wearing carapaces of old gold with muted rainbows on the wings became our carriages to fairyland. We borrowed vehicles and mounts from plants or insects, but we returned them before leaving the forest's kingdom. It was bad luck to bring them home. In the confinement of the farm, their magic could work against us.

Most of the time I was punished and stayed behind while all the other children went on their outing. *Papa Henri* stayed with me. A tall, absent man with a kind face, he never said much of anything, never spoke his mind, never intervened. He just worked, moving slowly but hardly ever stopping. He ate in silence, and in the evening sat for hours in front of the open fire until he blended so successfully with the furnishings that everyone forgot he was there.

Did you like Papa Henri?

I suspected him of disagreeing with his wife's cruel ways. I found out I had been right the very first time I was left with him. The others had only been gone for a little while when he spoke, teasing me about my long face. He told me jokes and made a funny face, forcing a smile from me. Seeing he had not entirely succeeded in chasing away my wretchedness at being left behind, he grabbed me, threw me up in the air and caught me back just before I hit the ground. Next he sat me down on the table and tickled me all over. I'd laugh so hard I could hardly catch my breath.

When time came for the others to come back, he retired to his dark corner beside the fire and it seemed like he never moved again until the next time I missed a walk. I felt somewhat guilty about our complicity, and that guilt stayed with me through school and church and love.

Your family didn't come to visit?

My father came to see me once. I was told that he had escaped from German prison camp with a small wound and he was on a leave. He took all of us children for a walk in the forest. Mathilde had warned him not to go too far, but it was very exciting to egg him on and lead him past the place where she usually made us turn back.

Suddenly and noiselessly a few men stepped out from the bushes and barred our way. They were carrying guns. One of them pointed his at my father. "*Halte*," he barked.

With a movement of his head he indicated for my father to follow him to a clearing a short distance away. We could hear a man's voice accusing,

"What proof do you have of your identity? How do we know you are not a spy?"

My father tried to explain:

"I don't have my papers on me, I left them in my room. But any of your men could easily follow me to the farm and check."

"What kind of an accent do you have? Italian isn't it?"

"It's a trap!" said another man angrily.

In the end, two men, one in front one in back of him, took my father farther into the forest where they disappeared from sight. Separated from him and very scared we obediently followed an armed man back to the road. He left us at the edge of the forest and ordered us to cross over to the farm, giving us a note for Mathilde. He watched until we stepped inside the gate.

My father came back very late that evening, we were all in bed. I heard him telling the story of how these men would have executed him if Mathilde hadn't gone to his rescue after reading the note. His Italian accent had made the Resistance men suspicious, but Mathilde was friendly with the chief of the *maquis*. He often came out of hiding to share our meal on Sunday and for him Mathilde cooked the best of what she had.

After lunch the next day the other children and I gathered around my father and listened to his stories of escaping from prison camp, eyes glued to him, mouths agape. He was our hero, we knew what that meant, hero and heroic had become part of our daily vocabulary. When my hero told Mathilde that she was also heroic, I thought he was very foolish. Or else, Mathilde had put a spell on him.

You believed she was a witch.

To myself I never called *Maman Mathilde* anything but *la sorcière*, the witch. I refined my hatred, imagining all kinds of tortures for the time, in the future, when I would have her in my power. This event would take place in my fourteenth year. I decided that I would secure the help of my brother's friends. Those powerful allies would help me capture the evil witch and tie her in the center of an empty room, leaving the rest up to me. I'd lash her skin with a razor blade and peel it the whole length of her body. I'd stick red-hot needles under her nails. I'd slice her eyes in two and collect the hard pebbles in the center of the viscous jelly like she did with rabbits' eyes when we had them for dinner.

She never softened towards you?

No, at times I tried hard to win her love. I bought her approval with mouthfuls of the pork fat I loathed but that she insisted I must eat. She boasted to the Resistance chief, "I sure cured that spoiled child, she would not touch meat before she came here, now she eats fat." Other times, sitting in the courtyard with Pierre, I conscientiously detached dead frog legs from their bodies. The frogs had been caught in the early morning by *Papa Henri*. I repressed my repulsion as they lay stomachs up in the bucket. If I touched the whitish skin inside the legs or their taut bellies, I felt sick. We wanted to please her, so when we finished a chore we asked to help her shell endless baskets of peas or string beans. We never hesitated for one second to execute the tasks she gave us.

Unannounced, my brother and his best friend Gigi appeared one day on their bicycles with sparkling wheels. Against all the grownups' advice they had decided to leave occupied France and ride to the free zone, with secret plans to join the Resistance if they could. They had been encouraged by our priest in Paris to keep some kind of patriotic connection from village to village, parish to parish.

Normandy was in the occupied zone and out of their way, but the priest had given them a message to deliver to the head of a children's boarding school not far from us, and Pietro wanted to see me. They arrived in the afternoon and spent the night, but would have to leave the very next day. Sobbing I begged Pietro to stay longer, but he said he couldn't and asked me if I could keep a secret. He revealed something about a message no one should know about, something about a boarding school that hid Jewish children under false identities. Somehow his friend and he were going to help, but he couldn't tell me more.

Why didn't you let him know about Mathilde?

I didn't tell him anything about Mathilde's treatment for I believed she was always within earshot and if she wasn't she could know everything anyway. She might kill me if I told on her, or make my brother sick to death.

That night after dinner, Pietro told Mathilde and Henri the latest war news, the advances and retreats of the troops, the defeats and victories. He described Germans marching in rows of eight through towns and villages, their field dress and metal helmet flashing, their faces impenetrable and impersonal, eyes wandering over the people, curious about the place where they would be stationed for months. Motorcycles came next, flanking the commandant's car, and behind them came trucks packed to the brim with large brown loaves of bread and other provisions.

Without letters or newspapers, since the post was no longer running, it was easy to forget about the rest of the world from where we lived in Cerisier. The village was in the occupied zone, very close to the demarcation line, but no German troops were stationed in our hamlet. They had made their quarters in the bigger village below and never walked the few miles to us. The radio was the only thing left to get the news, but the Germans confiscated the sets any time they walked through villages, so villagers hid them in the fields along with the hunting guns they were supposed to hand over. They listened to them at night.

Pietro continued to relay some of the adventures he and Gigi had on their way out of Paris a month earlier. "When people heard that the Germans were coming to occupy the city, they left in panic ahead of the troops. They were convinced that the soldiers would execute them all if they stayed. They had heard that the enemy locked people in churches and set fire to them. Everyone would be burned alive. Germans were barbarians. They would steal their food, rape their women and destroy their houses." Those were the rumors that were passed around.

It took the two boys a long time to get through, mostly because they helped tired mothers carry their babies, took the load of exhausted old people, pushed the carts that were stuck. Images stayed with me, even if some of the words escaped me. It made me feel very sad.

"I don't think most people had any place to go," Pietro said. "No home waited for them at the end of that ride, unless of course they had relatives down south willing to take them in."

"You could see a lot of them giving up hope even as they walked," Gigi went on. "Many of them could barely stand, it was people pushing from behind that moved them on. For those who hadn't left early there was so much traffic it was impossible to get out of Paris. Out of the city, there was not a hotel room left vacant anywhere. People slept on the side of the road, on the floor of cafés, in railroad stations. Crying babies were abandoned in their strollers on the side of the highway. What a mess!

"Further down cars burst with baggage, prams and birdcages. Furniture, mattresses and baskets of clothes were tied to the roofs. Horse-drawn carts of farmers who had abandoned their land to flee south, children and cattle in tow, crept towards the impossible miracle of food and safety.

"Even though people were jammed together like sardines, there was no complaining or shouting. Even the children were quiet. Only a low murmur rose from the crowd: sighs, sounds of labored breathing, moans and conversations held in hushed voices as though people were afraid to be overheard by the enemy. Roadblocks were set up to keep the road free for the troops, which only added to the confusion."

I can see it even now the images were so vivid. An endless, slow moving river flowing from Paris: cars, trucks, bicycles, animals, kids. Weary oxen and donkeys carrying household items piled high; a fragile scaffolding pushing forward and often collapsing. The caravan stretched for miles: people with their heads hanging down, women fainting and just left to lie there. No one had the energy to help them. They could barely walk themselves, so tired and hungry they were; but propelled by fear on this march of despair they continued to move on.

Pietro was particularly fond of relating the close calls, the near-misses. A plane suddenly appeared above their heads. He saw desperation in the eyes of those trapped on the road and a lack of courage to hope. Then they heard the thin piercing sound of the plane fading away. Everyone held their breath—maybe it had left for good—but suddenly it surged up again.

Next, they heard a close explosion; screams, blood, panic. "Thank God it didn't hit us," the surviving families said to each other, sighing with relief. We are lucky today. Afterward, they attended to the business of helping those who were wounded. The next day another plane flew low over the caravan showering it with bullets. Shrapnel grazed my brother's hair.

Another time Pietro hit a pothole and flew over his bicycle. An overloaded cart pulled by a donkey was coming downhill right behind him and the driver couldn't stop his animal. Pietro barely escaped being crushed, saved by Gigi who jumped off his own bike and pulled my brother off the road just in time.

Do you see now? It was as if all those close calls allotted Pietro some measure of immortality; each time he found himself facing death without fear.

I kept asking my brother for more stories, wanting to find a way to keep him with me in Cerisier in spite of himself. Maybe I could get sick, but how? Before I figured out how to do it, Pietro and Gigi were gone.

A jerk of the train brings me back to the present. I am suddenly aware of needing something to drink, but mostly I need to move.

"I'll go stretch my legs," I tell my mother.

I am not sure she heard me.

I end up in the *wagon-restaurant* ordering coffee. I need to be alone, take time to filter the past, decant it, get rid of the dregs, the toxins, in order to make it bearable. I write fast with a chewed up pencil in my small notebook. Something inside is making me anxious, something knocking on an invisible door. When I write I open that door and make room for what needs to be born.

Then suddenly I feel discouraged, disheartened. Do I need to put down on paper all those old stories? What use are they to anyone? What are all those questions about? Remembering serves only me.

THE LAST DAY IN THE HOSPITAL

I was five years old. I woke up in a white room. My family was around me. I didn't remember anything, except something about an operation. Oh, yes, it had to do with my ear. That ear had been mistreated before. I was prone to ear infections and the only remedy known at the time was to pierce the eardrum to let the infection drain. No antibiotics then. The process was so painful that I tried to hide the fact that my ear ached for the longest time. When my mother finally would catch on and ask the doctor to come for a home visit I'd be so terrified that I'd hide inside a closet or under a massive armoire where there was hardly any space to squeeze myself. But if my head could go, my body would follow, and *Maman*, doctor in tow, had such a hard time finding me the first time I hid there that they considered calling for a search party, believing I had somehow mysteriously managed to slip out of the apartment.

But this time it was different. This had been much worse. This involved someone else. Oh, now I remembered. I was at the farm when it started. The right side of my face doubled in size, I was boiling hot. I saw strange things. For weeks before that, whenever I told *Maman Mathilde* how badly my ear hurt, she had slapped my face. "Those are crocodile tears. You are making it all up so I'll send for your mother, but don't fool yourself, I won't."

My fever got so high that Mathilde worried I would die. She finally telegrammed my mother who came to the farm in urgency. The village doctor said, "You better take your daughter to a specialist immediately."

I keep remembering. More and more things I remembered.

I saw my mother taking me back to Paris on the very next train and Mathilde whispering to me as we were leaving, "You won, you little brat."

My mother carried me through the city, wrapped in blankets, feverish and thirsty—subways not running, taxis unavailable, specialists not to be found. I was not in pain any longer but couldn't see well what was in front of me. I had dream-like visions and talked nonsense to my mother.

A friend of the family recommended a Jewish specialist who was still practicing in the République section of Paris. A woman opened the door of the apartment and took us to the doctor's office in the back. The doctor took one look at me and said, "I think we will have to operate immediately. It may be too late already. I can't promise anything."

I remember! In my room all is white. A white nurse comes in and out. My ear hurts a little but doesn't throb. My father, my mother and my brother are around me. I smell funny. I try to recognize the smell, a mix of ether, sweat, fever and pus.

Now I remember the moment when my beloved doctor came into my blurred sight. My mother had carried me into his office, which looked more like a living room except for the consultation table. *Maman* told me his name was Doctor Schmidt. He stopped her and said I could call him Jean. He put me on his table right there and checked my ear.

I remember more. We took a taxi to a small hospital not far away. A nurse led my mother and me to a white room and took my clothes off. Then she put me on a gurney to roll me into the operating room. I didn't want to go. I screamed and hung on to my mother. I wanted her to come with me and wouldn't let go of her dress. She followed the gurney to the door of the room, but Doctor Schmidt stood in front of it. He put his hand up and gently told her she couldn't come in. I calmed down and let go.

A nice nurse put the ether mask on my face and asked me to take a deep breath. "It won't hurt at all. You'll see beautiful pictures, cartoons maybe, you will be flying," she promised.

And I did fly, but not in the way she described. Instead I felt myself inflating like a balloon, becoming bigger and bigger, as big as the world, then shrinking and shrinking into a tiny ball, compact and tight, and then even smaller. It was as though I had become a minuscule bug, or a microbe like those I had learned about from Dr Jean—as I called him now. Then I started expanding again, back and forth many times, becoming wider and wider until I expanded right out of my body. And I could see nurses and doctor disappearing at the end of a long tunnel. They were so tiny, so tiny.

I woke up in this room so tired, so tired. An immense weakness that smelled of whey. I closed my eyes and went unconscious again.

Now I feel strange inside as if I am not myself, like I have recovered a life that had been fading, a life now very far away from me. I can feel it all around, throbbing. I can feel it like the soft, warm, blue silk scarf my mother has tied around my neck as a present. That scarf makes me feel like a young woman who could be loved by a man. My doctor, my savior will come soon I am told.

My brother Pietro points to a silver speck on the horizon, moving across the sky with a soft buzz. Sparks fly off his pointing fingertip, exploding jewels in amazing colors, generating joy. Excited he yells, "Look, those are Allied planes. What a performance they give us!"

Then he explains, "Today we celebrate the liberation of Paris. See, the Allies have done it. We are free and victorious." Incomprehensible, but comforting words. They capture the joy snaking around the room like a shimmering *feu-follet*, a will o'wisp. The boundaries of the room burst. I become a dust mote floating in the sunbeam that drenches the floor. I feel so soft and tender I can do nothing but surrender to this moment.

The words of glee are painted yellow and blue. The sun outside the window, brilliant yellow; the sky above the roof, so calm, so blue, and my blue scarf that wants to meet the sky, and my brother's bejeweled fingertips.

I have nearly died; I do understand that. This is the day of my recovery. Around me, people keep repeating words like liberation, victory, Allies, but I know the celebration is for me. They are happy that the war will soon be over, but it's for my recovery that the family around me rejoices, and the whole city is celebrating it also.

Dr. Jean walks in. "We are so grateful to you for saving our child," my father tells him. Dr. Jean hushes him. I understand that the Allies are like my doctor, only they saved France.

Well-being. To have my family, the nurse, the doctor around makes me feel so safe. I love my doctor even more than my father who had been away in the army for so long I barely remembered what he looked like until he came to visit at the farm.

The doctor gave me back my life. I heard them say so. I know that it was an evil spell the witch had put on me, and that Dr Jean dispelled it. Just like the Allies disarmed the Germans. When I needed him he was not at the front, saving soldiers, like many other doctors, or busy fighting and forgetting about me like my father. He was not hiding as so many Jewish people, he had been there for me, to save me. My Doctor Jean knows me better than anyone; I promise myself never to forget him.

And did you stay in touch with him? Did your parents?

No I was too young and they too busy surviving.

He moves close to my bed, encourages me, "You can get up and walk around the room a little." He helps me but I can only walk very slowly for I feel so weak.

I stand in front of the window, my relatives happily tucked around me, laughing. I haven't known any wide opened windows. As far as I can remember everyone always kept their shutters closed and pulled their drapes. I don't have any memory of leaning over the railing and embracing the blue sky. I feel so big.

Warm currents tease my skin. A soft wind blows right through me. It's my first day on earth. My skin is new, a stranger to me. I remember words: *"Elle y a presque laissé la peau!"* Yes, I did leave my old skin behind, and now something is buzzing in the spring-saturated air, something shiny my brother points at. I would never have noticed that speck of silver if it weren't for that finger. My brother knows what matters; he is so much older than I. Something is up there flying, something vital.

I see sparks, fireworks of goodwill reflected in the eyes of the family embracing me, something that wets those eyes. I hear the word airplane, but I see no airplane in the sky, only this fly, buzzing, filling the room with happiness. I can hear its drone even with my bandaged ear. My ear now pain free, but still fragile for having been used as a weapon against Mathilde's sorcery. I have figured out why Mathilde—I'll never again call that dried up old witch *Maman*—whispered angrily that I had won. I had.

The sun shines on the iridescence of the fly. The sun so warm, so bright. Soft purring of love, happy fuzz of words. My mother cries and laughs. She thought she would lose her only child, but the good doctor saved me.

All of a sudden the whole building bursts into song. The sky becomes alive with silvery flying beings. Down below in the street, soldiers in formation stomp their heels to the rhythm of a big marching band, a huge parade swings from one side of the street to the other like a long wagging tail. The whole city is celebrating my recovery. I have made it. It's a great day.

Someone recites Verlaine's poem, *"Les sanglots longs, des violons de l'automne, bercent mon coeur d'une langueur monotone."* It's the poem they had all been waiting for on *Radio-Londres* as the harbinger of the good news telling everyone that the Allies had landed, that the war had been won.

Before I was sent away to the farm I had seen my parents listening secretly to the radio at night. They kept it very low so as not to attract attention. It reported our victories. Now the radio is blasting. I know that it's not just airplanes that chased the enemy away; I am certain that flies help airplanes fly.

How can you remember so many details of wartime? You were so little."

It might be all made-up memories, words that as an adult, I put to a child's feelings triggered by grownups' recall. I had heard adults constantly talk about The War even after it was over. My school friends and I were referred to as Children of War. My best friend's father had been executed by Germans, she was *Pupille de la Nation,* Orphan of War in local care. War was inscribed on our psyche.

Yes, you were the War's Children.

Orsolina

Music is a demanding mistress, you abandon her for years, you come back and find that she is gone. —*Sainte Némoise*

16

VIOLIN LESSONS – Leaving Les Fondettes

In which the train leaves Les Fondettes and the violin concerto from the next compartment reminds Orsolina of her initial infatuation with the violin and the people she meets on the street going to her lessons, the dog man, the bag lady, Bologna the lonely neighbor; where her violin teacher punishes her harshly and puts an end to her playing forever; in which in Guigniéres her despair becomes apparent and she invents a scenario to distract herself.

The train has just left Les Fondettes and we pass by the high walls of a small fortified farm. Someone in the next compartment has put a radio on loudly. I can hear it distinctly, a violin concerto, could be Schubert. It has been so long since I listened to any violin music. That old wound is still not totally healed.

I was six when I got my first violin. Walking with my mother and father one day I stopped dead in front of a shop window displaying instruments. I saw a violin and recognized it instantly. "It's mine," I said to my bewildered parents, "let's go in and get it!" They walked in and asked to be shown a violin my size. I caressed, enchanted, the beautiful instrument made of an exotic rose-colored wood fading into pale orange on the edges. I longed to put my chin on the black ebony rest and look towards the white ivory bridge that bit into the tender belly. When I did I knew where to place my fingers.

My parent's childhood in Italy had been fueled with stories of children prodigies and this sudden desire of mine to play violin was a sign they could not ignore. The most incredible talents had been discovered in just that way: a sign from God, a voice from the Virgin, a touch of a fairy's wand would blindly select a child for a great destiny, sometimes from among the humblest families. The voice of fate might even speak through the child directly. It could be what my parents hoped when I demanded the violin. So I got the instrument as my one Christmas present and a teacher to go with it: Monsieur Christmans.

A strange man who carried himself like my father, with elegance and dignity in spite of his short stature, Monsieur Christmans was unlike anyone I knew. He wore his black hair lacquered, combed back on each side of a perfect line, Tino Rossi fashion, a hairdo now totally out of style. His gold-rimmed spectacles gave him the air of being very learned and very wise. He played in a symphony orchestra and gave lessons to supplement his small earnings. His other students were hopeless, but he saw great potential in me and devoted time to my instruction outside of the paid lessons. I responded with enthusiasm at first. I wanted to learn to play well fast so I could impress Pietro and make him love only me.

When I start my violin lessons I am excited by the prospect of a walk by myself in the *quartier*. I have never been allowed to go that far from home on my own before.

It's really just a matter of crossing the *rue des Maraîchers* in front of our house, my mother watching from the opened apartment window and telling me when to go across. I follow the sidewalk until it bends sharply towards the *rue des Rasselins* for half a block, then turn another corner where it becomes the *rue des Pyrénées*. I don't need to cross another street.

As soon as I am out of my mother's eyesight I experience total freedom. Carrying my tiny violin, slightly apprehensive, I go by the huge black mouth of the carriage entrance that swallows up one of my friends after school each day. I hug the retaining wall of volcanic rock, and salute *mon arbre*, the biggest acacia I have ever seen. It always whispers sweet nonsense to me and at the right season, it dispenses scented flowers my mother uses to flavor *beignets*. The upper part of my street towards *rue de Belleville* is always deserted.

My mother took me through *Ménilmontant* and on to *Belleville* once, we went up and up on winding streets and stopped at a corner to listen to three sisters singing in harmony to swing music. *Maman* had a hell of a time getting me to go on.

Now all is quiet. No street singer. There are no more stores, shops, or cafés, no more people walking around in this part of the street. A dozen somber apartment buildings four or five stories high stand like soldiers baring their teeth. Often, the water is let out in the gutter to carry away garbage and debris. The hundred tiny voices of the water chat, hum, and murmur as they follow irregularly shaped cobblestones. Where the sun searches for its reflection, effervescent wavelets gush out, washing away the dirt.

Grateful sparrows come to drink in the stream and bathe with rapid, jerky little movements of their heads, legs and wings. Hopping and chirping, they preen themselves with jubilation. I want to capture all this, bring it back home to draw and paint it.

I stop. I see the picture I will make: a landscape framed in a window dressed in printed cotton, the curtain so light the wind blows it aside. The sun resting on the horizon is deep yellow inside, lighter on the edges, radiating out. The stream is dark blue in the middle, lighter close to the bank. A mysterious form sits under a tree, more like a shadow. I want a train in the distance and if the whistle can be heard, the painting will succeed.

I always loved trains, but the one I am on right now takes me on a mournful ride towards the last chapter of a family drama. Will I ever feel comfort in trains again?

"Trains are freedom," my friend Françoise used to say when we spent the summer at her Aunt Juliette's. Françoise wanted us to follow train tracks for hours because they led to great adventures according to her, and when a train chugged past us we waved at passengers with gusto, imagining that the greeted travelers would carry us with them over long distances.

The fear of being late for my lesson cuts short my contemplation, and I quickly resume my walk. I go by the tailor shop with its headless, legless mannequins. It is the only shop in this part of the street and I have never seen any customer pushing its door.

The twin sisters Lamie live in the building next to the tailor shop. Once, I met an old man coming out of there. He walked along with me awhile and struck up a conversation. Mostly, he talked about his dog. "How lonely life would be without him. People don't care, but dogs are loyal forever. They make you feel you have something to live for, someone to whom you are important. I sleep with my dog every night," the man added. "He keeps me company in my big, cold bed.

"Happiness is simple for a dog," he went on. "Dogs are like

children. They like repetition and expect a life based on rituals. Food, walk, treats, sleep, love. It's so easy to please a dog!" I agreed about all of that and told him extraordinary examples of dogs' loyalty I had read about. All along, I kept wondering where his dog was. How come the man didn't take his beloved pet along with him on his walk?

It's only when I met the man the next time without his dog again that I pried. He didn't give me a totally straight answer but I deduced that the dog had been dead for a few years already and that his master had him stuffed so he could continue to live with his old friend, acting like he were still alive.

I also meet a rag lady fairly regularly. My lessons seem to coincide with her promenade. She never talks directly to me, but walks slowly up and down the street, pushing a baby carriage with a broken porcelain doll in it, talking to herself, getting into animated arguments, or laughing uncontrollably. She does her early round at dawn, collecting rags and salvageable garbage before the trash collectors clear the street, but this is her late afternoon stroll and she wears her best clothes for it, tattered outfits with a remnant of grandeur: a moth-eaten boa wrapped around her neck, a threadbare velvet hat with long feathers hiding her hair, a sequined satin gown held by a string encircling her waist. Her legs are carefully enfolded in rags and her shoes yawn sadly. Thick make-up attempts to cover up her wrinkled crinkly skin, but it cracks when she smiles making it look like a dried-up mud puddle. She has been heavy on the rouge and the blue eye shadow, it gives her face the bewildered expression of a clown. She constantly casts fleeting glances around as if she expects an audience.

People say that she was once a famous actress who played in silent movies, but the sudden arrival of sound put an end to her popularity. She didn't have a good voice, couldn't add the necessary subtleties to her acting, and she stopped getting parts. Foolish and wild in her youth, she had spent all her money in extravagances. Like the grasshopper, she was left penniless and hungry. Her old friends abandoned her and soon everyone forgot her.

Now, alone to mull over her memories and look at a few yellowing photographs pinned on the walls of her damp garret, grief has gotten to her head. This story might or might not be true. There is one just like it in every Parisian *quartier.*

On the way back from my violin lesson I visit Bologna; everyone calls him that, but it's really the name of his hometown. No one knows his real name if he has any. He is one of the immigrants who left home to find work but never completely adjusted to life in the French capital. A bachelor, he lives directly above our apartment in a room partitioned off from the attic.

A tiny skylight pierces the sloping ceiling, the only source of ventilation and light for the room dominated by a gigantic iron bed. A coal stove Bologna uses for heat and cooking sits in a corner, and the few kitchen utensils needed to prepare his simple meals hang on the wall. A table and two chairs limp to the right of the bed. That's all.

The walls are not painted but might have been papered once. The floor made of rough pine boards badly fitted is neither sanded nor waxed. Next to the bed sits an enormous chamber pot which Bologna empties every morning in the between-floors toilet we share with him.

An area of darkness around his eyes gives Bologna the appearance of an owl. He wears a wide-brimmed hat all year around. I never saw him take it off, even in his room. He talks very little, grumbles a lot. Kids are scared of him. They whisper to each other that he hoards a treasure.

Whenever I meet him on the stairs he invites me into his room and offers me a fruit, even though he usually only has one or two in his bowl. When I knock on his door he is always pleased to see me. No one else but me ever visits him, and no one knows of any family that he can call his own. I eat my fruit in total silence for Bologna has no stories to tell. When I am finished I speak about my day, my violin lesson, the sparrows in the gutter, school. There are times of dead silence, but I don't mind.

Something keeps bringing me back to this naked, overheated room with the lingering stench from the chamber pot. I feel a sense of security in that smelly den, always warm and stuffy. I feel at home in it. My parents try to prevent me from going there; they are embarrassed about my intrusions, besides, they find Bologna strange. He always stops their apologies about my imposition with one small wave of his hand and keeps smiling, "She furnishes my room."

One day, they found him dead in his room. I don't know the details of how his body was discovered or who broke in, for we had been away when it happened. Someone at work had noticed his prolonged absence, he who had never missed a day of work in his life. He made so little noise that even we hadn't noticed his departure; he had been dead in there for four whole days. There was nobody to bury him, nobody to cry for him. No hidden treasure was ever found.

Bologna died in the room where he lived a solitary life for forty years, sitting under the shaft of sunlight coming from the tiny roof window. I shed a few tears at the time, sad because I had lost my friend and my warm refuge in the attic, empty with the oblivion he had already fallen into. I don't know if I loved him, I just accepted him without question, like a character in a dream.

Sometime around puberty my priorities switched and I neglected the violin. I became interested in boys, infatuated with this one or that one. I wrote and drew all the time: diaries, poems, paintings. . . and the violin came last. One afternoon, a totally exasperated Christmans struck my fingers with his bow with such force he broke it. My fingers throbbed; I left the music room in a rage and dropped the violin then and there for good, vowing never to touch it again. And never did.

Now on the train I am teary-eyed, crying for Bologna, for my dead brother, my father, for all the years spent in the *rue des Maraîchers*, for my little violin I held so tight. I miss its sound.

The train slows down and stops for a few minutes in Guignières, a small station with benches under a large arbor covered with wisteria in second bloom. It would be wonderful to rest in the coolness of the arbor, basking in the sweet scent while waiting, but we only have a few minutes' stop.

I invent a scenario to distract myself: I get off the train while my mother is asleep and hide in the station's bathroom until the train leaves. Later, I could say that I missed it. I would not go to Paris. I would sit under the wisteria waiting for something to happen, something to take me elsewhere. Maybe a Gypsy would come and kidnap me.

This would be a good place to miss all the trains and to stop for good. I could become deranged and watch people go in and out of the big door with the fluted glass awning that reminds me of a nun's headdress, day after day. And yes, why not, someone might walk out to change the course of my life. Or I might just wait here until I find oblivion.

 **émoise**

17

NÉMOISE WITNESS OF DREAMS

Je regarde, je suis témoin, je vois. I watch over Orsolina as she goes in and out of sleep with the rhythm of the train, and her imagination continues to unfold her dreaming during her short spells of wakefulness. I follow one of her visions because I was there, Angela was there, Simone and Pietro, Giovanni and Malva were there in different forms and personalities. *Nous y étions tous, et tous marqués!* A cell memory deeply embedded.

Water spraying, feet running, peals of laughter, rainbow-colored droplets falling down my face and shoulders. Waves of intense pleasure stream through my naked body as we run, holding hands, all women, so alive, all naked, our small strong bodies covered with golden down. My companions' crystalline laughter resounds through me, a sound of tinkling bells—these are my sisters, I love them as we run through the shallow side of a river, splashing water, bodies touching. There is a young boy by my side, Lukos, the son of my blood sister who died a mysterious death. He hardly ever leaves me.

Playing, making offerings for ceremonies and erecting elaborate constructions according to our dreams' instructions take a large part of our days. There is such an abundance of food that hunting, fishing and plant gathering use little of our time. All is done in the spirit of fun and games for we share everything. There is no storage of food, no cultivation, nothing that we put away for the future. Our Wise-Ones-Who-See-into-the-Future, advise that hoarding would damage our souls, and eventually destroy the love that sustains us. The spirit of community would be lost.

What would be the reason to stockpile anyway? Trust is one of the principles on which our culture is founded. There will always be plenty to eat for everyone as long as we honor every animal and plant we take in, as long as we give thanks, keep the rituals alive and walk in a sacred manner.

In our tribe men and women live in separate temporary villages, in dwellings made from the skins of bigger animals and thatch. We take those down as we move along throughout the land and put them up again when we stop for a while. The male and female villages are adjacent to each other and there is much visiting back and forth, also great joyful meals taken together around the fire in one community or the other. The children of both sexes spend one moon in the female village, one moon in the male one. There are exceptions.

The old people have their own separate township with no sepration of sexes. There, ceremonies and burial rites are held. We change location following the seasons, and when we come across other tribes there is great rejoicing.

But on that day, as we run and play in the river far away from our home we are stopped by a large group of men the likes of which we had never seen before—much taller than we, more hairy, with larger advancing jaws and sunk-in small eyes. They walk heavily, stooped shoulders, hands practically touching the ground. Quite frightening.

We know instantly that this is not going to be the joyful reunion we are used to when meeting members of other tribes. So we run to get away from them, but some of the men grab the women closest to them. I watch over my shoulder, still running, and I see them throwing the women on the ground, and without the preliminaries of the usual courtship ritual, penetrating them from the back like animals, grunting and hitting them the whole time. When they are finished, which is quick, they smash the women's heads with a rock and gorge on the blood and brain.

The rest of us keep running through the river, water splashing, tears rolling down our faces, panic squeezing our hearts. When a man catches up with me I kick him in the testicles as hard as I can and while he is screaming holding his crotch, I choose immediate death over the ignominy. I climb a huge boulder and plunge head on in the shallow water onto a rock.

Orsolina wakes up with a start.

Orsolina

Every human that walks the earth is a highly evolved being who has successfully achieved mastery in another life and is now on earth to accomplish something that can only be done here.   —Sainte Némoise

18

TATA JULIETTE – La Riche
In which the train leaves La Riche and Orsolina becomes anxious, recalls her early fears, the demons and monsters residing in her Paris apartment, the immunity she achieves by touching her mother who loves her so much, and the relief she gets by being cruel to animals; where she challenges the beasts, talks about the magic of aunts, about boys and their assumed superiority that really shows their vulnerability; in which she goes on vacation with her friend Françoise at Tata Juliette's in Champlitte and experiences total freedom; in which she sees Aunt Juliette as an angel of acceptance and her garden as magic; where Juliette's liberating ways validate girls as their pranks are accepted; where laundry days are a celebration, the family gatherings an excuse for jokes and the girls' candor gets them in trouble when they expose an illicit affair; where the question of Juliette's background is raised after she elopes.

BEASTS AND PROTECTORS

As we leave La Riche, the whistle of the train chills me. We are coming closer to Paris and I'll have to deal with my mother's anxiety as well as mine, also face Pietro's family feeling useless, unable to alleviate the grief.

Quand tu étais petite, les trains étaient des compagnons.

Yes, when I was a child, any train whistle merrily invited my friend Françoise and me to go on an adventure in the daytime, but at night, if it woke me up, the whistle brought all kinds of dread: abandonment, loneliness, war, death. The woeful sound of the train disappearing into the night scared me. I'd curl up under the blankets. I knew the train had nearly reached the end of the world by the time I stopped hearing it. The thought made me dizzy. I remembered that trains brought many people to their death.

Quelle imagination tu avais!

Vividly alive and not tempered by reason, my imagination reigned over a strangely animated world. Stories were being shaped from moment to moment and I made little distinction between the unreal and the real as defined by grownups. Terror was often hiding within fanciful visions, but I had angel protectors who could defend me from dark creatures, bad witches, and those Gypsies who were always attempting to slit my throat and take out my eyes. Those angels were my *tatas,* my aunts.

Tes tantes savaient t'écouter. Yes, aunties could hear my requests, they believed me and believed in me. They were magic like fairy god-mothers who could not be seen but were always around me. They gave me love, sometimes as an adult, sometimes as a companion I could play with. As far as I could remember, a fairy-aunt had always been with me even when I was still nursing. She was beautiful.

In my fantasy world, the hope of escaping the wrath of any dragon or demon that stood in wait lay in some magical rite, at times in cruel offerings. I pulled wings off flies to make a congregation I could control, pinned moths and butterflies to the wall, tied dogs' legs together to keep them submissive, or put sticky tape under cat's paws to see them walk crookedly. I also threw cats in water because I had been told that they were devils in disguise, that they hated water but needed to be cleansed.

All this pleased and appeased demons, but fairy-aunts disapproved of my behavior. Eventually I stopped and instead, I began defying those night monsters and dragons that took over our apartment when lights were off. To save money, no light was supposed to be left on in the rooms we didn't use. We mostly lived in the kitchen, the only heated room, safe and cozy with its shiny white and royal blue tiles, and with the purring coal stove on which my mother cooked delicious meals to make up for the privations of war.

The bathroom, located at the opposite end of the apartment from the kitchen, could only be reached by walking through a long line of rooms connected to each other, from the kitchen to the living room, to the entrance way, my bedroom, my parents' bedroom and finally to the bath-room. Those rooms, always kept unlit, invited all kinds of beastly beings to hide in them.

I'd watch out for times when my mother had to go to her bedroom or to the bathroom. I'd grab hold of her skirt from the back, bury my face in it, press the top of my head against her lower back and tag along behind her pretending to play choo-choo train.

She'd let me do it for the fun of it, and I knew she couldn't see the world of dragons and monsters in the darkened rooms. Not seeing gave her immunity. Her love for me was a protection no monster could break through, no matter what. Touching any part of her made me immune also. So I went through the dark, eyes shut tight, trailing behind my beautiful mother and making train noises for her benefit, all the while grimacing and sticking my tongue out at the beasts, challenging them under my breath, "You can't get me you crazy monsters, you are ugly, you are dumb, I am with my mother, you have no power over me. Nyah, nyah, nyah."

Et tu triomphais.

Oui, for a moment I was triumphant.

TATA JULIETTE

As I got older I began spending my summer vacations with my friend Françoise at her Aunt Juliette's. Before I met Juliette I only knew one aunt in the flesh, Rosina, my mother's sister whom I adored and whose house I ran to whenever things were difficult at home—this from as soon as I could walk. *Tata* Rosina always understood.

Aunts didn't act like mothers, didn't forbid. On the contrary they allowed, gave permission. Aunts could see monsters and many things other people couldn't; they believed in invisible friends, were in touch with spirits. They could reach inside your soul with their hands and fix the places that were wounded.

Tata Juliette vous comprenait bien et elle savait.

Juliette fit the picture. Françoise had spent her summers at her house in the Haute-Saône since early childhood and she loved it. Since we were best friends, she wanted me to share that paradise with her. She pestered her mother until the woman agreed to talk to mine, but it took some doing to convince my parents. They were still disturbed by the disaster at *Maman Mathilde*'s farm that had nearly cost me my life.

Françoise's mother adored her daughter and endeavored to fulfill all her wishes. She used the argument that it would be good for my health to get some country air during the summer vacation. She assured my mother that Juliette and her husband Léon were people of excellent character, and eventually my parents agreed. They wrote Juliette. An arrangement was made.

I must have been seven or eight the first time I went to Champlitte. I spent every summer at Juliette's after that, until my parents sent me to Italy instead, right after my grandfather Ferdinando died. I surmised later that it was my father's way to get even with his own father to not let him meet the granddaughter he was so anxious to know.

Te souviens-tu de la première fois que tu as pris ce train?

Another long train ride. Françoise's mother takes us to Champlitte, the small town where Juliette and Léon live. Pulled by a coal engine that blackens our faces when we lean out the window, the train takes six hours to get there. It stops at every small town and village.

As the train enters the Champlitte station a weight flies off my shoulders. *Tata* Juliette meets us at the station. Freedom! That same feeling comes back every year when we first arrive. We marvel that breathing can become so light a thing.

We wake up at dawn the next day and greet the garden on the way to the outhouse. A light breeze carries the smell of flowers that ripples joyously on our skin. We recognize every flower even when we don't know the names. The flowers' personalities, their language expressed in shape, color, scent, is engraved into our being. I could easily leave my body and fly with the birds, but the moisture of sleep keeps me inside my cotton pajamas.

At Juliette's we meet things anew each day. We forget the rest of the year, the heavy oak door of our dreary, stonewalled school in Paris, which locks us in every morning. There everything is old, regimented, and uninspired. Surely, if the impregnable door is double-locked behind us, if all the windows are barred with heavy iron, there has to be a reason. In that school we feel guilty because it seems like we are serving a sentence. Most schools in Paris are built that way and kids know they are in the wrong the minute they enter.

In general I know I am to blame. I am not a good girl and often make my mother unhappy. When I don't obey the rules I worry her. I am at fault when I refuse my meals because so many children in the world don't have enough to eat. More than anything I carry this uneasy feeling I have no word for: my parents love me more than they love my brother.

Pietro is the only one who sends me a package to Champlitte on my birthday that falls on the last day of our vacation at Juliette's. My parents don't make much of birthdays and hardly celebrate any of the French or Christian holidays. That is the case in many immigrants' households.

When we enter Champlitte's dream world, everything is a celebration. We leave burdens behind for the whole summer. All the windows are open at Juliette's and we can fool around with the shutter-clasps shaped into ladies' busts. To her we are always good girls no matter what, there is no space for guilt in her house. And we have so much autonomy there. She lets us play with sumptuous materials, the dense clay we knead like bread, or the soot forming in the inside of the fireplace, falling in slabs when persuaded by our probing knives. The flaky crust can be crushed and used for makeup.

We are also allowed to make a mess when baking cookies, use dyes, paste henna all over our hair or engage in any untidy projects of our choice. Retaliation is not part of the vocabulary at Juliette's.

Et le retour à Paris cela était dur n'est-ce pas?

When we go back to Paris at the end of the summer, our apartment seems too small as if it had shrunk. It continues to do so more and more every year, until it becomes so confining there is hardly any room for me to grow into myself. I start to dream of leaving for another continent.

A tall and slim woman with premature strands of silver in her black hair, *Tata* Juliette had married Françoise's uncle, Léon, when still a girl. They remained childless and it has been a heartbreak for Juliette who loves children. She is glad to take a few youngsters as boarders in the summer months to enjoy them and help enlarge her very small budget. She is especially fond of girls and absolutely adores us.

Sometimes she takes care of a little boy two years younger than I am, named Pierrot. He is head over heels in love with Françoise and me and follows us around. Juliette is kind to him but we can tell that she doesn't have anywhere near the same attachment to the boy. I feel sorry for him who doesn't get much praise. He reminds me of Pierre, the little red-haired boy who was Mathilde's scapegoat. Françoise likes to play tricks on him because he is a boy—she had decided to punish all boys because they wanted to boss girls around. To me he seems vulnerable and gentle, maybe not all boys are conceited, but Françoise is the leader.

One day Françoise decides that he has to prove himself to us by eating a chunk of baguette spread with chicken shit. We tell him it's cheese but he can tell and eats anyway. After that we decide to teach him girls' ways, we dress him up, we even put ribbons in his hair. Only then is he accepted as one of us.

Juliette shares all her thoughts with us about life, about love, about men. "Women are the support of men who are so vulnerable they could never get on in life without them. It's because they are trying to cover up that fact that men use a bullying voice to impress women." After an argument with her husband who is mostly absent, she mumbles, "It's a terrible place where people work their life away and don't have time to be human."

We venerate her and in return she gives us an unusual kind of love, a kind I had not seen adults extend to children before, a love that respects. She never makes demands on us and lets us roam from morning till night, not hindering in any way our freedom of movement. She does this, entirely trusting our best judgment. Her only requirement is that we be back for dinner in the evening.

Une journée de bonheur.

On a typical day we leave in the morning, walk down the road lined with chestnut trees just behind the house. The early light falls through branches, throwing a lacework of shadows on the ground. We pop chestnut burrs under our feet and the brown chestnuts push out, smooth, shiny and unruffled, their big white eye earnestly looking at us. We collect them into a bag to be used later in a fight against the village boys we'll surely come across. The chestnut branches form a vault that frames the train station at the very end.

Beyond the *Allée des Marronniers* the day stretches interminably across fields and over distant ridges outlined with pale light. When we get to the foothills we search the trees for nests and climb to see if their babies have hatched. We follow wavelets in the sand to a small river where we collect newts, crayfish and pollywogs in small containers we have brought along. We dip our faces in the cool water and silence closes around us. We remember the sandwiches *Tata* Juliette packed in our bag. We devour them.

Our sandals clatter as we leap from rock to rock to reach the island in the middle where some unknown predecessor has erected a stone igloo. Any ruin, any abandoned building holds a deep significance because it undoubtedly hosts some ghosts from the distant past, maybe a treasure we can uncover. We are explorers, adventurers as we conquer it.

When we skip back to the other bank we become queens of all flying beings. We cut down cattails and run holding them up. The seed puffs popping behind us are clouds of fairies dancing over our heads.

After a while we trek to the *baignade*, a deep place in the river where someone set up a diving board and a rope swing. There are bathers there. We watch from afar some beautiful young Parisians who come every day to sunbathe and swim. We observe the mysterious makings and unmaking of love's triangles. Later, when we get back home, we will act some scenes in the privacy of the garden, rehearsing every one of the Parisians' moves, every one of their words. In the love scenes Françoise is usually the man, being older and taller, and I am the woman.

We leave the *baignade* to go to the ruined tannery where hides were processed in the old days. It is late afternoon. The tannery, just behind Juliette's wall-enclosed garden and orchard, is our uncontested domain. The stench coming from the dark liquids left in some of the vats does not bother us. We have secret passages to forts we have constructed in empty cement vats where young chestnut trees grow. We bend the young saplings and tie them at the top to make a frame for roofs.

We carve tender branches, our pocketknives slicing into the juicy bark liberating two snakes that join heads on the pommel; and we have a cane. It was Pietro who first showed me how to carve wood in that way.

Between the vats and Juliette's house stands an ancient walnut tree. We jump up, grab a few green nuts from the lower branches and crack the shell with a rock. Indelibly staining our clothes and hands we push aside the green envelope and extract the milky flesh we fancy. The venerable walnut, decked with webs and insect carapaces hanging down like ornaments quivers and whispers; he wants our full attention.

Et puis c'est l'heure magique où il faut retourner au logis.

It's getting to be the magic hour we can never pass if we don't want to lose Juliette's trust, or turn into pumpkins as she says laughing. The sky is golden, the Angelus bells are ringing, shadows lap the dusky water of a nearby pond. Exhausted from our day of roaming we walk through a narrow passage on the side of a neighbor's house, which is a shortcut to ours. That's when we meet the song on the neighbor's radio.

We don't need a watch; the same radio commercial about a shoe polish tells us night after night that we are on time. It has become our emblem, the voice of our freedom. We sing it all the way home where we know Juliette's wonderful meal is waiting for us. "I am starving," we both say at once. We laugh and pinch each other for good luck.

The three of us eat on the porch accompanied by the last bird songs. Bats start to fly overhead. Juliette's husband Léon will come back from his late shift at the mill and will eat alone. Juliette always cooks the things we like. We serve ourselves the quantity of food we want, in totally unorthodox fashion. The plates don't match and we get a different one every night. We delight in trying to guess beforehand which pattern will be ours that night, the joyous rooster or the faded four-leaf clover, the bird of paradise, the peach blossoms or the intertwined gilly-flowers.

According to the mood of the moment we eat breakfast at night or lunch for breakfast, and we never have to sit down to a meal at lunchtime like most people do. "It's a shame how it takes a big chunk out of the day. It's never the same afterward," Juliette says. This refusal to conform reinforces our feminine complicity, our consent to an order of things which is only our own. We do the dishes when we want to, it never is an obligation.

After dinner we sit and watch recalcitrant draught horses bringing back the hay from the fields in top-heavy carriages.

Et vos parents venaient vous reprendre à la fin de l'été.

Our parents usually visit for a week at the end of our stay. During one of those visits a cartoon in the paper causes great hilarity at the dinner table. Two famous men, a writer and painter, Jean Cocteau, and an actor, Jean Marais, are pedaling on a tandem bike. The legend reads: Jean Cocteau and Jean Marais, *rois de la pédale* (kings of the pedal). We pester Françoise's father until he explains with great reluctance that besides meaning the part used to put your feet on to turn the wheels of bicycles, *pédales* also mean people who don't like persons of the opposite sex. They prefer to hug and caress people of their own sex.

Françoise and I burst out laughing. "That means," she says turning to me, "that we are pedals also." Looks of consternation and shocked surprise from the grownups. I know that Françoise is referring to the time in bed when after rubbing each other's back, we tickle, wrestle, brush against and touch each other's private parts, mostly out of curiosity.

We never made much of it, but our parents do. "You are impossible, an embarrassment to us all," shrieks Françoise's mother. "If you continue like that we will not send you to Juliette's any longer," threatens mine. "And from now on you are to sleep in separate beds," adds my father.

From the window of the train my mother and I ride on I notice tractors and big farm machinery parked in paved courtyards or in corrugated iron hangars that have replaced stables. No more beasts of burden. If there are animals they are invisible. *La pile de fumier n'y est plus.* The traditional dungheap no longer thrones in the middle of the courtyard, heating up. No more cattle, no more manure. I look at my mother. She is awake and smiles at me. She loves me so much. How easily I would have traded her for *Tata* Juliette when I was a child though!

Juliette called us *les filles*, the girls, and those two short words, in her mouth, had a heroic ring to them. For the first time in my life I felt the feminine condition to be an advantage, something to be proud of since it had gotten me Juliette's love.

Boys were always preferred at that time, thought to be smarter, stronger and much more valuable than girls. Girls were inferior, meant to serve, be obedient and please. However, in farmers' families, the corporal punishments were much more severe for boys when they disobeyed. A *martinet,* leather whip with leaded ends, was kept above the entrance door to be used regularly on the boys for petty trespasses. Discipline was milder on girls unless their sin was carnal. Educators warned families that any kids who hadn't had enough physical punishment would become delinquent.

None of that at Juliette's. She opened her house, her garden, her heart and the world to us as matter-of-factly as she made our beds upstairs if we didn't. "Nothing to it," she often said. She liked to air the bedrooms every morning while we sat at breakfast and sipped our morning *café au lait,* very little coffee and lots of fresh milk. Her muffled steps from upstairs added to the flavor.

Her pleasure was in giving, she didn't want anything back from us, never demanded time, respect or attention. And we passionately gave it all to her, in great erratic outbursts, cleaning and rearranging the whole house while she was gone, putting everything out of place. She never faintly suggested that our gift was not properly wrapped, a parcel to fall apart with much handling. On the contrary, whatever we did for her seemed to be what she desired, nothing less, and nothing more, just what she needed to be happy.

We lived in the bright sunshine of our mutual love with never as much as a minute of disharmony. What about Léon? He simply didn't exist, a ghost, a shadow. He worked long hours, the mill was about ten miles away, he left early in the morning on his bicycle and came back late at night. He ate breakfast long before we were up, and sat alone at the dinner table. He was a good, kind, and slow man.

His gun hung on a rack in the hallway. On his one day off, he cleaned and oiled it without a word. I never once saw him use this gun for hunting or practice shooting the whole time I stayed there. Juliette told us that weapons are the jewelry of men, but the town women we knew hardly ever wore jewelry. They kept what little had been passed on to them in small chests, to be given before they died to their daughters and daughters-in-law. But Léon had no son to whom he could pass on his gun.

Having pestered her for a week, we finally talked Juliette into seriously looking for the attic's key. It was the only part of the house we had never explored before because it was locked and the key misplaced. The place was inaccessible from the outside. We couldn't stand its resistance to our investigations any longer. Along with Juliette we turned the house upside down, looked in all the closets, in all the drawers and finally there it was like a question mark, rusted and heavy in *Tata*'s hand.

When she pushed the door of the attic open we were assaulted by the strong smell of dust, herbs, dried apples and old paper. She reached towards a light bulb and screwed it in tighter. The sudden light burst in the room, forcing it to reveal its mysteries: cracked shoes in a row, yellowed wedding gown on a hanger, faded baby caps, a Christmas wreath, Easter baskets full of bleached straw, shriveled apples strung overhead, a photo album, broken furniture and some trunks, a limping baby carriage all on its own, a bed. "All this is from a previous owner," Tata said. In the semi-darkness against the back wall, we noticed a huge pile of books. "Those are mine," she added.

"I have spent too much time with you already" Juliette declared. "Now that you got what you wanted I have too much to do to stay any longer. I have to get back to my loom and finish an order of lace curtains." That was another of Juliette's enterprises to add to her husband's meager salary. Those curtains, sold at the local store, decorated the windows of many villagers. Juliette wove lacy peacocks surrounded by intermingled climbing roses, representations of Dionysus amidst grapevines, or geometrical flowers dancing with snowflakes.

Delighted, we explored the attic alone. We played all day, putting on costumes retrieved from trunks, rearranging old furniture and giving life to the characters from the photo album. From then on our exploration of the countryside came to an end. We returned to the attic day after day for weeks and it was only when we got tired of rehearsing the past that we got to the pile of books.

All the forbidden books were there, bad ones and good ones, literature and trash, also tales of green goddesses leading unsuspecting men to the peak of sexual passion before terminating them. Unlike parents and teachers, Juliette agreed that we could read any of those books we wanted.

The books had a tendency to fall apart, so we cautiously took them to our bedroom one by one to read to each other at night. The one who read aloud got her back gently scratched. In the acrid smell of friable paper, fascination, jubilation and fear were woven together in gaudy harmonies. I never stopped reading after that.

JULIETTE'S GARDEN AND LAUNDRY DAY

When the horizon thins out, Juliette often takes us along to her vegetable garden all the way across town. She likes to work there during the evening hours when it is cooler.

Juliette sells her vegetables to townspeople, yet another enterprise to make ends meet, but she can never resist putting flowers in the vegetable beds, a thing unheard of in the village.

The garden pump has a sea-horse handle and drips into a huge oak barrel covered with water skitters that follow some mysterious patterns on its shivering surface. Sitting next to lace-lobed leaves we lend an ear to screeching insects in the torpid silence, we watch red and blue-winged grasshoppers unfurl their flags.

Tata Juliette never asks us to help her but we often do, pulling weeds so she can finish sooner. We walk back through town with baskets full of vegetables, stop at the fountain in front of the church to drink, watch people go by. The church steeple leans over like the Pisa tower, crippled from years of bending down trying to hear the prayers of a diminishing crowd of faithful.

We talk *Tata* Juliette into making a detour through the Montgin, a hill where the *oeillets de poètes* we love grow. They are also Juliette's favorite wild flowers. When we get to the top of the hill Françoise stretches her arms as if to take the measurements of the world. Having collected the poet's carnations we walk down through ryegrass fields, Françoise's arm around my shoulder.

Going back through the village we stop for a penny candy at the grocery store. We love to look at postcards displayed on a revolving rack next to packaged food whose labels glorify the country's modernization in red, white and blue. Seasons and all their significant rituals are represented on those postcards.

It is there that we learn about Easter bells dropping chocolate eggs all over the countryside, how fuzzy yellow chicks and daffodils come out of those eggs, how the twig of lily-of-the-valley offered on the first of May is a symbol of workers' friendship to each other, how at Christmas, the path to the brightly lit church is blessed by flying angels as the head of the family swings his lantern and leads the way through the crisp snow. In Paris we have none of that.

N'y avait-il pas un solitaire qui vivait là?

Monsieur Morin lives close to the grocery store in a dark, crowded house that is more like a cave full of books and treasures. He is the brother of the bookstore owner but never held a job. People are scared of him because he is strange, but we love to visit him for he is a good friend of Juliette. He shows us his treasures, antique objects, fossils, bones. His whole life, he has existed well on the edge of a society that does not recognize him in any way. He accepts that, knows that laws are made for others. He reminds me of Bologna, the old man who lived in the attic above our apartment in Paris. Juliette and *Monsieur* Morin have conversations about books. He lends her some to read.

Tu aimais assiter aus jours de lessive.

On laundry days a teenage girl from next door comes and helps Juliette with the load of soiled work clothes, heavy linen sheets and mud-caked outfits. It's a fair exchange. The girl gets pocket money she immediately uses on costume jewelry at the local store, and Juliette gets the help she needs to lift the big boiler for cooking laundry on to the stove, and back down again after it has boiled the clothes long enough.

With their pink cheeks and muscled arms, surrounded with a billowing cloud of vapor from the boiler, scrubbing and beating furiously on tenacious stains among glints of tin they make me think of angels. At times, they pull out from inside the pockets of Leon's pants, a nail, a screw, the movement of a watch or some other unrecognizable piece, cogs in a machine the man might have had in mind to put together some day, but never could remember why.

We are distraught when our parents arrive to pick us up at the end of the summer. Fortunately my brother Pietro and his young wife Simone have also come with two friends, Pietro's partner and his wife. They are young and lots of fun. We have a week to ride around on our bikes and adventure with them way out of our usual territory before taking the train back to Paris. It's a time of great festivity.

Oh la soupe à l'oignon de Juliette.

Juliette is well known for her onion soup, the best in the county everyone declares. I don't know what it is about that silky golden broth, but as it simmers, the scent of it makes us swoon from craving. When it finally is served, the delectable crunchy little toasts having soaked the flavor from the soup drip with the scrumptious filaments of local cheese our spoon has picked up. Our parents, like kids, beg Juliette to make the soup for them over and over. Often, neighbors and friends are invited on onion soup night to join in the eating and merry-making. Someone suggests that it would be elegant to dine by candlelight and everyone agrees.

After dinner, the adults are ready to dance. Françoise's father turns on the lights and cranks up the Victrola. When the music starts he turns off the lights again and they all dance in the semi-darkness, some sweeping from the living room on to the porch through the open French doors.

To bring in an element of surprise Françoise and I decide to put the lights on all at once. At a certain signal she is to turn on the kitchen and dining room switches, and I the living room and front porch.

The deck is in total darkness for there is no moon and no candle. When the light is suddenly switched on two forms held in a passionate embrace are revealed. I immediately guess that it is the wrong husband with the wrong wife, and quickly switch off again. I am dismayed. I think I recognize Françoise's father and a neighbor.

Even though few among the attendants noticed, an awkward moment follows. It seriously puts a damper to the party and terminates the fun. Françoise and I are sent to bed. Juliette comes to talk to us the next morning. "First of all I want to tell you that it is possible for a man and woman to have more than one love at the same time," she tells us. "But also," she adds, "I want you to be careful. Grownups have a lot of secrets and don't like them to come in the open. Churchgoers have a strong notion of sin and guilt and often see evil in the most innocuous doings. If you want to continue coming here for the summer just be careful."

"What's innocuous?" I ask.

"Innocuous means harmless or innocent. But I'll tell you what of your doings is not so innocent. Or maybe I don't have to tell you. I'll just give you a hint. It's about the outhouse."

The outhouse was built on a knoll on one side of the house, level with the garden. We had discovered, in the wall running down, a loose rock that could be removed. When we pulled it out we noticed that it gave on to the inside of the holding tank and as we looked up we could see the hole where people sat to relieve themselves.

We wasted no time in installing a permanent watch station, even inviting the neighboring kids to come and watch, for a small sum, the butts and genitals of adults preparing to move their bowels in what they believed to be total privacy. Somebody must have snitched for after a few weeks we found the rock solidly cemented into place. No mention of this was made to us.

"Oh *Tata*, we are so sorry," we both exclaimed at once. And she let us hug her, shaking her head, a smile on her lips. The fear of losing Juliette's love put an end to our erring ways.

I learned later that soon after Françoise and I stopped spending our summers in Champlitte, Juliette just disappeared one day. It was suspicious that, soon after Juliette's desertion, *Monsieur* Morin was never seen again.

As I got older I became curious about Juliette. Who was she besides being Françoise's aunt and our fairy godmother? How come she loved us so much? In fact she was not even blood related to Françoise. It was through Léon that she had become part of that family.

When I pursued my inquiries I learned that Juliette, who was a few years younger than my brother, had been raised in an orphanage. Her mother, a Parisian called Madeleine Saurin, had come to the Haute-Saône region to do union work and deliver the child she had conceived out of wedlock. Madeleine had died during childbirth. Her name rang a bell. Didn't I hear about a liaison my father had early on with a woman called Madeleine?

Est-ce que tu l'as souhaité ainsi, ou bien l'as-tu rêvé ainsi?
It just couldn't be.

émoise

19

ORSOLINA FLIES

Orsolina records another dream in her journal. *Je suis la voix du rêve, je suis le grand oiseau, je suis ses ailes.* I am the bird in the dream, I am the voice, I am Orsolina's wings, I am the dream.

I have been walking for weeks in a deep canyon where the sun hardly ever shines so mighty and tall are the peaks around. I am discouraged and feel that I never will reach my destination. I become aware of a benevolent being following me, invisible but very close. It sustains me on my difficult journey. I feel love emanating from that presence.

However, the journey is so long I am about to despair again when my invisible companion takes on a voice. "Follow me," he says, but remains invisible. I follow the humming guiding me out of the gloom, out of weeks of dampness and obscurity, and we climb out of the canyon on a long, painful and dangerous path. I don't entirely trust this path to be the right one; who is he who remains invisible?

When we finally reach the top of the cliff, the male voice commands me to stand over the chasm and jump down with him, "Have faith. If you go first I will be with you." I know this is a test of my trust, but I waver for a long time, then suddenly make the plunge into the void. A vertiginous fall. To my surprise I feel great wings unfolding and I begin to fly up and out of the canyon. Exhilarated I become aware that a large bird is following me. As it catches up with me I recognize my first love, Jean-Paul. I follow him.

We reach yet another level where the mountains are made of gold. Thousands of crystals break the light and stretch small rainbows between the mighty peaks. When the rainbows run into each other they become tiny winged creatures and change their course, weaving intricate patterns that reverberate on the celestial dome. I burst into a chant of gratitude.

I become aware that my bird companion has disappeared and doubts sneak into my mind again. Am I intruding in a place that is not meant for me? Will I be punished and plummet to the ground? But the voice speaks again. "This is the place you have been looking for, don't you recognize it? Don't you know when you are there at last?"

As my trust is renewed, my bird companion reappears and pours his being into me. We are one, I am whole and I can fly alone now.

Orsolina

Within the absurdity and insignificance of their lives mortals can find an opening into infinity.
                                                                    —*Sainte Némoise*

20

MEMORY IS A DRUG – St Pierre-des-Cors

In which Orsolina recalls her early years, her day-dreaming habit, her infatuation with childhood, the stories that shaped her consciousness, her tendency to live in the past, her tragic-romantic personality; where Orsolina talks about her mother's stress when changing trains, about memory being a trap as the immigrant worker joins them in their compartment and shows photos; in which she goes through recollections of the family photo album, reviews what her childhood street has become, how the old characters have disappeared and the new residents live anonymously.

For many, childhood is like an unpleasant cold shower, soon forgotten. Adolescents triumph as they leave those early years behind. A few decades later, the traumas of childhood unexpectedly crash on them like a bucket of water balanced on a door they opened by mistake. They have to deal with it.

But it was not like that for me. The story I told myself was that I had the best of childhood. I idolized that time when, unsolicited by past or future, I lived every instant as if it were the first or the last. Awed and enchanted, I entered the mystery with no hesitation. That was childhood to me.

In pre-adolescence, when I became conscious of losing my childhood I mourned, felt abandoned. A great melancholy came over me. I went on solitary walks, pressing my forehead against the rusted gates of abandoned castles, wallowing in tragic-romantic fantasies. I gave voice to my quiet desperation in poems, lamenting something I had not yet lost. That grief was entirely mine and made me feel special; it was the beginning of my writing.

Tu te souviens du Grand Meaulnes?

Oui. That tale widely read by adolescents at the time became my bible. It described the journey of a rebellious youth who broke his boarding school's rules and went riding alone through countryside and forest. He lost his way and was led as if by enchantment to a castle where a costume party was taking place. There he danced with a graceful cat-woman who removed her mask for an instant to show her perfect features. "I have been waiting for you," she said mysteriously. "And I always will. We are meant to be together, *nous sommes des âmes-soeurs.*"

He never was able to retrace his steps later but kept searching, devoting his days to finding the castle. After years of this, he enrolled the help of a shifty Gypsy and finally did find his paramour. She indeed had been waiting for him. So he married the love of his life.

No sooner had they settled however, than he took off at the call of the Gypsy who owned his soul because of a foolish promise the young man had made. He ended up dying during that adventure, and she was left pining for him.

Cest ainsi que tu t'en souviens, mais tu as brodé, comme d'habitude.

Maybe this is my own version of the story. In any case, I secretly wished that my search, like that of the hero, would end in my demise. I wanted to die a child rather than embark on the path of adulthood. What was I looking for? Maybe for that perfect moment liberated from past or future, free of mind, free of fear.

Ironically, the present moment became truly significant only if it took me back to a past experience through smell, taste, touch. Collecting *des moments parfaits* became my main interest, I did it as others might collect butterflies. I wrote about them. Memory was my drug. With no energy for the present, only disinterest for the future, I lived in a dream state.

During class the irritated voice of the teacher in the classroom attempted to reach me and bring me back. "Spiazzi, are you listening to me? Always with your head in the clouds! What did I just say?" And I always failed the test of the present, "well. . . sorry, I don't remember," I'd answer, looking around for help from the other kids.

A jerk of the train returns me to the present. I glance towards my mother who never concerns herself with useless questions; she had more vital things to think about during her childhood and adolescence.

The ruminations of her daughter always worried Angela. She thought me complicated and wild and I often envied my mother's simplistic view of life. If something bothered Angela there was a concrete reason for it and one did not have to go far to figure it out. On the other hand I thought that she unnecessarily worried over things.

Now Angela wakes up and starts fidgeting. I know what it's about. We have just stopped in St. Pierre-des-Cors, a train station on the outskirts of Tours with square pillars and a low veranda. We'll only stop in St-Pierre for two minutes, and then go to Tours where we will have to change trains with only six minutes to make our connection. That's a terrible worry to Angela.

I have explained over and over that we'll only have to take our luggage and walk to the other side of the same platform to board our connecting train. It should take us about two minutes, but that's not enough for her. She'd have preferred to get up at four in the morning in order to take a direct train. A change of train is a grave risk to her—any changes in fact.

We accomplish the transfer successfully. We find a place in an empty compartment. We get two seats across from each other by the window. Again she chooses to ride backwards, whereas I like to face the oncoming landscape. We are barely settled when the door of our compartment opens. A tall dark man pretends to be looking for a place to sit, but I know he is looking for company because the train compartments we walked by were nearly all empty. Why would he choose the one with people in it if not to talk? I quickly close my eyes pretending to be asleep. I will make my sleep so heavy the man will have to leave; but it doesn't work.

He sits down and strikes up a conversation with my mother. He seems pleased to find out that we are also going all the way to Paris. It doesn't take long before he pulls out photos of his wife and kids from his worn wallet. He is from Turkey. Another lonely immigrant worker.

Sepia photographs, ancient looking. They remind me of my parents', my grandparents' pictures, those I pasted in my first album, side by side with my baby pictures and those of my brother Pietro as a boy.

A trap for idiots this black and white past. "Things were better then!" the older generation would say. I got so tired of always getting places too late when I started traveling. "You should have been here fifteen, twenty years ago. It was totally unspoiled. That's when it was real.

It's so fake now," I'd hear from those who preceded me.

Too late, always too late. I obviously started living too late, traveling at a time when travelers changed from interesting eccentrics and adventurers to dumb tourists. The cultures of the world are now entertainment, just a stage set, a shadow play.

Ah, the good old times! *La Belle Époque*! One goes on, telling stories, squeezing a meaning, splitting hairs, cutting up slices of the past and pasting them onto a permanent page, one by one, in chronological order. I can remember every picture on that first album I leafed through it so often.

The first photograph of me, a dark-eyed baby, naked on a fur blanket. In the background, a painted set fakes the munificence of a mansion with a broad marble staircase. Poor immigrants look at those photographs of themselves and their children and can pretend they have made it. They left their home villages to make money, so they send those pictures to their awed relatives, the ones who were left behind, to show that it was not in vain they left, that they don't regret anything.

"Do you think that's their house?" the siblings and cousins ask each other. To those remaining in the villages the relatives who made it to Paris are rich. They send packages of used clothing, coffee, sugar, chocolate and cigarettes more than once a year; those luxuries are hard to get hold of after the war. Even postage must cost an arm and a leg!

I was part of many family gatherings during which photographs like these were passed around. Everyone present would get into the good ol' days mode, and I would get so bored. Nobody my age to play with. My parents had me late in life; the cousins and friends their age had grown children.

Et l'album de ta famille, tu l'as si souvent feuilleté.

Yes, I looked through that family album often. I was at the center of every page. The little girl with the enormous bow pasted next to the baby picture in the album was me. The baby photo was taken a few years earlier because our family couldn't afford to get photographed in grand style every year. The little girl stands in a white, finely embroidered organdy dress, holding a basket of flowers, the white bow sitting on top of her dark hair. She wears white patent leather shoes. There is a look of affluence about her.

On the next page, a photo taken in grammar school. Again I am that girl with the dark, sad eyes leaning on a friend who has put an arm around her. The two girls are delighted to be taken for sisters. At closer inspection flaws begin to appear like graffiti under flaking paint: mended socks, wooden galoshes, long unattractive winter coats cut from old blankets. Those are lean years after the war. The winter coat of the smaller girl opens slightly to reveal an impeccably clean plaid skirt, a hand-knit sweater with a border of reindeer pulling sleighs. Her hair is held on each side by two small, well-ironed bows. My mother sews and knits all my clothes.

Poor but clean is what we said about ourselves. Immigrants don't want to make waves and offend affluent people. Their pride in being clean is sufficient for them, and the ones-who-have like it that way because they don't have to feel guilty. Poor people in rags are disturbing, but once cleaned up they become invisible.

Someone in the neighborhood must have gotten hold of a camera because the next is a casual photo of our family taken in front of our apartment house in the *rue des Maraîchers*. *Papa, Maman et moi*. We are all so thin! One can read between the lines, guess behind the picture: long queues at dawn as soon as curfew is over in front of unyielding grocery stores. We wait to get our rations: a chunk of soap, two potatoes, half a quart of milk, two candles.

I remember standing in line holding my mother's hand in a cold not fit for wolves. I believe I can hear them howling in the background. "No, it's just the wind," says my mother. A leaden sky, shadows huddling close to each other or leaning against a wall, everyone infinitely patient. The line is very long. Around the corner there is no protection from the wind and the shabby characters stand out in the open. Once in a while someone falls, fainting from hunger and cold. Those nearby help the person up, but no one else makes a move. They are used to it; don't want to lose their place in line.

I must have dozed. The Turkish immigrant has stopped talking. I open my eyes. He is out in the corridor leaning out the open window and smoking. From the back he looks like one of my childhood characters.

Ça te rappelle la rue de ton enfance non?

Yes. Each time I come to France I have to revisit the *rue des Maraîchers*. The narrow street where our little two-story apartment house stands has hardly changed at all. Most of the rest of *la rue* is in great danger of being taken over by big housing complexes. There seems to be an urgent need to tear down the small houses crowding each other, air out the area and make it fit for modern living. People demand comfort, privacy and sanitary conditions nowadays, a bathroom in every apartment, no more shared toilets and communal showers.

From what I have gathered a catlady is still around, looking quite old and wearing an outmoded dress in tatters. Our street historians of the past, Nono and Bébert, are either in a home or else they have died. No one is left to tell. Once the street characters who kept the oral link are gone, people hardly ever talk to each other; they don't have time. They barely know their next-door neighbors; there are too many neighbors in those apartment complexes anyway, it's hard to keep track. Besides, what if they became nosy, needy or demanding? The advantage of city living is that you can remain anonymous and that there is no time for gossip. When the whole day is spent dealing with people at work and in public transportation, one wants be left alone at the end of it.

There is a split in the language. The private one is self-involved, the public one avoids what is personal, speaking in generalities so as not to disturb anyone. It's a language that does not move. In the past our street's oral historian would set himself at the center of great adventures and use his listeners as mirrors. The modern narcissist in his housing complex does not speak about himself to mirrors. He has become the mirror and eliminated others. He is his own reflection.

Farther down the street a couple of hotels with flowery names and verandas still rent rooms by the month. A few small country houses surrounded with gardens and trees also have survived. My mother told me that when Paris was much smaller, the twentieth arrondissement was a village set in the middle of vegetable gardens. Vegetables for the city were grown there. The *maraîchers* are market farmers.

Et les rues aux alentours, elles avaient de jolis noms.

In my *quartier* streets have names that create a picture. You can travel the world following those names: *rue des Pyrénées, rue de la Volga, rue de Belleville, rue de Ménilmontant.* In the *rue de la Croix St-Simon* the hospital where I was born hides behind the small church *style moderne.* When I was a child I loved to crush the boxwood hedge along the presbytery garden to inhale its pungent smell on my fingers. On Palm Sunday the priest blessed boxwood with holy water instead of palms because these were not available. Most families kept a twig of boxwood all year behind the cross over their bed.

The immigrant returns and sits down. I close my eyes.

Orsolina

Satan is man's foe battling to prove to God that he was wrong in putting his trust in a creature of inferior nature. —*Sainte Némoise*

21

FIRST COMMUNION – Leaving Tours
In which Orsolina, just after the station of Tours describes what a devout Christian and inspired mystic she was when, as a pre-adolescent, she prepared to do her First Communion; where she talks about her infatuation with the priest, her wedding with God, describes her dress and how she took the host; where she uncovers her disillusionment; in which she speaks of Lucien's mysticism.

As the train rolls along after leaving Tours, I fall into reverie. *Mes yeux tombent sur des photos dans Paris-Match,* I catch sight of some photos on a magazine the woman with baby—who took a seat in our compartment—is reading. A whole page about the wedding of some European princess. My generation tended to underplay marriage and I didn't wear a white dress for my wedding, everything was kept as casual as could be. On the other hand, the dress I wore for my First Communion was such a big deal.

Tu te souviens surtout de la jolie robe. You were so proud of showing it off.

We are thirteen-year old girls on a spiritual retreat to prepare for our First Communion. For three days we withdraw from family and school. We embrace prayer, silence and contemplation under the guidance of the new priest, a young handsome man who came to our parish from God-knows-where. The old priest was sent away for some scandalous reason.

Sitting on the grass around the young priest we follow every one of his moves, drinking every one of his words. He speaks in metaphors and parables. We climb the slopes of devotion and reach the peaks of ecstasy as he embraces the June sky with his long white hands flying up like angels.

A flame of passion hides in the pleats of his black cassock filling us with love and fervor. We feel ready for the great event that will flood us with light. I bury my face with more eagerness than anyone else in my illusrated catechism, marked on important pages with First Communion cards given by those who preceded us: announcements made by a dove holding a lily in its beak, pictures of Jesus' life, reproductions of stained glass or illuminated manuscripts.

We compete as to whose missal is most thickened by cards, a great sign of popularity with the older girls. Something in the transparency of blues and greens surrounding the Gothic letters in the missal, in the infinite line of the border reaching all the way inside itself and finding its way out, fills me with a longing. I want to decipher those symbols so strange and yet familiar.

While the priest expounds, I fall into dreaming of myself in the white lacy dress. The expectation of receiving the blood and flesh of the Lord for the first time is confused with receiving the dress. I know about the sin of vanity. I know I should not think about the dress so much, but it's impossible. The priest believes my interest to be more religious than aesthetic; I am one of his favorites. The other favorites are friends of mine who have the same fervor for the Gospels, the same longing for the dress.

Il aimait te prendre sur ses genoux ce prêtre.

Yes. The priest often takes me on his lap as he explains parables told by Jesus. His hands trace the form of the Holy Ghost in the air trying to unravel the mystery of the Trinity. He asks me to go to the table and take three candles, light them and bring the flames together, then separate them again. Three in One.

On the last day of our retreat we take a small exam about the life of Jesus. A more mature looking girl who got a bad grade blames the priest for failing her. "You just don't care about anyone else beside your pet," she accuses, pointing at me. "She always gets rewards she doesn't deserve."

Later at recess I bump into her by mistake and she hits me. I am about to hit her back when she screams for all to hear. "You think you can get away with everything because you are the priest's favorite, huh? You get better treatment only because you let him fondle you when you sit on his lap. I bet that you get all wet." The girls who are playing around us stop dead in their track. They all look at me. What am I going to do?

I am so stunned I can't find words. I stomp off in contempt as though she is not worth answering. Rage, humiliation and shame. I find refuge behind a building and try to figure out what the girl meant. Did she imply that I peed like an overexcited pup when its master pats it? The image compels me and stirs feelings of repulsion at the same time. I have to give up trying to understand because it's so disturbing. I turn it over to God, but never go near the priest after that.

When the retreat is over we go back home for a day. On the morning of the First Communion ceremony I wake up long before dawn. The moonshine falls in cold radiance through the window following me around from room to room, peeking in. It seems as anxious as I am to catch a sight of the magnificent garb that hangs ready for me in my mother's sewing room, all ironed and starched. I go in.

I follow with a reverent finger the finely embroidered flowers raised on the top of the pleated bust, let it slide down the pleats to the tulle of the belt. Up again my finger travels towards the fluted cap that will ring my face with an angelic aura and I caress the veil of gossamer. I try it on. It gracefully falls around me all the way to the ground. Happiness of white. White, not a color but a disposition of the soul. Happiness of the bride, shipwrecked in a sea of love on the morning of her wedding. Today I will be married to Jesus.

I reach into the alms purse of handmade lace and pull out the small transparent linen handkerchief with my initials embroidered in a corner. It's a present from my brother. Pietro gave it to me as a token, a way to remember that very special day forever. God, Jesus and the priests are very important to him.

I don't like that it smells so new so I put a few drops of lemon verbena cologne on it. Now the smell is too woodsy. I wash it with a lilac soap. Wet it fits in the hollow of my hand. I want the perfect scent, a scent of white. No, that's not exactly it. So I try other scents until I arrive at a smell so subtle and delicate it can only be perceived by me: a mixture of my favorite smells, of forest and garden, of the tame and the wild. When I succeed, I iron the handkerchief dry.

Et tu as pris l'ostie dans ta bouche. How about when the host touched your tongue?

The time has come for us to partake in our Lord's flesh and blood. The thought sends me reeling. An undulation of white defines the communicants devoutly filing in through the vaulted door to enter the heavily incensed atmosphere of the church. Blissed out and nervous we walk past the ornate pulpit to take our seats in the first few rows of pews while our families sit behind. I can hardly sing, overwhelmed by the rustling of white, of gauze, of whispers and sighs and by the Lord I will soon meet.

We gaze in the direction of the altar where we know our shepherd will appear. His vestments sparkle as he performs his dance before the tabernacle, bowing, bending, spinning. He swings his incense burner towards us, activating our repentance and our longing. When he walks past us to climb the five steps leading to the pulpit we are suspended, stunned by the succulence of so handsome a young priest in his robe of light.

During the sermon, his voice coming from up high penetrates me. I am the elected one. I am unique. His movements are fluid as he gestures, surplice flying over his cassock. He speaks, looping his language around his tongue, electrifying our souls.

Time for Communion. I am willing sacrifice, offering myself to the Highest in a passion of self-annihilation. I kneel behind the wrought-iron railing ready to be consumed by the Divine. Some of the girls have jutting busts under the virginal garment, but I am flat-chested and pure.

The priest comes closer, holding the chalice, raising the Host, signing and murmuring. I feel faint. I want to be assailed, bloodied, trans-pierced like Christ offering his bare chest, like the martyred saints giving their lives to God. With trembling knees I stick out my tongue, his pale hand only a shiver away from my lips. He gently lowers the host unto my thrusting mouth and deposits it on my tongue. I receive it like nectar. I am in love.

We all know the penance for sinful thoughts and frivolous behavior. Help me, Father, take pity on me, I am your child. God, help me stand this unbearable joy. Yes Father, I have committed a sin against purity, I'll do ten *mea culpa* for the image of your lips reaching for mine, twenty *Ave Maria* for your hand touching my skin. I'll walk twice around the Stations of the Cross naming my trespasses and accusing the flesh.

Yes, I have committed a sin against purity. Forgive me, but choose me again. I am beautiful and you know my faults. You smile upon me. You prefer me. You make my joy. I will uncover my face just a little more so you can see me better. Yes, see me, reach with your hands inside my soul, and touch me. I can't wait to ask for your forgiveness in the dusky confessional, to ask God for absolution.

At the end of the summer one of the girls is big with child. Soon after our priest disappears, sent away to another diocese. The girl who is an orphan raised by her older sister—an apprentice seamstress—remains alone and penniless to deal with her child. How will the sisters manage? Everyone whispers that the priest is the father. Then the story is hushed.

I never went to church after that.

Te souviens-tu que Lucien aussi est passé par là? Remember how Lucien also went through a time of religious fervor?

Yes I recall Lucien's mystical stage at the time of his First Communion. He even wanted to be a priest at one point. Pietro had to defend his son's fervor against his leftist family horrified at the thought of having a priest in its midst. "If my son has the vocation, I won't let anything stand in his way," Pietro declared. "One could be a socialist but retain one's faith, *les prêtres ouvriers,* those priest-workers, are such a good example of that."

As a priest Lucien could have become the infinite lover, an expanded identity that suited him well. His capacity to embrace and support would have been satisfied. Instead, as a young adult, he took that on in an unexpected way. He ran off with his high school English teacher and from then on wholly merged with the women he loved.

Angela's
Immediate
Family

Giovanni's
Family Tree

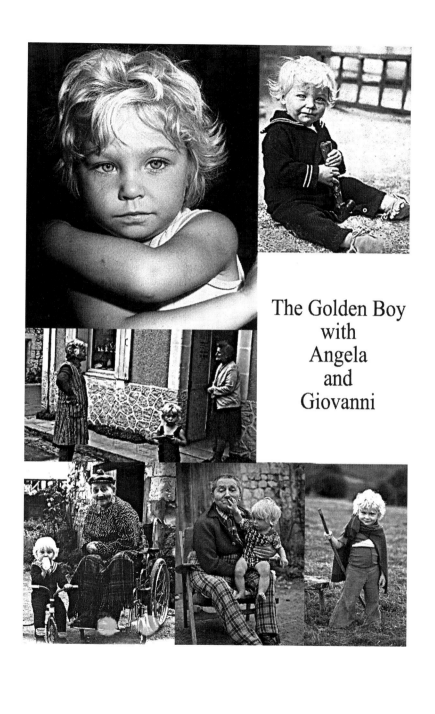

The Golden Boy
with
Angela
and
Giovanni

Lucien
Then and Now

# **G**iovanni

You have to love and forgive yourself before you can love anyone else.
—Sainte Némoise

22

THE BLESSED DAY
In which Giovanni relives a blessed day when Orsolina and he were in perfect harmony; where he goes back and forth, with the help of his teachers, between understanding the necessity of having gone through ten years of paralysis and the residue of anger that makes him vacillate between grudge, bitterness and the acceptance of his faults and mistakes; in which Angela gives him absolution and he accepts being dependant on her; where he remembers disclosing his wife's infidelity and the child that is not his to Pietro; where Pietro refuses to split up his family and Giovanni begins to take responsibility as he recognizes that in the end, it was Pietro who broke the ancestral spell.

Once, on a hot summer day, I had been immobilized for about six years, I was so dull and depressed I couldn't even lift my fork to eat. Orsolina was visiting us at the time, but no one had taken me out for days. To wheel me much farther that the three blocks that made up the main street of Lerné was difficult because the road became steep and uneven after that. Neither Angela nor Orsolina had the strength or the desire to push me up past the end of the village.

That afternoon after lunch Orsolina suddenly got up from the table, wheeled my chair in and helped me into it. She seemed determined and would not hear of any protest on my part. She put my sunglasses on my nose, my hat on my head, seized the handles of the wheelchair and vigorously pushed me out of the house into the courtyard. We went through the big portal that gives onto the street. She took the direction of Chinon, but at the end of the village veered right towards the forest of Thizay.

When I tried to tell her she could never make it up that steep hill she hushed me. I was aware of her straining, heard her panting. I could feel her sweat as if it were my own. She didn't say a word until we got to the top, at the place where the huge cross marks a fork in the road. Only then did she catch her breath, and we were silent for a while. Crickets hissed and the wind carried the scent of dry hay. It was my favorite spot, the place where village men gathered for pheasant hunting at the right season. I hadn't been there for years.

I could see the trail that led to our best mushroom spot in the forest. The farm where we got our milk stood alone in the distance surrounded by shade trees. The Gypsies were camped not far from there in the *friche;* I counted seven trailers. The sunflowers in the fields around us stood like armies, each *tournesol* a good soldier bravely standing up, head turned towards its commandant. Their heady fragrance made me sneeze loudly and that made Orsolina laugh. I remembered how much my own commandant had appreciated me in the army. It had been a long time for me without any appreciation.

"Long ago I came to visit the Gypsy camp with Pietro even though you had forbidden it," she said.

"You did well," I answered.

She laughed again and I laughed also. There was this feeling between us, of complicity and acceptance. It shimmered and quivered and changed something in me.

In the world where I am now residing, my allies help me understand that I was graced with forgiveness during such moments. Flooded with the light of acceptance I would let go of my resistance to things.

The chirping of birds and insects rising above the fields reminded me of my childhood in Italy. But there was even more to that moment. A streaming sensation traveling through my body eased me into the surroundings, and I stopped rowing against the current. I went with the flow. My long immobilization had been necessary, a time of reflection for me to reconcile with the people I had slighted, or with those I felt had slighted me—like Pietro who didn't fit my idea of what a son should be. That's why the voice had called me back to my body when I had the stroke. I had more work to do.

Orsolina stood there next to me, apparently filled with the same feeling of gratitude as I was. No more words were exchanged but we embraced, just as Angela and I had embraced a few days before when she leaned over to kiss me goodnight on the forehead. She said, "You have become so helpful and understanding. You are really able to show me your love now." Then she sighed and whispered under her breath, "Too bad it took this awful sickness." But I heard her and looked up at her, no longer feeling slighted because she stood over me. I wanted to put my head between her breasts still so full, but I just said, "I love you." And it dawned on me that I never had said that before except in the throes of passion. I opened my arms to her.

All my life I had held on to so many grudges, so many vindictive thoughts that it had obstructed my feelings—just as the disease impaired my physical activities. Even now I can easily slip back into that angry state, but when the rancor dissipates the fog of my past resentment lifts, and I see much farther. It seldom happened during my lifetime, but towards the end I was able to trust people and be generous without the fear of being used or taken for a fool.

It doesn't take much to plunge me back into bitterness and separation again though. In that way I go back and forth between loving understanding and fearful grievance. It was so hard for me to accept being wrong. The least trespass on anybody's part and I would feel terribly affronted, mulling over the ill treatment and making him or her responsible for all my misfortunes.

It took the journey through the tunnel for me to be able to look at my faults and mistakes. On this side I learn to accept responsibility for the events of my life. My teachers are many, always kind in their teaching, without judgment. Kindness is something I never appreciated in my lifetime. I called it foolishness.

Towards the end of my life however, on one of the rare weekends when Pietro came to visit me in Lerné, I was taken by an urgent need to go to the bathroom. I had no time to get out of my chair and grab my walker to get there. I called out to Pietro and without any hesitation he picked me up like a child—I had lost so much weight he had no trouble—and carried me to the toilet. We had never been so close. I could smell the cologne he used, felt his strong arms around me and was overtaken by a feeling of gratitude. For so long I resented Pietro's kindness as an embarrassing weakness and had never let myself feel my love for him.

All I had ever done for this son I called a stubborn idiot, was to give him one kind of warning over and over: he should be careful, he didn't give his wife what she needed and she was looking elsewhere. Was he impotent or what? But he never followed my advice, always helping others and often neglecting his own family.

Wasn't I the one who brought in the betrayer though, the partner who seduced Pietro's wife Simone? When I gave over the furniture making business I chose that partner because I didn't trust my son to run it well, and I wanted to put a sharp entrepreneur in place to help him with it. So I introduced a wolf into the sheep's den; the cunning businessman took over everything including the wife.

I ended up revealing to Pietro that I had the proof of her infidelities, that his youngest, Lucien, was not his son. He told me to get lost. I couldn't be quite sure about it since the slut was probably sleeping with her husband as well as her lover, but I had to let it out anyway. I insisted. Wasn't he going to do something about it? Was he just consenting to the family's curse? His mother was an adulteress who had brought dishonor to the family, bearing a child that could not possibly be mine, probably the priest's child. Would he let *La Strega's* curse continue to operate over generations? I was furious at him for his disrespect, and ordered him to break that spell or I would disown him.

Then I calmed down and offered to help him: Angela and I would take over the care of his two first born. He could easily take them away from the slut. The court would give him custody for sure because I had witnesses—but no, that stubborn son of mine refused. He told me to get lost for the second time. I could have killed him.

"What I will not repeat is the breakup of my family," was his answer, "and if you tell anyone about this you will never see your grandchildren again." So I was forced into silence. The secret got stuck in my throat making me angry and mean.

But that day when he put me on the toilet, everything changed. I forgave Pietro, started to forgive myself. It didn't last though. We butted heads many more times, my son and me.

I recall those arguments as my teachers in the afterlife encourage me to do, but I get carried away and forget the bigger perspective, forget my good resolutions. Rage grabs me all over again and I have to tame it out of me like a wild animal. What power it has even here!

Yet, Pietro did break the spell when he stayed with his family and willingly accepted to raise a son who was not his. It was keeping the secret that was the mistake. It renewed the curse's potency by damaging our family in many ways. It could have been aired out at the time and saved a lot of grief, but each one of us had much to learn. It was the only way we could do it.

# Orsolina

Redemption is complete release from the past: a true state of grace.
—Sainte Némoise

23

MY MOTHER'S STORIES - Leaving Blois
In which Orsolina confides the guilt she has about her neglect in view of her mother's immense love for her, that love which also subjected her to Angela's many fears and worries; where Orsolina recalls the enchanted days of early childhood basking in her mother's affection.

We are leaving Blois. My mother is dozing again, her head falls on my shoulder. I wonder how she came to have such devotion for me—a bad daughter.

Over the years of our early intimacy Angela's life story unraveled. When she got pregnant she was thirty-six and afraid she might not be able to bear a child; she had remained childless with her first husband. When she did get pregnant it felt like a miracle, she was ecstatic. After I was born she lived in a state of grace for a while, but soon, distrusting that much happiness—she who had so often been shortchanged in life—began to torment herself about any event that might have adverse consequences on her child. As I grew up she kept me close and dependent.

Angela feared and taught me to fear abduction, molestation, infections, infestations of all kind. She hovered over my every move, inspecting my stools in the morning, admonishing me never to flush or touch anything if by mischance I absolutely had to use a public toilet, because germs could splash out.

Later I joked about that, told friends that I had envisioned nasty little creatures jumping on me, determined to make me sick, but at the time the fear was real. Angela also examined my panties before I went off to school. They had to be impeccable in case I'd be in an accident and taken to the hospital. I imagined that if such a terrifying thing happened, the first thing the ambulance people would do before taking me in would be to investigate my underwear. If they were not clean, they'd leave me right there to die in the street.

My eyes come to rest on my mother who wakes up, smiles at me. The love I see in Angela's eyes pains me. I know my mother always meant well, but so often operated out of fear. Her only daughter had been Angela's reason for living. *C'est lourd parfois!* A heavy burden at times.

Overtaken by a wave of emotion my mother lowers her eyelids; her passion for the child she so desired is very alive even now. As an adult I still am her child.

Son enfant, toujours son enfant.

I know that it is the guilt associated with that heavy love that makes me react in irritation.

Even though I can describe my mother's dreads with humor, it remains the work of a lifetime to untie the knots, erase the fear that was inscribed at cell level. I want to help Lucien with that, I don't want him to fall into the same pits. I'll have a serious talk with him after the funeral about his mother's propensity to dispense guilt.

Besides public toilets and dirty underpants Angela also taught me to distrust Gypsies who stole children, and dark people in general because you never knew what they were up to. She discouraged me from forming close relationships with her adult friends, and even with children. Worried about losing my affection she worked hard on furthering our closeness and complicity.

She began telling me stories as soon as I could understand. *Les histoires nous rapprochaient.* Stories became our main bond. We went on walks along shaded boulevards, in parks and public gardens, my small hand holding my mother's. She made me into the childhood companion she sorely missed during her lonely early years in the house in Castel' Arquato.

Tales filled our days. Enchanted days when the desire of one became the need of the other. Angela didn't fear close physical contact with me at the time, she was not afraid of being overwhelmed by emotions. Now, when I hug her too long or hold her too close she stiffens and shortens the embrace that might bring out her tears. So many tears she has kept locked up inside!

I left her nest and went to live overseas. I don't call her often enough. She is lonely but she is brave, she has toughened herself. In the old days, the families of emigrants got used to the fact that as they made a new life in another country across the ocean, their relatives lost contact with those left behind. They might never hear from them again.

Angela can't allow herself to cry about these long absences or she might never be able to stop. There is so much to cry about. She might turn into a puddle. People going by would comment, "Funny, I didn't notice that puddle before."

Tu te souviens combien vous vous aimiez?

Yes I can recall a time before school when the love between us was like a radiant sun.

We are home. My mother sits close to the window at the edge of the light, embroidering or sewing. The sliding of her fingers on the cloth is a caress inside, a murmur, a warmth in my chest. From her presence, her patient occupation, her passivity, I derive an immense wellbeing. All my needs are fulfilled. She tells stories.

After she finishes the last story she says, "We can use some fresh air." To her there is bad air and good air according to how green, how high and well exposed the place is. Dark and dank valleys are lower on the scale, low and poorly lit areas in the city often are the places where street-walkers and bad women do their sinful commerce. Therefore our street at the foot of a hill climbing towards Belleville is without question a place with bad air.

She bundles me up and we ascend towards a small public garden on the hill, next to the Karcher brewery. There she sits on a bench while I play. She takes out her wool and knits, or else embroiders, waiting for me to return from my small ventures.

I can leave her sight and explore in all security, she fully expects my reappearance and her trust weaves a spell of safety—for that short time she does not fear for me—it's a reprieve. I order her not to move until I come back so I can radiate out, spread the warmth I draw from her in all directions, and know with certainty she will be there when I return. I have nothing to worry about, she'll be exactly in the same spot.

I come and go and from this motion new stories are shaped, circular, inconsequential and necessary. After a while I feel that she is ready to tell. I come back to sit by her and wait. She begins a tale as her fingers continue to move along her work. She stitches the words into the cloth, chain stitch, satin stitch, French knot, blind stitch, stem stitch, cross stitch.

She tells and I listen. It's our history she pearl-knits into words. We are in love.

émoise

24

Orsolina dreams. I am there.

It is the fourteenth century. I am one of three monks walking around the arched walkway of the enclosed garden, deep in meditative prayer after a long period of fasting and penance. One of the three is Giovanni, my father, although he does not quite look like him. The other looks like a male Némoise. We are given a vision that makes us stop and fall to our knees, awed. Bells ring all around us.

The vision is of souls happily playing in heavens and blissfully merged in total innocence. They have awareness neither of themselves nor of the creator. When God sends His voice forth, the divine action of light and sound draws a dividing line from the pure regions of the spiritual world and brings into being gases, liquids and solids. Structure orders matter and energy in space and time and the lower universes come to be. So we are made to witness the creation, and later we are given the full understanding of that vision.

We are told that during the structuring of galaxies and planets a rubbing occurs that brings a resistance to the velocity of the creative motion, which unchecked would overwhelm itself. That resistance is internalized by humans, often taking the form of obstacles to receiving pure joy. We as monks are given the task of removing those obstructions through prayer so we can put an end to the wounding actions and emotions perpetrated by one human upon another through filiations. We are to bring back love to humankind.

Prayers have such power.

Orsolina

Humans live in a system of awareness with all that exists.

—Sainte Némoise

25

THE FIRST WORDS

In which Orsolina recalls her first encounters with letters of the alphabet, words and animals, where she journals about her first memories of learning to read and how she meets the black panther; in which we learn that Orsolina misses her three children but chooses not to think of that during this time.

Dozing, sleeping, waking and dozing again, my mother and I keep succumbing to the tyrannical rhythm of the train. Once again I start falling asleep but one of the baby's sweet utterings wakes me up. I smile at the child. *Une vague de tristesse.* A wave of sorrow moves through me; I do miss my son and daughters left behind in California with their father. Right now I'd rather not think about them, they are in good hands. Their father is as good a mother as he is a father; they call him MaPa. At this time I can only be a bereaved sister and a dutiful daughter. I hardly exist as a mother.

A year ago just before my father died I brought little Jean-Luc to France with me. I wanted him to spend time with his grandfather during his last days and he was too young to be left behind. My daughters were in school.

Upon entering the room where Giovanni's body was kept, my son on my hip, I felt the pull of that other world on me and my child. A fog seemed to rise from the cracks on the floor enveloping us. A sudden switch in the light and a chiming of bells in my ears made me wonder if my father was trying to contact us. *Les oreilles me sonnaient.*

Jean-Luc extended his little arms towards his grandfather's corpse and called loudly, *Pépé.* I explained to my son that his grandfather couldn't answer now but that they would be reunited later. But he remained very sad and I was unable to convey to him the joyfulness I believed should be part of the death experience. It was my theory at the time, but now I feel no joyfulness about my brother's passing; maybe because Pietro and his family had not been able to accept it, maybe because of my own shortcomings. I am glad I didn't bring any of my children along this time and try not to worry about the effect of their separation from me, especially on Jean-Luc at such a tender age.

Have you been so engrossed in your memories that you haven't let yourself feel the ache of their absence? Are you ready to feel how much you miss them now?

Not ready! Fortunately, the woman sliding down the window a crack distracts me. The rich smell of barnyard and hay comes in. The child raises his little hands and I imagine that the baby is reaching out towards angels none of the people present can see. I silently ask those angels to protect my children.

When I change position I discover that my left foot is asleep. I can't put it down without the invasion of pins and needles. Thousands of ants crawling up and down. It makes me cringe. I massage my foot and my glance falls on my mother smiling faintly in her sleep. Those angels the child beseeched are flying around her and I want to send them to the help of Lucien, so stricken by his father's death and perturbed by his mother's denial.

How often are babies used as the mouthpieces of angels?

I reach into my purse and pull out my journal in order to answer that. There is always comfort in writing.

JOURNAL

Angels don't really need babies to manifest themselves. Any bright ideas that arise are most often angels passing through. Un ange passe. . . and laughter is the most powerful angel of them all.

I am still on the train to Paris with my mother. I have not been concerned with recording the events of this last month: my departure from California leaving Christopher and the children behind, Pietro's last days, his death, the preparations for his funeral. I can only write about what's in my head in the moment, but am often inundated with so many interesting ideas and strokes of inspiration that I am unable to put them to use. Sometimes I believe that the writing angels overwhelm me and don't give me time to put thoughts to word. The truths of yesterday are often the clichés of today.

There is an idea that keeps popping into my mind since the mother and baby came into our compartment; I imagine that language is an angel that flies too fast.

I remember how I struggled with language as a child, maybe beause I sensed that my mother's language was not her own and I didn't want to learn it. I didn't read till late. Powerless worshipper in a system adults seemed to have mastered, I was at the mercy of furies, unable to find my way in the forest of symbols.

I loved to be read to, and when no one had the inclination, I made up tales. After following some pixie to misty lands, I happily slumbered in enchanted castles, wishing to remain there forever. More often than not my parents were tired after a day of work, besides, they found it difficult to read aloud in French. My mother told me stories from her life, Pietro picked up the slack. I never wanted him to stop reading animal stories and fables.

There was a place for each animal. I recognized the cunning of foxes always ready to trick other animals and people. Sheep showed me the danger of being gullible, donkeys the consequences of being stubborn. Crows reminded me how one is easily fooled through vanity. Without gazelles I would not understand timidity. I experienced how the leopard got his spots, shed fake tears with the crocodile, and knew nobility and the true power of generosity from the lion.

I often talked to animals in my dreams and they gave me advice. One day, as a treat, my mother took me to the zoo. To see animals caged saddened and outraged me. Some children were teasing the black panther and it made me so mad I wanted to beat them up. As they continued their banter I felt like crying, but instead I stood in front of the panther's cage, my eyes fixed on her, silently talking to her. "Your hour will come," I told her. The panther paced back and forth, looking past the children, far away. Then everything inside me went silent. I joined the distant world of the panther, felt the sliding of her skin on her muscles as though it were my own.

Unexpectedly she walked towards our group and stopped right in front of me, staring me in the eyes. Oblivious of the noise and teasing she stayed there, gazing. I dissolved in those eyes. The kids went quiet and whispered. They gathered around me. "You sure have a way with ani-

mals," my amazed mother commented after a while. I ignored it all. But it lasted too long, my mother became edgy, anxious to leave. I refused to budge. She ended up dragging me away with the greatest difficulty.

As a teen, I took my nephew Lucien to the zoo one day and planted him in front of the black panther. This time there were no children. Without telling him anything about my own experience I encouraged him to softly talk to the panther. He did and the animal slowly slinked towards us, stopped in front of Lucien, staring.

"No one can say we are not of the same blood," I said. I wondered why I said that. It came out of my mouth so quickly it surprised me. To explain it I told Lucien that the same thing had happened to me with the panther. Then some vague recollection came to my consciousness, something I had heard about a family secret, some rumor I meant to dispel about my nephew's true lineage. I didn't really have doubts, but some questions remained.

I stare out the window biting my pen for more inspiration, but my mind drifts away. I look at my mother who has opened her eyes. She smiles and asks me, "Aren't you a little cold?"

"Is it OK if I close it?" I ask the woman, pointing to the window she had opened. She nods her assent. I stand and slide it up.

I believe now that my mother loves me too much, but when I was little it was just enough. I wanted to do everything with her. In the evening she was often too exhausted from her day of work at the sewing machine to read to me. I became tired of begging her. Pietro, my willing reader, was too often out with friends. So I decided to read for myself. I tried to put together letters and mouth the sounds, but it was painstakingly slow. I would easily have traded youth for knowledge.

Et c'est pourquoi tu as voulu apprendre à lire. Learning to read didn't come easily did it?

I PICK UP MY JOURNAL...

I am in class. The teacher writes on the blackboard and I meet the letters for the first time: a has a wide open mouth biting into an apricot; b sticks its neck out and puts a fist on its hip, looking quite stuck-up; d its mirror image, dances and makes merry wanting b to buzz with the bees; h is haughty like a tall English lady; i wants to take off its little cap and become I; f is a fancy sword handed to k who is a knight and likes to fight; m rises tall as a mountain against the sky; o a jolly old fellow, s is a snake that swings and hisses; t stretches its branches like a tree; v forms a deep valley; x crosses its heart and hopes to die. It's all fun and games, but how can I use those letters to make words if they already have a meaning on their own?

Now the teacher points to the blackboard where she has drawn a cat with the letters C H A T under it. She asks me to read the word. I believe that if I do say chat I would be faking it because I know I can't sound those letters together and read them as a word yet. She keeps insisting, showing the drawing of the cat. I am well aware that it is a cat, that the letters together probably form the word chat, but I also know I can't truly read the word. I only know that it says cat because of the drawing. If I pretend she would find out because she knows that I can't read. It must be a trick.

The kids behind me are getting edgy, they shuffle their feet and snicker, raise their hands to give the answer, pester the teacher to be given a turn. The teacher is getting angry. She thinks I am being a smart ass and defying her. I am close to tears and do not want the humiliation of crying in front of the class so I shut down and become rigid. I am sent to the corner facing the class and the teacher puts the donkey hat on me. Now I don't want to cry at all, I am strangling with rage.

The next time I pretend to know what I don't. One of the important lessons of life. To my teacher's great relief I say the words she wants me to, even though I only recognize them from the drawings.

It works! After a while I learn to read, and from then on I never stop. Anything written, whether on walls, tags, newspapers or instruction sheet has to be read. I read the label on the Camembert box at mealtime, down to the fat content. Not a word can be left unread for it is like condemning it to nothingness.

But as words killed the letters—since I never bother looking at letters singly anymore, only in relationship to others—grammar kills words. I am taught to see words in relation to each other; I disregard them on their own. Sentences show me a world full of significant connections.

In the spring, the first bumblebee buzzes to remind the sap to rise within the tree; it also invites the invisible seed to shoot up and bring to light the story of its subterranean travels; it spurs my heart to pump new blood, helps my bones expand.

The bean sprouting in a jar on my windowsill wants me to peek at the miracle of life, caterpillars become butterflies to show people all the wondrous possibilities of this world. The scent of lilac traveling on wind is a signal for yellow chicks and fuzzy ducklings to start pecking through their shell and come out of the egg; daffodils still hiding under the earth suddenly shoot out to show who is the brightest of them all.

On the forest floor the lily-of-the-valley jiggles its fragrant bells to be noticed and picked by Sunday promeneurs, so that on the first of May, workers of the world can have a sprig to give friends as a symbol of solidarity. The forget-me-nots are as blue as my true love's eyes in memory of all the tragic love stories ever told.

Yes, I had so many questions as a child, but one day I stopped asking. I didn't need adults to answer anymore. I knew that things and people had hidden doubles that lived a parallel life and that most grownups were unaware of this. I had a little friend, invisible to adults, who did everything with me; played with me, slept with me, even helped me with my homework.

Pietro said to me one day, "everything is about something else, it's all part of a huge network." I didn't totally understand, but it stayed with me. I readily accepted that nothing was just what it was. A dog might be a dragon in disguise, bums could be wizards and hoodlum princes, flowers walked along roads at night and you found them in another spot in the morning, mushrooms hid from people under pine needles and turn into milkmaids in the evening. It's my dreams that told me all about those things.

If I put my small mother-of-pearl cross under the right side of my pillow, lined up with the edge, I would not stop breathing during the night and my parents would stay alive. The cracks in the street's pavement, the spaces between cobblestones were really deep abysses I could fall into. They went right through the center of the earth and out the other side into space. One could keep falling forever, beyond planets and nebulas, never to be seen again. I was extremely careful never to step on them.

I, myself, was a planet, my skin was the crust of an earth where tiny creatures lived. I didn't want to take a bath for fear of creating a flood that would kill all my inhabitants. If I fell down it would create a devastating earthquake for them, so I stopped running. My mother knew nothing about all of that but she was worried.

As years went by I noticed that adults had lost the wisdom I once believed they had. Relentlessly they faced the burden of their meaningless routine, the endless pathway that had become their fate, dreary, empty, full of troubles until the time of their doom. I worried; my magic rituals might not prevent me from becoming like them. One day I took a solemn vow to find my personal truth and if I did, I'd also show Lucien how to avoid some of the pitfalls I had nearly fallen into. He was still so trusting and innocent.

Tu l'as trouvée cette vraie vie. Elle n'était pas ailleurs.

Eventually I found that truth that was entirely mine, a practice that recovered my inner voice one step at a time. . . and my authentic life began to unfold.

émoise

26

Orsolina dreams.

I sit by a pond feeling so alone. I hear a voice, "Look deep down into the water of the pond and you will see your twin sister." I look and on a lily pad I notice a lifeless form lying on a broad leaf. Something about that colorless little body reminds me of a school friend who was very sick and died. It has no strength, no energy. It's a girl, she looks like me in some of my earlier photos.

I extend my right hand towards the small bundle. Like a mirror image the girl very slowly extends her left hand. When our fingers join I feel a jolt of energy. We are in the center of a magnetic field that pulls her out of her inertia. From the moment the contact is made we start attracting everything to ourselves. We can move objects from one place to another without touching them. Our fingers only have to point to a thing to make it rise and trail behind us like the tail of a comet. Together we push the limits of the world we know and free ourselves from physical laws. We are full of joy and excitement. It's the best game we ever knew.

ngela

The meaning is in the plot, the shape of your story and whom you meet in the course of your simplest action, everything so intricately fitted into a larger scheme that all you have to do is to follow the signs.
—*Sainte Némoise*

27

THE ARCHED CASTLE OF MY VILLAGE – Leaving Orleans
In which Angela wants to tell her daughter the stories she was not interested in as a young girl, stories of the Italian relatives in her village of Castel' Arquato, the poverty-stricken family, the miraculous chicken, Angela's sister Rosina going to work for a rich household in Rome at the age of ten and coming back with presents, Giuseppe and the bad adopted sister Bruna; where Angela recounts her fears when alone in the old house with all the spirits and ghosts; where on the train she feels like one of them is lingering.

We have just left Orleans. One more stop in Etampes before we get to Paris. I am anxious. Thank God the motion of the train has rocked Orsolina to sleep. I no longer feel her eyes on me. I can open mine and look at her, so tired, so sweet in her sleep. I want to tell her my stories like when she was a little girl and I wished she would learn about my family from Italy. She didn't meet any of my relatives until later in her life. She loved my tales as a child but when she grew up she often cut me short, "I already know that one."

She preferred her father's stories. It was the witches and wild women of the Spiazzi tribe that got her attention. I wonder if one of their ghosts is around right now. Whenever I close my eyes a shadow passes in front of my face, but when I open them there is nothing there. Maybe some spirit is interested in my tales but doesn't wish to be identified, maybe Pietro.

Castel' Arquato, my village, sits on top of a hill crowned with a fortified castle. Our house, dug into the cliff under the castle wall was partly troglodyte. My family was so poor and our life so uneventful it didn't hold much excitement for Orsolina.

We owned nothing but the clothes we wore, a few kitchen utensils, a couple of beds and four blankets. We ate nothing but dark bread soaked in a soup made with the few vegetables our tiny garden grew and polenta my mother cooked twice a week. We didn't have an oven so we paid Frocolli the baker with vegetables to bake our bread—which reminds me, I am hungry. I brought some bread and cheese in my bag and can probably get to it without waking Orsolina. I don't really want to share a meal with her and talk.

I got the food out. God, it's good to eat. You always appreciate it when you haven't had enough at one time.

Once in a while on Sunday, my mother would make an omelet with the eggs from our chickens, some onions and cheese she traded for. I wouldn't mind having some of that right now.

Mostly we sold our eggs to pay our rent. I never tasted meat of any kind until I was twenty, but I don't complain, I never was starving, we had polenta to fill us up and I was rather plump. My father's family had owned property in the distant past but had lost it to the Church over some legal feud that resulted in confiscation. Since then our family had been fiercely anticlerical, which was unusual in our village.

I had two brothers and two sisters, but my older brother died before I was born. I was the youngest. Most village girls never went to school. They worked in the fields with their parents from the age of twelve on; earlier they took care of the younger kids, cooked, kept the house and garden. If they were lucky they were hired as servants in rich households instead of going to the fields. Boys left town at about the same age to find work in the neighboring farms, only coming back home on Sunday.

My older sister by five years, Rosina, was ten when she went off with a family that owned a country house in our village but mainly lived in Rome, hired as a nanny to their children. Rosina was anxious to experience some comfort, taste new foods and own better clothing, but I believe she left mostly to escape our older brother's beatings.

Giuseppe was two years older than Rosina and when he was hired as a farm hand in a nearby county he only came home every other Sunday.

Our eldest sister Pina, a year older than Giuseppe, stayed home to take care of me as a baby while our parents worked. When I was five Pina went into service in Piacenza, a town about fifty miles from our village.

She came back home fairly regularly, but on very short visits.

My parents worked in the fields as hired hands from dawn to nightfall. They made it back home long after dark if at all. Often, they worked too far to attempt the journey back, and after eating their polenta simply wrapped themselves in blankets to sleep in fields until the job was finished.

I was mostly home alone to eat my bread, alone to go to bed in our dark, dank and windy house. Alone and so scared I could not sleep, wanting to remain alert in case some ghosts came to sit on me and rob me of my strength. I had heard about those spirits that hid under girls' beds from older children. As soon as you fell asleep they'd sneak into your sleeping couch and land on your chest, trying to suck your soul out. If such a thing were to happen to me, Pina had told me to try at all cost to lever myself out from under the sitting ghost in order to regain some force and fight, but this was easier said than done.

I had a last weapon I could use to retrieve my endangered spirit if all else failed. The old wise woman who delivered babies had taught me to weave together with reverence the names of father, mother, grandfathers and grandmothers as well as those of my brothers and sisters. This would earn me love and protection from my ancestors. Then the spirit would have to leave and try its luck elsewhere. I did recite those incantations even though the spirit was not there yet. I shivered in my bed until I drifted off to sleep from sheer exhaustion.

If I had to use the chamber pot in the middle of the night I waited until I could no longer hold my pee before I got out of bed. As soon as I did, the darkness closed in on me and I passed from the reality I was familiar with into another of which I had no understanding.

That reminds me that I need to go to the bathroom. It has been bothering me for a while but I was afraid to wake Orsolina if I got up. Just like in childhood I tell myself that I can hold it a little longer, at least until she wakes up on her own and can keep an eye on the luggage.

As a child, when I had to get up I feared that I would never find my way back into my life. I would be stuck in an in-between place like this neighbor woman who had lost her only child. Day after day she held the boy's little coat open, calling his name in the direction of the wind. She had started doing this when the child was sick, before he passed away. If the wind had filled the coat, the mother could have buttoned it up quickly and taken it back home; her child would have been healed, but since the wind never filled it the child died. The woman couldn't accept the death and continued to offer the coat to the wind, day after day, no longer noticing anyone alive around her, only talking to the dead. I often felt the child's spirit lingering around. It was trying to get in touch with me, I knew it, but I was too scared to let it happen. So I closed my heart to any feeling that would let the ghost in.

Was it the angry child or some other ghost who made the racket in the attic? The creaking of the boards and beams in the ancient house, the whistling of the wind through the cracks terrified me. I kept watch so as to detect any unfamiliar sound for I had yet another recourse against a persistent spirit. If I held the cross the priest gave me—the one I hid from my parents—in front of me chanting a paternoster under my breath, no ghost would be able to get me.

Some visitors from the spirit world were much more of a threat than children's ghosts though; they were the lamenters. There was not much I could do against them once they started their lament, only to hide my face under the blankets, stick my fingers in my ears, shut my mouth and eyes tight lest the lament enter my soul. If it did, the lamenter would occupy the shelter of my body forever. I had to outlast that lamenting ghost, lock myself until it went away. If an owl mimicked the sound of the departing ghost and wounded the night by repeating it to the wind over and over, I got no sleep.

I can feel this unsettling feeling right now.

We had no money for books and no one in the family knew how to read anyway. I was alone so much of the time I entertained myself with making up stories and telling them aloud. Much later when I became a mother I told the stories I had invented to Orsolina. She was my only child and I was afraid she would suffer from loneliness like I had. As she grew she didn't seem to have much use for my tales, but one day I caught her retelling some to her little nephew Lucien. I guess she did care.

Such a bond between her and that nephew in spite of the fact that... But I can't mention it, it's a secret that must remain undisclosed.

The only animals our family could afford to keep on our very small plot were a dozen chickens wandering around freely, pecking what they could find. I was alone with them most of the time and put them in at night. I became very attached to a hen I called Kiki. It had sepia eyelets on its rusted feathers. Neighbors thought that attachment was silly, but my mother knew it was a special hen. And she was right for this hen saved my life.

Sitting on the front steps of my house one afternoon when my parents were home I was drawing some imaginary scene in the dust with a stick. I never had paper and pen. Suddenly Kiki, who had been scratching the earth for worms and seeds a few yards away from me, started to frantically jump up and down, flapping its wings, screeching in the direction of my legs.

Unsettled by this unusual display I looked down between my legs and froze in terror. Out of a crack in the old staircase a viper was crawling and flicking its tongue, heading for my thigh. The audacious chicken, all feathers out, jumped on the snake, grabbed it with its beak and broke its neck with one shake.

It happened so fast my mother who was standing close to the door didn't have time to make a move. The next day she went around announcing to everyone that would hear it that her hen had saved her daughter's life. Family and neighbors nodded approvingly as if they had known all along that Kiki was a unique bird.

I was ten when my parents, in order to bring a little extra money to the household, decided to adopt an abandoned girl, Bruna, and collect the allowance the government paid monthly to the guardians of such destitutes. They also thought that a girl would keep me company during the weeks when they stayed in the fields.

The adopted girl turned out to be a sneak and a thief, mean and devious beyond belief, but she only showed those nasty traits in the absence of adults. She loved to get the neighboring children or me in trouble, even Pina when she came home. When my parents were in the house, she became the sweetest little thing, obedient and gracious, but as soon as their backs were turned, she played all kinds of dirty tricks.

She often whined and complained to my parents about the bad treatment she got at the hands of the other kids. "They tease and mock me all the time," she would say shedding a tear or two to win their pity, "they make me feel bad about not having parents."

My mother became very protective of this girl who brought money to our home, for this allowed her not to work so hard and rest a little. She believed the girl's lies, distressed at the cruelty of her own children. I began to feel my mother's attachment to the new girl as rejection. "Poor girl. She never had a home, no brother or sister to play with, no one to care for her, couldn't you be nice to her? How do you expect her to know how to share when no one has ever shared with her? We have to teach her by being kind. She had a much harder life than you did, that poor child. She is so easily hurt. Can't you show her some kindness?"

The family became very distressed when the chickens stopped laying way before molting season. I suspected foul play so one morning at dawn I followed Bruna as she went outdoors. She snuck into the hen house and I peeked in through a hole without making a sound. There she was picking up one egg after another, making a small hole on the top and the bottom of each with a pin and sucking out its content. She gobbled all the eggs in this way, then buried the shells.

I was furious. Those eggs were the family's most precious food, our only treat. I gave the girl the beating of her life even though she was older, and I did not stop until her hollering woke up my mother. Once more she excused the girl. "Hunger has pushed her," she pleaded, forgetting that her own children also went hungry.

My sister Rosina became like our fairy godmother. Whenever she came home on a visit, which was rare, she always brought special treats for us all so we could have a feast. Often she would have a dress, a coat or shoes for Pina and me, only trinkets for Bruna because she was clothed by the agency, and even a little money to help the family out. My clothes mostly were hand-me-downs, mended over and over and so faded the prints were unrecognizable. I didn't often bother brushing my jet-black hair, which was totally entangled. I looked wild and tousled. Rosina would cut my hair, wash it and brush it until it shone.

On one of Rosina's visits Bruna snuck out of bed in the early morning and finished up all the leftovers we were saving. She stole my new dress and went to the village to show it off to other kids, came back the next day with the dress all torn up. Carelessness or viciousness I could only guess and even my mother started to have doubts about the innocence of the child.

At thirteen the adopted girl packed the few good pieces of clothing I owned and she took off during the night when everyone was asleep. No one heard from her for a couple of weeks. My parents didn't inform the authorities for fear of losing the tiny pension on which they had come to rely. Finally we got a letter someone wrote for Pina. Bruna had arrived by train to visit her in Piacenza. The girl seemed to have plenty of money and even took her out for tea and pastries, then to the movies. Pina questioned. Where was she getting all the money?

We got the answer when Giuseppe came home the next Sunday and found the lock of the small trunk where he kept all his savings busted open. The money was gone. Bruna must have worked the lock until it broke. Giuseppe could hardly contain himself, he wanted to find her and kill her but didn't know where she was.

What he didn't expect was for her to come back. She did the next Sunday because she had no more money and didn't know where to go. Giuseppe happened to be home again. Bruna denied everything, accused me of the theft. "Where did you get the money you spent with Pina?" he asked picking up a stick. He would have killed the girl if my mother hadn't bodily interfered.

Bruna never changed, she never learned. Kindness or beatings didn't make any difference. People said she was a bad seed, couldn't help lying, stealing, cheating. She was one of the bad women. She ran away with a married man a year later and was never heard of again.

When I told her that story, Orsolina commented that Bruna might have had an interesting life because she knew how to take what she wanted. She added that men fell for that. I believe that bad blood is bad blood, and I don't understand my daughter's fascination for wild women.

I can no longer wait. I will have to get up and go to the restroom, hopefully I won't wake up Orsolina.

 **iovanni**

The work of an individual still remains the spark that moves mankind forward.
                                                                    —*Sainte Némoise*

28

MY SISTER'S DEATH

In which Giovanni after he finishes telling stories to his grandson is back in his mother's presence in the world between incarnations; where he suddenly encounters his sister Estella who died at thirteen; where he recalls the story of his love for Estella and how their stingy father refused to get the doctor that would have saved her life, her agony; in which he remembers the guilt of his mother, Orsola, who excused her husband but later rejected and punished him by her silence; in which he describes healer-witches and magic in his village; where he starts understanding—through his mother's eye—his father's constant battle for freedom from serfdom.

As I finished telling stories to my grandson, the memories faded away and I was back in my mother's presence again. She embraced me by enfolding me in her light and was gone. I was distressed when she disappeared, but thought-forms reached out to me, caring and nurturing. I was informed that my mother had to leave me for now because I did not belong in the same group as she did. She was working on different things.

Then I drifted along on what seemed like pure white sand. I was alone. Not totally though. In the distance a light was moving fast towards me. "Oh my God," I shouted. "Is that you Estella?" I recognized the sister who died at thirteen because our stingy father refused to spend money on a doctor who could have saved her life. I loved her so much!

Estella was five years younger than I, always laughing. Her laughter was like the tinkling of bells. Even as a baby she had been my favorite sibling. I carried her on my back, sometimes all the way up to the high pastures. When I did she clapped her plump little hands she was so excited.

As she got older I brought little presents to her. On the rare occasions when we had dessert I saved mine for her. She slept in the bed next to mine and I told her stories to put her to sleep at night. I promised her I would save money for her so she could have a better education than any of us and go to the big city.

"But I love it here," she'd answer. "How could I leave *Mamma* and *Babbo* and the rest of the family? I want to stay here and marry you." And we would laugh. She never held a grudge and loved everyone. She felt so fragile to me, just like a flower, and that made me love her all the more.

Without warning I suddenly find myself at the scene of her death, but without the horror and distress I felt at the time. I have the distance of a storyteller performing for an audience.

It is early fall. I have just come back home from a summer in the high pastures. Estella wakes up in the middle of the night with an attack of stomach cramps. She is in such pain that I run to get my mother. Orsola takes one look at her daughter and immediately wants to hitch the horses and drive to the doctor in Sutrio, six miles from our village. My father Ferdinando—that bastard—convinces her to wait till morning and see what happens. "It might just be indigestion," he says. All night my sister moans, feverish, agitated, then screams at regular intervals with renewed attacks of pain. In the morning she seems to have calmed down and Ferdinando once again convinces *Mamma* to wait even though the fever remains high.

"It will pass. It's probably something she has eaten and not digested. You'll see. She will be getting better now. The doctor is a crook anyway, a crook and a charlatan. He asks for way too much money and doesn't know what he is doing most of the time. He has never been much use to us. He goes and writes prescriptions by the page so his dumb brother the pharmacist—that idiot who was not even able to get his diploma and be licensed—can get more business. We are better off calling the healer."

Through the next day, then another night, my father refuses to call the doctor even after the medicine woman brought to the bedside throws up her arms. "I don't think there is enough time for me to help with this," she says.

My sister laments, then falls into a coma suddenly broken by loud wails, calling for God to help her. She is burning. My mother keeps cold compresses on Estella's face and body, sprinkles salt on the her doorstep, prays to her favorite saints, but to no avail. The temperature will not go down.

I am by my sister's side holding her hand, paralyzed with terror. Her moaning begins to sound like a death chant, then a soft prayer, a secret worship in a tongue unheard of, suddenly interrupted by outbursts of despair. Besieged with pain, her faith shaken, she feverishly questions God about being forsaken.

We all beg the old fart so much he finally consents to get the doctor. When he sees my sister, the physician declares that it is too late to take her to the hospital. She would not make the trip. "A burst appendix has poisoned her blood. Nothing can be done," he declares.

Estella is unconscious. Family members who come to visit know the end is coming. I notice a radiance around the sick bed and Estella's features blurring, a glassiness settling on her eyes. A desolate feeling in my heart betrays the presence of the unwelcomed guest. Forgetting that I am there, people cross themselves fearfully and I run out of the room to sob. All things around me have gone flat as if their substance had been consumed.

I can feel *Mamma* pulled away from me, sucked into a vacuum. She has lost her usual footing and no longer seems the master of her own movements. That scares me so much. I hear her tell my aunt, "I don't know what's happening to me, the room is moving away from me, so far away it makes me dizzy. I see things and people as through the end of a long tunnel.

"I heard the call of the owl that last night," she goes on. "It hooted three times in a row not far from Estella's room."

"I am afraid it was the sign," her sister answers.

Orsola is the first to know when death steps closer to Estella's bed. She yells for it to go away, but it doesn't. When my sister takes her last breath a current ripples through the room, we hear a sound like a small chuckle, then something wriggles out of Estella's chest. There is a beating of wings like a little bird flying out. Fifteen women are in the room all agreeing to have heard those things.

Men are standing outside mumbling to themselves and smoking their rolled-up cigarettes of black tobacco. All the women kneel down in unison and begin praying aloud, exalted as if they had received the body of Christ. Many assure us later that they actually did see the tiny bird flying out, and that it was laughing.

Mamma collapses on the bed hanging on to my sister and sobbing.

I throw myself on top of my mother, clinging and sobbing also. Orsola calms down, gets up and takes me by the hand. She goes to the window and opens it, "so the soul can fly out," she says. Then she asks all the visitors to leave the room, she orders me to go to bed, and she locks herself in my sister's room all night.

The next day, without saying a word, she goes to her own room, bolts it and refuses to come out or eat anything until the time of the funeral, three days later. My father and my aunt have to make all the arrangements. Orsola's only other daughter, my sister Marietta, had also died at age thirteen five years earlier, her breath taken away by an attack of the croup. For weeks *Mamma* remains lost in deep thoughts, dead to the world.

I often wondered what happened during those weeks, and now that I can ask my mother questions, we have a wordless communication. At that time and in that place, every sickness, even minor, held the prospect of death. Orsola accepted that. Women dealt with this inevitability while men continued to plan and save for the future. But she couldn't forgive herself; she should have known to call the doctor when her daughter doubled over with the first attack of pain. She should not have listened to her husband. She should have taken it upon herself and made the decision.

She held herself responsible; it was not her husband's fault really, she had no right to hate him. Ever since he was born his life had been so hard, so totally lacking in anything but the bare essentials, so devoid of security and comfort that he had become obsessed with what he considered the only possible salvation: privation in order to save. For generations, the wolf had been at the door, the future uncertain. Who would have time for affection when they were responsible for their family's welfare, when they were expected to put food on the table?

It was often that way around our villages; most patriarchs expected utmost frugality from wives and children. Every penny that was not absolutely necessary for survival of the barest kind was saved, an effort so taxing that her husband had had to close his heart to any emotion that could lead to spending. Charity, compassion and even paternal love had to be erased from his realm of feelings. No extras were ever allowed. And she always thought that he was right. It had been such a trial to wring a living from this poor rocky soil. Just hanging on to the farm and the little land the family owned through famines, invasions, overbearing taxes from king, church and state had exhausted all desires for initiative. The heads of families stuck to what had worked for their ancestors, trying hard to beat adversity by accumulating and burying as many coins as they could.

She also knew that Ferdinando's obsession with saving had turned into an avarice that swallowed up all else and everything was subordinated to it. Could she forgive him that? She understood that he had to save in order never to be taken by surprise, save so his family would have the means to survive the times of hardship. So she excused him. He did need to save for lean years and keep feeding the kids, save so the two of them would not starve in old age if all their children went away, but she suspected that he had to have more than his neighbors so they would look up to him. He was so vain.

He was obsessed with having land and possessions, having known a time when not having any was a fate worse than death. With no land to call your own you didn't exist, you didn't even belong to yourself. Someone else owned you and this for all of your life. You were merely tolerated here and there in exchange for your daily toil, slaving from morning till night to earn a little food, a roof over your head, that's about all. The wages you got for your work, if any, were so meager it didn't allow you to provide for a family, therefore you had no right to one unless your masters agreed. Under their roof your children were born in servitude.

Once my mother asked Ferdinando for money to buy material to make the children new clothes. He went silent and after a moment of reflection said to her, "How can a man live in serfdom and remain a man?" The question didn't seem related to her request, but she understood then that the days of serfdom were not yet over in her husband's mind, that his pride was to be a free man. It was not clothes he wanted to buy for his children, but freedom from belonging to someone else. Besides, he would never let them go hungry or naked and this favor would be returned to him. It was the tradition. He would be taken care of and respected in his old age and this afforded him a measure of peace.

To his defense it had to be said that most of his countrymen were possessed with the same greediness, which under the disguise of working for survival dictated their every action. Survival was of real concern of course. There had been years of famine not so long ago. She remembered that once, when asked to make a donation to support the blind and the crippled, her husband answered the man asking for money, "Compassion is a luxury I can't afford." She never forgot that: in order to have freedom her husband could not afford the luxury of loving. In this way she went back and forth silently accusing him, then excusing him, then condemning herself.

She should have ignored him and fought for her daughter's life. What stupidity to think that putting a little bag of garlic around the girl's neck or sprinkling salt on her doorstep to fend off evil spirits would do the trick. Lighting candles to Sainte Bernadette, her patron, didn't work either. Those things often failed; on the other hand she'd heard that doctors and hospital worked miracles.

She should have known! A sickness that might not appear serious at first could easily and rapidly subjugate a person. During the fever, fairies could take the spirit too far away from the body and the patient could not come back. Herbs and potions no longer could help then. Only a very powerful medicine woman might reverse this process by undoing the fairies' spell. She had seen it done.

She should have eaten her pride and gone to *La Strega,* the only one powerful enough to perform this healing. No, not that. She should have insisted on getting the doctor who, since he didn't believe in magic, could win over it. When spells failed the doctor still had the power to heal. He could take the patient to the hospital and cut into the body to remove the cause of sickness while the witch could only show the spirit how to do that.

Yes, she should have known.

At midnight on the night before my sister's funeral the church bell started to ring. It rang for about fifteen minutes. The priest woke up and ran to the church to see who was there, but he found the place empty. To Orsola it proved that a holy martyr had died, and she worshipped her daughter as such.

She never totally recovered and remained aloof after that, but her bond to me became even tighter. She cut herself off from her husband and no longer excused his bad habits. She kept pondering about the miracle of the bell ringing. If her daughter was a martyr, then her husband was the executioner.

My mother faded away and Estella remained in energy form. She showed me the place where I should go next. There were other people around, blobs of luminosity, they looked friendly and they wanted me to join them. I knew I had been in contact with them before.

My sister, having enfolded me in her light much as *Mamma* had earlier—evidently a form of greeting in the in-between—left. Again I asked, "Why do you have to desert me?" The answer immediately came to me. She had only come to meet me; like our mother, she dwelled in a different place and worked on different things. Damn it, I wanted so much to stay with her.

Forgive me, but my old self can't help but swear!

ngela

*Everything hidden shows up when exposed to the light, and whatever
is exposed to the light becomes light itself.* —*Sainte Némoise*

29

RADIO DAYS – Arrival in Paris

*In which Angela worries about not being able to catch a taxi and Orsolina gets
irritated; where Orsolina asks the taxi driver to stop at the rue des Maraîchers in their old 20th
section; where Angela recalls the Sunday mornings in their apartment and how the neighbors
used their radio, what kinds of songs they played; in which she describes Pietro's wonderful
voice when he sings along.*

We enter the *Gare d'Austerlitz* in Paris. The train comes to a stop.
We are in one of the last cars and I am anxious to bring down my suitcase
and hurry out. Orsolina gently pushes me back down on my seat. "Let
people get out, we are in no hurry, it will be better after the crowd moves
off."

"But what about catching a taxi, there might be none left."

"I wish you would stop worrying about things like that, there
always will be taxis. You are a such a fussbudget."

Orsolina is a seasoned traveler. She doesn't realize how stressful
traveling is for an old person like me who hasn't moved for a long time.
She always wanted me to be someone I am not.

She is right though, when we get out there is a line of taxis still
waiting by the entrance of the train station to pick up passengers. We get
in the first one and on the spur of the moment Orsolina asks the driver to
go to *rue des Maraîchers*, the street in the 20th *arrondissement* where we
rented our apartment and lived until Giovanni retired and I stopped my

work as a seamstress. We raised Orsolina and Pietro there. But later, Orsolina moved across the ocean, maybe to get away from us.

"For old times' sake," Orsolina says to me, "it's not much out of the way to Simone's place." I nod my agreement. "Do you remember?" she adds, pointing to *Café Marius* where she used to visit her friend Huguette, as the taxi goes by. The two of them sat in the back of the café and painted strange dark subjects on large pieces of cardboard. Once I caught them smoking cigarettes. Marius, Huguette's father, a widower who hardly ever said a word, didn't care about the girls smoking. His daughter did all the shopping and cooking for him and as long as that was done, she was free to do anything she wanted; a bad influence on Orsolina who seemed to be attracted to those unconventional characters.

When we come to number 74, Orsolina asks the taxi driver to stop. She gets out to walk around but I stay in the car. The two-story building is now entirely occupied by offices. In our days *la loge,* the concierge's tiny office and quarters, was on the ground floor with two large apartments above it. The facade has been redone; cemented over, new metal shutters replace the old chipped wooden ones. I'm sure Orsolina hates it, but I don't mind. I think it's neater that way. In our days the front wall was covered with chipping plaster, black with age. The landlord refused to sink any money into the building and even in our lower class section it looked neglected.

I particularly loved the *rue* on Sunday mornings when Giovanni and Pietro lingered in bed. Orsolina who used to join her father in his bed decided that she was too big for that. A scene unfolds in front of my eyes right now.

Orsolina joins me in the kitchen where I am putting away the dishes from dinner. I have been up since six in the morning. I am unable to stay in bed past that time. If I do, I get headaches, even on the day I take off from sewing. I serve Orsolina breakfast and she turns on the radio as loud as I allow it. She knows if it's loud enough it will force her brother to emerge from his bedroom. She helps me with lunch preparations and while the sauce simmers on the stove we go to the window and watch people down below in the sun drenched street.

It's spring; people have put on light, colorful clothes. The birds sing and passersby start humming along. The last *Tino Rossi* song plays on the radio. "I remember when radios first came to our street," I tell my daughter. "One to begin with, and then more and more homes got them."

"But we had one, didn't we?"

"Not right away. It was too much of a luxury for us." I want to let her know that we didn't always have an easy life.

The first families to own a radio are mostly French. Italians immigrants don't have money for that kind of frivolous stuff. They'd rather save enough for a small plot just outside Paris, eventually build themselves a little house in the country. Besides, they have obligations, not like those who care little about family. They have to send money to relatives back home, feed their aged parents and grandparents.

The ones who own radios want everyone to know it. At first, only the four or five women who have nothing to do all day but fool around with other men because their husbands earn enough money to support them, own one.

"Good fortune only comes to the sluts," jealous neighbors sneer.

They turn their radios full on, leave their windows open. When more and more families get theirs the noise in the street becomes so loud it sounds like an amusement park. People complain, quarrel, but when *Tino Rossi* sings, harmony is restored. French, Italians, everyone agrees, *Tino* is great, a miracle of a voice. Radios are all tuned to the same station. Those who don't have a radio lean out of windows to listen, women smile, sometimes a tear rolls down their cheeks. Men nod their appreciation. Everyone is happy.

"Such a velvety voice is a gift from God! What *Tino* sings is so true, not the usual nonsense. It's something everyone understands, something that has depth," people tell each other. He really has everything. Besides the smooth voice, you can tell from posters that he is a handsome man, the eyes of a deer, black hair shiny with brilliantine. His voice sends shivers down the spines of the most respectable women and even little girls like Orsolina melt when he sings.

Tino's song is over. The following one tells the story of a man who traded his black winter overcoat for a light gray suit and fell in love on a glorious spring day. The morning sun streaming through our window lands on our big radio. Now *Charles Trenet's* voice fills the room. It's Pietro's favorite singer. He says that *Trenet* is a poet in the tradition of the troubadours. Orsolina is hopeful, her eyes stuck on Pietro's bedroom door.

Trenet always seems to skip along on a beautiful day, happy to be alive, to see and feel. He sings his pleasure and makes you feel like singing also. Men like him better than *Tino* whom they find a bit corny. Pietro always sings along. He knows every word of *Trenet's* songs and makes things come alive: dotted landscapes, ladies wearing frilly dresses and wide-brimmed straw hats, the play of light coming through lacy parasols, men in Panamas rowing on the river Marne. It brings to mind famous paintings. The sea has silvery reflections and villages with steeples and bells hold bittersweet memories; *Trenet* turns nostalgia into delight.

Melodrama follows. In *L'Hirondelle du Faubourg* a repentant doctor brings red roses to the tomb of a woman he has seduced and abandoned. The night before, at the hospital where he worked emergencies, a little girl died in his arms. Before she expired she asked him to put red roses on her mother's tomb the next Sunday, because it was *l'anniversaire de sa jolie Maman,* her mother's birthday. When the doctor asked for the little girl's name he realized that she was his daughter; her mother was the woman he had abandoned.

Mothers' tombs are a popular theme. In *Les Roses Blanches* a loving hunchback secretly brings white roses to his mother's tomb. On his way he chances upon a group of crude factory companions who jeer at him when they see the flowers, teasing him about his new girlfriend: is she a hunchback like him or is she missing an eye, does she limp, does her harelip make her hard to kiss? When they find out about the hunchback's mother they hang their heads in shame and ask the dejected cripple to forgive them. He willingly does because he is gentle and innocent. Those kinds of songs—as I recall them—always bring tears to my eyes. I think of my own mother who died so young, overworked and underfed.

My first husband's great favorite was *Mon Vieux Pataud,* a song about an old man who has only one friend, his dog. He saves pennies from his meager pension to feed the animal. One day, the mayor meets the old man and his dog on the street and announces, "Government money should go to the needy, not to the dogs." And he orders the animal shot. The broken-hearted old man expires on his dog's warm corpse, bemoaning his companion's loyalty. For some reason the old man who lives in our attic, Bologna, always comes to mind when I hear that song.

It makes me sad. It's as if all those tragedies happen to people I love, but fortunately, the radio gives up on gloomy songs to return to stormy adventures. I follow the flight of dragonflies along rivers. Now the *Soeurs Etienne* harmonize, "Storms only last a moment; the sun comes right after the rain."

I wish for Orsolina's sake that Pietro would get up. When he sings his favorite songs along with the radio it's like he shares the secrets of his soul. The room expands, dull familiar things take on a new dimension. Pietro sings countryside, forests, rivers and villages alive. He has magic in his voice.

ietro

Sensuality invites each person into the intimate experience of all feelings between all people.
—Sainte Némoise

30

STREET PEOPLE

In which Pietro sitting in between sessions on the second day after his death has total recall; where he follows the taxi that brings Orsolina and Angela to his old home in Bagnolet; in which he tosses memories of the apartment where he and his sister were raised, rue des Maraîchers, of Orsolina's friend Huguette the daughter of a café owner, of three noteworthy street people doing their antics.

In earthly time it is the second day after I passed away, late in the afternoon. I am following Angela and Orsolina in the taxi that is driving them to my home for the event that will take place tomorrow. As they go through the *rue des Maraîchers* and park next to the apartment where Orsolina and I lived with our parents when we grew up, I toss a memory at my sister.

Our apartment *rue des Maraîchers*, number 74, is on the first floor of a two-story building. The apartment is fairly stark because Angela has no use for frills or nonsense objects. She doesn't believe in decorating; just the bare necessities in this long row of linked rooms. The only one with privacy is the last, our parents' bedroom, but you go through it to get to the only bathroom. There is one more mysterious room we call *l'Autre Pièce*, the Other Room, that Angela and her best friend have made into their sewing shop. Giovanni had to cut a door through the wall to connect it to our apartment.

We live rather happily in spite of postwar restrictions. Angela is a great cook and she can make anything taste good. I work in my father's shop. He has three other apprentices and he often compares me to them in a disparaging way. It's hard for me but I let it go. I don't want to keep resenting a member of my family.

When I come home from work I often go to find Orsolina at her friend Huguette's place. My sister spends most of her time there. It's much more fun than being at home. Huguette's father, a widower, owns a café called *Chez Marius*, frequented by regulars. There is always something interesting going on there.

The girls usually sit at a back table, close to the kitchen of the small apartment where Marius and Huguette live. My sister and her friend paint intense scenes on huge pieces of cardboard. Huguette babysits a little cousin of hers while his mother is at work. He bugs the girls with all his attention-getting schemes, but I like to play with him. We build things together. His name is Lucien, a name I always liked. If I have a son I will give him that name.

Sunday mornings is a big day at the café. Locals are off work and they know there will be some kind of show going on. Their favorite street character, Bébert, wears a multicolor jacket two times his size. "It belonged to the fat grandmother who raised me. I patched it up myself," he told the patrons on a day when he was sober. He has been going from bar to bar on his daily round, telling stories. Eventually he gets to *Chez Marius* and starts dialoguing aloud with invisible characters, spitting at the end of each sentence. He reconstructs historical moments, mostly having to do with Napoleon, and jumps into the action at the right time, holding an imaginary banner, blowing a trumpet or beating a drum to keep up the morale of the troops. He runs to his superior who was about to get slain and saves him. "I was so handsome in my bright uniform when I accepted medals for my heroism," he tells the bystanders.

"'What do we do now?' Napoléon asked me when he felt that his troops were failing."

"'Leave it up to me,' I answered."

Tripping on pants too long for him, Bébert courageously grabs an invisible sword and rushes to the onslaught at the head of the troops. He gallops out of the café and into the street. One of his shoes yawns sadly, showing one big unsocked toe. He makes excuses for that. "The retreat from Russia you know. We were freezing, our shoes totally worn out, our *moral à zéro*." And he hands his glass out for the refill someone is always willing to buy him.

As he exits, some of the amused customers go to the window to follow his antics in the street until he disappears into a nearby café, *Le Bougnat*. He stays there just long enough for a quick one a regular customer orders for him. He carries on with the historical drama for a while then dashes into the street again and back to *Chez Marius*. He has been marinating in wine since early morning and usually falls asleep at one of the back tables before noon. He immediately begins to snore loudly. The rusty smell of the neighborhood's empty lots mixes with his pungent body odor and keeps people from sitting too close. To spice it up, a whiff of wine, cork and mustiness drifts up from below the bar where a trap door opens to the cellar.

That's the time when Nono, who gets up late, hits the bars, starting with *Chez Marius*. He looks down his nose at Bébert, deploring what he calls the execrable condition of this human reject. Nono uses good language as he is quick to point out. "This wretch has never been a hero," he adds. "All that happened during the last war is that he received a head injury from a black market butcher whose meat he was stealing. He hasn't been the same since. I should know a hero when I see one, for I have been in the Foreign Legion. *La Légion Étrangère,* that has some dignity!"

A profile à la *Jean Gabin*, he makes a show of being a hoodlum of the *Belle Époque*, the *Bastille-Apache* kind. Always dapper in his own way, a cap slightly tilted to the side and hiding one eye, red kerchief around his neck to show his affiliation with *Garibaldi*, navy-and-white-striped jersey, tight vest over a wide flannel belt rolled around his waist, bell bottom trousers and pointed shoes, he strolls along, hands in pockets, very erect, dragging his feet to demonstrate his nonchalance.

With his hooked mustache and long sideburns, a brownish cigarette butt perpetually hanging down from the corner of his lips, he sports a style that is now history. He orders a *calva* for breakfast, to warm up. "I was raised in Normandy," he explains in his Parisian drawl, "and that's where I learned to fight, with booze, the constant drizzle that drives the cold into your bones. Besides, it takes a strong alcohol to cut through the pounds of butter we *Normands* consume each day."

People say Nono is a *mythomane,* one who invents his life as he goes. Not satisfied until he has center stage, he doesn't just rely on his gift of gab but makes sure his audience is captive by standing in front of the only door. After moistening his throat, that prophet of doom drowns his audience under a torrent of well-chosen words, warning, lecturing and pontificating, advising or protecting according to his public. The hero of breathtaking adventures of bounty, duels and revenge, he also tells of nights spent in what he calls sex infernos.

Head over heels in love with *Edith Piaf*, he is convinced that he himself is the handsome mercenary smelling of warm sand she sings about. "She must have been hanging around the desert when I was still in the *Légion*," he states with conviction. And that reminds him of the sadistic officers he had to deal with. "Those brutes, those tyrants. They enjoyed making us crawl, torturing us with unfair punishments. But we enlisted men had our time of revenge during combat when we could shoot our superiors in the back." Nono lost his left eye in battle. "It's my gift to the *Légion*," he comments. "Now my missing eye makes me a living." He survives on his pension.

"When I first came back from Africa I found a small pad around the *Bastille* area." Nono narrates the following episodes of his life: the gang fights at night under the light of gas lamps, the duels between real men, heads of gangs, the sudden flash of the knife; the *Gros Fred* with his enormous head; *Roro les gros doigts, P'tit Louis*. When he gets going, he forgets his cultivated language and his extensive slang becomes hard to understand. One has to guess the meaning of words from the imagery.

"Later I joined *le Parti* believing along with my comrades in singing tomorrows," Nono continues. "Mostly though, the Communist Party was just a big party to my buddies and me. We went to every rally, every fair, just to drink and raise hell. One day we planned a big raid in a *bourgeois* town house *dans l' seizième,* in the sixteenth section. 'When we get there,' I told my buddies to give them the guts to do it, 'we'll eat the caviar and *pâté de foie gras de Monsieur* sprinkled with the best *Chateau Margaux* there is, and we'll fuck the *bourgeoise* in her big fancy bed, in between silk sheets.' But we never got past the concierge."

Nono goes on telling stories, talking *le patron* or *les clients* into buying him a shot here and there to moisten his throat so he can keep going. He often ends his tirades by raving about the future of the world, or rather, its lack of future, and usually finishes with a vitriolic harangue against *Le Parti*. "Those fucking Communists! They ended up kicking me out. They said I discredited the *prolétariat,* that I was too much of a drunkard, me who never once stumbled under the influence. According to them I didn't belong to a respectable working class, too much of a hood, a bad sort. Fuck the comrades. I raided the *bourgeois'* houses without them."

More often than not, in the middle of this torrent of imprecations, Titi bursts in, to Nono's great disgust. *L'idiot du quartier* interrupts his inspiration and the concentration of his audience. Nono regards this intrusion as a personal offense and leaves for another bar hoping that his audience will protest and ask him to stay, but everyone has had enough.

With his clogged brain, sluggish limb, laborious speech, Titi the simpleton always senses the right moment to appear, riding on Nono's coat tail when drinks are being passed around and glasses refilled. He believes he is a motorcycle and runs through *le quartier* making engine sounds. He stops at every bar to be filled up for he often runs low on gas.

Everyone knows him. His protruding, cabbage-leaf ears are the targets for small rocks boys fling from slingshots. Lameness embarrasses kids. They scorn and punish it severely. It's as though they feel, because they are fresh out of the oven themselves, that they barely escaped being cracked or crooked. A sympathetic onlooker usually nods to the boss to go ahead and fill Titi's glass, put it on his tab.

"Do you want to fill it up with regular *sans plomb*?" Titi nods heartily. The buyer picks up the glass and pours its content into Titi's open mouth, spilling some on his clothes. But *l'idiot* doesn't care, he starts the engine and goes roaring down the street.

When the taxi stops Orsolina leans towards her mother and begins, "Do you remember when . . ."

Orsolina

Our thoughts create the environment we are in. —*Sainte Némoise*

31

RUE DES MARAÎCHERS – Paris

In which Orsolina, after hiring the taxi to take Angela and her to Simone's apartment in Bagnolet for the funeral, asks the taxi driver to stop in the street where she was raised in the 20th arrondissement; where she describes the different ethnic groups, the characters that could be in B movies, the Communist friend of her brother with his endless theories, the dreams of the proletariat; where she talks to the café owner about the only one left, the cat lady, and where she mourns the changes that have taken the life out of her old street.

From the *Gare* we hire a taxi to take us to Simone's apartment in Bagnolet, but I ask the taxi driver to make a detour through the *rue des Maraîchers* and stop for a few moments across from number 74, "I was raised there and would like to walk around," I explain. "I might go as far as that café a block away, do you mind waiting?"

"I don't," he answered, "but I will keep the meter running."

My mother decides to stay in the cab and the driver gets out to smoke a cigarette.

74 rue des Maraîchers, tu te souviens?

So many memories. Today it's Sunday. I remember when Pietro refused to wake up on Sunday mornings and I, who got up early, waited for him to walk out of his bedroom. I felt so dejected and to pass the time I watched people from our living room window. Often my mother joined me.

In the 20th in Paris, the Communist proletariat, Gypsies, Arabs, and Italians share the pavement. Small shops, cafés, cheap restaurants offer deals to the workers, *les petites gens,* the small people. I watch and they become actors in films I have seen with my mother—we go to matinées every other Sunday—or films I invent.

Cheap hotels by the month, furnished rooms. It is warm and the windows are opened. Our street is narrow and we can see into the apartments across from us. The prostitute from a B-movie sits on an enormous bed in black lingerie, a cigarette hanging down the corner of her mouth. Next window, a hairy man with enormous arms and a red face leans out in his undershirt, calling by name in a gravelly voice some passerby to share a dirty joke. His lips are fat and oily. I put him in my movie. Behind him a frizzy haired woman emerges from the zone of darkness in a faded robe. She weaves in and out of the light, probably straightening up the place. I see her reflection in the mirror of a huge armoire half the size of the room. When she goes by him he slaps her bottom quite heartily and accompanies that with loud greasy laughter.

She shrugs, trying to get away, but he catches her, forces a kiss, then pushes her away with a pinch declaring loudly for anyone interested, "Madame is in a bad mood. Madame didn't get enough last night. Madame is asking for more." He is not letting on whether he is talking about sex or a beating. In my mind, sex and beatings are confused.

He turns to her as she walks away: "So! You don't like my hand on your ass anymore? It used to tickle you pink. What the fuck is the matter with you?" She hears the warning. Better make him forget her irritation, better submit to his fooling around or the beating is imminent. It happens regularly, sounds like a killing.

On the second and third floor, more movie couples; on the fourth and last, a respectable bachelor; next door, a woman with TB coughing her lungs out; behind the building, an albino family. The family lives in the shade of a four-story building, across a damp courtyard, in a dank, cave-like outbuilding where nobody ever ventures.

No one really knows how many members of the family are albinos, how many have one blue and one reddish brown eye. They are shy, wild like animals, you hardly ever see them during the day and they never look at you. They hide in their recess on the dark side.

The father comes home drunk and beats them all, they might know why, but no one else does. The mother's face, shrunken like a dried plum, has a deep purple tinge and her legs, swollen and puffed are turning black. She never wears socks all winter long. Her shoes are split open and the toes show. She wraps the same frayed coat around her skinny body, year after year. Her only mascara is the black bruises around her eyes. She walks, hugging the walls, trying to pass unnoticed.

The older sister is a fierce dragon, hostile, aggressive, strong as a horse. All the kids in the street are afraid of her. At home, she rules in spite of her repeated pregnancies. She beats her father with a two by four when he is drunk, terrorizes the younger kids, and once, she kicked her older brother in the balls so hard when he tried to rape her he passed out. That was the end of that. Her father and brothers screw all her sisters whether they are willing or not, but they never touch her.

She makes love to Arabs—her weakness—and displays that preference shamelessly. She regales the neighbors—those who dare to scold her for her outrageous conduct—with juicy tales of lewdness in a loud voice. She loves to shock those *petit-bourgeois*. Proud to be lower than the low, she plays with respectable people's racism, tells them that Arabs are better at fucking, more potent. Just what honest men always feared! She drives them crazy with anger.

Those are all stories that are passed around, whispered from one household to another. I don't always understand but I am all ears.

The albinos' landlord tends the café in the front building helped by his son, a gentle simpleton. The street's small artisans go there to breakfast on their *petit muscadet* a dry white wine that scratches the throat. At lunchtime, they switch to *pernod* and shoot pool in the back room. On Sunday they hang out all morning.

The next few buildings, more aware of public eyes, are kept up and shelter respectable families like ours, tradesmen, artisans, merchants, who live and work in the same street, often in the same building. You have the professions of the white dusty hair and stiff overalls, the builders, masons, housepainters; the ones of the dirty faces, black hands and soiled clothes; mechanics, plumbers, coal dealers; the ones of the golden shavings and sawdust on their hair and clothes, the woodworkers like my father.

During the week nomadic tradesmen preceded by their sing-songs walk the street calling out to people. The window-repair man carries glass panes on his back, the chimney sweep is all black to his cap, the rabbit skin, scrap metal and rag collector sings loudly calling for merchandise: *habits, chiffons, ferraille à vendre,* the knife and scissor sharpener rolls his wheel in front of him, the Gypsies show their baskets and offer to mend chairs.

Then come the troubadours, the hurdy-gurdy man with his dancing monkey, a woman singer with snotty kids hanging on her skirt, some street musicians, a young boy turning the crank of his big music box. They all stop at the *Bougnat,* a place where you can buy kindling, coal, charcoal, but also cheap wine and liquor as advertised in white on the black painted shop: *Vins, Charbons et Spiritueux.* That blackness invades the minuscule café with its soiled walls and grimy bar, *le zinc.* There is sawdust on the floor so everyone can spit unreservedly. The wine, *Vin du Postillon,* is delivered in casks on Thursday morning by the driver of two horses pulling a cart. Since school is out on that day I make sure never to miss the sight.

All the *Bougnats,* owners of those kinds of cafés are *Auvergats* and very miserly as everyone from that province is well known to be. They wear the same black cotton shirt and pants in all seasons, their sullied faces and hands point to a certain reluctance to waste soap.

My friend Françoise lives in a building two houses down from *Chez Marius.* Her father, Ponthieux, the butcher who delivered stolen meat during the war is a *bon vivant* disclosing his tendency to excess in the satisfied way he carries his huge stomach around. He handles the knife with fascinating dexterity, slicing into the meat with gusto as if it were a most pleasurable activity, the ultimate in all sensuality. I've spent a lot of time watching him, *l'eau à la bouche* as they say.

Next to their apartment building another café swarms with Italians. The end of the bar turns a corner and becomes a counter for the tobacco shop, stamp and lottery tickets retail. In the back you can play the *tiercé,* the three numbers for horse races. The agitation becomes intense on Sunday. If your horse wins, you can fulfill all your dreams. The *petits salariés,* underpaid blue collars, meet there to share those dreams, tell stories and dirty jokes, play cards. They understand each other, they are in the same boat.

The noisiest bunch of all are the Arabs who hide in a café across the street, behind drawn curtains. Whorls of belly dancing music ascend at all hours of day and night. The men's speech is harsh and guttural, we never see any women. Maybe they keep them locked up, or else leave them behind in their country. "They are men without women," people say, "totally unpredictable. You never know when they will stick a knife at your back to rob you or do whatever they want with your wife." Rumors circulate. Illegal gambling, quarrels, fights with switchblades, this bunch is really dangerous. Women hesitate to come home alone at night, they avoid walking in that part of the street even during the day.

Il y a beaucoup de cafés dans l'coin!

Every block has a café enticing another ethnic group; each goes where he feels the most at home and understood. Some Jews are grouped in three or four buildings at the very end of the street, but they are most discreet and don't frequent cafés. To hear some Communists talk you'd think that anyone is accepted in any of those groups, no matter what their nationality is. "Some are more accepted than others, that's all," jokes a neighbor. "And no love is wasted on those Arabs who never talk to anyone. Nothing personal but no one would like a daughter of theirs to end up on that part of the street."

After my brother wakes up I want all his attention, but often and to my great dismay a Communist friend of his shows up. He always seems to lecture about this and that; on that Sunday it's about the evilness of the cinema, another opiate of the people. "The proletariat is *à la mode* on film these days," he tells us. "There is no lack of movies about *les ouvriers*, but don't fool yourself. It's because the low classes will pay good money to see their story glorified, made into romance. A big movie goer this working class, there is so much it needs to forget!"

He goes on and on addressing my brother or my mother, but not my father who never goes to movies. "Sagas of the gutter are great favorites; prostitutes are redeemed through love and hoodlums softened by romance repent as they walk to their deaths. I bet you love that melodrama, but don't you see? All romances are doomed because the lower classes are not meant to believe they can win; that could make them unruly.

"They respond best to characters they can identify with, you see. So let them have that, get their money and keep them dreaming. . . but don't give them too much hope or they might get cocky and revolt against their condition." Getting in Pietro's face he concludes, "the movies are a tool of your capitalistic society, meant to keep you under, don't you understand?" My brother just nods, he agrees and he doesn't. My mother remains quiet, she only understands half of what he says, and I even less. And we love to go to the movies.

Que reste-t-il de tous ces personnages?

Of all the past street characters the only one still around now is a cat lady, as I find out when I enter in conversation with one of *chez Marius'* customers. Marius is no longer alive, but the café has been sold to a personable *Maghrebin* whom people call *patron*. My interlocutor points out the basement apartment right across the street where the cat lady lives with twenty cats, eight dogs and some birds with broken wings, he says. We watch a group of children playing ball next to it. One of them misses his mark and the ball goes right through her makeshift window. And that protector of innocence forgets that the hand that threw the ball had no ill intention. She gets out of the house yelling, and waves her broom at the kids, scolding them in a shrill voice—she is quite spry in spite of her age. They scatter like birds.

The *patron* joins in the conversation. "She sweeps the pavement for hours, mindless of passersby," he comments "but inside her house no order or cleaning is ever done. It looks like a zoo and smells like one too. She is not the kind to ask dogs to hold up their feet so she can wipe the mud off. She never wants to disturb her animals in order to sweep where they lie down. Where would they go anyway? The whole place is occupied, there is no floor room left. If she puts a dog or cat out, he'll come back through one of her windows made of plastic bags held by tape anyway."

So she sweeps the street as if all need for cleanliness was fulfilled in this act.

She still wears a long dress with a bustle that was in style in another era. Could it be the same as when I was a child? I remember that Nono, when he was still around, never failed to comment, "it must be moldy under that long skirt, and full of spider webs since no one ever scrapes the chimney."

Tout a bien changé n'est-ce-pas?

The *rue des Maraîchers* seems to have shrunk. It is even narrower than I remember, the houses smaller. The setting hasn't changed much but something is lost. Is it because the whole street is lined with cars? There were very few in my day. Some of the buildings have been cleaned up; one was torn down to make room for a newer apartment building that stands way back and out of alignment with the rest. But that's not it.

Qu'est-ce qu'il manque donc?

What's missing is life. There is no one walking or standing in the street, hardly any kids except for that bunch with their ball, now disappeared, nobody playing hopscotch in the middle of the street. The small artisans' shops are closed. There is no little corner store, yogurt maker, ironworker, furniture shop. No *Bougnat* where one could have a drink and get provisions of coal and kindling. I learned since then that all the *Auvergnats* who were the brunt of jokes about cheapskates were actually not from Auvergne but from the Aveyron. The poorest of the poor, they came *en masse* to Paris and got the worst paid jobs as servants and *serveurs* in bars and cafés. Hardworking and skillful at saving, they ended up owning most of the bistros in Paris. Next they brought relatives from their village to help. Now that they are well off, their offspring seek other, less demanding fields of work; Chinese or Algerian people are buying the bistros.

As I walk back to the taxi I see that the car repair shop is still there next to our old apartment building which has been turned into headquarters for the construction company that used to have one little office on the ground floor. The rest of the street remains pretty much as it was.

Places, people and their relation to each other make such a deep impression in childhood. It's as if children became what they are looking at; they have no boundary. I slowly walk back. The deep mystery in which I would plunge to draw life's essence as a child is gone.

When I go back to the taxi I see that my mother got out and took her own walk. She is now coming back. When we're all in, I ask the driver to take the *Cours de Vincennes* and turn on the *rue des Pyrenées* so I can get a look at my old school. It has hardly changed, the same thick walls, the bars on the windows, but the façade has been sandblasted like most buildings in Paris, as part of Mitterand's cultural signature. It doesn't look quite so severe and dark; some cheery brickwork I never noticed around the windows has become visible.

There is so much I never noticed.

Pietro

Your identity includes all that is without and within yourself.
—*Sainte Némoise*

32

VISIT TO GRANDFATHER

In which Pietro speaks on the third day after his death reflecting on his relationship with Lucien hoping his son's spirit will hear him; where in the process he realizes that openings had been made by Lucien and Orsolina to tell him the truth about his sickness; in which Yamill his guide suddenly appears, encouraging him to remember the time when he was in Lerné waiting for an operation that would never take place, and during which he had a first honest talk with his sister about hurt feelings from a year earlier when he felt displaced; where he remembers talking to his sister about his village and the attempt his mother Malva made to reconnect, but how she was cruelly interrupted by his grandfather; in which he reveals his suspicion that when Orsolina, against all warnings, visited with La Strega's forbidden family, she incurred the curse.

My ability to be in many places at once still fascinates me. One part of me is in the bedroom where my body is kept for the wake. It is the third day after my death. I watch the family gathered around, so distressed and confused, Lucien especially. He was the only one who would have had the guts to tell me I was dying had he been allowed. He didn't want all those lies between us, wished to talk to me openly but ran into great resistance from the rest of the family—nearly all of them except Orsolina. She agreed with him all the way but believed it was not her place to force the issue.

She gave me an opening once, told me that if I wanted the truth on any subject I just had to ask and she would not lie. But I didn't really want to know. I was afraid it would open Pandora's box. There are things I'd rather not delve into even now, not so soon.

My poor little Lucien, I did want so to be his father, a good father who was always present for him. I didn't want him to learn the truth at the time of my passing and be even more confused than he already was, so I went along with the lies of my family. I didn't know then as I do now that it is truth that heals. Although surrounded by my close ones, I died totally alone.

I am able to communicate with Lucien in a different way now, tell him what my sickness was about, where the wound that plagued my life came from. It's not the obvious, not the brutality of the kidnapping, not the separation from my mother, but something else which happened before I was born. We all have a wound, the healing of which our lives are about. I would like him to understand why it was so important to me to be a good father to him. I want to open up all the subjects I have stayed away from. I know his spirit can hear me. He will have my story inside of him when the time comes for him to know the truth.

My guide Yamill suddenly appears as if summoned by my thoughts, "Go ahead, don't be afraid," he conveys to me. "Go back to the memories you have avoided all your life. You are safe now, no longer powerless. That will be your work for a time. You don't have to start at the beginning and go to the end in the way stories are told on earth. The stories themselves will find their own truth and order."

I was supposed to have an operation that would fix me. On my doctor's recommendation I left the hospital in Paris to go rest in Lerné where I could regain some strength before the intervention. I suspected that the doctor was just buying time and that the operation would never happen. How could they operate on someone as weak as I was? But I tried not to think about that. Since no one in the family wanted to talk about cancer and death I buried what I knew as far as I could and pretended to myself that I would get better.

I was sick, so sick. The sickness had become my whole life. It was like a jealous lover wanting to possess every part of me. It didn't leave room for anything or anybody else. I could feel myself becoming weaker by the day. I could no longer walk, had to use a wheelchair to get around. The sickness filled me to such an extent that I couldn't retain any food. I avoided looking in the mirror because what I saw was the death mask. It had taken over my features—sunken eyes, cheekbones sticking out. I was skin and bones, my stomach bloated. I could tell that it fascinated and repulsed the village folks. "He is reduced to nothing," they would say with great pity. At first I refused to be wheeled around the village because I couldn't stand to be looked at with curiosity and pity as a living corpse. I only wanted to stay inside the house or in the garden, but after a while I no longer cared.

Some days were a little better than others and on those days I could still fool myself. Orsolina sat by me in the garden. More often than not we were silent. I dozed in and out, rehashing things. I still had bitterness about something that happened the year before, during Giovanni's last days. I could not get over the idea that my sister had dislodged me from my rightful place on my father's side when he was dying. Up till that moment I had always felt in total accord with my sister, but suddenly I resented her for the first time in my life.

Yamill unexpectedly comes into my sight. He lets me know that I have the possibility of knowing how it was for Orsolina at the time. So I felt her hunger for powerful experiences, her unwillingness to share the privilege of father's last moments, her desire to drift into the far away place with her *Papa*. She found justifications for that—the other members of the family were not honest with him, still pretending he was getting better when they knew he was dying. The family's denial was loathsome to her. Because of that she ignored our right to go through Giovanni's death our own way.

I see us on one of those days when my sister sat silently by me. Out of the blue she decided to break through the wall of silence.

"I have to ask for your forgiveness," she blurted, tears rolling down her cheeks, "I was so selfish at *Papa's* death, totally self-centered. I took over and didn't leave you any space for your own resolution."

"I have to say I was hurt. What pained me most was a small thing you might not even remember. Simone and I had come to Lerné to stay for a few days because we knew *Papa* was dying. Two of our children, Lucien and Amélie had arrived the day before and were sharing the bedroom that had three beds. Angela used a small room with a single bed downstairs. You were ensconced in the master bedroom upstairs, the only one with privacy. We fully expected, since your own family was not there with you, that you would leave us that room and sleep in the other one with your nephew and niece, but you couldn't make yourself do it."

Orsolina choked, "I was so distressed I could only think about my own grief and my need to be alone."

"Yes. Because of that Simone and I were forced to share a room with our two children and sleep in a double bed while you had the queen one. It was not the first time I felt disowned, you know."

"Oh Pietro! Are you telling me that you carried this hurt around for close to a year without letting me suspect anything of it?" She was sobbing by then and my tears started also. We ended up in each other arms, crying together for all the pain that had piled up between us. One pain brings on all pains.

That day in the garden I could not sustain my sister's embrace for very long. I was so thin and fragile even a hug hurt me. I gently pushed her away and sank into my pillows. When her tears abated Orsolina started to recall, "Before your marriage with Simone there was only love between us. I was just a silly child. I begged you not to go through with it but to wait for me to catch up so the two of us could get married, remember?" She giggled, suddenly embarrassed, and I laughed with her. "We would have made a great couple," I whispered.

The door of honesty had opened just a slit. Changing the subject I confided, "To begin with I thought what was causing me such terrible pain was cancer." When I realized that she might confirm the cancer, I got so scared I shut the door.

She hesitated, "And what do you think now?"

"I don't think so any longer. My doctor would have told me," I said very quickly in order to close the subject.

To my relief she started talking about other things. "I think that you've kept too many things inside for too long. You must learn to talk about painful things to others in the family just as you are doing with me. There is nothing wrong with that."

"Remember," she went on, "how you always invited people to hand you their troubles? You were always ready to nurse their pain, help them heal their wounds. Meanwhile your own were left unattended. I believe that's what your sickness is about. You can still heal those wounds, you know."

I answered: "I know I can."

When Orsolina got up and gently started to rub my shoulders, I let her do it; until that moment I had resisted anyone's attempt to massage me. My skeletal body embarrassed me. Rivers of tears were damned up in that body of mine. I might drown if I let go. As she massaged she noticed my hands quivering on the blanket. She took one in her own.

Unexpectedly and to my own amazement I blurted out, "You know, at times, I think that *La Strega* from Noiaris did this to me. She put a spell on me. I should never have gone back there, never. Every time I went on a visit I got sick. I tell you, I have been under a bad spell."

"The witch? How do you figure that?" she asked in total surprise.

As suddenly as it came out I took it back. How could I, a grown man, talk such nonsense? "Oh! Don't pay any attention! I was just being lame. Sometimes the sickness makes me delirious."

"Why did you say it though?"

"Oh, I have been thinking about my village, my mother Malva. She was related to *La Strega* you know."

"Yes, I know. But more than half the people in the village are related. What about your mother? I always wanted to ask you about her but you avoided that subject. It must have been so hard when you were taken away from her as a child?"

"I don't really remember much—just what the family told me. She was a bad mother, ordered me to bed early because she wanted to go whoring; she held me out of our second-story window and threatened to let go to keep me quiet. I could never play with my cousins after dinner; if I protested she beat me up."

"Were you angry?"

"I don't know. I was told how I felt. She was bad. I was happy to get away from her because she abused me and might have killed me. I did what I was ordered to do. I don't remember much."

"Did you ever want to see her again?"

"*Papa* sent me to Grandpa Ferdinando's house in Noiaris one summer when I was about thirteen. Remember the house, a big chalet nestled at the foot of the mountain, with the vegetable garden and orchard in front? One day, I stepped out to go fetch water at the pump. My mother Malva owned a field next to Grandpa's garden and she was in it, scything alfalfa for the animals. I saw her. She saw me. I did what I had been told to do. I turned away from her.

"'Aren't you going to say hello to your mother?' she called. 'Come here. Come kiss your mom.'

"She held out her hand. I walked towards her. Just as I was about to reach for her hand, Grandpa came out of the house and spotted us. He swore like a madman, yelled for her to leave me alone, 'Don't touch him, you bitch.' He started running towards us.

"She grabbed my hand and pulled me as she began to run. He picked up an ax leaning against the wall of the house. 'I'll catch up with you and cut your hand off, you dirty whore,' he screamed. I stumbled. He was gaining on us. I could hear him, closer, closer, louder. I knew he would do it. Her hand would be left, in mine, forever. I jerked my hand out.

"She let go and continued to run, terrorized. Grandpa took me by the hand she had held and led me back home. I was shaking. He patted my

head to appease me. 'Good boy, good boy. You did well,' he compli-
mented.

"It was the last time I saw my mother—except of course when I
went to Noiaris with my family for the grand reunion not too long before
she died. *Papa* had sent me to Grandpa's a couple of times more after that
episode but I managed to avoid Malva completely. But you know what?
As soon as I'd arrive in the village, I'd get sick. It happened every time.
Papa declared that Malva was in cahoots with the witch and refused to
send me to Noiaris anymore.

"When I asked Giovanni why I could no longer go to Grandpa's
house, he answered: 'that witch with her two different color eyes will get
you every time, just like she used to get me. She was sexy in my day, she
got men that way, but although she is starting to lose some of her appeal,
she still has all her powers.'

"Even later as a grown man, when I went back on vacation with
Simone I got sick. I took to my bed the very first day. Do you remember?
You were there also, thirteen or so. My vacation was ruined.

"Meanwhile you ran around with the witch's daughter, a girl about
your age. *Papa* had absolutely forbidden you to have anything to do with
any of *La Strega's* family but you disregarded that—a wild one you were.
The witch's daughter had the same name as you, not just the last name,
which was not unusual since more than half the village was called Spiazzi,
but the first name also. She fascinated you, that girl with the same name as
yours who lived in the witch's house.

"*La Strega,* who has since become an old scary hag from what I
hear, had some appeal at that time. You were attracted to that family. You
even went to their house, ate some of their food. What a fool you were! If
Papa had known about this, you would have received the beating of your
life. Do you realize that going over there you gave them power over our
family?"

"No I didn't. I was just a silly girl playing witches."

"Do you remember showing me some iridescent beads the witch
had given you that summer? I can still see that string of beads as though it
were in my hand. You wouldn't still have those beads somewhere, would
you?"

Orsolina shook her head and looked at me as though I was
delirious, "No why?"

I didn't answer. I felt so discouraged suddenly, feverish, out of it. I
believed that if she had kept the beads we could have removed the spell. I
went unconscious after that and they had to carry me to my bed.

The fever was with me all the way back to Paris where an ambulance transported me to the hospital, then back to our house in Bagnolet and finally through the passage to the other side where it left me, right after the tunnel.

# **O**rsolina

The only difference between the angels in heaven and the angels that walk this earth is that the angels in heaven know they are angels.

—*Sainte Némoise*

33

THE EXPERT STITCHER OF LIFE - Bagnolet

In which Orsolina and her mother continue to visit all the significant spots of their past in Bagnolet where Rosina used to live; where Orsolina recalls how her aunt taught her to embroider while her husband was asleep, a charmed life where there was lots of time for everything and in which the clock marked the minutes of a life forever fecund; where she understands by watching the public writer that she writes in the same way she embroiders and can continue, when she slows down and listens, to catch the magic of moments.

Cela m'a tout l'air d'un pélerinage!

Yes. This is a pilgrimage. I want to visit all the significant spots from my childhood. Obviously my mother also wishes it. After our stop in *rue des Maraîchers*, I ask the driver to go by my old school *rue des Pyrénées*, and my mother suggests we go by the *rue de la Liberté* in Bagnolet where we lived until I was three and where my aunt Rosina resided for so many years until she moved to an assisted living place not far from there.

We cross the *Boulevard Davout*, drive by the low-cost housing compounds and through the funky section where the Montreuil flea market sets up on weekends. When we arrive in Bagnolet and drive by the small three-story apartment building that I loved to visit as a child, I tell the taxi to stop again for a few minutes. In my memory my aunt Rosina is still young and full of spunk.

Rappelle-toi quand elle t'a appris à broder.

Yes. It's summer, a bright day. My aunt wants to teach me how to embroider, something she does for a living along with fancy ironing of priests' ceremonial vestments, nuns' habits and headdresses, pleated gowns and lacy undergarments, communion and wedding dresses. She has shown me a few stitches I practice, and now she sits in the semi-darkness in front of the door kept ajar for light, embroidering on her own work. She embellishes the hems of linen sheets with tiny stitches, grows miniature gardens on large tablecloths.

Sitting on a small stool with my little napkin, I concentrate on my work while watching the advance of hers. My work is difficult. I am sweating, the needle slips in my hand. Stitches are too loose or too tight, the material puckers, I lose a stitch and my thread knots. Without a word, Rosina takes my work and puts it all back in order, making it possible for me to continue.

I watch her, marveling at the precision of her hand as she sews knowledge with those little stitches. This time, when I get back to my work, I let go of my forceful concentration and the miracle happens. I haven't been thinking and my fingers have embroidered the outline of a wildflower, a stitch at a time. I look for the mistake, but there is none. One whole flower has come alive in the spring bouquet drawn on the material, more real than any flower I have ever touched or smelled. The stitches are regular, the line smooth.

Now I know how to embroider. An hour ago I didn't, now I do. A metamorphosis has taken place. I have left behind the incompetent, messy little girl and entered the chain of embroiderers, knitters and crocheters, the expert stitchers of life. My life is charmed. I am so happy to have yet so long to live, so many things to learn.

Rosina continues to embroider, stitching complicated filigrees into the daily routine, linking each thing to the next, and perpetuating our union to the earth. She looks up and smiles at me in recognition and I welcome this complicity of ours, the womanly secret we stitch in our work, a secret that demands the total enjoyment of my occupation. I stop for a moment to look at her, marveling at the variety of silk threads she employs in the realization of outlines. I let my glance wander from my embroidery to the brightness outside, trying to preserve this feeling of well-being.

My uncle André is taking a nap in the only bedroom of their tiny apartment. They are in love, it shows when they look at each other. Now he swims in the sleep of oblivion and she does not say a word to me. She insists on being quiet about this complicity we share, this secret that is only revealed when man's hustle and bustle is appeased: we, women, are the bridge on which man can cross safely to the other side.

Within their couple and to a superficial onlooker, Rosina might appear to be standing in the background, unassuming, discreet, silent, a tribute to her husband, but in reality she is the warp of a cloth of which he is the weft and he can only make patterns on what she has solidly set.

She sits at the edge of time while her man, the loud mouth, the show-off, sleeps in the shadow. He is the activity, the laughter; he has the bright feathers. He is generous, works hard and gives her everything he makes. He is the one who talks, the one who tells stories, but her hands are forever fecund; she needs to give, cannot help herself. Life pours through her and she has no choice but to pass it on. She doesn't need any recognition. She sits at the threshold of light, guiding our vessel of cool shade into the immensity of summer, drawing back her sleeping lover from the penumbra in which he might dissolve.

The big clock in the hallway, the heartbeat of the family, scans the minutes of a story forever improvised; here at my Aunt Rosina's place I have all the time in the world to push the needle through with my little thimble, slide it out of sight and bring it back up from the other side, picking up each moment along the way, balancing it, stitching it and letting it go. A stitch in time.

I get out of the taxi and walk around. Red brick is the favored material of this lower class suburb. Things haven't changed much except that the centenarian who lived on the ground floor, *Madame Guérin,* has long passed away. She was the landlady for whom my aunt did chores; she always had great candy and told fantastic stories.

Across the street in the window of a tiny storefront that didn't exist in my childhood there is a sign: *Écrivain Public.* Public writers have made a comeback now that more immigrants who hardly speak French have created colorful ethnic villages in those low-class suburbs. Rather than trying to embroider on the white page the precise words, the strong verbs that might open Rosina's spirit to others, I would be more useful offering my services as a public writer.

I see the public writer through the shop window, sitting at his desk, chewing on the end of his pen, apparently dreaming, or looking for inspiration, unhurried. A colorful African woman wearing a turban sits across from him.

Alors tu voudrais prendre sa place?

Yes, I could be there writing love letters for others. Instead, I trace on the white page words that I hope will slow down the world for me, linking each thing to the next, connecting sentences, creating stories. Too often these days I catch myself lamenting, "If only I had enough time." Time runs short when one lives in America.

In Rosina's house, however, I had all the time in the world to start things, all the time in the world to finish them. My aunt never said, "I have so much to do, I don't know where to start!" or, "I'll never be finished!" or, "I want to be done with this!" because all that had to be done was done in its own time of day, week, year, at the time set aside for its execution since the beginning of times. The delight I felt at the succession of days with their undisturbed rhythm turned into a subtle pleasure in her house, a wish for more of this meaningful repetition.

The sap of the joy Rosina passed on hasn't run dry; I still find it when I think of her. I found it then in the languid flow of honey she poured in my verbena tea, in the tang of her sourdough bread, but find it even now among torpid buildings and drowsy stones, when the air throbs and branches tremble, when I come across a blazing display at the end of the day.

I find it in the rasp of a garden hoe, the faint whistling of the pruning shears, the lowing of cattle, a rustling of wings, the drone of a bee, or the triumphant arches formed by foliage at the end of provincial avenues. I also find it when children knead the mud like flour and shape new people, new stories. I find it every time I take time to look and listen.

ngela

The longing for wholeness, an almost irresistible urge for union with the opposite energy, has its root in the spiritual, a yearning for the end of duality.
—*Sainte Némoise*

34

MY SISTER ROSINA – Bagnolet

In which Angela asks to make a detour through the place in Bagnolet where her sister Rosina used to live, not far from Simone's house; where she remembers how in childhood her brother Giuseppe beat Rosina, how she got away from the nuns and moved to France; where she relays to her daughter how she came to Paris from Italy after her parents died to live with her sister and husband André; in which she tells how she met her first husband Aldo and later, Giovanni; in which she describes the harsh side of Rosina and her way to cajole men; where Rosina's insatiable appetites and many husbands are mentioned along with her reputation as a husband killer.

I have suggested going the long way to Simone's, through the old part of Bagnolet where we lived after Orsolina was born, close to my sister Rosina's place. My daughter agrees and when we stop in front of Rosina's old building, I remember. . .

In Castel' Arquato Rosina always had the hardest time with our poverty. She loved to own things, loved to give me little presents. When she still lived at home she befriended girls whose families were better off and in her sweet whiny way extracted gifts from them. She didn't even wait till she was twelve to leave home and be a servant in a rich household so tired was she of sleeping on a straw mattress with her two sisters.

Rosina, who knew how to cajole and get her way with just about anyone, had no hold on our brother Giuseppe. In fact her act as a fragile and needy little flower, her playing up to the rich folks, drove him crazy. When Rosina didn't get her way through her charm she dug in her heels and became obstinate.

Giuseppe beat her mostly because she refused to help in the vegetable garden or in the fields. "I'd rather be a servant inside than a peasant outside," she'd declare. And that statement enraged our brother so much that he took it upon himself to force her to do the work she despised. "You are going to turn the ground and weed the garden if I have to kill you," he'd yell. "Household chores are easy and should be left to your younger sister."

I remember one day when they locked horns more savagely than usual. He went mad with anger, picked up a stick and beat her with it. I was so scared. I begged him to stop and eventually he did, but Rosina still wouldn't get up and hoe the soil in the garden. She held her ground, didn't even cry. So he got a rope, tied her up, dragged her to the spot he wanted her to cultivate and strapped her to a post. "You stupid mule," he yelled giving her a kick as he did. "You'll stay there until you do the job." I was sobbing so hard he untied her and let her go in order to console me.

Giuseppe was gentle, loving and caring with me. He never once raised his hand to me, never once ordered me around. Because I was the youngest, he wanted me to have the childhood the other kids never had: no back-breaking work, no servitude, enough schooling to at least be able to read and write. All my other siblings as well as my parents were illiterate.

Orsolina often tells me that if you don't have enough language you don't know how to define yourself, so that your only motivation for conversation is survival. She probably is right. There was not much conversation happening around the hearth of our old tumbled down stone house. No stories around the fire, everyone was too exhausted from their day of labor and often went to sleep to forget their hunger. Silence was king.

Our brother expected us all to obey him for he was the man in the family. My father was too tired and often too sick to do much discipline, and when he was home he mostly slept. Rosina's contempt for farm work never ceased to provoke our brother. So it is that she followed a family vacationing in our village back to Rome to be a servant and nanny. Rome was very far from home and she could rarely visit us.

Rosina yearned to be a wife long before she wed. She felt incomplete without a partner; she wanted a protector, someone she could look up to, someone who would indulge her. She knew how to be charming, and men loved her subservience and helplessness, her young coquette act. As long as she had no mate, she grieved the absence of him. Along with the protection a man offered she wanted the prestige that marriage promoted. But she swore she would never marry a peasant.

In Rome she served one family after another, leaving to get better conditions as her expertise grew, until a prominent Roman doctor who had a sister in Paris hired her. Rosina had heard that many Italians immigrated to France because there were plenty of jobs there and they could make good money. She wangled her way into the good grace of the doctor's relatives when they came on a visit and left with them for Paris. They paid for her trip, but it was supposed to be repaid by taking money out of her meager salary every month. So she got room and board but only a few coins for pocket money beside that. The few hours of freedom she was allowed on Sunday afternoon she spent looking at shop windows. She had to be available at any other time.

My sister never tired of retelling the story of her meeting with her first husband, André, to whoever wanted to listen. It happened on a beautiful winter afternoon. She was taking her usual solitary walk, daydreaming about a handsome man asking her to marry him. She was starting to cross the street when a motorcyclist coming around a corner nearly ran her over. He was wearing a red woolen hat down to his eyebrows and the collar of his thick coat was up, covering most of his face. His eyes were protected with goggles. She had no idea what the man looked like but a voice in her head clearly stated, "This man is going to be your husband." As he disappeared she noticed his *canadienne,* a leather coat with beaver collar.

A week later she chanced upon an older Italian from her village sitting at a café terrace, talking to a younger man. They invited her to join them for a drink. Her acquaintance's friend was introduced to her as André. She immediately noticed the red woolen hat on the table next to his coffee, and the worn leather jacket with the beaver collar on the back of his chair. Her heart missed a beat.

André was French, didn't speak a word of Italian, but he looked intensely at her the whole time they sat there, so much so it became rather embarrassing. When she got up to leave, the young man said something to her she didn't understand, but her acquaintance who had been in France a while and could speak the language, translated. "He is asking if you two had met somewhere before." She replied through the acquaintance that she didn't think so, and André asked for her permission to accompany her back to her place. She accepted, but wouldn't get on the back of his Vespa. So he walked her and they communicated through mime, hand gestures and laughter.

When he left her, André, conveying things with drawings on

paper, asked for a date. She accepted to go out with him the next Sunday. From this moment on they saw each other every Sunday and since they couldn't communicate much they kissed quite a lot.

One Sunday afternoon André declared that this could not go on. He couldn't live without her, couldn't sleep. He mimed putting a ring on her finger, she nodded her acceptance and they were married within a month. For the first year—until Rosina learned some rudiments of French—the newlyweds communicated with hands, drawings and kisses. They had a great time of it, often laughing so hard the neighbors complained about the noise. As she told the story, Rosina also hinted that it was the noise of their lovemaking that was most disturbing.

A small giggle escapes me at that thought. Orsolina who was looking out of the taxi window turns to me questioningly.

"I always wondered why there is such a strong bond between you and Rosina," I tell Orsolina, breaking our long silence. "She is a rather subservient, whiny woman always looking for sympathy and protection whereas you are strong and independent."

"When I was a little girl it was her ability to play like a child that won me over. I remember that as soon as I could walk I wanted to go down the few blocks to *Tata* Rosina. She was my *Tata* and in my mind aunties and fairy godmothers were one and the same. To me she had extraordinary powers, and her drawers were full of small treasures she kept pulling out just for me. In her eyes I could do nothing wrong, she trusted me, and that made me courageous. I have that kind of relationship with Lucien."

"Yes I can tell. Though I often wonder why him when you have other nieces and nephews that are more . . ." But Orsolina's harsh stare makes me change the subject. She is so touchy when it comes to Pietro's children, like it's a taboo topic.

"I remember that whenever you were angry with me you ran away to Rosina and she let you stay. I always knew where to find you if you were missing and we would laugh about your escapades—but I held a grudge."

"What was it about? You two were so close early on. What happened between you?"

"Something I thought I would never forgive. When I came to her all excited with the news that I was pregnant, she snapped, 'so you are going to have a bastard child.' I was shocked. True, Giovanni and I were still living in sin. We couldn't get married yet because he hadn't been able to get his divorce. But to hear that from my own sister!"

"Was it jealousy that made her say that?"

"Probably. She had been unable to get pregnant and was envious. After you were born though, she loved you so much and we lived so close to each other, I had to forgive. Your father however, never did."

"Didn't you live with her and André before you moved in with your first husband?"

"Yes, our parents died one year apart, worn out from work and lack of nutritious food. I was only seventeen. André wrote a letter some-one translated, offering me to come to France and live with them. At the time I worked as a seamstress and embroiderer in the convent where I had done my schooling, to repay for it. One of my favorite nuns pressured me to join their ranks and take the vows. I didn't feel I had a vocation and I wanted so much to be a mother. So I accepted André's offer."

"You never seemed to put much faith into the Catholic Church anyway."

"I lost my faith when the village priest attempted to force himself on me. I told you that story I think. I was totally disillusioned and decided to leave all that religious stuff behind. But there was something else I never told you. A very handsome naval officer and I had fallen madly in love. He asked me to promenade with him around the *piazza* on Sunday afternoons, but when his family found out they objected and he cut our meetings short. I was heartbroken, but had to accept that I was not of the same class and could not expect marriage."

"You never told me about that. It makes me sad. What a coward that man was, but I guess it was the way in those days. The class barrier was unbreakable."

"It's still that way. I could tell you stories. . ."

"Did you get along with Rosina and André when you moved in?"

"It was not easy living with them in their tiny apartment. I had to sleep on the couch and didn't get along with my sister too well. André was kind and courteous with me, and that made Rosina jealous. She was afraid I would take her husband away.

"Ever since we were children she had a hard time with people's comments about my beauty. After I moved in it disturbed her more. Myself, I never thought much of that beauty people raved about, I didn't really know what it meant to be beautiful. When I looked in the mirror it was just me. My features were harmonious, there was nothing discordant about them but all that beauty people talked about hadn't served me when it came to keep the man I loved. So what was the use of it?"

"So did Rosina make it difficult for you?"

"It was obvious that she wanted me out of there. Besides, she was convinced that single women entirely missed the boat and she constantly pressured me, 'Why don't you marry one of the suitors who keep telling you how beautiful and smart you are. Bring them home, André and I will know how to decide for you and get the man we choose to become serious about things.''

"You took that to mean she wanted you out of there?"

"Yes. Also, I was anxious to leave. I felt like an adopted child who turned out to be more trouble than she was worth."

Orsolina tells the taxi to go on. She points to our first apartment building as we drive by. Pensively she says, "Yes, the unwanted child story is one that repeats itself in our family it seems. So, how did you choose your first husband?"

"I was shy and didn't speak French very well, but the neighborhood was mostly Italian. There was a good friend of Rosina's husband, Aldo, who obviously fell in love with me the minute he saw me. Within weeks he asked me to marry him. He was gentle, kind and generous, tall and not unpleasant looking. I believed he would make a good father and provider. Rosina and André agreed. I accepted.

"I left my sister's house and for the first time I had my own place a few blocks away. I played house for a while, knitted for a baby, but the child never came. And after a few years of relative happiness Aldo got sick. I nursed him through seven years of suffering with a cancer that devoured his mouth and palate."

"Did Rosina help you through that?"

"Not really. Yes, a little I guess. She had quite a busy life with André. He had set up a shop of varnishing and lacquering and was very successful. Rosina and he traveled to Italy yearly and visited the family, stayed in fancy hotels. Even though there was a lot of trouble and restlessness all over Europe none of us saw the war coming."

"You never told me any of that before."

"You never asked."

"I remember that André died rather young. What was it that killed him?"

"A bleeding ulcer, people did die of that in those days. But Rosina didn't waste any time in finding another companion. I saw her through three more marriages. She never left a man, nor was she ever abandoned. Her husbands died of natural causes. A rumor started that she killed them all. The joke was that it was her insatiable sexual appetite that did it. Even now, in her eighties, she has a next-door neighbor ten years younger who is so devoted to her I am sure he is her boyfriend. Whenever I visit he is always at her place. Can you believe that she defends the purity of their relationship? 'We are just friends, we don't really have that other thing going,' she tells me, and under her breath she adds, 'he can't get it up anymore.'"

Orsolina and I giggle like two schoolgirls. I love it when we have that complicity.

"Please stop here for a minute," says Orsolina leaning over to the taxi driver.

We are in front of the apartment house where Rosina lives nowadays. My daughter runs in but comes back alone.

"She is not there. Someone already picked her up and drove her to Simone's."

Orsolina

Brief and elusive glimpses of love are possible whenever there is a gap in the stream of mind.
　　　　　　　　　　　　　　　　　　　　　　—Sainte Némoise

35

MOTHERS AND DAUGHTERS – Arrival at Simone's

In which Orsolina, in Simone's living room reflects on her early fears, her nightmares, the murderous Gypsy, the lion, her rejection of Pietro's family lifestyle and of the grownup world, her mother's determination to eliminate her daughter's sexuality, which brings Orsolina to defend herself fiercely, resisting, rebelling.

When we arrive at the door of Simone's apartment in Bagnolet I ask the taxi driver to stop and I help my mother out. Angela rings the bell while I pay the taxi, Simone answers the door and carries her luggage inside. I follow with mine.

"Do you remember," Simone asks after helping us to the room my mother and I will share in her house until the funeral, "how you wanted to come to our house all the time as a young girl? You even learned at an early age to take the métro and bus by yourself to get here. Our family was a happy one and you were always a big part of it. Then in adolescence you suddenly dropped us. We hardly ever saw you. I always wondered what happened, if it was something we did."

"Nothing you did, just that the teen years got me!"

I recall that coming out of childhood and into adulthood was like climbing over a fence and looking at a totally new landscape. There was no room for magic or metamorphosis in it. I had no choice but to jump because ferocious dogs were barking at my heels. Many of my friends hurt themselves badly when they landed on the other side and never totally recovered. Others picked themselves up immediately, surveyed their surroundings to understand what the game was about and began playing it. Others, although injured, managed to lick their wounds and function somewhat awkwardly, nursing their infirmities.

"You and Pietro had been part of my childhood magic but it didn't work anymore, something else got my interest."

"That's a nice way to say that we were passé."

I hug her but don't answer. Simone seems lost, drowning and gasping for air. She'll grab on to anything not to deal with what's in front of her. She rushes over to one of her children after another, nervously talking about what needs to be done for the funeral. Frantically she tries to fill in the gaps, saying the wrong things at the wrong time, anything but silence.

Simone is right about me. I remember the exact day when something changed, when she and Pietro stopped being models. I had been hanging out with the neighborhood's tough kids and learned how they played the game, a tough uncompassionate game.

So I began playing also. Nothing was sacred or serious. I challenged all beliefs. I remember a weekend when Pietro and I were at my parents' house in Lerné. One evening I convinced him to go with me to the Gypsy camp outside the village in spite of our parent's interdiction. I shocked my brother when, on a challenge, I kissed a young Gypsy on the mouth. It was the kind of thing I started to do, my method for being in charge and daring. If I had to play the game I was going to do it my way.

At the Gypsy camp I sensed how scared Pietro was. I probably was also, but I didn't admit it; the handsome young Gypsy had aroused my combative spirit. That night I won the game and my brother was lost to me. I realized that he could never save me from the disillusionment of being stuck in a world without magic, among people with little imagination.

Played with humor, the game of life could be fun. Pietro and his family were no longer of interest, but Gypsies and fringe characters had become fascinating.

Ever since I was little and this in spite of the fear my mother had instilled in me, Gypsies fascinated me. I wished to live like them, move from place to place like them, free to be vulgar like them, say bad words, scorn people I didn't like. When I was a child my mother and I would often go visit my aunt Rosina in Bagnolet on Sunday. My mother dressed me up like in a photo I still have: white organdy dress embroidered and starched, enormous white bow on top of my head, white patent leather shoes.

I strutted along pretending to behave but watched with envy the

Gypsy kids running in and out of abandoned buildings. They were dirty and free, no one told them what to do. Anyone who dared to scold them, whether man or woman, met with a string of insults, and the culprits disappeared in some dark hole under a tumbled-down house or behind a pile of debris. They kept an eye on me, giggling and snickering in my direction. I knew that if my mother wasn't there they would throw mud on my dress and tear down my starched bow to bring me to be one of them. I wished they had.

When I reached adolescence I wanted to be different, wear hip clothes, meet interesting people and explore a world of new ideas. I wished for adventure. The small, narrow world of family life bored me. Marriage, work, children, the same daily routine, three weeks of vacation at the same place, in the same family cottage. It made me cringe.

What a disaster adult life seemed to me! Like neurotic moths hitting the windowpane over and over and hurting themselves without ever learning, grownups slept, ate, worked, got depressed, fooled themselves, got depressed again and questioned how they got caught in a vicious circle that was always taking them where they didn't want to go. Some found refuge in a religion that taught them to be masters of denial, others embraced lucidity and cynicism, others yet became wage-slaves and stopped thinking. Children believed their parents and in turn deceived their children.

To me, Pietro now seemed common, uninspired, working his life away and letting his wife raise the children. It was only when Lucien, my brother's last child was born, that my interest in the family was somewhat renewed. There was an aura of drama around that birth, something different, something worth writing about. Writing had become part of my daily life.

I began collecting new kinds of friends: people of the edges, beatniks, hipsters, gentle outlaws or iconoclasts, all Gypsy-like to me. That was the family of my choice.

Early on my mother had made me aware of three enemies: Gypsies, vipers and the sea, all three Damocles swords hanging over our heads. Gypsies stole children and used them for begging, vipers lay in wait in fields and forests anxious to introduce their deadly venom into our bodies, and oceans churned up overwhelming waves to drown us. In spite of her warning I talked to Gypsies anytime I had a chance and came to understand that to be a Gypsy was more a philosophy than a race, not so much a culture as a chosen way of life. I wore snake rings and sailed the ocean with a bunch of daring youngsters.

My stubborn attraction to fringe characters saved me from my mother's fears. When in class I read about some innocuous beetles that attach themselves to frogs from below the surface of the water and slowly suck out their insides, I immediately thought of my mother. Once emptied of my own substance I could be filled with her fears. It was her way to keep me on a leash.

After I had made the jump into young adulthood I perceived all grownups as wanting to lock me in. I saw that even Simone, whose talent as a mother I admired, had neurotic ways of controlling her children. When Lucien was born I decided not to let him be molded into the conventional role of French middle class male; I would help his spirit be free.

My fringe character friends showed me I was not the person my mother had described to me. And the painful process of separating from her and her views of life began. Even in my crib I already had adopted my mother's fears when, night after night, a tiny rust-colored malevolent animal rolled around my pillow trying to get me. I understood later that it was a feather from my quilt.

Later nightmares began: two recurrent ones. In one a Gypsy chased me with a knife, intent on taking out my eyes. I tried to run as fast as I could but fear sucked out my energy and my knees buckled. In spite of my determination to flee I could barely stay ahead of him. Then, totally drained, I could no longer run at all, barely walk, becoming heavier and heavier, unable to utter a sound. The Gypsy was catching up. Finally, unable to move at all, I used all my will to call for help and woke up screaming in terror as the Gypsy was about to grab me. My mother rushed to my bedside and I only calmed down when she agreed to sleep with me.

In another nightmare it was a lion chasing me ready to devour me. This went on for years. I was about twelve or thirteen when I mustered up the courage to turn around and face the Gypsy with the knife. To my amazement he lost all his viciousness and when I asked him what he wanted he said he wanted me to look at him. When I looked he seemed familiar, friendly. After that he never came back.

Soon after that I tried a similar method on the ferocious lion. When he was just about to close his huge jowls on my neck I turned around and calmly put one hand on his upper jaw, the other hand on the lower one and kept him from closing his mouth. I had enough strength to do that. The lion became as tame as a pet. These were two battles I won. There were many more.

At Simone's everyone sits around in the living room, silent, mournful. Simone busies herself in the kitchen. I overhear my mother talking to her as she helps. "Yes, she was looking for it! Now she is pregnant and he dumped her. God knows where she'll end up. I don't feel sorry for her, she was a little slut even at thirteen."

I don't know who she is talking about, probably one of the Lerné farm girls, but my reaction astounds me. Even now as an adult and a mother those kinds of statements make me want to strangle her; as if it's always women who are in the wrong! I walk over to the kitchen and snap, "Don't talk about people you know nothing about." She looks hurt but does not say a word.

"You are hard on your mother," Simone tells me later.

"Believe me I know," I answer. "My judgment of her is enormous and I dislike myself for that."

I judge her ignorance; I judge the impersonal language she uses, a language that has never fostered an original idea, a language of convention. I know that it's also a tribal language of difficult times, the language of the oppressed, that she is just repeating what has been passed on to her, but I don't want to be included as one of the victims of that oppression.

Simone nods her understanding, but I don't know if she really understands. She has been branded herself. Once in a while I even witness that same language slipping into my own speech when I talk to my children. Horrified, I recognize my mother's voice. I see that in spite of all my resistance I have become more and more the woman she wanted me to be. Her unremitting efforts, day after day, to form a good person, a safe person, have won after all. Now I can measure the force of her will to make my body, my thoughts and my soul take the shape she had decided on. I was her occupied territory.

Tu dois te rendre compte that Gypsies and lions were the guerillas hiding in the woods and fighting to free your country.

Maybe, but by the time I was old enough to judge her standards of morality and defend myself, the seeds Angela had buried had sprouted inside. I had the courage to face the Gypsy and the lion, but later it was hordes of faceless beings that ran after me ready to tear me apart, screaming, "you are guilty." Things my mother had judged dangerous or sinful were cancelled from my choices. Still I saved parts of myself.

You jumped into other realities. Psychedelics helped you.

Yes, but I was stuck in her reality for a long time. Her version of life came from novels that had been in vogue in her youth, or propaganda in Communist publications. There were episodes to be followed from week to week in which the heroine was seduced, impregnated and abandoned by her lover, ending up dying of tuberculosis in the gutter or becoming a prostitute in a sinister bordello, venereal diseases eating away her insides. Orphans were exploited, abused, beaten by cruel foster parents, servant girls raped by their masters and thrown out in the cold when they were tired of them. Rich and elegant *grands-bourgeois* took advantage of credulous country girls, they deflowered and desecrated them.

My parents were not strictly *engagés*—committed to the Communist Party like adherents willing to do militant work, but they were registered. They believed that by being united they would have the power to fight the capitalist system and make the world a better place. They were told that the church was the opiate of the people and that confirmed their own views.

But the Communist Party was just another church, and those realist novels often set in slums had their own morality just as insidious as the church's. The poor were exploited by the rich, the weak by the strong, but things would change. In the *bourgeois* world, man was the hunter and woman the prey; even poor and helpless men who were used by more fortunate ones had power over women, but in the Communist world women became the equals of men, and all men were brothers. . . supposedly. . . however...

My mother added other moralistic ingredients into the picture. Who knows where she picked them up, maybe from her early days with the nuns. If the heroine succeeded, against all odds, in remaining a good girl, if she could make people forget she had this unfortunate, unprotected opening between her legs into which the masculine desire could force its way, then she stood a chance. She would become a sort of saint, a Madonna, a Virgin that men would respect and want to betroth.

The scums wouldn't dare touch her before marriage then. My mother loved to see unblemished purity win over base desires. She loved seeing good girls getting the proof of men's true love and respect: the patience to consummate only after marriage. . . she who had lived in sin with my father! But that of course was only so she could conceive me.

After all, the future husband could be patient since he would be the first one to open the passage on the fateful night, the first to spill her blood, snug in his belief that he would also be the only one to ever have his entries.

From observation I knew something different. Once the hymen was broken under the force of a man's battering, someone else could enter and no one would know. Suspicious future husbands asked for guarantees in the Italian villages my parents were from. Those were given in the form of an irreproachable female ancestry. My father hadn't looked for guarantees close enough and he got a bad woman.

Tu ne comprends donc pas? Do you not see that man represented death for your mother, a fear of abduction and rape as ancient as the world, a fear women transmitted to each other. Very early on women's destiny had been to be delivered to the invader as young virgins, pierced and penetrated or brought to the dragon without any way of protecting this hole that led to the inside of them and could bring on the creation of a new being. They were defenseless. The entrance to this second heart, the womb, could be conquered in hatred. It had no teeth to bite the invader, no lid to close it off. Not even a word to protect it, a word that would be good, sacred. It's a fear as ancient as life itself.

Most girls I knew went wild upon discovering the power of their hole to give pleasure. My mother was well aware of that and she labored to close mine off permanently. If she made me frigid, she would as securely fasten this opening as those mothers in other parts of the world who sewed up their daughters'. With no warm fluid to lubricate it, the opening would become inaccessible.

Angela worked hard at convincing me that I didn't have a vagina. I was not denied a mouth however; I used it quite freely to kiss boys. I got my pleasure that way. On the other hand, I was never allowed to forget what came out of my anus. Stools might reveal a sickness even before it declared itself. It was of utmost importance for Angela to check and consider my bowel movements daily when I was a child.

Since I couldn't have a vagina, no mention had been made of the blood and when it came, nothing was offered in the way of explanation. The night of my first period I was horrified, thinking at first that I had peed in bed. I had heard about girls getting their *règles* but nothing about blood, it terrified me. Those were private matters best not talked about so, never alluding to the stained sheets, Angela took them off my bed the next day. She left a cotton *serviette hygienique* on my night table with a medical booklet as an explanation. However, I overheard the two apprentice seamstresses that worked for my mother whisper about it in the Other Room, and even giggle as though it had been talked about.

Il faut l'excuser! She was embarrassed and so afraid for you, she was trying to do her best.

In other areas, my mother didn't hesitate to intrude on my privacy though. She believed she did it for my protection. A closed door never meant a border to be respected by her, the confidentiality of a diary not something sacred. But no matter how much she desired to intrude on my thoughts, I could preserve the privacy of my mind through silence. I never let her in, told her nothing about my life.

Many of my friends who have been subjected to the brainwashing of the time have not made it: lost in combat, killed in action, turned into salt statues, locked up by a man or buried in a tomb with someone else's name on it. I still meet some of those women in buses, subways, in the streets, young or old, women cracked, cracking up, breaking down, unable to stand the drill. They are told that things have changed. They are told they are paranoid and need help, that this oppression they feel is a thing of the past. And they are handed the small pill of oblivion.

Rappelle-toi! There was a time not so long ago when exceptional women were put away because their vision disturbed the conventional one, because they refused to accept the ancestral tradition that denied them any power in this world. You are lucky to have escaped that destiny this time around.

Yes, I have escaped that, but it's more insidious now. Women don't have to be put away, they can be obliterated by the beliefs they bought, they can destroy their true selves obsessively following the fashion of the period. It took me a long time to discover the hoax, the tortures women endured to have small feet, the corset to have a tiny waist, the implants to have big tits, the torments we, as young girls, underwent to become beautiful, perfect, to be nice and pleasing to men, torments inflicted by our mothers, as any good mother would, for our own good—to find a husband.

Anything to discourage pleasure though: tribal mothers still perform clitorectemies on their own daughters with a broken piece of glass. Elsewhere they partly sew up the hole because women are alive to pleasure men but not to get theirs. A self-respecting woman of my mother's generation would never acknowledge having an orgasm.

Did your mother?

No, my mother never did acknowledge having one. It might have given me ideas. She let me believe that she was frigid. She wanted me safe, therefore immobile, not making any waves. In order to preserve essential parts of myself I reacted by ferociously defending the occupied territory using the enemy's own weapons against her. I screamed the forbidden words on the forbidden grounds. I said fuck; I said cunt; I said cock and piss and shit. I ignited her anger anytime I could. I enjoyed making her lose control, driving her crazy.

We had horrific fights. She hit me with the stove poker and I kicked her in the stomach. Although we never hurt each other very badly I knew it was a fight to the death. I never asked for a truce or made deals with the enemy she had become for the sake of a status quo. I would not be beaten into submission, nor shamed into confession. I spat on the Catholic Church. I could take responsibility for my sins myself. I would not be victimized.

So, what did you gain from all of that fighting?

I met and integrated my faults and that gave me self-confidence. It brought forward qualities in me that only showed up when flaws activated them. Mistakes and failings were useful tools, energizing, dynamic. They combatted shame and guilt. There was power in them. I wanted to recognize each one, name them.

Si tu retournes à ton enfance. . . go way back, do you see a woman who helped you, a shadow woman? Malva, the bad woman you never met often came to your rescue.

I certainly do recognize that. Following the bad woman's example I used my faults instead of suppressing them. My faults were my qualities; they silenced my mother's voice within. She deceived me unknowingly. I hurt her unwittingly. I have compassion now, I forgive us both.

# iovanni

*If you keep on saying that things are going to be bad, you have a good
chance of being a prophet.*   —*Sainte Némoise*

36

THE STROKE

*In which Giovanni visits Pietro's grieved family on the third day after his son's death
then continues to recall the days after his own death, his journey guided by Senja, his visit back
to earth after seven days; where he describes the stroke and his enlightened state in the
hospital where Orsolina and Lucien visited, his insights about his life, his guide Senja advising
him to go back into his anger until he begins seeing his part in the family drama; in which he
returns to his anger about the stroke as he has been instructed; where he talks about looking
for a savior in the medicines he takes, his manipulative and inconsiderate treatment of Angela,
this until Orsolina's son, Jean-Luc, appears and becomes Giovanni's redemption, also the tool
of reconciliation with Lucien, the grandchild Giovanni suspects of being a bastard.*

When seven earth days after my death had passed, my teachers in
the in-between told me that it was time for me to visit my family and
friends again. My guide Senja reminded me that I would have to continue
recounting events from my life to an invisible audience and forget about
telling stories to the golden boy for a while. When anger and resentment
came up for me, I was to let it out and allow myself to be my old self
again, even use my rough language. It would act as a cleansing.

Now it is the third day after Pietro's death. My wife Angela and
our daughter Orsolina are staying at Pietro's wife's place while awaiting
the funeral. The family is sitting around the table, including Pietro's older
son with his wife and kids. There is a discussion about how old I was
when I had the stroke. One of the young ones says dismissively, "Oh, he
was very old." It makes me angry.

I would like the members of the family to know I am there with them, to hear me, but all my efforts are in vain. They don't sense my presence even when I brush against them. I can't make objects move even though I have been told it is possible.

I was seventy when I was struck down. Still in great shape, energetic, independent and fun loving. I liked people. I loved life. I enjoyed building things. And suddenly I was confined, relying on everyone for everything. Was it really ten years sitting in that chair as my family recalls when they still talk about me, which is rare.

Christ, it seems that it's all they remember of me, these ten years. Maybe they don't want to think of who I was before that stroke. They don't want to bring to mind the loudmouth, the womanizer, the tyrant.

They all seem to have forgotten that I made a big effort right after my stroke, before I became totally immobilized. I had my heart set on overcoming my handicap. How hard I tried to walk, to talk, and to do things for myself so I wouldn't be dependent.

What none of them realized—not even I—is that it was my true nature that struck down the aggressive personality I had developed as a result of my beliefs about the world. The stroke and the ten years that went by were necessary for me to resolve the old grudges, and to soften. My guide Senja instructed me to consider that.

Angela and I were still living in Paris. My body was failing me. I had liver problems, blood clots in one leg. My digestive system malfunctioned. There was something wrong with my prostate. For some time I had suspected what Angela and Orsolina were hiding from me: they had found out I had cancer.

Orsolina talked long distance to her mother daily. She wanted me to go to Italy for Laetrile, an alternative treatment for cancer not available in France, insisting that it would cure me. I don't think she even really knew what kind of cancer I had, but like most of us at the time, the big C diagnosis was enough to send her into a panic. It meant that one was condemned to die in the worst agony.

There were stories going around of people screaming in pain day and night when dying of cancer. We had heard an agonizing woman who lived a block away from us begging her family to kill her. Our next-door neighbor lowered her voice when she talked about an acquaintance with cancer as though it were a shameful disease.

So Orsolina convinced her mother to fabricate a story about the urgency of getting the Laetrile treatment for my general health, but they decided to keep me in the dark about the cancer. I went along against my doctor's advice because I was scared, even though I was still dealing with blood clots.

It was customary for physicians not to let their patients know they had cancer so as not to throw them into despair. My doctor didn't believe in alternative treatments and was mostly concerned about the clotting so he wanted me to stay put, but the cancer is what terrified us because my father had died of *'la prostate'* in great pain. That's what people said then, "he died of the prostate," as though it were the prostate itself that was the killer.

Angela and I made the trip to Italy and I came back exhausted. We had been back no more than a week when a cold wave hit Paris. The temperature dropped to forty below. The city turned white, the windows grew flowers of ice. Parisian fountains froze solid while running. My wife and I didn't get out of the house except once, to see my regular doctor about the clotting. When we came back home I couldn't get warm for hours.

The next morning I woke up abruptly at dawn as if struck by lightning. Gigantic fireworks exploded in my brain. An unbearable brightness and then total darkness. In this blackness I saw indescribable things, horrors, tortures, calamities, wars, devastation, cataclysms. People's prayers and supplications formed a thick fog around the earth. Far from reaching their intended destination, God, they got lost in the atmosphere. It was much more than I could handle. All went dark.

I tried to get up but fell on the floor. I called Angela who was still asleep, but no sound came out of my mouth. "I must be in a nightmare," I thought. This kind of thing had happened to me before. I made an effort to wake myself up but to no avail.

As if aware of my silent call, Angela suddenly sat up like she had been stung. When she saw me on the floor, opening and closing my mouth like a fish out of water, she yelled. "Oh my God, what happened to you?" The blood drained from her face. I could clearly see every detail as though looking through a magnifying glass. I looked at her in panic; it was no nightmare.

Within moments I lost all clarity, no longer sure whether I was in the same room as she, whether she could see me or not. She seemed so far from me. All of a sudden I was above it all, looking down. I watched her kneeling next to a body that might be mine. Her panicked questioning echoed from miles away. She shook that body.

Now I was in Angela's mind. Looking at my distorted face she felt that the unavoidable had happened. She had always feared she would have to nurse her second husband, as she had had to look after the first. She would be nailed on that cross again. She tried to pick me up. I was dead weight and she couldn't move me. She ran to get help.

Sirens. Ambulance. Men in white. In the hospital, I moved in and out of my body. I could hear people in the next room as though they were right next to me. I was floating above myself again. Next I was in the operating room witnessing a difficult operation. I heard the jokes of the surgeon and his assistant nurses and knew the patient wouldn't survive. Then all of it stopped. I felt complete emptiness.

The world was breaking down into particles. Everything was vibrating. I noticed a buzzing sound which got stronger and stronger as though a jet was taking off. The sound threw me out of my body. I was moving through the roof, through the atmosphere. Then the noise fell away. I traveled through layers of silence, out of our solar system. I didn't know where I was going but felt safe. I was vaguely aware of my life on earth. The personal history of this small human being down there had little to do with me.

I saw stars, nebulas as I traveled for a very long time, very fast. Then I became aware of sounds, an extraordinary music, bells, a clinking of crystals making the most beautiful harmonies. I went towards the increasing sound. I was conscious of the world I had left, but felt totally detached from it.

I heard a voice in my ear. "There are still things for you to do, you are not finished. You can't stay here, but this place will always be there for you, it won't be lost. You must go back to your family now." Whether it came from within or without I didn't know.

I started traveling back through stars and nebulas. As I approached the earth the beautiful music became so low I could barely hear it anymore. Upon reaching the earth's atmosphere I was hit by the saddest sound. It was the prayers of the people again, like a pleading and moaning that never rose beyond the material plane and had no chance of reaching the god they addressed. The horrendous airplane noise started again.

I didn't want to go back down, but I heard the voice again. "You have been in the peaceful place. You know the way there, but now you are back on earth and need to adjust to its reality. That is what your work will be."

Reluctantly, I went down through the roof, into the room and into my body. I didn't stay long in it. I found that I could move out, hover again and go through walls if I wished to. I explored my surroundings, but didn't get very far because suddenly it was over. I was falling back into my body this time for good. I was like a lump in my bed. A great tiredness came over me.

The next morning the doctor came to my room and announced that I had had a stroke. My whole left side was paralyzed. I was seventy years old. I would never be the same, but with lots of will power and physical therapy I could regain most of my faculties he reassured me.

Orsolina arrived from California two mornings after that and came to the hospital immediately. Pietro's last child, my grandson Lucien, came along because he also wanted to be with me. There was a light around them, a flickering blue light. They didn't seem solid, more like transparent projections of themselves.

That nine-year-old grandson I had always neglected because I knew he was not of our bloodline, peered at me with tear-filled eyes. I saw so much love in them. At that moment I felt closer to him than to my other grandchildren, his brother and sister who were related to me for sure. Maybe my blood was running in his veins after all.

The year was 1968. Orsolina had the morning paper under her arm. She put it on my bed. I remembered that the uprising going on in Paris had greatly disturbed me. People were afraid, talked about civil war, there was some bloodshed. I had seen the horrors of two wars. I had gone through fascism and I couldn't take much more.

In the paper I saw pictures of the insurrection, students taking over universities, uniting with workers to occupy the streets and vandalize the *bourgeois'* cars. Before my stroke I had been outraged at this behavior. How could anyone feel right destroying private property? So irresponsible to damage what people had worked so hard to get. Orsolina and I even had a fight about that. I yelled at her, "Those fucking students are just spoiled rich kids who always had their way and use drugs to escape reality so as not to deal with anything difficult. They have been given too much of everything and they never will be satisfied."

But now I understood something else. I knew what those kids were looking for: freedom from the rules, from restrictions, manipulations, hierarchies, and hypocrisies of the *bourgeois* world. And they had the right to that freedom. They no longer wanted a society based on the exploitation of the masses for the benefit of a few. I knew about that; I had fought for the same things. I had been a Communist. The psychedelics—as I heard their favorite drug called—allowed them to travel in a meaningful world, a spirit world, not unlike what the stroke had done for me. For them, it didn't have the permanent consequences of the stroke.

I talked to Orsolina about all of it in a jumbled, broken speech, but she understood even my silences. She and I were able to communicate with a few words. I could see her amazement at my change of heart. She kept hugging me, and Lucien joined in the embrace. The tears rolled down his cheeks. That much physical contact hadn't happened between my daughter and me since her girlhood, and it had never happened with Lucien.

Christ, it felt good!

RESENTMENT, REFLECTION AND REDEMPTION

After I came back home it was not long before my old self took over. I became more and more embittered by my condition.

Damn the stroke that caused me to spend the next ten years either sitting in my armchair or being wheeled around by Angela. I can't say it enough: when I had retired a year earlier, I was strong, I remodeled my house, grew my garden, and was sociable, always ready for a game of *belotte*, or *pétanque*. I hunted during the season and even took up fishing.

Screw the sickness that turned me into a total recluse. I was fucking ashamed. I had lost my manhood. My body slowly began shrinking. My cheeks became hollow, my skin like wax paper, my high cheekbones protruded. My hooked nose seemed to have lengthened; my eyes were pulled into a slant. Holy shit, when I looked at my face in the mirror one day I saw that my skin had taken on the cloistered appearance of nuns'. I shattered the stupid mirror with my cane. I even started growing boobs!

So I sat all day long with my radio on, dozing. I never really listened to the radio, never really read the newspaper sitting in front of me on the table. They were the last vestiges of my life as a healthy man, and I just liked having them around.

I hardly touched any of the food Angela put in front of me. At the beginning I tried to walk, but the fucking walker gave me the creeps. I had become an old man overnight.

I bought a motorized three-wheeler and took Angela for rides. But one day I lost control of the damn thing around a curve and we ended up in the bushes. Angela had to run for help because she couldn't lift me. That happened twice and I gave it up. I couldn't even talk straight. I only spoke out of necessity, mostly to order Angela around. What a hell of a life for both of us.

For a while I tried to walk with a cane, but I fell a few times and again Angela had to run to get help. I lost heart. I didn't want to get up from my comfortable armchair anymore and I used the walker only when absolutely necessary. I started using the wheelchair more and more to get around.

I didn't want to walk. I didn't want anything. As I look back on that period, everything seems enveloped in a thick fog with a few vibrant clearings here and there, mostly when Orsolina and my grandson were around. Little snapshots. And then the fog again, my mind always clouded, my thoughts disconnected.

When it was time to take my medicines though, I came alive. The devil knows why. All my attention and energy went into the daily ritual of pill taking. My doctor prescribed many of those pills, to make me feel well taken care of I presume. They were all different colors and sizes. My mind was a blur for Christ sake. I could hardly remember things from one minute to the next, but I knew all those pills by name, size, color, and hour of day. Nothing else was of interest to me.

I see it now. Among those brightly colored pills a savior might have been hidden. I didn't put it in these words, but hung on to that belief. I had given up on saints to intervene on my behalf, but I still hoped for a redeemer. If I moaned, complained and asked for justice, constantly bargained with the Big-Father-in-the-Sky, I could win His pity, me, so small and defenseless.

But the pills didn't work. Was it then that I really gave up? I can't clearly remember. Even in the place where I am now, things are often blurred, out of sequence or unreliable when I try to recollect—as my teachers advise me to do.

Damn it. Instead of getting easier to move, as I was told it would be if I kept exercising, it became more difficult. My words became more slurred, and only those who lived with me could understand what I said.

The more helpless I became, the more my distrust of life and people increased. I was such a bastard, demanding utmost devotion from Angela. She had to tend to all my needs, run to my side when I called. What an asshole I was, impatiently banging my cane against the floor or the wall to get immediate attention. This went on for ten years.

Angela took care of me way beyond what should have been expected of her. Devotion was a vocation with her. It allowed her to feel good about herself I believe. She never expressed resentment and went about her business looking tired, full of pity for her poor husband.

I fucking resented the freedom she had to walk around when I couldn't, to enjoy things I couldn't. I was in a constant funk. I set up emotional snares and used everything I could think of to entrap her.

Convinced she was involved with another man I spent my days

trying out maneuvers to find out what the hell was going on behind my back. My obsession was to wring more pity out of her, more devotion. If she tried to get me to do things for myself I growled. I made visitors feel uncomfortable so I could have her to myself. I couldn't stand to have her attention go to others.

Orsolina came from California every year for a month or so. Not really enough I complained. She tried to get me to overcome my handicap, urging me to do the things I still could do.

"People in worse condition and much older have succeeded in getting over their disability," she reasoned. What a bunch of crap, I thought. I fucking hated reason and I half listened, waiting for her to be finished so I could ask her to help me with something I could easily have done for myself.

Lucien asked his parents if he could spend some of his school vacations with us in Lerné. He wheeled me around and willingly did any favor I asked of him. He was the only one in the family who didn't tell me I should do things for myself.

All the strength I had left went into manipulating the family around me. I perfected my skills and became a master at controlling others from my chair, using my wits to have my whims satisfied. Holy shit! I succeeded most of the time.

This went on until the golden boy, Orsolina's child, was born. Then I saw the light, or rather a new light was shed on things. Lucien, when he was in Lerné, loved to play with baby Jean-Luc. It cracked me up the way he threw him up in the air to make him laugh. Together we tried to teach the baby new babbling words.

As Jean-Luc grew into a toddler he loved to sit on his little bench right next to my chair. We played together with beads, coins or blocks. When he built something I liked, I gave him one of the green pastilles he adored.

So the sun began shining in my life. Under that new light I looked at my passage on earth. Wasn't I responsible for having brought a partner into the family furniture business instead of passing it on to Pietro? Trouble was, I didn't trust Pietro to be able to handle it on his own.

Didn't I damage my son's self-confidence by berating him so much of the time? I overworked him. Didn't that cause him to neglect his wife? I came upon the new partner and Pietro's wife in a passionate embrace one day. Why didn't I get rid of the man right then? When Lucien was born, convinced he was not Pietro's son, I decided to reveal what I knew. How could I be so sure?

It was the first time in my life that I looked at my mistakes, the first time I felt partly responsible for the way things had turned out.

One summer, when Lucien was visiting us and Orsolina had come to Lerné from California with my little Jean-Luc, I asked Angela to bring me some of the things that were precious to me, things I had made, a cane with two snakes wrapping around and joining heads on the pommel, a mandolin encrusted with mother of pearl designs, a box covered with carvings that locked with a silver key, a hand-carved frame with the only photo of my family in Italy. Then I told Angela to ask Lucien to come to my room. He came holding Jean-Luc and sat him down on the bed. My golden child began playing with some of the objects. "Hand this to Lucien," I told him, showing him how. One after another the objects were given to Lucien in that way. He looked at me questioningly.

"Here," I said, "those are all things I made when I was still a good craftsman. They are yours now. When Jean-Luc grows up you can share them with him if you want."

So I began to see the work I had to do.

Orsolina

We are what we are looking for. —*Sainte Némoise*

37

PIETRO DECIDES TO VISIT MALVA

In which Orsolina confronts her feelings upon meeting members of the family and sits with her brother's dead body that has now relaxed; where she tries to start a conversation with her dead brother about what he really knew of his wife's illicit liaison and the child that might not be his—Lucien; in which she recalls the last days of Giovanni when Pietro takes advantage of his father's weakness to confront him; where Giovanni for the first time in his life has some kind words about his first wife Malva; in which Italian relatives help Pietro decide to go visit his mother after all these years; where Giovanni surprises everyone by approving of the visit.

Simone's apartment sits on the ground floor of a three-story building in a residential compound within a small park. On the morning after our arrival I take a walk and when I get back some family members I haven't seen for years are standing outside the door talking. They have come for the wake and wear a somber look befitting the circumstances. I feel my mother stiffen as she goes to greet some cousins. I walk by everyone nodding to them, and straight to the room where the corpse is kept in an open coffin. I hug Simone who is standing at the door, take a chair and sit by the coffin, making it obvious that I need to be left alone.

Pietro's face has relaxed now; he seems to have accepted his death even though there was much left unresolved in his life. However, he did see his mother one last time, and forgave his father.

Maybe you can talk to me Pietro, you must know much more than I do now. Were you Giovanni's son or were we not related at all? The thought is appalling, but it is not entirely inpossible. Could we have lived

*the romantic love I fantasized was ours as a child without breaking any
taboos or was that picture some remnant of another life?*

*Did you know about your wife Simone's liaison Pietro, and that
your son Lucien might not be really yours? I believe that for years Simone
lived with the fear of being uncovered but consoled herself with the
thought that at least the family was spared any suffering. Did you know
that Pietro? I suspected that you did and that your children somewhere did
also.*

As our father grew weaker, the confrontations between him and
Pietro were constant. Towards the end however, when Giovanni understood it was death he'd have to surrender to, he tried to make friends with
his son. To tame the fear of his demise, he entreated death to have compassion, "Get me soon but be gentle about it, come get me in my sleep,"
he'd say, not a bit embarrassed to be thought a softy and to talk openly to
his death in front of Pietro and me.

Over the weeks Giovanni removed himself more and more, and
Pietro who was ready to confront his father for the first time in his life,
became incensed to find no one to battle against. In a last effort to get a reaction out of Giovanni Pietro tried something new. One day he announced,
"I am going to take Simone and the kids to Italy to visit my mother."

At this the old man nodded. "You are doing what's right," he
answered as if it were something he had already thought about. Pietro just
about fell over.

A week later Pietro was lecturing our father about being so hard on
Angela. "Give her a break. Do you want to kill her? She has been such a
devoted wife, has done so much for you. She keeps taking care of you
even though she is exhausted, and she never complains about your
unreasonable demands. Not many women would do that," he said.
Giovanni interrupted with a wave of his hand and softly whispered, "Your
mother would have done the same."

"What? My mother would have done the same?" Pietro repeated the
words in total disbelief. Our father nodded, "Yes, you have heard it right."
Was it the old man's last joke or a step towards redemption? We never
found out, for Giovanni refused to say more in spite of all our questions. It
was at that moment that Pietro started to seriously consider going to
Noiaris with his family.

For better or for worse, the gossip road back and forth from Noiaris
to Paris was kept opened by strings of visiting relatives with news and
presents. "Your mother is not getting any younger," his cousins kept tel-

ling Pietro. "Lately, she has been mentioning your name a lot. Her dearest wish is to be able to see her oldest son again before she dies," they added. This insistent shared voice eventually made its way in. Pietro arranged to go to Italy with his wife and children to see his mother that very summer.

From what I heard, Malva had had a few other children from different beds, but her firstborn, the one who had been taken away from her, was the one most present on her mind at that time of her life. She had raised her other children alone, asking for no help. The flourmill her father had left her when he died supported them. As years went by it had become more and more difficult to make a living at it. People bought their bread already made and much less flour needed grinding. But she had taught her children well.

"An exemplary mother," our relatives reluctantly admitted after decades of considering her an outcast. Her courage and initiative in all circumstances, her heroism during the war earned her the esteem of the villagers. Our uncle, Giovanni's brother, wrote Pietro to convince him to visit his mother. All our relatives and Malva's family members joined in their effort to engineer the reunion. A Parisian cousin of Pietro returning from Noiaris after a vacation brought back a message from Malva asking her son for forgiveness and pleading for a meeting.

Pietro's response was a note with these few words, "We are coming."

 # ietro

It is through hunger that we participate in the cosmos.

—*Sainte Némoise*

38

PIETRO AND HIS FAMILY VISIT MALVA

In which Pietro describes how he is made to witness his mother Malva on the day she waited to be reunited with her first born after thirty-seven years, his surprise at his father's change of heart about his first wife; where we see how he makes the decision to go to Italy and see his mother.

While dwelling in the restful place, scenes from my life come to pass in front of me not always of my own volition. I see Malva as she waits for me, her fifty-year-old, the son she hadn't seen since he was thirteen. I see me driving my family towards her after thirty-seven years of avoidance. Earlier, when I had mentioned Angela's devotion to him Giovanni replied, "Your mother would have done as much for me. It's a good idea for you to go visit her." I was stunned and my decision was made right then.

Malva knows I am coming. She couldn't sleep all night although I was not due till the next evening. It's dawn now; she gets up, dresses carefully and walks to the front door. She notices how badly chipped the paint is; too late to do anything about it. She pushes the door and stands on the threshold, leaning against the wall. After a while she goes down the four steps leading to the yard, walks across and opens the gate to the henhouse. The hens immediately get out and busy themselves behind the rooster, mimicking him as he shows them how to peck their way through the yard. *As though they can't figure it out for themselves,* she thinks.

Without a rooster it seems that hens wouldn't know how to scratch the ground for food, maybe not even how to lay an egg. Females, always needing a male to lead them! As if agreeing, the rooster crows proudly over the flock he protects.

"You've got to get males off your eyeballs before you can see for yourself," she whispers throwing a handful of corn to the hens. Her eyes linger on the sun-stroked feathers scalloped around the wings, the eyelets like scales around the neck. A tense swish suddenly warns her. A quick side-glance catches the angered coxcomb, the green sheen on the sharp blades of black moiré. The rooster is coming at her. She picks up a stick to defend herself, but the rooster changes direction at the last moment, jumps on a negligent follower and pulls on the neck feathers. The hen's screeches drive Malva away.

She goes back and resumes her station by the door. She follows the flight of seven crows on the tangerine sky. Their raucous cries echo into the hills, shrieks of alarm tossed back and forth. Tales of disasters and sorrow that took place in those hills come to her mind, old stories buried deep in dark earth and oozing out from rusty scars on the mountainside. It's already getting hot in spite of the early hour, but a cool breeze comes up and relieves her anguish. She feels as if she is just now being born to the world.

Dawn retrieves rocks, trees, animals, and buildings out of obscurity one by one. Pink fingers point towards the hills where ochre layers piled up by time crumble like too rich a cake a giant spat out after taking a few bites. The heat rises slowly. Dewdrops enfolding tiny rainbows suddenly let go of the leaves they were clinging to and fall on Malva's hair. The grass winks, alive with hundreds of sparkles. She feels a tickle on the tip of her tongue and her body seems to expand. She steps back and looks at the valley below. A small apron of earth between two branches of a tumultuous torrent catches her attention; she believes she sees every small pebble, every tiny insect.

Frogs begin their orchestrated croaking and startle her. All at once they jump into the pond on the other side of the yard among a nimbus of ripples. *They must have a director to be in such unison,* she thinks. The lily pad is in full bloom. She desires one of those lilies intensely in the same way she longed for things as a child, a craving so deep it hurts. That longing had always been there.

She picks a rose from a bush climbing on the side of the house, fondles it and nibbles on one of the petals, then lets it slip through her fingers. The air temperature continues to rise; when it matches the one of her body, her outlines melt away. It's like being woven into the dancing light along with birds, flowers, pebbles, dew drops. She is one with this festive world and doesn't make a move, for any movement may prevent her son's car from getting there. It needs all her attention to materialize. A gust of wind comes up again and takes away her concentration. She looks around. It's like she has never seen this place before, this place she has tended since the day of her birth, this place she has never left even for just one day.

Her life seems to spin away from a tilting world. Something had prevented her from looking at things as they really were. In the first part of her life her wild longings and desires made her forget everything else. In later years, she sought refuge from the overwhelming passions of youth into a life defined in terms of routine and chores: breakfast, lunch, dinner, the mill, the children, the animals, the fields—so busy she never noticed the joy of it all.

She tries to imagine the car that will bring her son back to her. If she lets go of her vigil it might not appear. She will make it come true by the sheer force of her will. She'll stay right there on that spot and guard that image.

She remains in silent contemplation for hours, eyes intently fixed on some point of the horizon. Members of the family, as they get up, don't dare interrupt. No one offers her any food, afraid they might break the spell.

A sudden splash in the pond. She turns and sees the water lapping the bushes. Her dog Sabbio has jumped in. The smell of stagnant water leaves a taste of silt in her mouth. Her throat is dry, she is thirsty but won't move. Sabbio swims after some ducks; she doesn't bother ordering him to come back.

The early afternoon heat closes in. She is dripping. Water voices murmur into her ear, each voice with a story to tell. As she listens she notices her thirst again, but she is used to it by now and ignores it. A beetle climbs the rough bark of the big apple tree. It opens a path into her memory. She remembers me as a child. Her first baby, my first steps, my first words and then, the awful day when I was stolen away from her.

She sits down on the last step and she stares for hours, oblivious of herself. The day is reaching towards its end when the long-awaited car appears on the road. She follows it as it goes out of sight around the last curve before entering the village, and then reappears on the dirt road coming up to her house. When it stops, the smell of exhaust delights her nostrils. She relaxes her watch, pulls out of her trance. She has succeeded.

The car bringing her son back has materialized.

She catches sight of me at the wheel, a middle-aged bulky man. She watches the car slowly coming to a stop. When I get out, hesitating, unsure of my next step, she stands. I face her but can't look into her eyes. I wait for the rest of the family to get out. My youngest son Lucien comes out first and pushes me towards her. I feel as embarrassed as a young child who doesn't know what is expected of him. Slowly, I make my way towards her who stands there not moving. Before I reach her she senses my body in her own—a husk around one intense little seed in the center. Only when I get close do I look up at her. The seed inside explodes, the husk bursts open. Little slivers rush madly back and forth stirring up ashes that were still hot.

More explosions and my heart starts racing wildly along with hers. Whole parts of myself I'd believed dead or nonexistent come into life. Knots are untied, seams come undone leaving me torn, caught between outrageous joy and unbearable pain. I want to laugh, I want to cry. I'm shivering all over. One more step and I will reach her, but I stop, flushed and confused. The rest of the family remains a few feet behind. I feel their presence as a huge load I must carry forward.

For a minute she remains there, pale as death. Everything is suspended. Then, very slowly, she extends one hand towards me as if to help me up the steps. It's the signal I was waiting for. I race up the stairs and finding her arms open to receive me I forget my bulk, fling myself against her with no thought of sparing her.

She braces herself to receive the shock. Her arms close around me. She trembles. I can't say a word and begin sobbing, little sobs, hiccough-like. She pats my head gently as if to reassure me. Soon her tears join mine, big tears silently rolling down her cheeks.

Normally, I'd tower over her, being a tall broad man—and she, such a small woman—but I must have shrunk for in her arms I feel so small. She strokes my hair, murmuring sweet nothings like a young mother to her little son. Her womb aches.

There we stay, oblivious of others, crying, unashamed, as the rest of the family waits for a more formal introduction.

I watch us, mother and son, crying. So many tears to wash away the bitterness of thirty-seven years. How long to fill the huge hole that sucked everything dry, so dry the source had been depleted and the shrunken container leaked. It has to expand again before it can keep water in. When it fills up, the crying subsides.

Orsolina

*Become the watcher of your own marionettes, sustain your attention
and bring about their transformation.* —Sainte Némoise

39

MOLESTORS

*In which Orsolina recalls how in pre-adolescence she fell in love so easily but soon
rejected the objects of her infatuation, how she despised good boys and good girls, how she
came to distrust men and develop cynicism; where in adolescence she looks for love in off-beat
places and how she encounters exhibitionism at a neighbor's whose daughter plays strange
sexual games; in which she describes the perverts and sexual deviants her friends and she got
used to in the city, and how the penis becomes an object of repulsion; where we learn that her
distrust of men even includes her father and brother.*

Tomorrow the funeral will take place. My mother has relaxed and
is taking care of Simone who is a nervous wreck. I mostly stay in my
bedroom to write in my journal or read, but I was in the living room when
one of the neighbors stopped by to offer Simone his support. There is
something sleazy about that man. It brings to mind an early experience I
had with an exhibitionist, a next-door neighbor I had long forgotten about,
or whose memory I had buried.

I was thirteen. I had never seen a penis in my life. On that day I
found it revolting and all men became suspicious to me.

The attic where Bologna had lived and died had been remodeled
into a new comfortable apartment. A nice family, the Verrails, had moved
there; the daughter, Michelle, more than a year younger than I, the father,
an engineer who traveled often to Africa, and the mother, a plain house-
wife from a well-to-do provincial family.

Michelle befriended me and often wanted me to come upstairs to their apartment because her mother was reluctant to let her out of her sight and play with the street kids as I did. The game Michelle wanted to enact with me took a turn that intrigued me as well as shocked me, but I was not going to let myself be surprised by a girl nearly two years younger than I was. Where could she have learned about all that stuff though, such a protected little girl.

In childhood, my friend Françoise and I had done much exploration of each other's body, at first giving one another innocent backrubs, later frequenting the municipal showers where we played at being girl-friend and boyfriend, caressing each other all over. At that time in the lower class sections of Paris no homes except the rich households—and for some reason our apartment—were equipped with a bathroom. People went to the baths on Saturday to get clean for the week. The rest of the time they took sponge baths. My mother found it strange that I wanted to go there since we had our own bathtub, but I told her that I preferred showers to baths and that all my friends went there. It only cost pennies.

But Michelle explored in a totally new way. She made up stories: she was my boyfriend and we stroked each other all over, kissed and wrote enflamed letters. At times she would pretend I had my period. I was a late bloomer, I very recently menstruated for the first time and knew next to nothing about it. She said she loved my blood so much. She pretended to caress the bloody spot between my legs, to smear it all over herself and lick the blood that had dribbled down. All of it was just imagination and story telling. Only a very small part was actually enacted.

One day I went up to the Verrails' apartment to return a pan my mother had borrowed. I was hoping Michelle was there, but she had gone shopping with her mother. Monsieur Verrail was alone at home. When I knocked at the front door he yelled that it was open and to come right in. The door to the kitchen was ajar and I saw him sitting at the table reading a magazine. I told him about returning the pan and he asked me to come and see something. He was pointing at the magazine. I came closer to look at it but he took my hand to direct it not to the magazine, but to his exposed penis under it. My hand actually touched it.

It looked and felt like a slug to me, veiny and slimy, horribly ugly. I don't think it was hard. I had never seen a penis in my life. I jumped back in horror and ran back to the front door. I was so distressed it took me a few seconds to fumble with the latch, time enough for him to shout, "don't tell anyone."

And I didn't. Shame seeped inside of me like sewage water. I felt dirty all over. I wanted to crawl in a hole and be buried. It took me two weeks to tell my mother. When I did she was appalled, but in the end not totally surprised. She asked me not to say anything to my father because he was capable of going up and shooting the man with his hunting gun. And the silence closed in on the secret. I didn't mention it another time, but never again played with Michelle.

Later that month, my friend Françoise and I were taking the trash down to the downstairs hallway when we noticed a pile of small publications on top of the big garbage can. Curious, we looked through them; they were the porno magazines of the time, not very graphic, mostly naked women playing with naked men, but a lot of it involved naked children. We had never seen such things and giggled the whole time as we paged through. Was it Mr. Verrail who left those for me to find? If so, I didn't want him to think I had picked them up, so we left them exactly as we had found them.

After that incident the penis became an object of repulsion and all men were sordid to me, not to be trusted. Even my father and brother; I never wanted to be left alone in a room with them. I avoided kissing them good night, stepped away when they put an arm over my shoulder.

Once, during a family vacation at friends I had to sleep in a dorm situation, on a cot next to a girl and a boy my age, in the same room as a man in his forties. I became convinced the next day that the man had snuck into my bed during the night and impregnated me while I was asleep. I was distressed for weeks.

Tu es devenue assez cynique je crois. Didn't you become quite jaded soon after that?

In pre-adolescence, following a couple of devastating realizations about male figures I respected, something insidious made its way inside me, cynicism.

In adolescence, good boys repulsed me. If they dared being attracted to me either for friendship or romance I battered them like a cat a mouse. I had no pity for the opposite sex. Hadn't they enslaved generations of powerful women? They deserved what they got from me. I regularly fell madly in love with some boy with beautiful eyes, beguiled him and then dropped him when the novelty had worn off.

On the traces of the *existentialistes,* the *zazous,* the hipsters with whom I danced be-bop or swing in the *caves* of St-Germain-des-Prés, I looked for passion. I tracked the boy that would become my hero for a while.

I am sixteen. I hunt for love in my long black sweater, heavy skull medallion and tight jeans. I wear my school clothes when I say goodbye to my mother, but then I go downstairs to the basement where the garbage is kept and change into the hip outfit I had hidden from her.

I stride towards the *caves* on the Left Bank where I go dance when school is out. The hot tongue of jazz rising from the bowels of the earth licks my skin and floods my pores, enticing my ballet-slippered feet down the steps.

I am looking for my echo, my other, in the ensnaring solo of the tenor sax that enters my chest like a sexy voice, descending into my belly to light a slow burning fire. Who can resist the deep penetration of sound?

I am looking for my other, the sister I never knew, the soul brother who betrayed me. I recognize the love of my life, he has green eyes, he plays saxophone. I haven't met him yet. He is a sailor. He'll open the world for me, and all its mysteries, he'll render legible the unfathomable strangers that inhabit Paris. He'll show me what drives painters, authors, musicians and poets to the creative impulse. He'll show me what a gift it is to be a woman.

I am looking for my other, but I don't know him yet, I catch only the echo of an echo of myself. I am looking for the love before love in every good-looking boy with fiery eyes, and I taste the breath that makes me woman on the tongue of many handsome youths.

I am looking for love; it used to be easy. Even as I pushed through the passage on the horrendous journey towards birth there were others to accompany me. And then, there was my mother's breast pulsing under her light flowered dress, the tit I could take in my mouth, the love I could milk. Soon there was the sentient teddy bear bestowing affection and acceptance, but it was never enough. I wanted a sister, a twin, a lover.

My dance partner is already there. He is not my other, but I desire the flow of desire that turns my body to water as the jazz takes possession of our feet. We dance to find love, in a circle of longing.

Et puis un jour ta mère t'a suivie.

Indeed. One day, my mother snuck behind me and followed me to the left bank where I met my bohemian friends. She waited until we were walking down the *Boulevard St-Michel* and pretended to come across us by chance. I was outraged to have that happen in front of my cool friends and asked her what right she had to follow me. We had an altercation and she slapped my face. I didn't forgive her for the longest time; I believed she had greatly affronted a woman wiser than she was.

By then my girlfriends and I were so used to voyeurs, exhibitionists, men exposing themselves in the *métro,* in parks, in front of the *pissotières*—those stinky Parisian street urinals revealing the piss-soaked bread under the feet of the men that relieved themselves—that we made a joke of it all. We threw a few worthless coins at the feet of men who exposed their penis, snickering and joking that their show was not worth much more than that. We had become hardened city girls, sarcastic, cynical.

As I got older I became wiser about disillusionment. Whenever I encountered someone I perceived as a hero or a god, someone who deified me also, I made sure to cut the relationship short so as not to be disenchanted. I wanted to leave this perfect being with a glorified image of me. I knew that if I stayed around too long the real me would start showing and I would fall off the pedestal—and so would he. Like Humpty Dumpty, none of the king's horses or the king's men would be able to put me together again.

Tu ne te demandes pas quand ton amour pour Pietro a tourné à l'indifférence?

Yes, I do wonder. When is it that my love and infatuation for Pietro turned to indifference and even repugnance? When is it that we fell off our respective pedestals, and when did the golden cloud on which we had placed our mutual admiration burst into poisonous rain? When did we absent ourselves?

Is it when Pietro married Simone or is it as a consequence of that neighbor so rudely uncovering his organ, soiling my hand and deflowering my eyes?

Pietro was lost to me when he became just another man in my eyes—all of them wanting to possess and dirty my body, bury my soul inside of them to use it as they may. I started to believe that men wished to kill women's spirits so we could become their slaves.

ietro

Your job as a keeper of memory is to have a good time, be clear about who you are and the assignment that has been given to you.
—*Sainte Némoise*

40

FOLLOWING THE HEARSE

In which Pietro and Giovanni are following the hearse together and where we witness Pietro's happiness at being missed so much, although he finds some room for regrets and is concerned about his father; where Orsolina and Lucien walk hand in hand reminding Pietro of lovers, where he reflects on the fact that Orsolina and he might have been lovers in another lifetime and how he influences Lucien to ask questions.

My father Giovanni and I follow the hearse that brings my body to the church for the funeral service. My funeral is very well attended. How good it feels to see family and friends shedding so many tears and, judging by the amount of flowers and wreaths sharing the hearse space with my coffin, I am well loved and missed. I still care about that. It touches a place I now realize was starved all my life. I hope my father does not feel slighted by this display, he who had such a small congregation following his coffin.

I must admit that I do have regrets about not attending every moment of my life as fully as I do now. Yamill told me that here there is no room for regrets, but how can I avoid them when I was not really living my life but the life of someone else. Principles that were not my own and rules that I didn't make governed me. I wanted to make everyone happy, be loved, but since I was really that other Pietro no one knew, I never felt loved for myself.

Giovanni directs me forward, it's like a gentle force pulling me. My awareness goes to Orsolina and Lucien walking together holding hands. Heads together, they are whispering to each other. They look like lovers.

I stay behind them and follow my sister's footsteps. At the place where she puts her feet down, the pavement holds her shadow memory. When I walk in Orsolina's steps I am filled with her inner self and become one with her physical being. I experience all her thoughts, feelings, memories, emotions.

That's what we wanted to achieve in our lifetime and never could. Orsolina might have wanted to break the societal taboo and be lovers at one time. She never clearly said so but I believed she suggested it. Or is it I who made that up? Did I dream the whole thing?

I have learned since that we were lovers in the life before this last one, but our relationship couldn't work because of the betrayal curse in our ancestry. In the life before that we were twins but we were separated by cruel circumstances. Will we have to go through the torture of separation again or have we learned enough to move on?

I don't feel Giovanni's presence any longer. He led me here and disappeared. I probably had guessed right. It might have been hard for him to see how much more grieved I was than he had been. I know that he will come back when it is time for us to do more work together.

For a while now Orsolina has been able to pick up the memories I send her. I try the same technique on Lucien. I want him to learn more about our family. To my surprise he is the one to ask Orsolina the things I wanted him to know about. It is that easy to reach him.

 **ucien**

To fear death is an insult to life.   —*Sainte Némoise*

41

ENTRE NOUS

In which Lucien asks Orsolina what she remembers about her change of name and of Pietro as a godfather; where she tells him what a good father Pietro was to his children but to her also, how she missed him when he went away with friends; where Pietro introduces the idea of the instability of memories.

"I seem to remember something about your last name not always being Spiazzi," I ask. "Did you have a different last name in your early childhood? What was that all about? It always seemed like such a taboo subject. Wasn't *Pépé* your real father?"

"It was never talked about, so I didn't question," Orsolina replies. "I accepted what I was told about my father being at war and all that. It was only in my teens that it dawned on me: the banquet following my change of name and my baptism had also celebrated *Papa*'s and *Maman*'s wedding. Giovanni had finally obtained a divorce from his first wife, Malva, your grandmother, and that was big cause for celebration. For my benefit however, the story was different, and it made sense to me at the time. *Papa* had been in the army fighting the enemies when I was born, and he was unable to come back for my birth and give me his name. So I was registered under my mother's. I didn't find anything wrong with that."

"Kids at school didn't ask questions? Were you teased about changing your last name? No one ever pointed out the oddity or questioned your paternity?"

"At that time and in our *quartier*, there were lots of immigrants with strange customs and strange names. To us kids, one name was as good as another. Typical French names like, *Desmoulins, Desjardins, Delacroix, Ducimetierre, Boulanger, Belavoine, Deschamps, Dubois,* usually designated something. The teacher explained to us that way back, people's last names were often their profession or the place where they lived. An abandoned baby might be given the name of the place where it was found. I loved when our teacher took the roll every morning, because so many last names raised pictures of country scenes, mills and gardens, oak trees, a cross in a cemetery, a baker with good oats, a hamlet by the well, the edges of fields and forest. Foreign names didn't have any meaning we knew of, and we accepted them as such."

"So in the end what was the truth about your name change and your late baptism?"

"I guess that in those days the man who wanted to give his name to a child had to be present if he was not married to the woman giving birth. Besides, your *Pépé*'s divorce from Malva was not finalized, so my mother put her name on the birth certificate."

"And it was all hushed because your parents didn't want you to know that they lived together in sin, right? What were you told exactly?"

"When my father came back after the war, he took matters into his hands. That's what I was told. To prove he was my real father he had to present his case to the authorities and they made him produce complicated documents he had to send to Italy for. In fact, he was waiting for his French nationality so he could get a divorce. After years of efforts he was allowed to give me his name, also your father's name. I was pleased about having Pietro's last name."

"Didn't Pietro become your godfather at that time?"

"Yes. Since an illegitimate child could not get baptized, we had to wait for the baptism until I legally became my father's child. When it finally happened I was old enough to answer myself the questions Pietro and Simone, as my godfather and godmother, would have answered for me had I been a baby. Pietro was so proud of me. He praised me for being one of the few children able to take responsibility for my own baptism. He assured me that it was an unusual honor. I understand now that he wanted to make me feel all right about the peculiarity of being baptized at that age."

"Was he a good godfather?"

"In my mind a godfather was a more complete version of a father, a younger one. Pietro fit the picture. He was the only person with whom I could talk about God. And God interested me no end."

"He loved to have those kinds of talks with us also."

"I know that Pietro was a great father to you kids, and he was to me also. When he still lived at home he came back early from work in the evening to be with me. We talked, played games, and often he read me stories, a thing my parents hardly ever had the time to do. He never raised his voice or forced me to obey the rules. I did what he asked me to because I loved him, just like with my aunts. He always found time for me even when he was in a hurry. But Sunday was his day to be with friends. I had the morning with him, but in the afternoon he left me behind. His friends came on their bicycles with sparkling wheels. They were like a flurry of birds. They whizzed by, swept my brother away before I could even say goodbye. And I was left alone for the day, left to find ways to entertain myself."

"So did you feel very sad?"

"After a while I learned to distract myself with other occupations besides morosely swinging a pendulum back and forth to the great distress of my mother: to the right, he will come back soon, to the left, he will never come back. I drew, I colored, I painted. Later I began to write a diary, but I kept waiting for him. If the day was sunny they didn't come back until late afternoon, their bicycles decorated with bouquets of the flowers that were in season. I mostly recall the daffodils—such a ray of sunshine. If it started raining I was happy. They came back early."

"It was the same with us, Pietro was a great father but so often absent. On weekends he was always working to make extra money. Mother was a spendthrift and they could never make ends meet. But there was more to it, I sensed a discomfort about being home. Something weird was going on in our house. It disturbed me, made me sad. Do you have any idea why Pietro became such a workaholic? Also, why was my older brother so hard on me, so angry all the time, and why did he leave home so early? And why, tell me, why was Simone's love for me so excessive and suffocating?"

Orsolina is just about to answer when a woman interrupts her and starts walking along with us, offering me her condolences, then sharing her memories of Pietro.

Pietro

Death doesn't extinguish life, it enhances it. —*Sainte Némoise*

42

REAL LIFE IS ELSEWHERE
In which Pietro ponders the validity of humans' memories as he sits in the church next to Orsolina and Lucien during his funeral.

In my travels through time I have learned that the memories of mortals are very unstable, so much so that the accurate recall of past events is practically impossible. Someone can easily be influenced by another to create a memory of something that never took place; once the memory is repeatedly seeded by someone of authority, the person accepts it as his or her own. Different witnesses to an event will remember things entirely differently and be sure that their version is the right one. Life on earth is but a dream, real life is elsewhere. Lucien will not find out at this time what he needs to know. It would only be one version of it anyhow, and those kinds of things are supposed to remain *entre nous*, between those already in the know.

Orsolina, the chatty woman and Lucien walk inside the church to-gether and find a place in the first row. Giovanni has come back and we sit next to them in our invisible form. No one will offer us their condolences, but we have our way of getting a kiss, a hug that was destined for someone else: the grieved widow, the offspring, the sister. We steal that kiss, moving in front of the intended receiver. A kiss on both cheeks, two times on each, as though we had a body—better even, for we appreciate so much this last physical contact. We deserve it, we have worked for it.

Orsolina

*Your work as a conscientious objector is to change the paradigm
and confuse everyone about what they think they know.*

—*Sainte Némoise*

43

CONSCIOUSNESS
*In which Orsolina contemplates her early life and her disillusionments, her
rebelliousness as she observes adults and her determination not to become like them; where in
her sleeplessness she reflects on writing, on old age and death; in which she has a dream.*

In the bedroom I share with my mother at Simone's I cannot sleep.
Angela is gently snoring in the bed next to me. She will easily put everything unpleasant behind her, reject what she does not like and continue
with life. Those are things that happen; survivors learn to accept and go
on.

But I am not like her. I take my thinking much too seriously. I still
suspect that rude encounter with our neighbor's penis to have tainted the
following years. After that first disillusionment about men, I went from
disappointment to disappointment in the world of adults.

Starting to write my first journal saved me from feeling sorry for
myself when a friend ditched me; with my second journal I found that
when I wrote about secrets they ceased to be a terrible burden; my third
was about resisting the grand adult scheme to make us docile so we would
embrace the beliefs of the exploited masses.

I had an ally, Huguette. *Métro-boulot-dodo, le cauchemar.* The
subway-job-sleep syndrome was our nightmare. Just to make sure not to
forget, we regularly took the métro early in the morning at rush time.

People were packed, the last ones pushed into the already crowded car in order to get in and allow the doors to close. The smell of sweat, sour socks, the disgusting promiscuity that allowed dirty old men to place their wandering hands, as if by mistake, on pubescent asses, the crusty eyes, the unbearable heat, all that sealed our solemn promise: we would not succumb. We would not be slaves. We would never take a nine to five job. If perchance one of those drifting hands ended up on Huguette's bottom she would grab it and hold it up asking very loudly, "whose hand is it that feels me up?" And everyone would stare at the offender who wiggled away in humiliation and got out at the next stop.

Fascinated by *la bande à Bonnot*—a group of young anarchists who became bank robbers—we embraced radical ideas and rebelled. We had very little respect for instructors who we believed were part of the conditioning. Huguette was a great comedian and mime. She could imitate any of our teachers so well she would have the class in stitches. When we studied *La Commune* and the French revolution, we talked the other students into coming to class wearing red ribbons around their necks. Red ribbons symbolized being ready to make heads fall, our history teacher told us. It was fun to see her look of alarm in the morning.

The written word became my companion. Writing was like a breath of life, a tool to learn about myself. Soon I discovered poetry. My hand moved, liberated from the encumbrance of my will, free from planning or thinking. It was like a direct intervention from the spirit. I loved the forgetfulness that movement brought when it was not controlled by the mind. I witnessed the birth of sentences that bypassed my will and showed up on the page. They taught me something new, something I didn't even know I wanted to learn. Painting had the same kind of movement. Suddenly the brush would move of its own accord and I was more myself than ever; blissful, I followed that brush guiding and supporting me. I no longer felt that real life was elsewhere; I was in it.

I still can't sleep. I hear steps in the hallway. Someone coming home late or it's an insomniac like me. I look at my mother sound asleep next to me. She has this fortunate capacity to sleep through the worst events of her life, a blessing that has allowed her to remain healthy in her older years.

It's easy to forget that old people were once young, that life is pitifully short. Sometimes I wish to die right now so as to get to my end instead of rushing towards it, so as not to witness my loved ones dying. I want to be finished with all the activities that inevitably lead to old age and death.

But let's not go into that. I make my breathing fit the rhythm of my mother's and after a while I fall asleep. I wake up the next morning and catch this dream as it is just about to dissolve.

I am standing on the edge of a precipice with another pregnant woman who is due at about the same time I am. I have been cautioned not to venture too close to the edge, not to go farther than the roped off area, for if I do I might not be able to get back. But I don't obey rules. I talk my friend into going with me a little farther beyond the line, to the place where some narrow steps carved in the rock vanish into the earth.

Suddenly the ground starts shaking violently. We are both thrown down the stairs into a narrow passage. Rocks fly all around and hit us from every direction as we tumble farther down the tunnel, landing in the bowels of the earth. No sooner do we reach the bottom than we are ejected again, thrown against walls, churned around and swallowed up. My terrified friend and I end up in a sort of grotto, sorry not to have paid heed to the warning.

The heat is unbearable. The sides of the small niche where we have taken refuge slowly close in on us until we are squeezed so tight we can neither move nor breathe. We believe we'll be crushed to death. There is no choice but to pray and surrender. Suddenly, the sides open up and we are free from the pressure, but it's not long before the upheaval starts again. Around us, other beings are also struggling. We cannot help each other. Everyone has to go through this passage alone and eventually my friend and I lose sight of one another.

All of my instincts are enlisted to avoid a fatal blow. I duck and flatten against the ground, then race ahead again before the burning magma catches up with me. All of a sudden the pulsing in my ears stops. I step back. Everything goes quiet for a moment and a new pathway opens up. I become one with the quakes, the eruptions and cataclysmic explosions. I feel their rhythm and begin to discern a pattern. Breaks happen at regular intervals.

A shower of fire again. I take shelter in another cranny. Looking up I detect a roughly hewn set of stairs on my left that leads out of the grotto. I measure the space between eruptions in heartbeats and succeed in escaping just before the boiling lava covers my feet and the sides of the cave close in on me. I reach a protected place. I wait. Twenty-four heartbeats to reach the next ledge, twelve to find the protection of a crevice, seven to crawl in. Proceeding in this way I make it to the top of the stairs. There, things are less hectic.

At the very top a light shines under a door. When I am about to reach it I hear a familiar voice. "Quick! Open the door so she doesn't burn her hand on the handle." I laugh to myself. They must be kidding. Burn my hand on the handle? Surely they have no idea what I have just been through.

How many of those others who struggled underground along with me made it? I'll never know. We each have our separate set of stairs, our different doors through which to get out.

As I reach for the hot handle the door is pulled open wide from inside. A bright light falls on me, so bright I am blinded in my left eye. I take a breath, but a burning pain shoots through my body. I stop breathing, but a big hand slaps me on the back, forcing a scream out of me. When I open my eyes again I am bathed in the green light of two loving eyes. The burning stops, my breathing comes easily.

The tall man with the green eyes in the dream was Pietro, I am sure of that. He laughed with delight, caressed my cheeks, reassured me with soothing words. "There, there, you made it. You are okay. Don't worry, we'll take care of you." Others were there, smiling and welcoming me. The joy in their eyes was a salve on my body.

# **O**rsolina

Heavens is where everything fits.　　　　　　　　　　*—Sainte Némoise*

44

A MOMENT OF PERFECTION
In which Orsolina and Lucien muse about life.

From the living room window I absently watch a group of children on the playground of the apartment complex. My chest tightens. I miss my children badly, but quickly stop myself from thinking about it. I will be back with them soon enough.

I look up and notice Lucien looking at me over his coffee. I smile at him. *Un tendre moment.* I recall how I took him under my wing when he was my son Jean-Luc's age. I was barely out of childhood myself. "Do you remember," I ask him, "how we played mother and son when you where a child?"

"What makes you think of that?"

"I guess I miss my kids."

Lucien sits down and drowsily contemplates the golden light falling on the sleeping cat.

"I am overwhelmed by the absurdity and insignificance of it all," he tells me.

"Yes, life is short and of relatively limited consequences. Ours until now have been good to us. When it gets too hard, I try to find a moment of perfection like this one. It's so quiet you can hear the wind rustle the leaves outside the window. Each sip of this coffee is sublime. It's like entering the mystery, an opening into eternity."

ngela

You must place your routine on the background of the infinite.
—*Sainte Némoise*

45

ANGELA MUSES ABOUT OLD AGE
In which Angela reflects about her relationship with her daughter Orsolina, how dismissed she feels; where she considers old age, how reduced to insignificance by society at large when one needs the most courage, how it really is the apex of one's wisdom if one can make friends with death; where she describes reclining and merging with the surroundings.

Orsolina gets so impatient with me. Sometimes it makes me so sad I retreat inside myself like a snail in its shell. I don't mean to do that, it happens. I only feel safe when I go far enough inside to the place where I can't be reached. I absent myself, become numb and do not utter another word. I can tell Orsolina feels bad, guilty of the pain she has inflicted, but she pretends not to see it and I pretend not to feel it. I act as though her attacks don't touch me.

She thinks I am boring, she thinks I am too slow, she thinks I spend too much time reclining on my lounge chair doing nothing but staring at the sky. She is still too young to know that as you get to be my age reclining is a worthwhile activity, letting the body relax and totally fill its own space. It merges with everything around. Your outlines disappear and you enter a world where there is no pain, no drama, no chores or hard labor. You are floating. Finally you rest after a lifetime of hardship.

Orsolina once more left her journal open on the table and I started to read: *There is so much neglect in my impatient soul and the stallion of my heart keeps devouring the miles ahead, forgetting the life right under its hooves. My mother inspires me most when she is far away from me.*

That's just it. My daughter cannot see me for who I am when I am too close. She thinks I am spineless but does not realize that old age is not for cowards, it is the biggest challenge of life. One has to enter it with care if one does not want to replace the passionate and wounding drama of life with the degrading drama of sickness and suffering, substitute passion with dispassion and even despair.

I remember one of my friends joking: "don't stand when you can sit, and don't sit when you can lie down." The joy of lying down, surrendering to the comfort of a bed or overstuffed chair, feet up, contemplating the heavens, that is the pleasure of older years. No thoughts, just an immense *bien-être*, body dissolving in the warm broth of life in which everything is alive, benevolent, and willing to merge.

I recall when in my seventies I first realized I was an old lady. I was in such good shape I laughed at the discovery. How could this happen to me? But I knew that younger people believed I was finished. It's around that time that I realized that youth was not all it was cracked up to be; in fact the elder years were much better. It's like trading your *Deux Chevaux* for a Rolls Royce, I heard it said—difficult to handle until you learn the commands and feed it the right gasoline.

To accept old age is giving up resistance and being oneself with total abandon. It's like with the first love, everything new and fresh. To begin with I was full of curiosity and laughter about getting older, I was willing to go through it with courage.

But as we got on in years, my friends and I started to talk mostly about our ailments, just like the ancient ones we made fun of as children. Obsessed with our illnesses we stopped living, for to live had become dangerous. We forgot about this new land we had been curious about earlier, fear took over. We were diminished, some of us dependent, invalids, and our children failed to understand that to lie around and join in the flow of life was the only life we had left.

Our children didn't know that to merge is a way to welcome your own death.

ucien

Our acceptance of what is guides us to our true destiny.

—Sainte Némoise

46

THE MANUSCRIPT - Twenty years later

In which Orsolina, twenty years later, meets Lucien in a Parisian café and reminisces, together with her nephew, about the time when they sent off samples for DNA testing; where Lucien retells how he stole a lock of his dead biological father's hair and the psycho-magic act his teacher asked him to perform, and how he punished his mother; in which Orsolina and he get into a small altercation about the past and her role in it, about the girlfriend who ruined him; where Lucien tries to describe how things are when your identity collapses from under you.

Orsolina rushes across the little *Place Jean Moinon*, a setting for small restaurants and cafés with terraces shaded by three venerable plane trees. She spots Lucien sitting at a table, sunspots falling on him through the new foliage. Light and dark, she thinks, so much like Lucien. She walks towards him with determination and gestures for him to remain seated as he starts to get up upon seeing her. She leans to kiss him on both cheeks, then pulls up a chair and sits down, slightly breathless.

"Sorry I am late. I got a little lost. How did you ever find this place? Charming, you'd believe you were in a sleepy provincial town. But hell to find. To think that I was born and raised in Paris—didn't leave till I was twenty-two—but never knew anything about this section of the city. From the look of those I met in the narrow streets coming up here, I guess it's an Arab and African section." She points at the surrounding streets, "A few African stores, some specialty groceries, women in bright outfits with turbans matching, men in djellabas, all very local color. You've always loved this kind of place, haven't you?"

She goes on without waiting for an answer, "Anyway, have you been here long?"

Lucien settles in his chair and leans back, balancing on the two back legs, "No, just ten minutes. I thought I gave you pretty good directions. I believed it would be worth your while. I love to come here, read or put down ideas for photos. This section is not yet taken over by yuppies; it's still cheap. I am thinking of trying to find an apartment around here.

"So, what do you want to drink, I'll call the waiter." He waves to a young *branché* wearing baggy jeans hanging so low the top of his pretty boxers show; his hair tips are bleached blond.

"If you want to, when we are finished with our drinks I'll take you for a walk to discover more of this section, through the gardens of the *Hopital St-Louis* and along the *canal St-Martin.*"

"Yeah, great, I'd love that. But let's not go to the *Hotel du Nord* on the *canal.* I hear it has become the new hangout for the in-crowd since old movies are in style again."

The *garçon* comes to their table, tray balanced on one finger. "Would you like to order?"

Her right hand goes up, one finger extended as though trying to catch some inspiration, then tapping her forehead. "Oh, I don't know. What are you having Lucien? Oh yeah. Bring me a *kir* please."

The waiter leaves and Lucien pushes a stack of a few hundred printed pages towards her. She pretends to discover the title on top of the first page and reads it aloud. *Entre Nous.* I didn't know if I needed a title for this piece of writing I never meant to publish, but it came to me one day because all this was supposed to be just between us, right? Not supposed to leave the family circle. Did you finish reading it?"

Lucien, letting his chair fall back on all four legs, puts one elbow on the table and looks into her eyes slightly irritated, "What do you think? Of course I did. Isn't that why you gave me this story? Come on, what a question? But somehow I did wonder why you thought it would help me, I am not in it hardly at all."

Orsolina gestures dismissively, "Yeah, you're right. It's a stupid question; just a way to make small talk on the way to the big talk. It's true that there is little about you in there, but I believed that by getting to know the family members better you might understand them and have compassion."

"Well I do to some extent."

"I'm surprised you didn't ask to meet me in the back room of one of those dark little cafés you seem to have a special fondness for. I was expecting it and would have been more at ease maybe than in full daylight. Remember the last one where we sat together two years ago? We had sent the check to pay for the DNA test. Your brother had agreed to be tested with you to determine whether you had the same father, because the lock of hair you had pilfered from the corpse of Gilles—your might-be father—turned out to be unacceptable in terms of the law. The test was very expensive, you made a first payment but it had taken you a while to get the rest of the money together. The results were in a lab in Germany waiting for your last check to disclose the truth. Such a momentous day, do you remember?"

Lucien ignores the question and his face tightens, but Orsolina nervously goes on.

"And earlier that day, when we went to the bank to get that international check, I'll never forget. It was like a ritual. We held hands as you talked to the clerk. Then we put the check in an envelope, you licked it closed and I placed the stamp. We put it in the mailbox together. Right after that you took me to the café and we sat at a table in the back."

"I remember well, believe me."

"It seemed like nothing had changed since the war in that place, not even the boss with his enormous paunch standing behind his bar, looking ancient and cranky. He brought us our drinks as though he resented us for interrupting his concentration."

Lucien nods, sips on his *kir* but remains silent.

"And a few weeks later, when you finally did get the results, you called me to meet you in the little Arab café down from where you worked. It was crowded and hot in there. The belly dancing music was loud, but we spent the evening talking it over." The memory brings a smile on Lucien's face.

"You are not very talkative today are you? So here we are. You finished reading the story I wrote at the time of Pietro's death. Like I said when I handed it to you, I just let the Spiazzi's voices come and speak through me. When you told me on the phone that there were some things that pissed you off in there, I wasn't sure you would finish reading. I know that you are angry at many things right now. I see that your anger is directed at me also."

The *garçon* comes to their table and puts a *kir* in front of her, "*Voilà, Madame.*"

"*Merci.*"

Lucien picks up his glass and raises it towards her. She does the same, they toast. "Here is to our karmic connection, whether through blood or not," Orsolina says. "In a way you are more my nephew than any of my blood related ones."

"I believe that," Lucien answers. "Actually I couldn't put your manuscript down. I do understand what you had in mind when you wrote those pieces and it probably will help me in the long run. But let me tell you how it is for me because I want you to write something from my point of view. I am sure you can get into my head-space like you did with those others and let me be a person also.

"Do you know what it's like to find yourself in your mid-forties with no identity, no roots, and no firm ground to step on? Imagine. I was told, or rather didn't need to be told for it was implied since the day I was born that I was the son of my father Pietro. And of course I accepted that." He pauses and sips on his *kir*, she does also.

"But all of a sudden things in my life no longer worked. I had been wondering for a while why this life of mine, which had started off in such a promising way was now at a standstill. It no longer came together no matter what I did. In fact, it was falling apart. Nothing fit for me, neither relationships nor work, and an insidious voice kept whispering that there was something wrong with me, something I'd better find out about and straighten out or I'd be stuck forever. I suspected there was a lie somewhere and I had to force the truth out of my family, for they'd rather have continued to fool me."

Orsolina raises one hand and with a firm downward movement slaps the table to punctuate her words. "You are not going to change things by ramming your head against the wall or hitting everybody in the family over the head trying to get them to change. Believe me, I have learned the hard way myself. The only change you can effectively accomplish is within yourself and if you are successful, people around you will start changing also, especially the ones you are closely involved with. You'd be surprised. It's like you open a door inside and everyone's inner door responds in kind. It might be a door you have been pushing on for years, but no amount of pushing the wrong way will open it.

"I have held your hand through highs and lows throughout the ordeal of discovering you were not the son of my brother. I was the first one you questioned remember? You put it bluntly, 'Do you know anything about Pietro not being my father? Please don't lie,' you said. 'I desperately need the truth.' And I told you what I knew."

Lucien raises his head aggressively, "Yes, you did. You were honest with the young bull I was at that point. And that's why I took refuge with you when the truth was tearing me apart and I could no longer function. After everything I'd built collapsed, I came to stay with your family in California for a while.

"But still, you don't seem to really get it. I want you to imagine breaking down and your family offering no support. Yes, imagine. They all believed there was something drastically wrong with me and I scared them. Imagine overhearing them discussing your state, 'He needs something more than a shrink.' And eavesdropping on your mother, 'He's so disturbed and smokes way too much of that awful stuff. I am so afraid he'll end up a junkie, maybe even a homeless,' she whined." Lucien becomes more and more agitated as he speaks. Then he suddenly stops, points to the pale moon in the day sky.

"See the moon over there on the other side of the street, just above those two trees? It's missing a piece, just a little corner, as though it were bitten off. And that little piece prevents it from being called full moon, but everyone accepts this bitten off moon, some even find that it has a special charm that way. They all trust that the moon will go through its cycle and come together again, be full sometime soon. So the partial moon is just a stage, something the moon has to go through before it becomes whole again."

Raising his voice, "Why is this fucking French society so stuck that it will not accept the stages of a being? So stuck in a system that supposedly brings security but rules and regulates everyone's life to the point where there is no freedom. So stuck in that *bourgeois* sense of safety that it can't condone the stages of man. They say that I am too old to go through this, that I should have been finished with all that after my teens. They think it's an adolescent's crisis. Don't they know about mid-life crisis?"

Orsolina signals with her hands for him to lower his voice because the patrons are starting to look in their direction. She speaks calmly, tapping her chest, "I know about mid-life crisis. I know about all kinds of crises, believe me. You see this?" holding the manuscript in one hand and shaking it at him. "It's something I never showed anyone because they would think me crazy. I wrote it when I was confused and devastated and needed to understand something more about death, about the Spiazzis, about myself. I didn't just want to go through the customary motions and forget the whole thing as quickly as possible. As I told you earlier, I asked some members of the family, whether dead or alive, to speak through me, you understand? And they did. I discovered things I didn't know about each one. I understood that I had them all inside me and would carry them forever, that in their own way they would advise and guide me. I thought you might benefit from knowing them better. You were still young when it happened, only a little more than eighteen, you had very few tools yet."

Lucien fidgets, rolls a *métro* ticket between his fingers, then pulls up his chair and leans forward as if he wanted to be closer. "I appreciate that you entrusted me with your manuscript. But let me tell you—you who like stories so much—how I came to be where I am now. You are responsible for the lie as much as anyone else, you know. I am finally close to this place I call the acceptance of my unacceptability. Believe me, it has been a long journey to get there. You think you know at least the beginning of it, but not from my point of view. I want you to write about that.

"OK. I will."

"When I was born you were already sixteen or so. I know now that you'd overheard that I, the last child of your brother, probably was the bastard from an illicit affair. There had been much commotion about my mother trying to get an abortion that was unsuccessful and nearly killed her. At the time abortions were totally illegal and the few doctors who took the risk of performing them wanted a lot of money for their service. They usually operated without anesthetic and I was told that many of them enjoyed inflicting pain on sinful women.

"The only other choice was to go to Holland, Switzerland or Morocco if you had the money and the contact. But if you were poor and not very worldly you ended up going to one of those women abortionists who got the fetus out with a coat hanger or made the pregnant woman ingest a foul potion that would bring on a terrible fever. That's what *Maman* chose to do.

"I understand now that the whole story was very disturbing to you. You loved your brother, you had come to love his wife, you loved their new baby and at that point you thought their marriage was perfect. So you chose not to believe the rumors and put everything neatly away. After all, you had better things to do—probably totally involved in your first love.

"Your father—my grandfather—on the other hand, was fuming about the whole situation. You confessed to me that more than once you heard him spewing out venom about my mother's unfaithfulness, bemoaning the family's curse. You chose to discount the truth as an object of his paranoid imagination." Then in a whisper, "Poor grandfather."

Orsolina, waving apologetically, "I thought he was seeing his own story repeated over again as though there was no end to it and that he overreacted."

Lucien finishes his drink and signals the waiter for another one. He raises his voice again. "That's what you told yourself because you were just a chicken shit like all the others who knew and said nothing. Sorry, I guess you were not like the others really, it's just that you didn't concern yourself with the concepts of morality and immorality. It's obvious to me now that you were a budding beatnik on the way to becoming a hippie. It was freedom from sexual repression you were after, from the moral judgments of a repressive society. You wanted nothing to do with the narrow minded, restrictive patterns of behavior that were considered common decency; you were sick and tired of the blinders everyone around you wore. Didn't you tell me that yourself later?"

Orsolina again motions for Lucien to lower his voice, then raises her empty glass catching the waiter's attention and asking him to fill it up also. "Yes. I probably did. I always liked to expound during that formative period of my life. Monogamy was a moral code I didn't adhere to at the time, so unfaithfulness was not so dramatic in my eyes." The waiter puts a full glass of *kir* in front of each of them. They thank him. "You were my little nephew, cute and interesting," Orsolina continues. "I loved to play with you, influence your development. Whether you were really the fruit of my brother's seed or not was not of great concern to me."

"It should have been. It wasn't the situation in itself that was so dramatic. What was, were all the secrets that got created around it. Think about how it was for me. I loved Pietro whom I considered my father without a doubt. He was big; his was a presence that filled me with a sense of self. He was absent much of the time, always working, but when he was present he made up for it. He had little ego and gave us kids a sense of our own worth; his mark on us was minimal."

She pensively takes a sip of her *kir*. "Yes, he was like a channel for the life force and he let it flow through his children without standing in the way so they could be filled with their own true nature."

"So you understand now why it was of utmost importance to me that I should be a product of this man's seed and no other? He had given me a sense of my own self. I wanted that ability in my genes. Who else could do that for me? Certainly not that crazy man, Gilles, *Papa*'s business partner, my godfather, who managed to imprison my mother in an illicit affair for twenty years. Twenty years, and no one suspected. Even Giovanni didn't know that it actually lasted that long. It continued until about the time of *Papa*'s sickness. Can you imagine what it meant for *Maman*? Twenty years of secrets and lies, twenty years of sneaking and hiding, twenty years of drama and probably looking at me, her last child, as the adored fruit of her sin, the source of her deepest guilt. I couldn't help but pick that up even if it remained unconscious.

"When she finally admitted to everything, Simone told me that I was the son Gilles desired more than anything but never was able to beget before—a wish he had never been able to totally put aside come true. I was the son of a passion that so enflamed him that he was ready to kill his lover and kill himself in order not to let her slip through his fingers. Gilles started as *Papa*'s partner, then became a friend of the family, then *Maman*'s secret lover, and finally my godfather. My grandmother told me that when the guilt was too overwhelming, Simone wanted to put an end to the relationship, but Gilles would go mad when she mentioned it. She was scared of him."

Orsolina puts her hand down on Lucien's fidgeting fingers and holds it there. "Yes, Simone's mother, your grandma, loved all that drama, and the gossip. It's from her that I learned that Gilles stormed into Simone's apartment gun in hand one day when your mother was alone with you, a toddler. He threatened to kill all three of you if she dared end their relationship. He made her swear she wouldn't. Your grandmother also told me that he did that more than once. He threatened to kill himself in front of Simone so as to coerce a promise from her to leave Pietro and run away with him. He was ready to take on all three of her children for among them was his son, his own blood, he was sure of that. But in the end she couldn't do it. She loved Pietro also."

Lucien removes his hand from under hers. "That's why I kept asking *Maman*, 'How could you and Gilles be so sure that I was the fruit of your passion? Didn't you also sleep with *Papa* while this affair was going on?' She admitted to me that she did sleep with Pietro at the same time, but she knew for sure that I was Gilles' son. She couldn't explain why she knew.

"The idea of *Papa* raising a son that was not his made her decide to abort. Can you imagine how mad Gilles must have been about that? He must have begged her to keep the child. He must have threatened again."

Lucien slumps in his chair and remains silent for a few moments. Then he raises his head defiantly, "You know what? I don't have much compassion for her. She was caught in her own web of betrayal. As for me, I wouldn't give in, I refused to be annihilated. I held on and remained in the womb until term. I wouldn't let go of this chance at life that was given me. What was I so anxious to come here and prove exactly? That I was strong, that I could survive all the secrets and lies? That I could be bigger than life being loved by two fathers?

"Before I became conscious of all this I was so arrogant. My unconscious always knew of course, but I kept the truth from surfacing, just like everyone else. My strength and self-confidence were built on sand though; the foundation was weak. Arrogance only mimics self-confidence but when you try to build on it, it can't hold up and the whole edifice collapses. My poorly placed pride, to this day, sabotages everything I try to build whether in relationship or work."

Orsolina puts both her hands on the table, "your girlfriend Malvina, the gorgeous model, also helped sabotage everything you did."

Lucien, as if stung by a bee, starts to get up from his chair then sits down again. He is about to protest but she interrupts him, "Oh, come on. You know that's true, we've talked about it. Malvina didn't want you to photograph any other woman but her, and when you did use her as a model for your assignments she hated the pictures you took of her. You ended up blowing off all your big accounts with top magazines and when Kodak sent you to Egypt you came back with hardly anything. You didn't know it at the time but the Spiazzi tribe referred to her as vampire because she was sucking you dry and besides . . . she absolutely hated garlic.

"I actually liked her, such a character. Interesting that her name was nearly a homonym to Pietro's mother Malva. She was so tall she towered over most French men and patted them on the head in her patronizing fashion, calling them *mon coco,* cutie pie. And the way she threw all your clothes and cameras out of the second floor apartment when she was angry. And she was angry a lot, wild when she. . ."

Lucien pulls his chair up. His voice is low, "That's enough. Let's not talk anymore about Malvina. What I was going through had only little to do with her. She was just another symptom. It was an identity crisis . . . and what a crisis! I went all the way down into the blackest pit. The dark night of the soul—supposedly a spiritual crisis that comes to show you that there is more to life than the material world. Mine was different, though. I could no longer avoid what had been nagging at me since childhood. All the unsaid. All the whispering. And certain looks that denied the words that were spoken, denied what I was told.

"How can I deal with all that betrayal? With the fact that my god-father was my biological father. Can you fathom that? So much desire for an offspring, and then you surround him with lies. That much desire for possessing a son and then you don't let him know he is your son. Every weekend I spent with him and his wife at their country house playing family. And Gilles' wife was not supposed to know that her husband was my mother's lover. And I was not supposed to feel any of the conflicted emotions that were thrown at me: the most desired son, the undesirable offspring, the reminder of passionate love, the reminder of deadly guilt, and for *Papa*, his last child, the child of his infinite tolerance, but also the child of suspicion, the child whose blood line he couldn't be sure of. And all was supposed to be ducky?"

He pauses, takes a drink and calms down. "Do you remember my teacher and spiritual mentor Alejandro Jodorowsky? I took you to a gathering when he was giving readings some time ago."

"Yes, that Russian mystic prophet. I remember him quite well. He is bigger than life, made quite an impression on me."

"Recently, he tried to make me reach some kind of resolution, reconcile me with all those contradictions and recommended that I accomplish a task, one of his famous magic acts.

"You remember that after coming back from California I reconnected with my godfather Gilles. I had lost track of him and his family long ago, but now that I suspected he might be my father I wanted to get his story, develop a relationship of sorts. Gilles had had a stroke that left him paralyzed and he had buried that old story so deeply he couldn't, or wouldn't, dig it back up. 'I'd love to keep seeing you but please, don't bring that up. I have already hurt too many people including myself with that story,' was his excuse. Soon after that he died.

"I was floundering, wondering who I was, still making my mother pay for her lies. Pay! Literally! I borrowed money from her—my photography business had collapsed, I was always broke and never had the funds to pay her back. I borrowed her car because mine broke down and I couldn't replace it. So I drove her car and kept accumulating parking and speeding tickets, which were sent to her address. And she would pay." Lucien's voice becomes angry again.

"I made her pay in more than one way. I sat her down and pushed, and pushed, digging into all the recesses where she might still have secrets, things she had not yet revealed about herself, her feelings, things she had nearly forgotten. She was terrified of me, terrified of my inquisitions, my demand for total honesty, afraid she would say something that would hurt me more, damage me more. I laid her bare, she who all her life had been so discreet, unassuming, secretive, and with so little self-esteem."

Orsolina takes a sip of her drink and moves her chair back. "I remember. It practically killed her. I was angry with you for being so harsh, uncompassionate. I was very judgmental of you. Here you were, complaining about those *petits-bourgeois* and their stuck ways, but taking from them, needing their help to survive and not hesitant to use the pressure of guilt to get what you wanted, then, biting the hand that helped you."

Lucien drums on the table. "Believe me I felt your judgment, but I ignored it like I ignored my contradictions. I was on survival mode. Anyway, Jodorowsky spelled out my task. Always horrendously difficult those tasks he called magical acts, bordering on insanity. I was to talk my mother into coming with me to her husband's grave with a picture of her lover in her hand. I was to take with me the lock of Gilles' hair—which Jodorowsky knew I had taken from the corpse during the wake—along with a photo of him.

"My intention when I took the lock had been to have the hair analyzed so I could ascertain my true genetic line. At the time I still didn't know for sure and I believed that to know would straighten everything. During the wake, looking for an opportunity to cut off the hair, I stayed in the room where the corpse was displayed until everyone was gone. When I was left by myself I looked over my shoulder to make sure no one was lingering in the darkened room. I inspected every corner, then quickly took out my pocketknife, grabbed a lock of hair and cut it off. I found out later that I would have needed to pull the hair by the roots in order to get a good result. Besides, Gilles' wife's signature was required for the analysis.

"But anyway, knowing about this, Jodorowsky gave me the task of digging a hole under *Papa*'s grave and stuffing the lock of hair into it, then *Maman* was to push the photograph of Gilles into the hole while asking forgiveness aloud of both men. This was supposed to integrate all the pieces. I practically drove my mother crazy with worry and fear at this weirdest of ceremonies, but in the end it certainly improved my relationship with her. And I started to see the benefits of having two fathers."

"Then you thought you could put all that behind."

"Yes, after all that I decided that I didn't have to know who my father was and didn't have to do a DNA test. But I chose to tell my brother, sister and mother that I had done it, and that it indicated Pietro as my biological father. I wanted to put their mind at peace. That's how I wished it to be and I was going to create my own reality. After the turmoil created by my earlier revelation about Pietro possibly not being my father, the news made everyone very happy. The bombshell I had dropped when I opened up the secret had ripped the family apart, and now everyone was ready to settle back into their small, undisturbed routine, their limited understanding and comfortable blindness, ready to pretend that nothing at all had happened."

Orsolina nods in discouragement and takes a drink.

"But that was a false resolution. It was not really finished in any way for me. I still couldn't get my financial scene together. I still couldn't keep a relationship. I still didn't have a place of my own and was unable to accept the status of vagrant, anarchist and worse, destitute. I still couldn't pay monthly child support to my ex-wife. I still wasn't able to prove to my family of *petits-bourgeois* that I was a productive member of society. I couldn't settle into the Gypsy, outlaw and iconoclast misfit image, but couldn't accept being one of them, *petits-bourgeois,* either. I became obsessed again with knowing for sure who my father was: Pietro or Gilles."

He finishes the rest of his drink in one gulp. "It took me another two years to put the money together for that test—the money that you and I deposited with great ceremony. It's true that my brother and sister helped me pay for it, but I had to force their hand for they would've rather not stirred up the shit again. They were worried about our mother cracking up, and they sent her to a shrink who recommended tranquilizers. So again Simone had found another way not to deal. I couldn't find compassion in my heart for any of them, especially not for my mother. There was a scene from the past I could never forget or forgive."

Lucien swallows hard, falls silent as if overwhelmed by the memory. Then, taking a deep breath he goes on, "You witnessed it, remember, it was the night before *Papa*'s death. I had been arguing with *Maman*, also with my brother and sister about whether or not to tell *Pietro* that he was dying of cancer. It was obvious that there was no longer any hope, but the doctors had advised us not to reveal his condition to him and I was not yet ready to act in accordance with my beliefs."

Orsolina shakes her head in disapproval. "I sure remember that. I was totally in agreement with you but felt that I didn't have a voice because I was only Pietro's half sister and had to respect the wishes of his close family. He didn't even know he had cancer. The doctors called it all kinds of other things. One of them, a specialist, actually said he would no longer treat Pietro as a patient if we told him the truth, because that would take away all his chances of survival."

Lucien gets agitated again. "What chances I ask you? But they kept giving *Papa* hope and even trying to fool us about his probabilities of survival. I was in a rage about it. Let's be honest with one another. This is the end; let's not leave a lie between us. Let's say a clean good-bye, let's cry in each other's arms. But no one would agree. 'Okay, you do what you want but I am telling him,' I yelled ready to storm out and go into his room. My mother, who had been standing by, clutched her heart, fell backwards onto the couch. 'Pretty soon it will not be one corpse you will